Sam Parks, a.k.a. Sam Gale, moved from the US to the UK to pursue her love for writing. Now she's settled there, writing romantic stories and going for long walks with her golden retriever Kirby. In the little spare time she has between working full-time and writing books, she likes to play D&D with her friends and dress up like she could stumble into a Ren faire at any moment. She also reads as much as life allows, documenting her reading and writing on her YouTube channel.

www.samanthaparks.com

- tiktok.com/@samparksbooks
- youtube.com/@searchingforsamantha
- instagram.com/searchingforsamantha

YOU'VE GOT CHAIN MAIL

SAM PARKS

One More Chapter
a division of HarperCollins*Publishers*
1 London Bridge Street
London SE1 9GF
www.harpercollins.co.uk
HarperCollins*Publishers*
Macken House, 39/40 Mayor Street Upper,
Dublin 1, D01 C9W8, Ireland

This paperback edition 2024
First published in Great Britain in ebook format
by HarperCollins*Publishers* 2024

1

Copyright © Sam Parks 2024
Sam Parks asserts the moral right to be identified
as the author of this work

A catalogue record of this book is available from the British Library

ISBN: 978-0-00-868558-4

This novel is entirely a work of fiction. The names, characters and incidents portrayed in it are the work of the author's imagination. Any resemblance to actual persons, living or dead, events or localities is entirely coincidental.

Printed and bound in the UK using 100% Renewable Electricity
by CPI Group (UK) Ltd

All rights reserved. No part of this publication may be reproduced, stored in a retrieval system, or transmitted, in any form or by any means, electronic, mechanical, photocopying, recording or otherwise, without the prior permission of the publishers.

For everyone who's ever played pretend with me.

CHAPTER 1
CAPTAIN MORGANA SILVERSWORD

Captain Morgana Silversword was dying. She could feel the life leaching out of her with every laboured breath as she lay spent on the stone floor. And as the fight continued to rage around and above her, she regretted that her death wouldn't be more ... heroic.

Dying in battle was never glamorous; Morgana had seen enough of her fellow soldiers fall to know that. But to die from friendly fire because she couldn't manage to get out of the way? That was particularly embarrassing.

Bone-tired, she looked around at the combat still unfolding in the small cave. The necromancer's apprentice had retreated into the corner, looking spent. Calamity, who had been responsible for the blaze of fire that had taken Morgana down, had backed herself into a corner. The halfling bard Yorick peeked between her legs as they both fired off spells at three undead enemies advancing on them. Then there was the hulking half-orc Gorlag, whose great axe swung at their enemies from behind.

Morgana smiled as her eyes fluttered closed. They were no

longer outnumbered. She may not make it through this, but at least her friends would.

Just as she was sure she couldn't possibly hold on any longer, she felt a hot breath on her face and two hands on her. A searing pain ripped through her at the contact with her wounds, but it melted away quickly as healing magic coursed over her. She caught a whiff of stale ale and incense, and something tickled her face; she opened her eyes to find it was a wiry dwarf beard.

"I thought I smelled your rotten dwarf breath," she joked, and Thrormir looked down at her in relief. He offered her a hand, and she took it, staggering to her feet.

Morgana didn't have much strength, but she had enough to finish what she'd started. She made a beeline for the apprentice, slicing a massive gash in his leg with her great sword. The man dropped to one knee, clutching at his now-bleeding thigh.

"I surrender!" he shouted, his hands held feebly in the air. The sinister superiority he'd shown when he'd raised his undead army against them was now completely gone. "It's in the fae realm! The catacombs of Thelanoris!"

Gorlag lowered their axe in triumph. They'd all come here for the location of the Supremacy Sphere, created long ago by the apprentice's master. Now they could let the city guard deal with this nobody whilst they continued their search in Thelanoris, right?

But Morgana didn't trust it. It had been too easy. And as her companions gathered around the man, interrogating him further, she saw his hands twitch slightly. She readied herself, positioning her weapon again so that the moment a spell formed on his lips, she could strike.

"You'll never get what you're after," he spat. "Many have

tried, and many have failed. You won't find a soul alive who's lived to tell the tale of their attempt."

Calamity scoffed and crossed her arms next to Morgana. "We'll take our chances."

"And so will I," the man said, his hands already starting to glow with magic, a spell on the tip of his tongue.

Morgana didn't hesitate even a moment, bringing her sword down directly on his head, splitting it into two.

CHAPTER 2
MORGAN

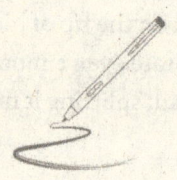

"Yesssss, Morgan!" Chloe whooped.

"Thank you, thank you," I said, miming a bow from my seat at the end of the table as the rest of the group golf clapped. I needed to leave soon, but these post-game moments, reliving the glory of whatever we'd just achieved (or, just as likely, the hilarity of whatever hijinks we'd got up to), were some of my favourites.

"I genuinely thought that was going to be a TPK," Fatima said, sighing in relief. I'd never experienced a "total party kill," but apparently it wasn't out of the question.

"Only terrible DMs kill their whole party," Phil said, and Fatima stuck out her tongue at him. He responded by shoving a brownie at her; she spluttered at first, then accepted it.

"From death saves to killing blow is a pretty badass combat moment." Grey tipped an imaginary hat to me. "Well done."

"Indeed," Jack said, and I gave him a half-smile in return. Only half, though; too much eye contact with Jack was almost always guaranteed to knock me off course.

"Sounds like we should do stars and wishes?" Fatima interrupted, bringing the table to order. She was our gamemaster – or Dungeon Master, but that always felt a bit kinky when not abbreviated – so the table in front of her was littered with papers, dice, and open books. The rest of us had our character sheets – some paper, some on phones – and our own dice. For me and most of the others, that meant just a couple of sets. For our resident dice goblins Grey and Chloe, that meant literally dozens of sets of dice: some sparkly, some made of metal, some oversized. Of course, they seemed to always reach for the same ones, but pointing that out had only resulted in death stares. I also had my tablet with me like every week so I could doodle as we played. I put it on the table in front of me, switching it off so no one would see my poor renditions of their characters.

"Ooh yes, me first," Phil said, raising his hand like a student in class. Fatima nodded at him. "Star is for Morgan's kill, of course. Wish is that we get a cute pet faerie in the fae realm, please."

Everyone nodded their assent. Cute non-player characters, or NPCs, were always high on everyone's wishlist. Animals and small creatures preferred, of course.

"Friendly reminder that faeries are people in D&D, not pets. But I'll see what I can do," Fatima said, writing down Phil's wish in one of her many notebooks. "Grey?"

"I'll start with my wish," they said. "I know cleaving is a fighter attack manoeuvre, but my great axe would be perfect for it, especially if we're likely to be in more battles like this with lots of smaller enemies. Could I pretty please take it as a feat during our next level up?"

"I'll look into it," Fatima said, and Grey's face lit up. It had taken me months to reconcile their tough exterior – buzz cut, dozens of piercings, denim biker vest with a million patches – with how much of a puppy dog they actually were. They liked to dye their buzz cut different colours every time they trimmed it; at the moment, it was a neon blue. Their best friend Fatima was the far opposite: restrained femininity. Her long brown hair was tied into a low ponytail with a mink-coloured velvet ribbon, and her round, gold-rimmed glasses perched daintily on her nose as she took notes with a maroon gel pen, her posture offensively good.

"And since Phil took the obvious one, I'll say my star is the excellent religion checks Jack rolled tonight."

More assent from the group, me included.

"Ah yes," he said, "the impressive skill of dropping resin dice onto the table." Jack was simultaneously the most physically imposing and least socially imposing person at the table. Even sat down, he was a full head taller than me, a far cry from his dwarf character. He was two for three on the tall, dark and handsome, in fact, with one of those faces that would be universally acknowledged as good-looking. But there was no dark and brooding aura; every part of him was golden. Golden tanned skin, golden blonde hair, and a bright, wide smile lighting up a chiselled yet friendly face. He looked like he'd just stepped off the front cover of some 90s surf magazine.

"Star for me is how quickly we solved that puzzle to get in the door," Chloe said, and everyone laughed.

Fatima grinned. "Given that I usually just Google 'logic puzzles for ten-year-olds', it's about time you found one of them doable. So yes, well done on being smarter than my students." She turned her attention to Jack, who was next in line.

"I think my star was getting to use that new healing spell for the first time, especially when Morgan went into death saves."

I couldn't help but feel a flush of pink creep up my neck at hearing my name come out of Jack's mouth, even though some part of my brain acknowledged it wasn't a compliment. If anything, it was highlighting my ineptitude.

"My wish is that we get some time to explore Thelanoris," he added.

"Depends on how quickly you piss off the locals," Fatima said, not looking up from her notes. "Which, if the last city is anything to go by, will be about ten minutes. And Morgan?"

"I know it's technically been said, but given that it was my kill, I'm saying that held action was my star."

"Fair enough. And your wish?"

I wracked my brain for what I might want from the next session. But I was still so new to the game that I struggled to imagine what could come next. I liked it that way, actually; every week was a new adventure. But that was definitely way too cringe to say out loud, so instead I opted for a joke I knew would get a reaction.

"I mean, for what the game is called, there have been far fewer dungeons than expected..." I said. "...And nary a dragon."

The table erupted in cries of outrage, wondering why I would wish a dragon on our level five party, but I assumed Fatima understood how unserious I was being, given the lack of note-taking happening at her end of the table. Jack just tipped his head back in laughter.

My tablet lit up in front of me, at the same time that I felt my phone buzz in my pocket. It was a text from Cara. A series of texts, actually, and I read them one by one as they came through on my tablet.

> so sorry moggy, but I've got bad news

> my mentor told me at lunch I should avoid taking big blocks of holiday during my rotation in sales if I can help it

> apparently it's really easy to fall behind

> so annoyingly it's a no-go on America this autumn :(

> didn't you say there are other ren faires though? lemme know what other dates we should look at

> not now though, i'm at the pub xxx

It was my best friend Cara's first day at her new job at some mega agency in London, where she'd moved yesterday. We'd been making plans to go to a Renaissance Faire in America sometime in the autumn, but apparently that wasn't happening anymore.

"Well, good job tonight everyone," Fatima said, bringing me back into the room again. She scooped the scattered papers in front of her into her hands. "Sorry for going on so long. I know it's already a bit later than usual, but I wanted to get through that combat."

I was actually grateful for the extended session; it was my second night alone in the house, and if the sad, empty feeling of the first was anything to go by, I didn't exactly have the time of my life waiting for me at home.

But I was sure the others were less thrilled. I knew they always went to the pub after our Monday games. I was always invited, and Chloe tried her best to get me to go each week, but I'd always had Cara waiting at home for me, something delicious simmering on the hob and whatever reality show we were bingeing queued up on the TV. And plus, the rest of them had been friends for years, and I would have felt like a clinger to force myself into their social traditions. Chloe had invited me to play when Fatima's boyfriend had had to drop out, and I knew what I was: a stand-in for him.

I packed my tablet, character sheet, pencils and dice into my backpack and stood up from the table to go.

"Oh here," Grey said, pulling a book out of their bag. I'd loaned them a romantasy novel I'd read last month.

"That was speedy!" I said, putting the book into my own bag.

"Yeah, well, you were right – I couldn't put it down once I'd started. I'll have to bring you one I've got that's similar."

"Ooh, yes please," I said, smiling, then waved as I moved to leave.

"You sure you don't wanna come to the pub?" Chloe asked, batting her eyelashes at me and pulling her rosy lips into a puppy dog pout. "Just for one?"

Honestly, it was tempting. If I were ever going to take her up on her invite, now would be the time. I glanced around at the others; Fatima and Grey were in a side conversation, and Phil was in the kitchen cleaning up the cake tin he'd brought the brownies in. Only Jack was paying attention, and I caught his gaze for a brief moment – was there a bit of hope in it? – before he looked away.

I took in a deep breath to respond, but Jack interrupted me.

"Don't pester her," he said to Chloe. "You do this every week." The breath whooshed out of me as my chest fell.

"She can answer for herself," Chloe said, chucking a cork coaster across the table at Jack, who lifted his hands defensively. She looked back at me pleadingly again, but I'd got Jack's message. I didn't really want to go that much, anyway.

"I can indeed," I said pointedly to Jack, then turned to Chloe. "But no thanks, I'd better get home."

Chloe pressed her mouth into a disappointed line, but she nodded. "See you at work," she said.

"Yeah, see you," I said, slipping out the door, waving as I

went; but they'd already moved on, and their laughter trailed out after me into the warm evening air.

∼

Just as the last of the light was leaving the sky, I pushed through the front gate of the tiny terraced house I had shared with Cara until yesterday. I checked the letterbox on the way in; there was a water bill I'd need to take a picture of and send to Cara's mum, and a postcard from my mum. It was a vintage-looking blue and yellow Big Sur print, with a message scrawled on the back:

My darling Mo, today I woke up next to this view. Van life has its perks. Love mum xxx

I kicked off my shoes and felt myself exhale in relief; Mum might be living it up on the West Coast, but this house was my happy place.

But it was also the first workday I'd had since Cara left, and I immediately felt the gut punch of what was missing: her noisy greeting, asking about my evening and if I finally let Jack flirt with me; the smell of whatever she'd made for dinner wafting through the small space; the dulcet tones of Carole King singing the *Gilmore Girls* theme song in the background.

Cara's parents had bought the house when she started uni nearby, and I'd found her post for a housemate on our university intranet, not wanting to brave the halls. Over the three years of uni and the four years since we'd graduated, we had made the place our own. There were not one, or even two, but *three* different rugs layered on the already-carpeted floor. The green velvet sofa we'd rescued from the side of the road was piled high with cross-stitched cushions and heirloom quilts. Fairy lights wound along the rod above the bay window, which was framed by thick, velvet brocade curtains and huge stacks of books, overflow from the bookshelves that flanked the wood-burning fireplace. It was my heaven.

Tonight, there was no noisy greeting, no homemade dinner, and no Lorelai and Rory, because Cara was gone. There was just me, and an empty bedroom upstairs I couldn't even look at these last few days. Without her, the place felt empty. Which was saying something because of how aggressively full it was.

After a sad microwave risotto – Cara had always been the cook, so I'd have to learn how to feed myself properly – I settled down in my usual spot: the bench seat built into the bay window. I leaned back against some of the dozen or so cushions lining the seat and opened my tablet to resume the drawing I'd started during the game. But I'd lost interest, so I started scrolling on my phone instead. I scrolled past an ad for handbags (as if I had anywhere to take a handbag, or the inclination to use one even if I did), a reminder to take a deep breath to which I nodded along, but then got bored halfway through my inhale and kept scrolling, and a morning routine video that I bookmarked as if 5am was even remotely within my capability.

But my finger stopped swiping as I landed on a video of two best friends in the US entering their local Renaissance Faire hand-in-hand, dressed in cosplay from head to toe. The shorter of the two wore a green cloak fastened with a leaf-shaped brooch, whilst the tall one was clad in what looked like a chain mail tunic and plate armour. I'd seen enough of these videos to know it was probably all plastic, maybe even 3D-printed, but it looked pretty legit to me. The caption underneath said "Less than 4 months until Ren Faire is back!" with a faerie emoji and a litany of hashtags underneath.

Over the last few months, I'd been getting more and more videos about cosplay, and specifically about Renaissance Faires. I was sure it probably started from my many Google searches at the beginning of the year when I was first learning D&D – "paladin vs fighter" ; "what does 5e mean dungeons & dragons" (fifth edition, or 5e, it turned out, was the active edition of Dungeons & Dragons); "do fighters have spells 5e" (no); "which is better battle master or champion fighter 5e" – but by now it was taking up at least half of my social media real estate. It was pretty dreamy, to be fair, and my starry-eyed watching of every video served to me by the sacred algorithm probably had something to do with the volume I saw. I had dubbed this particular genre of content "nerd shit". It was a broad genre with many sub-categories: people prancing around in fluffy dresses, inventing custom scenarios for their D&D games they called "homebrew" content, and even "great weapon workout routine" videos that involved people swinging around what looked like single-ended barbells.

This was how I'd been introduced to the concept of Ren Faires, and to say I was obsessed would have been an understatement. When I'd first tried to explain it to Cara, she'd just nodded and said "like a medieval festival?" referring to the dinky weekend affairs characteristic of small towns all across Britain.

"It's nothing like that," I'd said, mounting quite a passionate defence. "It's like a whole medieval village, and everyone who works there is in character. They heckle you, and you can buy old-timey food and drinks, and people dress up in costumes."

I wasn't convinced she'd ever really understood the appeal, but she'd got excited anyway, immediately diving into the research needed to choose one for us to go to. For my birthday in March, she'd made a big deal out of gifting me a pair of elf ears and saying they were to tide me over until she could get us tickets to the Ren Faire.

But now that was off the table it seemed, which was probably for the best if she was only into it for my benefit. I'd just have to keep rolling the literal dice each week to see if anything as exciting as those videos would happen to me. Or to Captain Morgana, anyway.

I bookmarked the video, adding it to the graveyard of saved content I'd never revisit, and kept scrolling.

The internet quickly lost its allure, but I was still craving the adventurousness I'd felt during the game; the high of completing part of a mission. Of doing something epic. So I walked over to the bookshelf and picked up my worn copy of my favourite fantasy novel; one I'd read half a dozen times but never failed to make me feel that high. And for now, whilst my own adventures were limited to three-hour sessions on Monday evenings, that would have to do.

CHAPTER 3
JACK

I fought the urge to stare out the window as Dad went through the plans with the client for the third time. I knew why he did it – I'd heard him complain enough times about a poorly scoped job or a bad choice of materials – but it didn't stop it from being boring as hell.

I'd got in trouble for staring out the window all through school, but it wasn't my fault that what was happening inside was infinitely less interesting than what I could see outside. Even now, I could make out from the corner of my eye the blue of what I thought was the first cornflower of the season. It was a damn shame they'd be getting rid of half their lawn for a stupid extension; the house was more than big enough, and they had a veritable meadow out there. But that wasn't my job to say.

It actually wasn't my job to be there at all – until recently, I'd been just carpentry and joinery – but Dad had been taking me along for more and more quotes lately, and even taking the first stab at pulling them together, at least for small jobs like the extensions. It wasn't my favourite, but he seemed satisfied enough, which was good; Dad was always in a better mood if I did a good job. He took a lot of pride in his work.

Back at the site, the guys had all left for the day, so we were just rounding up tools and cleaning up after them before heading home. I took advantage of Dad being round the other side of the house to check some messages on my phone; he hated phones being out on the job site, but Chloe and Phil had been trading jabs in our group chat, and it was entertaining as hell to read.

The two of them had been my best friends for well over half my life; Chloe even longer. She had grown up on the next farm over, and we were always so close that Mum thought we'd end up together. But I was the only one who knew that, from the time we had crushes at all, hers had been on her own girl next door, who devastated Chloe by being straight. Then there was Phil, who had come barrelling into our lives in year seven and turned our duo into a trio, a swirl of seam tape and the smell of freshly baked cookies trailing after him, even then. If he hadn't been such a lad, he might have been bullied for his homemaker tendencies, but instead he was just the coolest guy in every room he walked into.

I'd never lost touch with the two of them, even when I left on what was supposed to be a gap year, following what I thought was my future all around the globe for almost six years. And when that didn't work out, and I came home broken and directionless, they didn't let me pull away. Even as I was walking around like a zombie, doing nothing but working on my house and going to work, they were there, force-feeding me takeaway and a film at least once a week.

It wasn't until I emerged from my post-breakup fog that I met the other two. Grey was a university pal of Phil's, sliding into the friend group like they had always been there once I came up for post-breakup air. And Fatima came with Grey, especially when she realised Grey had a group of pals who were desperate to try their hands at Dungeons & Dragons, dragging her boyfriend Jared with her.

We weren't an inherently nerdy bunch, but we'd thrown ourselves headfirst into the game, and now we'd been playing together every week for almost three years. We were quite sceptical when Chloe suggested one of her colleagues join us; most of us had only ever played together, and none of us believed that Morgan would be as keen on bringing her work life into her personal time as Chloe insisted she would be. But Jared had suddenly had to move to Manchester for work, and we were getting ready to start a new campaign, so we decided to give it a try.

I'd be seeing all of them over the weekend – well, other than Morgan, of course, but that was a given at this point. I wasn't sure why I felt so disappointed every time she turned us down for drinks after the game or an extra hang over the weekend; maybe it was what Chloe always said, about her not having many friends. It was why she'd wanted to invite her to play with us in the first place.

Or maybe, if I were being more honest, it was the feeling I got in my stomach whenever she smiled at me. But I didn't examine that too closely.

"You'd better not let your mum see you in that," Dad said a bit later as he heaved the last of the rubbish into the skip. He dusted his hands off on his filthy jeans and pointed at my t-shirt.

"She'll be fine," I said, but I crossed my arms as if to cover it up from him, despite the fact that we'd been working together all day. I had to promptly uncross them as Dad handed me a bucket with a trowel in it, both still caked in plaster, of course. I knew he would lay into someone about it tomorrow, but for now it was up to me to clean it off when we got back to the workshop.

"You'll need a shower before dinner, anyway. I suspect the both of us do."

I managed to get a whiff of my own odour as I gripped the grab handle and lifted myself into the van; Dad was right.

"Still," I said as he put the van in gear, "it's been years. I feel like she should just get over it at this point."

The black t-shirt wasn't inherently offensive; in fact, the crumpled takeaway coffee cup illustration with "LEAVE NO TRACE" written across the side was downright polite. It had been a part of a campaign my ex had started – or, well, one I'd started, but she'd promoted – to clean up outdoor spaces. All the proceeds had gone to wildlife charities, too. But despite how long it had been since the breakup, Mum and Dad still treated it like a sensitive subject, and the t-shirt was just another reminder apparently. Maybe it had something to do with just how deeply I'd spiralled after it happened, but that was beside the point.

"Your mum just feels protective. I'm not saying she's right to be that sensitive. Just that you ought to change before dinner."

"Will do, I promise."

Satisfied, Dad turned up his heavy metal music, and I unzipped the backpack at my feet to get to my massive noise-cancelling headphones. Turning them on woke my phone, which was still paused on the podcast episode I'd started that morning; a deep dive into emerging materials in sustainable architecture.

Dad and I enjoyed this sort of company – each of us doing our own thing, but together. We saw each other at work almost every day, except when the job he was on didn't need me. To just sit together on the drive home, each of us listening to something we enjoyed, was an ideal way to transition from boss and employee to father and son.

Mum was different. Where Dad was measured, Mum was manic. She was always making mountains out of molehills. This could be a good thing depending on the context – birthday celebrations for my sister Amy and me, and even Chloe, had always been next-level – but on average days, it could be exhausting, even for me, who had inherited more of Mum's anxiety than I cared to admit. I wasn't sure how Dad managed it. And as we pulled up the long drive to the house, we could both see Mum out in the garden weeding – something she only ever did when she was worked up. She was very passionate about rewilding, so when she was on her hands and knees ripping native species from the earth, it was a pretty good sign she was worked up.

"You'd better go," Dad said, turning the music down. "I'll get that plaster bucket cleaned up."

"Is the shirt really that big a deal?"

Dad sighed. "She's taking Amy's breakup hard. Don't wanna set her off."

I rolled my eyes – Amy was twenty-two; messy breakups were her prerogative. And we'd all known this guy wasn't going to last; he was some fancy project manager in the city nearly ten years older than her. But Mum took it so personally when it didn't work out, as if she could have protected Amy from it.

But still, why should I suffer now about a breakup of mine that happened years ago just because Mum took Amy's love life way too seriously?

But I knew Dad was right; it was best for the equilibrium for me to just go home and get changed, so I got out of the van, grabbed my backpack and started the walk to mine. On the way, I fired off a text to my sister – "Mum's really tweaked about your breakup. You ok?" – after reacting with an eye-roll emoji to the message she'd sent me earlier containing my horoscope. She only ever sent it to me when it was dramatic, and today it read, "a shake-up is on the way, and it's up to you whether it will be welcome or not."

Honestly, a shake-up sounded like the worst thing I could imagine. I'd been shaken up enough for a lifetime, thank you. I'd basically designed my life around preventing future shake-ups. And Amy knew this, which was why she loved taunting me with supposed pending dramatics. She didn't immediately start texting me back, so I pocketed my phone again as I crested the hill and my house came into view.

Technically, I didn't live with my parents. Sure, we were on the same land: over a hundred acres that had been in my dad's family for generations. His brother – Uncle John, after whom I was named – still farmed most of it. But Dad had never been a farmer, nor had I. So whilst Mum and Dad lived in the old farmhouse, and Uncle John lived in a modern build over the hill, when I had moved home four years ago I had chosen a tiny spot down in a dip in the crop fields that was blocked from view from any of the other houses. I designed it in a fit of creativity fuelled by heartache and IPA, learning everything I needed to know about building code and utilities and all the rest. After years of bending to someone else's vision at every turn, I'd needed it to come wholly from me and what I wanted.

After that, it had taken me almost six months of full-time work and trial-and-error, but I'd built every inch of my house with my own two hands while I'd grieved my failed relationship. Every nail I hammered in, every roof tile I lay, every swipe of plaster inside, all had the angst and hurt and despondence I'd felt, both whilst I was getting over the breakup and, if I was being honest, for months before it had finally happened. It was a long and arduous project to commemorate the end of a long and frankly arduous relationship. And by the time I was done, I'd worked through most of my hurt, built myself a paradise to live in, and finally felt light enough to enjoy it.

Inside, I stripped off my clothes and turned on the walk-in shower. The rainfall showerhead sent well water cascading over me, a bit cold, but a refreshing change from the heat outside. It took almost five minutes of rinsing myself off before the water ran clear.

In the kitchen, my bath towel wrapped around my waist, I made myself a cup of chamomile tea and headed to my back deck, which overlooked a small wildlife pond formed in the little crook of the hilly farmland. It was the reason this part of the land hand never been utilised, and the reason I chose it as the perfect spot for my home.

I moved aside a magazine I'd been looking at before work – the May edition of the monthly journal put out by the Royal Institute of British Architects – and sat in my rocking chair, sipping my tea and thinking about Chloe's birthday. It was still a couple of months away, but since we were kids Phil and I had gone in together on a present for her. This year she'd requested an old-school slumber party, so we needed to figure out what that would look like.

My phone dinged with a response from Amy:

> Yeah, fine. Coming home in like 3 weeks, so hopefully she'll see I'm okay.

Three weeks was a long time to deal with Mum in this state,

but maybe that was the promised shake-up. Maybe I'd need to keep Mum from losing it.

Three weeks was also plenty of time for me to fit in my first camping trip of the year. I'd been thinking about what I wanted to do this summer, and along with some time on the water – the levels had been way too high over the winter to get any paddling in safely – a trip to the Brecon Beacons was at the top of my list. I'd been every year since I'd come home, and it was becoming a bit of a tradition for me; a way to kick-start the summer. So as I finished my tea and got dressed for dinner, I made a mental packing list, hoping I could shave a bit of weight off last year's load, and went through my sparse calendar in my mind. There was Adam's stag do, Chloe's birthday party, and ... well, not a lot else. Which was just the way I liked it.

I walked back up to the main house for dinner, my black t-shirt long gone. I let myself in through the front door to find Mum setting the table. My stomach rumbled as I spotted the sausage and mash; it was my favourite that she made. I knew the gravy would be from last weekend's roast, and the sausages from the farm up the road. Maybe besides Phil, Mum was the best cook I knew. He'd learned from her, after all.

"Looks great, Mum," I said, giving her a kiss on the cheek.

"Thank you, darling." I could hear the edge of anxiety in her voice, but I very much did *not* ask her about it. She'd end up talking all through dinner about Amy, and how worried she was, and how badly she wanted her back. I wondered if that was how she'd talked about me when I'd been away.

Dad came in a moment later, also freshly showered, and plonked down in his seat. Mum and I sat down with him, and we all tucked in. The food was just as delicious as it smelled, which was heavenly.

"How are Phil and Chloe?" Mum asked as she poured me a glass of red wine.

"Yeah, fine," I answered, my mouth full of food. When she glared at me, I gulped it down before continuing. "Sounds like Ethel's memory isn't getting any better, but Phil seems to be in good spirits."

"I'll have to go sit with her one of these days," she said. "I'm sure poor Phil could use a break."

"Yeah, probably," I admitted. Phil had been caring for his nan full-time for a couple of years now, since she'd turned eighty and promptly broken her hip, as if it had reached an expiration date or something. She'd raised Phil since his parents had died; Phil had only been eight. "Same as Batman," he always joked. But I knew it was still hard for him, even now, two decades later.

"And Chloe's okay? She's not dating anyone, is she?"

I laughed; Mum had only ever met one of Chloe's girlfriends, over a year ago now. "No, Mum, she's not."

"Oh well that's lucky," she said. "Cynthia at work has a daughter who's a lesbian, and I thought maybe we could set them up."

"I'm sure she'd love that," I said, knowing full well Chloe would *not* love that. "You can let her know the next time you see her."

We almost got through the entirety of dinner without bringing up Amy, but in the end it was Dad, who'd hardly said anything all night, that opened that particular can of worms. Mum was asking him to fix part of the pergola that had come loose, but apparently he'd left his toolbox in Manchester when he'd moved Amy out of her ex Chris's place and into the flat share she was now in.

"Oh that's okay," I said, "you can borrow mine."

Dad levelled a gaze at me so pointed it sent a shiver up my spine.

"Or, you know," I said, "I could do it?"

He nodded.

"Oh thank you, darling," Mum said, grabbing my hand across the table. "And Alan, I'm so glad you did leave it, because I've been thinking one of us ought to go up and check on her. This gives us an excuse."

Dad sighed. "I'll be fine without the toolbox, love. I'm a contractor. I've got tools coming out my eyeballs."

"But still," Mum insisted, "she's so far away, and heartbroken up there all alone."

"She's coming home in three weeks for a visit, isn't she?" I asked.

"Is she?" Mum looked surprised, and I wondered for a moment if I should have been keeping that to myself. But no, Amy would have to stay with Mum and Dad. "Oh, she doesn't tell me anything," Mum continued. "You'd think I'd be the first to know about that."

"It's only because I asked," I lied. "I'm sure she'll be texting you any moment to let you know."

I pulled out my phone under the table and fired off a quick message to Amy letting her know she needed to do that.

"I just want the best for you two," Mum said, in a complete non sequitur. "I really thought she and Chris might make it."

"Well, maybe don't go on about it to her," I suggested, and Mum frowned.

"Well, one of my kids needs to give me grandchildren one day," she muttered, and I sighed, loudly enough to make sure she heard it for the admonishment it was.

"Now, now," Dad said, always reluctant to get involved, "let's leave it. Jackie here is doing plenty for this family."

"Thanks, Dad," I said, raising a skewered piece of sausage to him in salute.

"He'll barely have time for babies of his own once he takes over the family business," he continued.

I lowered my fork. I'd been training up for the last few months to do some of Dad's jobs; when I'd come home, the deal had been that he'd get me trained as a joiner if I took over for him one day. I'd always thought he was just trying to make sure I wouldn't move away as quickly as I'd moved home, but when he'd announced last year that he'd set a target retirement date, I'd realised he'd been serious.

Mum and Dad had done so much for me, Dad especially. I'd built a house on their land, eaten their food, used Dad's business as a backup plan when full-time travel hadn't worked out. It would have been ungrateful not to go through with it.

But every time he mentioned me taking over, I felt it in my chest. Like I couldn't breathe; like it was being cracked open. And the best I could do was try to make sure he couldn't tell.

CHAPTER 4
MORGAN

I'd thought when I started working at an animal charity after uni that there would be a lot more ... well, animals. But instead of cuddling kittens and playing with puppies, it was mostly spreadsheets and being hung up on. Sure, I'd read the job description – "the Fundraising Manager's role is to help create and maintain a pipeline of regular contributions to the organisation" – but I'd assumed the animal part came with the territory, even just in tiny doses.

Not that it mattered; I would have done pretty much any job if it meant Cara and I got to work together after uni. But now, four years later, Cara was gone, and I'd yet to be given an opportunity within my working hours to do anything with the animals themselves. Instead I ate lunch at my desk twice a week so I could use my break to go walk dogs at the actual rescue a few streets over.

Today I had Chloe with me for the first time – Cara had always been my Friday dog walking buddy – and we were walking four sausage dog mixes between us named Eeny, Meeny, Miny, and Moe. We were walking along the path that followed the River Wye through town, and even though it was only late May, the sun was beating down on us as if it were the height of summer. I was also being blinded by Chloe's glossy red hair as the light bounced off of it.

"Last session was great," Chloe said as we paused for Moe to do his business against a tree trunk. I tightened my grip on Eeny and Miny's leads as they angled towards the river.

"Yeah, it really was," I said. "Honestly, it's pretty addictive. I wish I could play every day."

Chloe laughed. "I'm sure you'd get sick of us," she said, "and poor Fatima would have a full-time job preparing for our sessions. She spends enough of her time wrangling children; she doesn't need five full-grown ones to deal with."

"Very true." But still, spending as much time as possible in that fantasy world, where I was strong and brave and badass, sure beat chasing down tiny pledges from people who didn't even remember signing up to sponsor the charity, especially now that Cara was gone. At least I had Chloe, who had joined about a year ago.

Chloe turned around and started walking backwards in front of me, her bright red lips turned down in a frown, clearly picking up the angst I was putting down.

"Are you doing okay?" she asked. "I'm sure Cara leaving has been really hard."

I scoffed, ready to brush it off. Chloe and I had never been close in that way; I'd never talked about my feelings with anyone but Cara, and even then it had always been half-veiled in jokes. But Chloe seemed to genuinely care about my answer, so I paused mid-shrug and nodded instead.

"Yeah, it's been hard," I admitted, "but she's only in London. It's not like she's moved around the world." I didn't mention that, in the five days she'd been gone now, she'd only texted me back once, and missed two different FaceTime dates.

"Yeah, but you lived together and everything. Must feel like quite the change, even if she's only a couple of hours away."

"Yeah, I suppose."

We rounded the corner back towards the rescue, and I reached out to grab the door, Eeny and Miny's leads tangling in front of me as I did.

"Well, if you're ever in the mood for company," Chloe said as she strolled through the door I struggled to hold open, "the rest of us in the game hang out on the weekends sometimes, too. We're actually going away this weekend – you should come if you're free!"

I remembered hearing about that – hell, they'd planned it in front of me. Grey had a voucher for some holiday rental company that was expiring soon, so they'd picked a place less than an hour away on the river to spend the bank holiday weekend. They'd asked me then if I wanted to go, but like the pub invites, it had felt like a formality.

Luckily Lauren, whose shift at the front desk had apparently started whilst we were out, interrupted before I had to turn down the second invitation from Chloe this week.

"I'm glad you came back fast," she said, flinging her head to the side to get her short, floppy blonde hair out of the way, presumably so she could better see the clipboard in her hands, where we'd signed in earlier. "We've got a couple of new dog arrivals that could use some love."

"These guys only have little legs," I said. "We figured they probably didn't need as much as the bigger dogs."

She looked up at the dogs we'd brought back, then at me, then at Chloe, where her eyes lingered for a fraction of a second longer than they had on me.

"Well, I've got some more little ones for you," she said, leading us down the corridor of pens, back to business. We passed some of the rescues who had been there for months, most of whom were mongrels and senior dogs, and then a few pedigrees and puppies, who I knew would get snapped up straight away. She stopped at the last pen, inside which two small, long-haired dogs cowered in the corner. Their biscuit-coloured fur was tangled and matted, and they curled into one another as they looked up at us. A printed sign on the half-door said "Pablo & Percy".

"Were they surrendered?" I asked as Lauren let Chloe and I into the pen. She nodded.

"Left on a local walking path, tied to a tree with a piece of paper tacked to it that said 'Free to a good home, a.k.a. not mine'."

Chloe and I caught each other's eye, and I could tell she was also trying not to laugh at that. It was horrible, yes. So horrible. And a teensy, little bit funny.

"So obviously we don't know much. Pablo is definitely older than Percy by a good bit. Percy's practically a puppy. We've ordered a DNA test, but the vet thinks they may be mostly Shih Tzu."

"Do they need walks today?" Chloe asked. "We should have time for some more little guys." But Lauren shook her head.

"Honestly, they've been through enough in the last couple of days. It would be really great if you could just sit and try to help them open up? Maybe give them a cuddle if they'll let you? They've probably got fleas – they're getting haircuts this afternoon to help – but they need a bit of love."

"We can definitely do that," Chloe said, winking at Lauren; I just nodded my agreement. Lauren wished us luck and shut us into the pen, looking back at Chloe as she left.

Chloe and I sat down against opposite sides of the pen, waiting for the pups to come to us. We made the compulsory kiss noises at them, but their disdain made it clear this would be a long game.

"Are you sure you don't want to come this weekend?" Chloe asked as we settled in for the wait.

"That's really kind of you," I said, "but that's in, like, fifteen hours, isn't it? Plus, don't feel like you have to invite me to everything."

"I know I don't *have* to do anything," Chloe said, giving me a no-nonsense look across the pen that made me sit up a little straighter. "I mean, if I'm making you feel uncomfortable, just tell me and I'll stop. But I'm inviting you because I think you would enjoy it. And we would, too."

I wasn't sure how to respond. Sure, until this week I'd had a perfectly good reason to turn down the invites. Cara and I had spent pretty much every evening together, and weekends, and holidays. Well, okay, I hadn't actually taken a holiday in a few years; Cara had always wanted to go someplace interesting, and until the Ren Faire idea came up, I'd never been up for something that adventurous.

But now, that reason wasn't there anymore. And if the invitation was genuine ... well, that gave me something to think about, at least. Including how the others would feel; would Jack feel like I was being intrusive after his comment the other night?

Chloe took advantage of the lull to pull out her phone – "just wanna make sure Simone isn't onto me for taking a double lunch," she said – so I pulled mine out, too; maybe the dogs would be more likely to come to us if we were distracted. I did my usual rotation of social media apps, not lingering too long on any one thing. Then I opened up my email, making sure there wasn't anything important in my work inbox before switching to my personal account.

There I found an email that made my blood run cold. It was from Cara's mum, and the subject line was "Next steps for the house".

The first question I'd asked Cara when she'd said she was moving away – well, after gushing about the new job and asking what I was meant to do without her – was about the house. She'd assured me they had no intention of renting it to anyone else, and that my rent was just enough to pay the mortgage. So I told myself as I psyched myself up to open it that it was probably just them reassuring me that I could stay on my own as long as I liked.

But apparently Cara had had no idea what she was talking about.

We're so sorry to spring this on you so shortly after Cara has left, as I know the transition must be a challenge. But we've been advised that now is the best time to jump on this opportunity, so I'm afraid we'll need to move fast. I'm afraid we'll be selling the house now that Cara has moved out, so we'll need your help with making sure it's available and readied for viewings. Since you're already on a month-to-month verbal agreement, I assume this won't be an issue.

The first step will be having the estate agent come round to take pictures and measure in two weeks' time. Please let me know some suitable times that day to have her come over; you'll need to give her a spare key for viewings.

Thanks in advance for your help on this, Morgan.

The pen around me felt like it was closing in, and I was glad I was sat against the wall, because everything started to blur slightly. I realised I was breathing fast when I noticed Chloe scowling at me.

"Morgan, are you okay? Do you need some water?"

She held out her bottle of water to me, but I waved it off. "I'm okay," I said, which was a lie, given that I couldn't seem to take a proper breath.

Out of the corner of my vision, I saw a brown smudge come slowly over to me and settle on the ground beside me. It was Pablo. And not only did he lay down close enough to touch me, curling up like a little croissant, but then he stretched his head back and flopped it to the side, resting it on my thigh.

I reached over to pet him, slowly rubbing down his neck and across his side, and I forced myself to match my breathing to the strokes. In, out. In, out. After a moment, everything came back into focus, and I found that he had closed his eyes and seemed to be asleep.

"That's incredible," Chloe said, and I looked up to see her staring at me with wide eyes, her phone held up in front of her to take a picture. I did my best to smile, leaning my head down to be as close to Pablo as possible. I was sure it was a horribly awkward photo, but I did feel better, and it was pretty incredible that he'd come over to a stranger to help me calm down.

"Seriously, you're the chosen one," she said. "I'm so jealous." She reached out to Percy as if to try to even it out, but Percy just backed into the corner and bared his teeth again.

"Smart dog," I said, smirking at Chloe.

"Har, har," she said. "But seriously, sorry if I stressed you out about this weekend. If it's going to be uncomfortable, I can stop inviting you to stuff."

"No, it wasn't that," I said, scratching under Pablo's chin as he tilted his head back further towards me. "I just got some bad news."

"I'm sorry," she said, sitting forward in mild alarm. "Do we need to go?"

"No, no," I reassured her, and she sat back again. "Just something I didn't want to have to deal with."

"Well then, sounds like you could use a distraction," she said, holding up finger guns.

"Hah, maybe," I said offhandedly. But then again, maybe I *could* use a distraction. I thought about going home and spending my first full weekend alone in the house – and a long one, at that – not only without my best friend, but also knowing that I was about to be kicked out of my home. I had no plans, which meant I'd have to spend the whole weekend cleaning for the stupid listing photos. It sounded like a recipe for a breakdown, which I clearly was on the verge of already.

"Are you *sure* there's enough space?" I asked.

"Yes!" she said, clapping her hands together. "Does that mean you'll come?!"

"And the rest of the group would be okay with me being there?" An image of Jack flashed through my mind, and I snagged ever so briefly on the idea of spending the entire weekend with him. But Chloe's enthusiasm cut right through it.

"Absolutely!" she practically shouted, clapping some more. Percy, clearly thinking she was playing, came over and jumped up, putting his paws on her hands. She squealed with delight and waved her hands to make him dance around. "See? It's clearly meant to be!"

"Clearly," I said, smiling as I continued to stroke Pablo, who snoozed contentedly on my leg. I wasn't sure if it was "meant to be" so much as "a passable excuse to avoid my house", but either worked for me in the moment. Either one was a welcome escape.

CHAPTER 5
JACK

I pulled up to the wisteria-covered cottage – though it was far too big to really be considered a cottage – and paused the podcast I'd been listening to, having completely lost the last five minutes or so because I was thinking about the weekend ahead. I saw that I had a message waiting; it was from Chloe to the group chat we had with Phil, Grey, Fatima, and Jared. Our old gaming group chat. I was sure we'd all acknowledged at some point that we should add Morgan, but we mostly used it to chat shit, so no one had pulled the trigger.

> Change of plans - bedroom reshuffle because I convinced Morgan to come along this weekend! That means Phil and Jack have to share a twin room. Soz.

I stared down at my phone in my hand. *Well,* I thought, thinking back to the horoscope Amy had sent me, *that's certainly a shake-up.*

I thought back to Monday night, when Chloe had been pestering Morgan like usual to come along to the pub, and she'd looked so trapped and freaked out. I'd tried to give her an out, but I couldn't come to work with Chloe every day to keep her in check. I was sure Morgan had plenty of better things to do with her weekend, but it seemed my best efforts to keep my golden retriever best friend at bay had failed. I opened the back to get the groceries, and like the cliché I was, I overloaded my arms just to avoid taking a second trip, eight different reusable bags digging into my forearms as I closed the boot with my foot. This posed a problem when I got to the front door and needed to fetch the lockbox code off my phone, and three of the bags ended up on the floor of the stone porch so I could get to it.

I unloaded the groceries in the big, beautiful kitchen and got to work on dinner, which we'd eat as soon as everyone else arrived. I slipped into a bit of a Zen state whilst doing the chopping for a big pot of early summer vegetable soup; Phil was usually the cook, but he was coming with the others, so I'd offered to take one for the team. I decided to explore the house instead of just sitting around stewing along with dinner. I spent a while admiring the way the modern extension, where four of the bedrooms were, blended seamlessly into the no-doubt-listed building. I found the room Chloe had assigned me, wandered through the vast walled garden, and stood on the bank of the river that I knew just forty minutes away flowed through town.

I'd been perplexed when Chloe and Fatima had first suggested the weekend away – sure, they'd had a voucher, but was it worth using it to go less than an hour down the road? But I still got that holiday feeling as I closed my eyes to the breeze and took a deep breath. It was definitely an upgrade from Fatima's, where we usually hung out. Not that her house wasn't nice – she and her boyfriend Jared had bought it with the express purpose of having lots of people round – but it was our usual haunt, and it was nice to switch things up.

An alarm sounded on my phone after a while to let me know the soup should be ready, just as I heard the sound of tyres on the gravel drive. The two cars pulled up in a mini caravan, and I put on my best royal wave as I walked around the house to meet them.

I greeted the others casually as they got out of the cars, but my breath caught in my throat when I saw Morgan. She always wore dungarees and jumpers and graphic tees on Monday nights, with her ultra-curly hair piled on top of her head. It was actually quite cute, the slightly dishevelled look she rocked most of the time.

But she didn't look cute now. She was wearing a green floral summer dress, the sleeves fluttering down over the tops of her arms and the V at the front dipping low enough to create the tiniest bit of cleavage. Her brown hair hung in shiny, perfect ringlets, creating a halo of curls around her.

Why the fuck was I *so* taken aback? It wasn't like I'd never seen a beautiful woman before.

Her eyes were hidden behind dark sunglasses, so I wasn't sure if she'd clocked me, but then she smiled, and my brain short-circuited, taking me a moment to smile back. She moved around the car towards me, her leg poking through a high slit in her dress, and I might have actually gulped like a cartoon character.

"Fancy seeing you here," she said, casually enough, but the best I could do in response was jab my thumb back over my shoulder towards the house.

"I made soup."

She nodded and smiled tightly, as if she were holding back a laugh. "Is that so?"

"Veggie," I said, nodding and looking out at the surroundings. Anywhere but at her.

Now she didn't even bother hiding her laugh.

"Okay, well, I look forward to trying it." She put a hand on my arm as she moved past me, patting it a couple of times, and I felt my face go instantly red.

"Smooth," Phil said from the boot, and I picked the finger I thought would best express my thanks for his contribution and held it up to him, then tried my best to bury my embarrassment. I had a highly anticipated soup to serve.

"Fuck me," Morgan whispered under her breath, and I had to release my breath super slowly to keep my cool. The floral sundress had since been discarded, but her hair still fell over her now-bare shoulders, and the impulse to reach out and tuck it back behind her ears was strong.

With our bodies just inches away from one another on the floor, I reached out towards her, my hand trembling slightly, and plucked away the middle of the three cards in her hand. She let out a small sigh of relief once I'd chosen, and when I didn't immediately lay down a pair, she cheered.

"You're going down, Evans," she said, taunting me. And sure enough, on her turn, she lay down a pair of twos, proceeding to stand up and do a victory dance in the middle of the circle – one that involved an awful lot of "stanky leg", as Chloe proclaimed. In fact, it was probably a good thing she'd ditched the dress for her pyjamas given the moves she was busting. She still looked great, too, though closer to her usual cute than the bowl-me-over moment from earlier, which was a relief. One could only endure so much humiliation.

It had only been a few hours since we had eaten what had turned out to be a very mediocre soup, but since then Morgan had really seemed to come out of her shell. She'd never exactly been shy – she'd always gone along with the jokes and bits on Monday nights – but this was different. No one was watching the clock. She wasn't hiding behind a character. She was just ... here. Sure, she'd had a few drinks, but she seemed mostly herself, just *more*. And as she transitioned from stanky leg to Soulja Boy, I couldn't help but smile at how at ease she seemed.

The game continued post-dance break, until I found myself the last person with a card: the Old Goat. We were playing Old Maid, but Fatima had insisted we subvert the gender – apparently Goat was the opposite of Maid; who knew? – and now I was staring down at the lecherous lone King in my hand. And it was a good thing I wasn't at all competitive, because I was getting aggressively (and poorly) trash talked by the group.

"Honestly mate, my nan has a better poker face than you do," Phil said.

"Your nan literally taught us to play poker," Chloe retorted, and I laughed. I still remembered that night, shortly after we'd met Phil, playing Hold 'Em in Ethel's dining room, wagering loose smarties and lemon sherbets.

After that we all dispersed, and I went back into the kitchen to get the ice cream out of the freezer to go with the crumble Phil had made. I started when I turned around and saw that Morgan had followed me in.

"Sorry," she said, noticing the way I jumped slightly at seeing her.

"It's okay. Help me dish up?" I held the ice cream tub out to her. She nodded and reached for it. We dished up portions into coffee mugs – me scooping the apple crumble, then her adding ice cream to the top – which she carried into the lounge for the others. But when she came back in for hers, she sat down on a barstool instead of going back in, leaning back against the island as if a wave of exhaustion had suddenly hit her. I sat on the stool next to her and swivelled in her direction.

"Having fun?" I asked, thankful to have my dessert to focus on, but I couldn't help but glance over at her as she perched on her seat, her legs crossed, her foot less than a centimetre from my calf. I didn't dare move, even as she pulsed her foot up and down. Naturally, she took a bite at exactly the same moment I asked her the question. "Sorry if Chloe was a bit intense," I carried on, trying to give her time to get it down. "She's like a dog with a bone."

"She's great," she said, her mouth still full of crumble despite my best efforts. "And I'm glad I came, actually. I'm really enjoying myself."

"Well, we're glad you're here."

"So, what's on the agenda for tomorrow?"

I shrugged. "Grey's in charge of tomorrow. Knowing them, it could be anything from a video game tournament to a ten-hour hike."

Morgan tilted her head to the side and pouted in consideration. "A hike could be fun."

My interest was piqued. "Yeah? You like hiking?"

She scoffed at me. "You don't have to sound so scandalised. Do I not look like I like hiking?"

I rolled my eyes and smiled slightly. "I was asking a question, not challenging you. Promise."

"Well, in that case..." she trailed off, pressing her mouth into a thin line. "I've never actually been hiking before. Or walking, or whatever. Other than just, like, around town, obviously."

"Really? Even when you were a kid?"

Morgan shook her head. "Never. I know it's weird, but my

mum was never super outdoorsy when I was growing up, and by the time she started being a bit more adventurous, I was already at uni." She shrugged. "I take it you've been then?"

"All the time," I said. "I love it."

"Why?" She didn't sound critical, or disbelieving, just curious.

I debated how honest to be, but there was something about the tired-yet-interested look on her face that made me want to match her, so I angled for earnest. "Honestly, for a long time, it was the only time I got to feel like I was having the kinds of experiences I wanted for myself."

She paused with her spoon halfway to her mouth and put it back into the mug, a puzzled look on her face. "That felt loaded in a few places. Care to unburden?"

"My ex."

"Ah, gotcha."

"We used to travel together full-time. We took what was supposed to be a gap year after our second year of uni, and she started posting online about our trips. She got a bit of a following, and within a couple of years she was a full-time content creator." I couldn't help but sneer when I talked about Aria's work; it had been the bane of my existence for years. "She always wanted to get the perfect picture in these hard-to-reach places, but she never wanted to do the work to get there. Like when we went to Macchu Picchu, I did the hike, and she stayed in Cusco a couple extra nights before taking the train. In Japan, I hiked to the top of Mount Fuji whilst she took the bus. Hell, she even took the train to the top of Snowdon. And that was just a day trip."

She cocked her head to one side and squinted. "I mean, did she just not like hiking? Because I'm a girl's girl, Jack, and we don't shame other girls for not being 'one of the guys'."

"No, not at all, it's not like that," I said, my face burning red as I looked away. I was *not* explaining this well. "She'd pretend online like she'd done the big hikes, but it was all a lie. It felt like she just didn't want to do it with *me*. But really we had a lot of problems, and her lack of interest in hiking with me was small potatoes compared to the rest."

I looked up at Morgan to find her eyes glued on my face, her mouth turned down and forehead creased in a look I knew all too well from talking about my ex: sympathy.

"Don't look at me like that," I said. "It was a while ago now."

"How long?"

"Four years."

She shrugged. "That's not that long. Not if it was a bad breakup."

"It wasn't that bad," I said. "It was over a long time before we actually ended it."

"What's her name?" Morgan asked suddenly.

"What? Why?"

Morgan shrugged. "You said she's a content creator. I consume a lot of content. Maybe I know who she is."

I shook my head. "Nope."

"Oh come on," Morgan said, clasping her hands together in front of her as if she were praying to me, jutting her lower lip out in a pout. "Pleeeease?"

I rolled my eyes. "Okay, fine, but I'm telling you, you've not heard of her. Her name's Aria. Aria Mar—"

"You dated Aria Markham?!" Morgan asked, gasping. *Ah, fuck.*

"Yes I did." *Play it cool, play it cool.*

Morgan punched me playfully on the arm. "You said I wouldn't know who she is, but she has like five million followers. Including me."

"Does she?" I asked, trying to sound nonchalant, but that was impressive. It hadn't even been half a million when we'd split up.

"Uh, yeah," Morgan said. "She's basically a celebrity. I'm pretty sure she was at the Grammys last year with her boyf—" Morgan must have seen how glazed over I'd gone, because she had the sense to stop. She actually clamped her hand over her mouth. "Sorry," she said through it. "You probably don't want to know about that."

"It's fine," I lied. I really didn't want to hear about her, but I didn't want Morgan to know that. "Like I said, it was a long time ago."

"That sucks," she said. "She really does act like she's the queen of the outdoors. She even used to post those hiking guides."

That made me laugh, which startled Morgan. "Yeah, well, she's not. I wrote most of those."

"Sorry she was a dick to you." Her face went soft, and she offered a sympathetic smile.

"I was a dick sometimes, too," I said, but for some reason, having Morgan take my side meant something. Not that it should have.

"More drinks!" Chloe called from the dining room, rescuing me from my little stumble down memory lane.

"Coming!" Morgan called, but as she stood up to leave, she looked over at me and gave me that sympathetic look again. But I made myself meet and hold her gaze this time, and I could tell that there was no pity there.

"I know we don't know each other that well," Morgan said, "but you seem like a good guy, Jack. I'm sorry things haven't always been great for you."

I just muttered a quiet "thanks". But then she smiled and

leaned in, stepping slightly between my legs to wrap her arms around my shoulders, and I went stock still. Her chest was pressed against mine in a way that made my breath hitch. And as she nocked her chin over my shoulder, her cascade of curls was directly in my face, smelling of citrus and bergamot. I wasn't sure I'd ever touched her before, and certainly not like this. It was paralysingly novel.

I knew what a normal person would do: accept the hug, wrap their arms around her, and then move on. But I just froze. She was clearly tipsy, and I doubted she would have gone from zero to hugging on a normal day. But even if she would, why did that freak me out so much?

I wasn't super touchy-feely, but I was fine with hugs, and I didn't shy away from affection when it felt right. Hell, I'd only known Fatima for a week before we'd walked down her street arm-in-arm belting "Rest in Peace" from the musical episode of *Buffy the Vampire Slayer*. So why were Morgan's arms around me, and her words about me being a good guy, making me clam all the way up?

By the time I mustered the wherewithal to respond appropriately, she was already stepping back, and all I could do was watch her walk away as I kicked myself internally.

CHAPTER 6
MORGAN

I was so very, extremely, tragically hungover.

Genuinely, it took me a solid minute after waking up to convince myself to open my eyes, and then another minute to determine that I was not, in fact, dead, despite the bright light attempting to blind me. This was made more difficult by the fact that I appeared to be in a granny's house, with blue chintz wallpaper and needlepoint wall hangings galore. The curtains, which I could now see I'd not sufficiently closed, were so aggressively frilly that I thought surely they were hung ironically. Then I remembered my new friends and the embarrassing dance moves I'd done for them. Or was it *with* them? God, I hoped it was with them.

Admittedly, it probably wasn't right to call them new friends – we'd known each other for months at this point. But we'd never spent time together like we had last night. I mean, we had actual inside jokes now! I'd screamed "Superman that ho" at the top of my lungs with Grey! Chloe had challenged me to see who could eat a full mug of ice cream faster without succumbing to brain freeze! If those weren't friends, what were they?

But mostly what felt different was my head, in that it felt like a small gremlin was trying to chisel its way out of my skull.

So I rolled reluctantly out of bed, shoved my loose tit back into my pyjama top, and lumbered out to the kitchen. I groaned as I clocked the smart home tablet embedded in the fridge, which aggressively displayed a time of only half past six. I really should have shut those curtains better.

The sound of the kettle was both the most grating noise I'd ever heard and the most beautiful one, given the promise of cobweb-clearing caffeine. I leaned forward as it gurgled away and rested my forehead against the marble worktops, the cold stone a relief on my warm, sweat-soaked forehead.

The first thoughts of my situation, which I'd managed to keep at bay for most of yesterday, crept in as I lay bent over the worktop. My house was being sold. I was going to have to move. And I had no one to help me navigate that.

I'd made the mistake of looking up listings online the night I'd found out. Any of the flats that looked reasonable were way out of my budget, and any I could afford looked more suitable for a satanic ritual than a quiet single professional. The properties for sale looked even more laughable; I'd been frugal over the years, but my little nest egg was nowhere near enough for a deposit.

Simply put, unless I found a housemate or a suitcase full of money, I was screwed. Selling photos of my feet online had never seemed like a viable option before, but it was seeming less and less outrageous by the moment.

And then there was the fact that Lauren had tagged me in the rescue's post introducing Pablo and Percy yesterday morning, which meant I'd spent most of the drive to the cottage mentally calculating the even worse odds of affording a place that would let me have a dog. I'd made the photo Chloe had taken of us into my phone background, so now the reminder was near-constant.

The ache in my head grew stronger as my mental and emotional agony joined the physical. As the kettle switched off, I begrudgingly left the makeshift cold compress on the worktop, poured the boiling water over my teabag and one sugar, and looked out over the grounds whilst I waited.

The river – the same one I'd walked along with Chloe just a couple of days ago – was just visible through the gate of the walled garden. Back in town it was muddy and wide, but here it looked smaller and clearer. *Almost swimmable, even*, I thought, remembering what Chloe had said about swimming in it as a kid. *That would certainly beat a cold shower...*

I scoffed. I wasn't a swimmer – not spontaneously, anyway – and certainly not in front of people who may be new friends but had never seen my bikini line before. Plus, it wasn't a lido. It was a river, teeming with life, some of it potentially hostile to scaredy cats like me.

But all of the reasons not to go for a dip were easily disputed. Everyone else was still in bed. The river looked placid enough. And, last I'd checked, no one had made the local news for river-dwelling wildlife encounters ... right? Though maybe that kind of news wouldn't have made my particular For You Page. What *had* made my For Your Page were dozens of videos of people wild swimming and being seemingly fine afterwards.

Plus, it did look rather refreshing. Some might say the perfect cure for a hangover, in fact. So why the hell not?

Before I could talk myself out of it, I abandoned my brewing tea, walking back to my room at least twice as fast as I'd left it. I'd definitely over-packed for the weekend, having had no idea what was in store and not wanting to ask too many questions, lest it destroy my image as someone who was totally chill and up for anything. So not only had I packed a huge swathe of options for daywear, but I also had workout clothes, hiking boots, and – crucially – a swimsuit. Two swimsuits, actually, as I hadn't been sure what water-based scenario I'd be likely to encounter, so I'd brought one sportier one and a bikini. I didn't suspect I'd be doing laps in the river, and the sporty one gave me an impressive case of camel toe, so I opted for the bikini.

I reached into my bag to pull out a t-shirt to put on over it, but then I realised with horror that the only spare one I had was a black one with the words "LEAVE NO TRACE" on the front, which I'd bought from a fundraiser run by none other than Aria Markham. I didn't fancy giving Jack's ex-girlfriend any more airtime between us if he saw it, so I shoved the tee back into my bag and nicked a towel from the shared bathroom on my way out instead.

I slipped through the front door and trotted through the garden in bare feet, the dewy grass cool beneath my steps, the morning air already warm and humid in contrast. At the riverbank though, I lost my nerve slightly, freezing in place a few paces away.

At first I pretended to myself that I was trying to find the best way in, but once I spotted the well-trodden path between the rocks that eased into the water, I had to admit that I was just stalling. I mean, weren't there issues with parasites in some UK rivers? Sewage, even? Sure, the water looked clear enough, but I wasn't a scientist. I tried and failed to muster the courage and spontaneity I'd felt inside.

"Gone fishing?" I heard from behind me, and I jumped approximately a full mile into the air, trying to grab my towel and cover myself for some reason, as if I'd been out here skinny dipping. When I turned around and saw Jack standing in the grass, my face went flush.

"Just going swimming," I said, placing my hands defiantly on my hips to try to seem totally chill and up for anything as planned.

"Looks like you're *thinking* about swimming," he said, closing the distance between us. "Very different."

I shrugged. "So what if I was thinking about it?"

He smirked at first, but then he started taking off his top, and I was no longer looking at his facial expression. His torso was as tanned and toned as the rest of him, but he didn't posture or flex like other guys might have in that situation.

"What are you doing?" I asked as he tossed the t-shirt on a rock and started untying the waist of his joggers.

"Going with you," he said, "if that's okay." As his joggers came off, I saw that he was wearing swim trunks underneath. I refused to acknowledge the part of me that was mildly disappointed by the reveal.

I'd once read that women preferred dark-haired love interests in books because dark hair was associated with virility, danger, and masculinity. I couldn't speak to Jack's virility, though the mere thought of it made me go light-headed for a second. But in terms of danger ... let's just say I definitely felt very alert all of a sudden. And masculinity was subjective, but I was certain Jack's abs fit my own personal definition at least.

Jack splashed into the water confidently, and I knew if I wanted to maintain my adventurous air I would have to follow him in pretty quickly. But it took me a few deep breaths to psych myself up before I found myself splashing in behind him, my feet instantly smarting against the pebbly bottom.

I was all the way up to my hips when the temperature registered, and I couldn't help myself; I let out a Wilhelm Scream-style screech. *I definitely should have gone for the sporty swimsuit*, I thought amidst my pain. The water was like icy daggers against my skin, and as I forced myself in deeper, my teeth actually started chattering. Jack was cackling at me from the middle of the river, where he was fully treading water – all six-foot-whatever of him.

As I lowered myself further in, I easily imagined meeting a similar fate to a different Jack, picturing my body sinking into the cold water like Leo's whilst the real Jack watched from the surface on a definitely-big-enough-for-both-of-us door.

"Just breathe," real Jack said, meeting me halfway as I shakily paddled out to him. It was too deep for me to stand, but I saw him lift up in a way that told me he could still touch the bottom. He grabbed my arms and began rubbing up and down, which had the unfortunate effect of bobbing me up and down in the water. I was far too cold to think of personal boundaries, so I reached my hands out to stabilise myself against his chest. Eventually my teeth stopped chattering, and my breath regulated a bit – just enough for me to be embarrassed at how I was clinging to Jack like a child learning to blow bubbles in the water.

"I'm s-sorry," I said, and the embarrassment had the fortunate side effect of warming me even more.

"You're fine," he said, his voice deep and soothing. "Just keep holding onto me, and we'll go in a little bit deeper so your arms can adjust. Is that okay?"

He waited for me to nod before taking a long, slow step backwards, and sinking just a couple of inches further into the water. Then he paused.

"Just checking, you can actually swim, right?"

I rolled my eyes, already feeling a bit better. "Yes, Jack, I can swim. Don't worry, no mouth-to-mouth needed today."

He laughed a bit, but I was pretty sure I detected a slight flush passing across his tanned face.

Because the water was so clear, I could see a refracted version of both our bodies below. They were close – probably too close. But I actually couldn't push myself away very easily, since I was now upstream from him, and the gentle current was pushing me towards him as he stood grounded on the riverbed. If I let go of him, I could have swum backwards slightly and created a bit more space. But for the sake of both warmth and stability, I wasn't ready to do that just yet, so I let the current push us together until we were almost touching.

"You're up early," he said.

"Didn't close the curtains all the way."

He nodded in sympathy.

"You, too," I said.

"Yep, every morning. I could stay up until five, and I'd still be up at half six."

"Lucky you. I have to drag myself out of bed kicking and screaming most mornings."

He chuckled, and I felt the sound reverberate through him beneath my hands. "Who do you kick if you're the one doing the dragging?"

I shrugged. "Mostly Cara. Looks like I'll have to get a cat for all my kicking needs."

He let out a perfunctory laugh – more of a bark, almost. "You're funny," he said.

"Thanks, I practise all my jokes in the mirror."

I closed my eyes and focused on the feeling of the water moving around me, which I was surprised to find no longer stung me the way it had a few moments ago. My head no longer throbbed, either. I had been right; the swim was doing wonders for my hangover.

"Better?" Jack asked. When I nodded, he reached up and put his hands under mine, lifting them away from his shoulders. I tried not to be embarrassed about the fact that he was literally removing me from him.

I swam into the middle of the river and did little laps back and forth, getting more and more acclimatised to the cold water as I did. When I closed my eyes and leaned back, holding onto one of the rocks breaking the surface, all I had was feeling: the movement of the river around me, the sun on my face, and the contrast between the chill on my back and the warmth on my front.

And then, just as I began to feel as relaxed as I ever had, I felt something brush against my thigh.

"Nopenopenope," I said, my tone pitching upward as I repeated the word, immediately pushing myself away from the spot I'd been floating in and swimming back to the riverbank.

"Did something happen?" Jack asked, a bit of alarm in his voice.

"Something touched me," I said, scrambling up to sit on a rock just on the water's edge and drawing my knees to my chest. Jack laughed.

"It's a river, Morgan. Of course there's stuff in there. Fish, kelp, probably a few types of water spiders..."

I shook my head. "Yeah, that's all a big nope from me, thanks."

"Honestly, what did you expect?" he asked as he came to sit next to me on the rock. It was small, and we were close enough that our shoulders brushed against one another. I leaned into it.

"I don't know," I said. "I've seen people rave about wild swimming, and Chloe was going on about the river the other day, and it looked so refreshing this morning, and I wanted to try it. Just take a few steps in, even if part of me was convinced there was a river monster waiting to drag me into the depths."

With how close he was beside me, I felt rather than saw Jack shrug his shoulders. "Well then, it sounds to me like you did what you set out to do, because you definitely took more than a few steps into that water."

"Oh," I said, surprised to realise that he was right. I might have run from the river like a baby, but I'd technically exceeded my initial expectations.

"I take it you've never done it before then?"

I shook my head, and my wet curls brushed over my shoulders, sending a fresh chill through me. "I'm not the most adventurous person, to put it lightly."

Jack smirked, and I rolled my eyes, but I also chuckled.

"Not what I meant."

He shrugged. "I know. But still, what makes you say that?"

"I mean, I've never even been out of the country."

"I have," he said. "It's overrated."

I laughed. "The whole world is overrated?"

"Okay," he said, "not what *I* meant. But we do live in one of the best places in the world for adventures."

"Such as?"

"Well, swimming," Jack said, gesturing at the river. "And hiking—"

"Your favourite," I said, remembering last night.

Jack nodded. "Well, my favourite would technically be camping. And then there's kayaking, climbing..."

"Okay," I said, "I get it. You're Mister Outdoors."

"I mean, it's not *that* hard to get into. Maybe don't jump straight in with climbing, but you literally just have to start walking and you'll hit a hill you can walk up. Get some XP so you can level up to the next thing."

"Sorry," I said, "get some *what* now?"

"XP," he said, then paused, as if I would know what he was on about. "Experience points?" I shook my head. "They're a gaming thing. You get enough XP, you level up."

"We don't use that in Fatima's game," I said.

"No, we use milestones. But they're pretty common in D&D, and in video games and stuff. You get it from combats, loot, important interactions, all that. As you level up, the gaps between levels gets bigger, so you keep having to do new things to keep levelling up. So maybe now you're going for a swim, and next time you go for a hike, and the time after that you stay out camping..."

"So, baby steps?"

"Yeah, I guess," he said, frowning, "but that's a way less interesting way to say it, you've gotta admit."

I nodded. "Interesting. And how does one get this XP in real life?"

Jack waved his arms around him, nearly hitting me in the head in the process. "Pick a direction, and I'll tell you something you can do. It's all around you."

I looked around as if a quest marker were going to appear somewhere. But I knew he was right – I'd been telling myself for years that I should take more advantage of where I lived. The town we lived in was nestled in the Wye Valley, spanning part of the southern border between West England and East Wales, with some of the most beautiful scenery Britain had to offer. I just ... hadn't actually seen much of it. Cara and I had always talked about doing more, but none of it had ever come to fruition.

"Okay, that way," I said, pointing off to my right, down the river. Jack thought for a moment, squinting his eyes as if he really could see the quest marker I'd been imagining.

"Well, that's towards Abergavenny," he said. "You'd have to go over the Black Mountains, part of the Brecon Beacons, which are my favourite. I'm going there next weekend, actually."

"Ooh, fancy," I said. "So I guess you've managed to dissociate hiking from your ex?"

He scoffed. "Helpfully, I'm way past any hang-ups from that relationship."

I rolled my eyes. *Yeah, right*, I thought. Nobody got rid of all their breakup hang-ups, especially when it came to relationships as long-term as the one he'd been in.

"You're telling me you don't have *any* baggage from that relationship?"

He shook his head. "None."

"Okay, so what was your last relationship like then? How was it different?" I felt determined to catch him out – I was feeling awfully vulnerable perched here with my midriff and lack of experience on display, and I wanted to hang him out with me at least.

"That *was* my last relationship."

"Okay," I said, "then the last person you dated, even casually?"

He shook his head again. "I don't date."

I frowned. "Like, at all?"

He shook his head again.

Got him.

"So you're telling me that you don't date *at all* anymore, and that's not baggage? Because I know you're not having trouble pulling anyone." I didn't even care that it was obvious; I leaned back to take in the full, shirtless picture of Jack Evans, gesturing at his body and face. He looked like a Greek god, if they'd all had blonde hair and fewer daddy issues. I could practically hear the local population of dating app users crying out in agony at what they were missing.

"That's right," he said. "I just figured out what works for me. And when it comes to dating, the cost/benefit analysis just doesn't work out."

"Cost?" I asked, scoffing.

"People always hurt each other," he said. "It's human nature in romantic relationships. So I've built a life that means I don't need them. I have family and friends that I love and care for, and that's enough for me."

I definitely didn't mention that there were other needs friends likely wouldn't be able to take care of, and certainly not family. I knew I wasn't one to talk; I hadn't exactly been in a relationship, either. But I also hadn't written off the entire concept.

"And you can talk to those other people in your life the way you would to a partner? Chloe? Phil? Your family?"

"Sure," he said, shrugging. "Of course I do. I mean, there's not much to talk about. I've built my life to look exactly the way I want it, so there's no drama. Nothing to bother people with." *Fuck's sake*, I thought. *This guy has so many blind spots that he shouldn't be allowed on the roads.*

"And when things aren't going well?"

"That's the thing," he said, plastering on a grin that felt somehow forced. "When your life is exactly the way you want it, there's no way for it not to go well. Not enough to make a whole thing of it."

I narrowed my eyes at him, taking in his hunched shoulders, his slight lean away from me. He was feeling super defensive, that was for sure. Clearly I'd touched a nerve. And as curious as I was, now wasn't the time. And hell, I probably wasn't the person. This was only the second real conversation we'd ever had.

But I couldn't help myself being a bit sarcastic.

"Sounds like I'm not the only one due a bit of self-discovery," I said. "Maybe you need some *emotional* XP."

Jack scowled at me, and I scowled back.

"Breakfast!" Phil's voice called from the house, and we both turned our heads to look back in that direction.

"Look, Morgan," Jack said as I looked back at him, "you're barking up the wrong tree with this emotional XP stuff. If you want me to show you around a bit this summer, I'm happy to. But I promise you there's not some big, dramatic truth to uncover here."

I narrowed my eyes at him; I did actually like the sound of having him show me some local spots. I didn't believe him about there being nothing to uncover; he wasn't self-aware enough to be a credible source. But I couldn't exactly say that to him. So instead I just nodded.

"That would be nice, thank you."

"Great," he said, hopping up from the rock and offering me a hand to help me down.

I paused for a moment as he grabbed his clothes from the ground and walked back up to the house, admiring again his tanned skin and golden hair. If I was going to have to push myself, try new things, then at least I'd have a bit of eye candy along the way.

CHAPTER 7
CAPTAIN MORGANA SILVERSWORD

Gorlag the outlander and Yorick the bard, whether through bad luck or ineptitude, couldn't seem to find a single path through the thick underbrush.

The party had finally found a portal to the fae realm, which transported them to a lush meadow in the middle of a dense forest, with seemingly no paths out. It was just the latest in a series of confounding hurdles since the adventurers had been tasked with fetching the legendary Supremacy Sphere so the Queen could prevent it falling into the wrong hands.

"Why would there be a portal here with no paths to it?" Calamity asked.

"There should almost certainly be animal tracks if nothing else," Thrormir said, but Gorlag shook their head.

"None big enough for even the little guy here."

"Hey," Yorick said, smacking the side of Gorlag's leg, which was as high as he came on the half-orc.

"You want animal tracks," Gorlag said, "you find them."

"Maybe I will," Yorick said, turning his attention back to the perimeter of the meadow.

Morgana took the opportunity to look around at the trees, which looked to be completely wild; there were no straight lines or indications of pruning that might suggest intervention or maintenance. There were pockets of space towards the canopy where branches and leaves seemed to bend out of the way, but they were so high up that Morgana couldn't imagine what creatures could have reached them. Creatures they would want to encounter, anyway.

"Thrormir, come have a look," Morgana said, wondering if maybe he could detect any magical influence on the voids. The cleric of Chaius was one of the most useful of her companions, and the most even-tempered. He was also magically adept, like Calamity and Yorick.

But when he examined the space she pointed out, he just shook his head. "They're not magical."

"Look how the void continues," Morgana said as she looked closer, pointing away from the grove. "They're not just pockets. They're tunnels."

"Tunnels for what?" Thrormir asked, but Morgana just shrugged. She pictured all kinds of monsters and beasts, but none that would make a tunnel quite like that, so high up in the trees.

But then she thought about where they were. Maybe there were different beasts in the fae realm that she didn't know about? Maybe there were...

That's when it hit her.

"They're for travel," she said.

"How are we supposed to travel through those?"

But Morgana just shook her head, because they weren't meant for them to travel through. They were meant for the people who lived here: the faeries.

They were flight paths. And one of them, she was almost certain, would lead them straight to Thelanoris.

CHAPTER 8
JACK

When Monday came, we were all sat around the kitchen table for a too-early farewell breakfast. Seriously, what sort of rental made the guests vacate by nine?

We were all a bit worse for wear, but Phil had rallied us all for the 7am wake-up by promising us French toast. I was usually the rise-and-shine type, but even I needed bribery. And now, as I shovelled the fried, ricotta-stuffed goodness into my mouth, I suddenly felt capable of facing the drive home.

Morgan had fully, annoyingly wormed her way into my head. It hadn't helped that I'd been shitting myself the entire time we'd been in the water, with her floating so close to me we were practically pressed together. And then on the rock, with our shoulders touching almost the entire time. I'd felt my guard go up so fast that I'd been surprised we'd been able to have a conversation at all.

But I couldn't stop thinking about how she'd kept insinuating that my decision not to date anymore was some kind of emotional hangover. Was it nice to know she thought I could pull women if I wanted to? Sure. But I didn't love the implication that it was all some post-Aria defence mechanism. I'd worked really hard to get over Aria, and to build the kind of life I wanted. The kind where I didn't need relationships like that to feel fulfilled and accepted and supported. And the implication that I wasn't emotionally self-aware because of it? Fuck that.

So why had I kept playing the conversation on repeat in my mind since then? I'd thought about Morgan and her emotional XP nonsense all over this stupid cottage, including:

- When I was wedged against Phil in Chloe's wardrobe for almost an hour during an intense game of hide-and-seek
- At lunch, as I'd watched her build an absolute monstrosity of a sandwich – chicken, blue cheese, honey, and English mustard – and determined she had disgusting taste and I didn't need to listen to her
- As we all huddled in the dark lounge for a *The Lord of the Rings* marathon; she'd started singing the remixed version of "they're taking the hobbits to Isengard", and I'd admitted to myself that maybe she did have taste after all.

And not only had I been thinking about emotional XP, but also about the fact that I'd somehow ended up offering to be her adventure buddy over the summer and had to now come up with beginner-friendly stuff to do together.

~

FATIMA HAD IMMEDIATELY STARTED ASKING campaign-related questions as we tucked into breakfast. In direct contrast to me, she'd barely touched the food in front of her.

"I have this arc all planned out already," she said, "but I'm starting to think about what comes next so I can start planting some seeds now. So if you want something in particular, or if you're not sure about your character, I can make sure we move in the direction you prefer."

"Maybe everyone can be a little less cliché with the tragic personal histories?" Grey said, and everyone groaned. Sure, it was a bit of a stereotype that every D&D character was an orphan with a tragic backstory. But I wasn't the only one who'd played into that stereotype.

"I mean, I feel like I get a pass," Phil said. "Actual trauma earns you the right to create whatever backstory you want, I feel."

"At least you're not all murderhobos like in the last campaign we did," Fatima said. "Well, except maybe Calamity, but you all keep her in check."

"I love my character," Chloe said, sitting across the table from me, flicking her red hair over her shoulder to get it out of the way of her breakfast. "She's so chaotic."

"So just a natural extension of you then?" I muttered, and Chloe punched me a little too hard on the shoulder.

"Hilarious," she said. "Says the guy who named his character after the worst *Lord of the Rings* character."

"Don't you disrespect Sean Bean like that," I retorted, pronouncing it like *Seen* Bean, which was half inside joke and half instinct at this point. "Also, we've been over this; I didn't mean to do it. If I had meant to make an LOTR reference, surely I would have gone with Gimli? Or Thorin? Something more suitable for a dwarf?"

"Well at least you didn't give your character your exact name plus a single letter," Morgan added, and everyone laughed.

"I just assumed you really liked rum," Phil offered. "Captain Morgana?"

"I don't know why I thought it was a good idea," she said. "It was my first time, and I was worried if I zoned out a bit I wouldn't know you were talking to me unless it was basically my name."

"Well, I'd love to do some more spooky stuff," Chloe said, bringing us back to the actual question. "I loved all the eerie bits with the necromancer, so more creepy shit please."

As soon as Chloe said "spooky stuff", I saw Morgan's face drop.

"I can do creepy shit," Fatima said, "but only if everyone else is okay with that."

She looked around the table at everyone one by one, and everyone else nodded or voiced their assent. Morgan tried her best to nod casually when it was her turn, but Fatima narrowed her eyes and cocked her head to the side, her DM/teacher intuition kicking in.

"Not a fan of creepy shit?"

Morgan inhaled sharply and winced. "Not really," she admitted. "Not actual horror, anyway. The necromancer stuff was fine, but anything starts to feel like a haunted house and I won't manage."

"Do it," Chloe said, rubbing her hands together. "I love freaking out the scaredy cats."

"Not a chance," Fatima said. "Otherwise I'm going to start using all those character voices you hate again."

As she started in with the horrible Australian accent she'd

used for an NPC one time, I got up to get seconds. Phil stood and followed me.

"Wanna tell me why you're so fixated on that end of the table?" he asked quietly as he came up next to me in the kitchen. I'd come to get seconds of the French toast.

"Fuck off, Phil," I muttered in what I hoped was a casually dismissive tone, but I could feel a pink flush rising up my neck. "I have no idea what you're talking about."

"Oh yeah? How was your little swim yesterday?"

"Nothing happened, I've told you. We mostly just sat on the rocks and talked."

"Please," he said, keeping his tone low but mocking. "I was watching from the window from the moment you left the house. I saw your little face-off in the water. The only thing that was missing was a bunch of crabs and fish singing a daytime rendition of 'Kiss the Girl'."

I looked up at Phil's smiling face – he really did mean all this in good fun – and I saw when he realised I was growing genuinely annoyed.

"Hey, sorry, man. It's just banter."

I sighed. "I know. It's fine."

"But if it weren't," Phil said, "that would be okay, too."

I turned my glare back to him. "She's lovely. But I'm not interested."

"Or you won't let yourself be interested," he said. "In her, or in anyone for that matter."

"I'm not having this conversation," I said, finally putting another piece of toast onto my plate and walking away. I had to walk behind Morgan to get to my seat, and I saw that she had a video pulled up on her phone of someone in a very historically inaccurate suit of armour.

"Whatcha looking at?"

She looked up at me and then shrugged. "Just some cosplay stuff."

"Ooh, I love cosplay," Chloe said from the other end of the table. "I do a killer gender-bent Milo Thatch."

"Oh, I don't do it," Morgan said. "Or at least I never have. This is someone at a Ren Faire."

"I've always wanted to go to one of those," Grey said. "They look so cool."

"Well," Morgan said, "I was actually supposed to go this autumn, but my friend bailed."

"Aur naur!" Chloe shouted in a parody of Fatima's bad Australian accent. "Cara?"

Morgan nodded. "It's okay though, we hadn't booked anything."

I could see in her face that it wasn't okay; she was actually disappointed. And maybe after what she'd said at the riverside, I wanted to push her a bit. But I was still willing myself to shut up even as I started speaking.

"We can go with you," I said. "I know Chloe's always looking for the chance to throw on a corset."

"Are you airing all my kinks, Evans?" Chloe asked, but she looked genuinely thrilled by the idea.

"Oh no, that's okay," Morgan said, waving her hands in front of her. "You don't have to do that."

"Yeah, sorry, I was kidding," I said, instantly backpedalling. Because I didn't actually want to go to this thing, did I? It was certainly an escalation from agreeing to take her hiking.

But Morgan glared at me. "Well, hold on now," she said, clearly determined to catch me out. "Maybe I do want some travel buddies."

"Really?!" Chloe squealed.

"Really." She was calling my damn bluff. I glowered at her, but she just smiled wider. "Let's go to the Ren Faire."

"Wait, we're going to a Ren Faire?" Fatima asked.

"I'm so in!" Grey added.

"Fuck it," Phil said, sauntering over from the kitchen, "I'm in, too."

Chloe smacked my arm, as if waiting for me to agree. I sighed and nodded. "Fine. Let's do it."

I could tell from the way Morgan lifted her chin that I'd live to regret this. And to add salt to the wound, Phil had a smug look on his face, too.

"Great," Morgan said, settling back against the cushion. "Let's fucking do it."

"I can make costumes?" Phil offered, and everyone gasped in excitement.

"But won't that take you forever?" I asked. "And, you know, cost a fortune?"

"I mean, I'll want help with material costs," he said. "But I've got plenty of time this summer. Honestly, I've been looking for a project."

"I mean, if you're sure," Grey said. "It sounds incredible."

"Right then," he said, bringing his hands down on the table in front of him. "It's settled. Start thinking about what you want to wear so I can start."

"I can help with that," Morgan said, and everyone looked from Phil to her. Maybe it was just that we'd watched *The Lord of the Rings* yesterday, but it felt like an "and my axe" kind of moment.

"I mean, I can draw people's characters so you have something visual to work from if you want."

"Is that what you're always doing under the table during games?" Chloe asked. Morgan nodded. "So exciting!"

"It's just a hobby," she said, backtracking a bit, clearly trying to manage our expectations. "But it might help you visualise what you want. I'll show you next week."

"Sounds like a plan coming together," Chloe said. "Should we make this shit official and pick a date that we want to go to America? And, you know, actually choose which faire to go to?"

"Well, not to be that person," Fatima said, pointing to herself overhead, "but I'm a teacher, so it'll have to be half term."

"Don't you fancy private school teachers get two weeks?" Phil asked.

"Yeah, but only one weekend in between them," she said. "I assume these are weekend affairs?"

Things got very official very quickly, with Grey producing a sticker-covered laptop seemingly out of nowhere and starting a spreadsheet. There were dozens of Renaissance and medieval festivals in America every year, but only a handful that were really big and had autumn dates. We narrowed it down quickly to one in North Carolina, with direct flights, proximity to an airport, and our target weekend available. And by the time nine o'clock rolled around, we had to scramble to get our things, but we had something resembling a plan in place.

"How much XP do you reckon?" Morgan asked me as we reconvened outside to load the cars. She leaned into me conspiratorially, and I had a flashback to pressing against her on the rock yesterday morning. I had to step away slightly so I could focus on literally anything else.

"For the Ren Faire?" I frowned as I considered the question. "Two thousand?"

"Is that a lot?"

I nodded. "Worth a level-up all on its own in some games."

As she walked away and loaded her bag into Grey's boot, I

saw a huge grin on her face, which made me grin, too. As annoying as I'd found her line of questioning yesterday, I enjoyed putting a smile on her face. And I figured that, if the next few months could help do that, then maybe I should actually try to make them worthwhile. For both of us.

CHAPTER 9
MORGAN

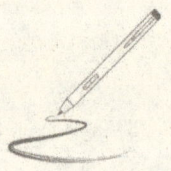

Tuesday brought with it the rudest awakening possible in the form of a performance review at work. At least I'd got to go play with Pablo over lunch; his pal Percy had been adopted as soon as the website had been updated to reflect that he was a Lhasa Apso puppy, which was much rarer. I'd come to terms with the fact that I probably wouldn't be able to find a pet-friendly place in my budget, but at least I could make sure he wasn't lonely in the meantime.

I dropped my sunglasses at my desk in the "fundraising corner", as it had been dubbed, which was made up of four desks smushed together into one big table. The six of us in fundraising – well, now five without Cara, as her role still hadn't been filled – took turns in each spot so no one would be permanently stuck in the seats that straddled two desks, or the "manspread desks" as we called them.

I grabbed my laptop and exchanged loaded glances with Chloe before heading to my boss's office; her review was later in the day. Simone was waiting for me, scrolling through a document on her computer that I recognised as my review form. I'd filled out the self-reflection a few days prior, not sure how to professionally say "I meet my quotas, but I also couldn't give less of a shit as long as I get paid, and I'm sure that's clear to everyone around me."

"Have a seat," Simone said, tilting her head down to look at me over her reading glasses, pointing to the chair opposite hers at her desk. Her tone was casual enough, but I still felt like I'd been called into the headmaster's office, causing me to perch nervously on the edge of the chair rather than settling into it like I normally would.

We went through the form together in a way that told me she could tell I didn't give a shit, but she also didn't give much of a shit, so it was fine. I would be getting a pay rise in line with inflation, and my quota was going up by ten percent like it had every year since I'd joined. It was the world's most monotonous performance review, which was fitting for what felt like the world's most monotonous job.

Until it wasn't.

"What's your vision for your future here, Morgan?"

I actually blinked, trying to figure out if I'd heard her correctly.

"You mean for, like, my career?" It was the most idiotic thing I could have uttered, but my brain hadn't processed the break in status quo yet.

"Yes," she said, a twinge of exasperation in her tone.

"I'm not sure," I said, sitting forward, wracking my brain for anything at all that would be professionally appropriate. But the only thing I could find for several seconds was "I have no vision for anything in my life, much less this dead-end job." Thankfully my still-mildly-hungover brain managed to filter that one.

"Well," Simone said, throwing me a much-needed lifeline,

"have you ever thought about moving into events?"

I somehow managed to keep my nose from actually turning up at that comment. I'd helped on the autumn gala last year, and it had been the worst three months of my life. "Not specifically," I said.

"Well, Aaron from the events team is going on parental leave at some point soon," she said. "And between you and me, he's let me know that he's unlikely to come back. So there could be a promotion up for grabs."

I didn't like where she was headed, and my leg bounced nervously in front of me.

"Now, you helped Aaron with last year's gala, did you not?"

I nodded, swallowing hard.

"Well, I'd like you to cover it this year, in addition to your usual work. And assuming it goes well, as soon as Aaron makes his departure official, his job would be yours."

I knew she was expecting some gratitude from me here; the Event Coordinators made almost ten grand a year more than I did in my current role. And who actually liked being a glorified telemarketer? So I saw disappointment settle over her when I didn't immediately begin thanking her.

But then I remembered my current predicament. I'd be moving out soon, whether I liked it or not. With any luck, the gala would come and go without a moving date, and I could save enough to tide me over in a more expensive place until the promotion became available. This could be a game-changer for me in terms of what I could afford on my own. Maybe I could even get a dog-friendly place...

So I smiled.

"I'm in," I said, trying to project the confidence I thought she was looking for.

"Brilliant," she said, bringing her hands down on the stack

of folders on her desk. She grabbed one of them, clearly placed conveniently on top for this conversation, and handed it to me. "Here's all the collateral from last year: the invites, the programme, the menu. Aaron will have everything else. I'll have him put a meeting in your calendar for next week to get started."

"Thank you," I said, standing up to go.

"You're the right person for the job," she said from her seat as I left the room. "I know you can do this."

I smiled and nodded thankfully as I left the room, but the smile dropped as soon as I shut the door behind me. Because I knew she was right; I could do this. But I also wasn't being given a choice, as was the case with most things in my life, it seemed.

BY THE TIME the weekend rolled around, I couldn't ignore the cleaning any longer. The estate agent was officially coming round in a couple of days, and I figured I'd better get started. So I put my headphones on, put on the audiobook of a new rom-com, and got to work.

I started by throwing a load of whites into the washing machine, which meant changing my bedsheets. Then, riding the wave of momentum that created, I boxed half the throw pillows and stashed them in the gross storage cellar; I hated to admit it, but the lounge looked significantly less cluttered as a result. I scrubbed the kitchen from top to bottom, and even dusted the skirting board, which was so dusty that I wondered if it had ever been dusted at all.

Then I took a step back, looked at the downstairs through the eyes of a prospective buyer, decided most prospective buyers were probably boring, and decided we probably didn't need all three rugs. I tried to get the most garish one out from under the sofa, but I couldn't do it alone, so I changed my mind and decided the boring buyers would just have to deal.

I was just putting another load of washing on when a text message came through, the ding of the notification so loud in my headphones that it made me jump. I pulled my phone out of the chest pocket of my dungarees and saw that it was from Chloe:

> Really glad you came with us this weekend! And now we've got the ren faire to plan, yay! Xx

I tapped out a reply:

> It was so fun! And yeah, lots to plan! Let me know when I need to send you money for the flights and stuff

This was new; Chloe and I had never messaged outside of work before. I hadn't had a texting buddy other than Cara in forever. Not that one text constituted a texting buddy, but still ... it was a start.

I smiled a few moments later when another notification pinged, letting me know I'd been added to a group chat called "Wench Please".

I sat down on the sofa for a break, and the second I did, I felt all the motivation drain out of me. So instead of doing the half dozen other things on my list, I grabbed my tablet and went over to my window seat.

Instead of resuming the character portraits though, I opened up a new file and just started drawing as lines and colours flashed in my mind: some grey shapes, some green grass, and finally some squiggles that could be water. It was the river. Now that I knew what I was doing, I went back and refined some of the shapes, then debated how to approach drawing the water, which had been so crystal clear; I'd never tried to draw anything quite like it. But eventually I got there, focusing on creating reflections and refractions instead of the water itself.

And before I realised what I was doing, I was adding more shapes to the scene: one taller and more golden, the other paler and smaller, as close as they could be to one another in the water without touching. The negative space between them was almost more conspicuous than contact would have been. Looking at it, I could remember what it felt like to have the current moving around me, pushing me towards him, his eyes on my face, his body heat at my front...

Nope, okay, that was enough of that. I turned off my tablet and chucked it away from me faster than if it had burned me.

I shook off the memory, but I couldn't shake the sense that something important had happened. Jack was right: it had awakened a desire to do something more. Something interesting. Whatever had come over me that morning that had made me want to go swimming, that didn't seem to be going away.

I pictured myself doing all of the things Jack had talked about. Hiking, camping, kayaking... I'd never done any of it, and I would have said just a couple of days ago that it was too far out of my comfort zone. But how could I say that for sure if I never tried?

Then again, how exactly did one go about going on a hike when one had no car and no survival skills?

I only knew one person who would be able to say for sure, and luckily I'd just been added to a group chat with him.

I took a deep breath and looked down at the list of group members, using process of elimination to find Jack's number;

there were two that didn't have names next to them, and one of those had a picture of a blurry figure with a lilac buzz cut. So I tapped on the other one – the one without the photo, though I could easily picture the golden blonde hair and chiselled face that should be there – and messaged Jack, trying to suppress the images that flashed in my mind from my little replay a few minutes ago.

> So how does one... hike?

Then, for good measure, I added:

> (This is Morgan, btw.)

And then, probably not good measure anymore but equally urgent:

> (I got your number off the group chat. Sorry if that's weird.)

I regretted the last message almost as soon as I'd sent it; of course it was weird that I texted him within ten minutes of having access to his number, and no amount of apologising would make it less so. But the only thing worse than the message would be deleting it and having him be able to see that I'd deleted a message. So I stuck to my guns, staring at my phone as if I could summon a reply.

Nearly two minutes later, it worked. He started typing. And ten seconds after that, his message came through:

> One finds a hiking buddy. Free Friday evening?

> Also, +200 XP for asking. Nice one.

CHAPTER 10
JACK

"Pass me that, will you?"

Chloe reached into the Defender for the bug hotel I'd made for Mum out of some scrap lumber, foraged twigs and paper straws. She heaved it over the low hedge bordering the front garden, and I was surprised yet again at how heavy it was, despite the fact that I'd made it. It was massive for a bug house, nearly a metre tall, but she'd insisted she needed one that size for the back garden, and arguing with Mum was almost always futile.

"I hate these things," Chloe said, dramatically shivering as she handed it to me. "They just get covered in spiderwebs, so they trigger my arachnophobia *and* my trypophobia all at once."

"Well, helpfully you don't have to look at it anymore," I said, placing it on Mum's front step facing away from Chloe. I walked the long way round through the gate back to the car where Chloe was waiting in the passenger seat, then drove it back up to drive it over the hill to mine.

"I need to say hi to your mum," she said. "I haven't seen her in ages."

"Yeah, well, gird your loins, because she wants to set you up with—"

"Let me guess," Chloe said, "her friend's daughter recently came out as gay?"

I shrugged. "I don't know about the recency, but I'm afraid it's a colleague, not a friend."

"Damn," Chloe said, smacking her thigh. "So close. It's fine, I'm emotionally unavailable either way."

I rolled my eyes. "Are we talking about that girl from the Rescue?"

"I can't stop insta-stalking her," Chloe said from the passenger seat, turning her phone to show me a picture of her current crush.

"Don't shit where you eat," I said, not even looking. I'd seen half a dozen pictures already since I'd picked Chloe up.

"She works at the actual rescue, not the headquarters," she explained for the third time.

"Doesn't matter," I said. "Seems complicated."

I could practically hear Chloe roll her eyes as I put the car in park. "Every form of romance is too complicated for you. You're hardly the barometer I'd use for normal dating habits."

She had a point; romance generally *was* too complicated. It was like I'd been trying to tell Morgan on our weekend away; there were too many opportunities to hurt one another, and you never got enough back for the trouble.

But even if I was all the way at one end of the dating normalcy spectrum, Chloe was way at the other end. She was so chaotic in who and how she dated. She'd never been with anyone for longer than a few months, but she would go through an entire long-term relationship cycle in that time. She would swipe through profiles on the app like she was trying to win some kind of competition, and she'd flirt with men at every opportunity despite being wholly uninterested. But she'd never approach a woman she didn't already know, just obsess over them from a distance, imagining an entire fictional life together without ever having spoken. And heaven forbid they actually speak to *her*; she'd find the tiniest thing to get hung up on and throw the whole idea of that person out the window.

Come to think of it, I wasn't sure how she'd ever managed to actually find a relationship at all.

What she was very good at, on the other hand, was packing Tetris.

Over the years, she'd earned the honour of packing my rucksack for my solo trips; not that I couldn't do it myself, but she loved to help, and she was a bit of a prodigy at it. Each time I'd think I'd found ways to trim weight, making it lighter and easier to carry. But she was next-level ruthless. Last autumn she'd even snapped the end off my toothbrush.

But now, as she looked at the supplies I'd laid out on the floor of my lounge, she seemed stumped.

"Honestly, Jack, I think we might have achieved perfection."

"Not a chance," I said, spurring her on, but I was, of course, stumped too. Over the years I'd collected lighter-weight clothing and state-of-the-art gear, and I couldn't spot a single inefficiency among the bunch. Except the pad of paper and pencils, but Chloe knew by now not to question that.

"What's the chance of rain?" Chloe asked, and I knew what she was thinking: could we lose the rain gear?

"I thought of that," I said, "but it's fifty–fifty. And it is Wales after all..."

Whilst the cost/benefit analysis of dating didn't work out, the cost/benefit of being prepared for rain certainly did. I'd been caught out once without the proper equipment, and it was the only time I'd understood why some people didn't like the outdoors. It had been miserable.

"It'll all have to stay then," she said, then turned to me. "Well done, grasshopper."

She knelt down and started folding and stuffing, adjusting and analysing as she went. Within five minutes, my rucksack was meticulously packed; I put it on to find the weight perfectly distributed. We really did have this down to a science.

"I still don't understand why you love doing that so much," I said, adjusting the straps so my hips took all the weight rather than my back.

"It's the ultimate sense of achievement," she said, standing up. I decided not to ask her for the umpteenth time why, then, her flat was such a tip all the time.

"You sure you don't want to come? Surely the achievement is better when you get to experience the impact of it?"

Chloe placed a hand on the strap running over my right shoulder. "See, that's where you're wrong," she said softly. "The satisfaction comes especially from *not* having to exert myself after. All the fun, none of the fitness."

SEVERAL HOURS LATER, I was walking along a low ridge in the Black Mountains north of Abergavenny. It was an area I'd visited several times, and sometimes I'd get questions about why I didn't go further afield, but I loved this route, just over the Welsh border. The Wye Valley and the Brecon Beacons were, in my fully biased opinion, the best place in the world to live. And given that I'd seen a lot of the world, I felt pretty entitled to that opinion.

Plus, I knew enough about the local flora and fauna to get

more out of the experience than the average outdoor enthusiast. I'd learned a lot of it from Mum growing up, when she'd taken Amy and me walking or camping, but I'd learned a lot on my travels, too, always a bit homesick for the birdsong and foliage I'd grown up with.

I tried to walk a slightly different route each time I came to these hills, but I was somewhat limited by my camping spots, which I had to clear with the land owners ahead of time. I would have preferred to wild camp like I had before in Scotland and Dartmoor, but it wasn't allowed, and Dad knew one of the landowners here. Still, for the past few years, I'd been able to escape to a place where I knew I'd have to interact with nothing and no one but the weather and terrain.

Except apparently my brain was determined to make me interact with Morgan, whether or not she was actually here. We were going on a hike in just a few days – admittedly a much tamer hike than the one I was on now – and I hadn't been able to stop thinking about it since she'd texted me. On the one hand, I'd been the one to suggest we could do things together this summer as a way to help her level up. (God, I still cringed at how cheesy that analogy was, but it had seemed to resonate with her.) But honestly, I hadn't expected her to take me up on it; certainly not so quickly. There was a part of me that had done a happy jig – internal, of course – when she'd texted. But most of me went directly into overthinking it. Was she just that desperate to try something new? Or had the heat I'd felt between us in the river, despite the cold water we'd been swimming in, not just been in my head? Was she interested in me that way, even after everything I'd said about Aria and about dating in general?

A cynical part of me wondered if maybe she *was* into me, but only *because* of Aria. That would be typical; everything coming back to her. She'd been a black hole for attention our entire relationship, and maybe now was no different.

But no, Morgan had been a bit flirty with me before she'd found out about Aria, hadn't she? Or had it just been my brain short-circuiting? Inferring interest where there wasn't any? Assuming that the tiniest bit of physical affection from a tipsy woman meant more than it did, just because *I* had felt something when she'd stepped between my legs and pressed herself against me?

Suddenly a familiar weight began to pool in my gut, and I felt sick to my stomach. I had to stop walking and catch my breath, which was unlike me. I didn't like the way it made me feel, thinking about Morgan that way. Thinking about *anyone* that way, actually. It was why none of the dates I had been on – the ones I hadn't mentioned to Morgan – had worked out. Any time I felt a spark, it was doused in this anxiety.

But I was determined to get Morgan out of my head, so I popped in my earbuds – always a last resort, but I was desperate – and focused on moving forward as quickly as I could. The further I walked, the more I felt myself unravel inside, even as my calves cramped and my glutes burned from the incline. My head cleared enough for me to take out my earbuds and enjoy the sounds of nature, like the coo of a wood pigeon and the wind blowing through the ferns in the gullies. I spotted several sets of dog tracks in the mud on one path, and even some for a fallow deer near a small grove, which was a nice surprise. And just as I began to fatigue, I came around the corner of a large rock formation and saw my campsite.

The reservoir was nestled in a little valley similar to my pond at home, but on a much larger scale. A dam at one end held back what seemed like an immense amount of water from flooding through the valley beyond. It was owned by a friend of

Dad's, and since it had been decommissioned as a drinking water source, it had become the destination for several popular walking routes. It was quiet now though, with not a soul in sight.

I made my way to the far end where the hillside folded around it; it was the most sheltered and secluded spot, with hills on both sides and a few oak and ash trees for cover. The longer grass was pointing the same north-eastern direction as the shorter grasses, so I knew, as raindrops began to fall, that I'd need shielding, both from the south-westerly winds that would sweep down over the hills and the driving rain that would come with them.

My tent and fly were at the very top of my pack – thanks to Chloe, of course – so I was able to get them up and put some water on to boil for my dinner before the rain started in earnest. I rehydrated the curry I'd packed, for which Phil had loaned me his fancy dehydrator, and sat in my tent looking out over the water, where the rain was coming down so hard now that it was hard to find the line between it and the surface of the reservoir.

As I looked around, it struck me for the millionth time how interesting the mountains here were. There were so few trees and bushes; it looked almost barren. The small oak grove I was sitting in was the only part that actually looked lush, despite the fact that I knew the grasses contained an immense amount of biodiversity. Because of the sparse look, any bothys and buildings that had been constructed, most made out of stone to combat the wind blowing against the side of my tent, stood out like sore thumbs on the landscape. What would it look like to build something that actually looked at home out here?

I pulled out the one inefficiency I always allowed myself on these trips: a pad of paper and pencil. It wasn't a fancy sketch pad or artist's pencil, but I began to draw anyway, reflecting the image that formed in my mind. A house built into the hill opposite me, just below the road out, with a live roof and a dark blue timber facing to match the colour of the water. The drawing didn't have colour, of course, but it helped it come to life more in my mind.

Before long I had a mostly accurate sketch of the hill opposite me, but with a new structure in perfect harmony with its surroundings.

It wasn't the first time I'd done this; in fact, my weekends away were some of my most inspired times. I'd started doing it when I was with Aria, taking in the different architectural styles we saw when we were travelling. I'd expected the inspiration to wane when I'd moved home, and especially when I'd started working for Dad, but if anything, it had deepened. Knowing how buildings came together had added a new level of consideration to the sketches, and I found the British landscape super inspiring.

But it was just a creative outlet, nothing serious. So I shoved the pad back in my pack and continued to watch the rain until it was time for bed, hoping it would clear up in time for my hike with Morgan.

CHAPTER II
CAPTAIN MORGANA SILVERSWORD

Morgana hadn't expected to actively battle faeries when she'd come to the fae realm, but as she watched Gorlag cleave their axe upward to take out three who were positioned above them, she was glad she hadn't ruled it out. She swung her sword at the archer, then ducked out of the way as the mage fired off a splash of acid at her.

"Let me out!" cried the faerie trapped in the cage; the reason they'd entered the fight to begin with. They'd been bushwhacking through the underbrush beneath a flight path when they'd heard her shouts for help – as heroes, they couldn't exactly say "ignore that" – and they'd found her locked inside a cage under an outcropping of rock, surrounded by other faeries with weapons drawn. After a failed attempt to negotiate her release, and being told not to meddle in the affairs of the fae courts, Calamity had opened fire. Literally.

Now Calamity was trying to get the cage unlocked, whilst the rest of the party fended off the others. Yorick played his lute in the background, bolstering them, and Morgana used that bolstering to skewer the mage on the end of her sword. She flung it off the end and went for the archer again, but this time she missed. Gorlag took out the ones swarming them, but the archer got Yorick in the back, and he broke a string on his lute as he stumbled.

"Thrormir, help!" he called. He hadn't taken many hits, but the wound on his back was starting to bleed.

"You're fine," Thrormir yelled, as the final faerie flew straight towards him. He cast a spell, and suddenly a spectral version of his warhammer was floating in front of him. He used it to attack the faerie in front of him, then cast another, and the faerie fell to the ground, clutching its ears. Morgana took the chance to step forward and finish it off.

"That was unnecessary," Gorlag said to Thrormir. "I could have finished it off."

"It was fine," Thrormir said. "And honestly, it was nice to get to use those spells. All I ever do is heal you lot."

"Some of us actually need healing," Yorick said, standing up and dusting himself off.

"If I recall," Thrormir posited, "you've got some healing spells of your own you could use."

"I'm really better as a motivational force," Yorick said, but Calamity cleared her throat for the party to pay attention. They looked over to her to see that she'd freed the faerie who'd been trapped. She hovered a few feet above the ground so that she was eye level with Morgana and Calamity. Her dark hair fell in a braid over her shoulder. Her skin was green, and she wore leather armour over her green dress, a trio of daggers sheathed at her side. She was dressed and armoured like a thief.

"Thank you," she said, her voice high-pitched and musical. "My name's Clover. Welcome to the Spring Court."

The party all introduced themselves, and when Yorick

stepped forward, posturing slightly, Morgana rolled her eyes. He had a habit of trying to charm his way through situations.

Calamity caught Morgana's eye, and she nodded. She knew what Calamity wanted to do, and it was worth a try.

"Could you help us get to Thelanoris?" Calamity asked. And as she did, Morgana could hear her voice slightly doubling; a thieves' cant that only a trained ear could hear. She knew Calamity would be asking about the catacombs, where they now knew the Sphere was. She couldn't understand it herself to know for sure, but she'd encountered the Thieves Guild in the Capital enough times to recognise what Calamity was doing. She only hoped it would translate to the fae realm, and that Clover was indeed a thief.

"I see," Clover said, understanding dawning on her face as she looked them over. Morgana sighed in relief. "I think I can help you get where you want to go."

"Thank god," Gorlag said under their breath, but then Clover smirked.

"For a price, of course."

CHAPTER 12
MORGAN

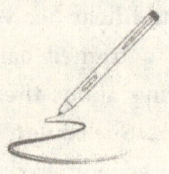

By the end of the following week, I had a pretty solid to-do list for the gala compiled. What was less solid was the budget – Aaron had gone over in almost every area where he'd actually managed to do something – but that was Next Week Morgan's problem. By five o'clock, Today Morgan was wholly concerned with the tall blonde man in a plaid shirt and hiking boots greeting Chloe at the front door.

When he saw me walking over to him, Jack stood up straight and gave a stilted wave. He looked as unsure of how to greet me as I felt about him. As I got close, he opened his arms out to the side in a gesture that could have solicited a hug or could have just meant something like "ta-da, I'm here!" if I wasn't keen on a hug. I indulged it though, wrapping my arms partially around his middle as he folded his around my shoulders.

As he did, I couldn't help but relax into the warmth of his chest a bit. He was a great hugger; not too tight, but tight enough that it felt intentional. Wanted. Way better than my fumbled attempt at a hug on the weekend away. And he smelled so good: like sawdust, and a hint of something deeper, like amber or musk. I'd never been a scent guru, but whatever this particular smell was, I was a fan.

And then I had the tragic, humiliating realisation that I was hugging Jack for the first sober time ever and was actually sniffing him. Like, full-on inhaling through the nose multiple times to get a good whiff. Was I even capable of not humiliating myself in front of him?

I was instantly desperate to save face, so I pulled away and tried to confidently meet his eye.

"You smell like sawdust. Did you come from work?"

Jack smiled, and I got the sense he had noticed the sniffing but decided to ignore it. "I went home first. Trust me, if I'd come straight from work, there would be a lot more actual sawdust in my wake. But the smell does tend to linger."

I smiled back, thankful for the save.

"You ready to go?"

I lifted my bag in answer. "Sure am."

"Have fun you two," Chloe said, and I looked back at her to find her smiling in a very strange and disconcerting way.

I followed Jack back out into the sunshine and to his car, which I recognised from the weekend before. It was a retro Land Rover Defender, with army-green paint on the lower half of the sides and a white top. The big black roof rack on top was empty today, but I imagined Jack used it regularly from what he'd said about his hobbies. I climbed into the passenger seat through the door Jack held open, nodding my thanks before he shut me in and moved around to his own side.

He offered me the auxiliary cable; the car was old enough that it didn't have Bluetooth, I guessed. I plugged in my phone and chose a playlist I thought would be good, pressing shuffle; a Death Cab for Cutie song called "No Room in Frame" came on.

"Not this one," Jack said, and it took me a moment to realise he was talking about the song. I looked up at him to see that he was pressed fully against the seat, his arms tense against the steering wheel. I skipped to the next track, and as Noah Kahan poured through the speakers, he visibly relaxed. *Weird.* I filed that one away for later speculation.

Happy with the music at last, Jack put the car in gear and turned out onto the A road. He had told me it would be nearly an hour until we got there, so I hung my arm out the window and let myself relax into the moment. The shopping centres and suburban estates gave way gradually to rolling hills and patchwork farmland, the lush greens of the grass and trees accented by pops of yellow gorse. I'd seen landscapes exactly like this hundreds of times in passing, but this was different. Maybe because I was here specifically to enjoy it, I noticed it in a way I never had before: the different types of hedgerows demarcating the farmland; the shadows cast over the fields by the tiny, fast-moving clouds; even the potholes in the road getting more and more prevalent as we got further out of town. And I looked over at Jack every now and then, admiring that view, too.

Before long, we found ourselves on terrifyingly tiny one-lane tracks, where the branches of trees we passed or from the hedges lining the road came dangerously close to scratching the car. The passing points were few and far between, and even then I doubted another car would be able to get through. Yes, we were essentially in a tank, and I had no doubt we'd come out literally on top if anything happened. But funnily enough, picturing those scenarios didn't exactly make my grip on the door loosen as Jack barrelled down the roads, slowing only when we came to sharp bends or junctions. We only encountered another car once, and thankfully we were only a little ways past a passing point, so Jack reversed a hundred metres or so to let them squeeze through. And I knew it was a cliché even as it was happening, but when he put his hand on my seat and looked over his shoulder to reverse, I swooned a little.

Miraculously though, we made it to the car park without incident, and I jumped out of the car onto the ground, pulling the sweet, slightly manure-y country air deep into my lungs. Jack offered me a bottle of suncream, and I applied it as he shuffled things around in his backpack.

"I brought you a water bottle," he said, holding it out to me. I took a sip and then handed it back, where it disappeared inside his bag again. If I'd had a competence kink, it would have been over for me then and there; he was clearly operating at Scout levels of preparation.

And then we were off, heading up a well-defined path that went straight up a hill. The gradual incline followed a ridge overlooking valleys on either side. I easily matched Jack's pace as I walked behind him, to the point that I suspected he was shortening his gait considerably for my sake.

A long while later, just as I was wondering if our previous conversations were a fluke and the silence of the drive here would persist the whole hike, the trail opened up a bit wider, and Jack dropped back to walk next to me instead of in front of me.

"Thanks for suggesting this," he said. "I haven't hiked with anyone else in years."

"Well, I need all the XP I can get before October, don't I?"

"True," he said, smiling softly. It was nice to see him so at ease; so in his element. "But I'm still grateful for the company."

The scenery was beautiful, with views over the blue and green landscape for miles and miles around. Our steps fell into sync as we climbed the hill, which was now getting steeper and steeper. I intentionally dragged my heels as I walked, timing my inhales so the sound of my shoes in the gravel would mask my embarrassingly loud breathing. I wondered if continuing to talk would make it better or worse.

I asked about his family, so he told me about his parents, and how different they were, but how sometimes he would still catch them snogging in the kitchen like a couple of teenagers. About his sister Amy, whose most recent breakup was basically a non-event for everyone but their mother. And he brought up Chloe and Phil, too; I'd known they went way back, but I hadn't realised just how close they'd been, and for how long.

Our fingers brushed against each other briefly a couple of times as we walked, setting sparks flying through my hand.

"What about your family?" he asked.

"Well, I don't have a dad," I said, pleasantly surprised at how unlaboured I sounded. "I was a donor baby. But Mum and I were always close. Until she decided a few years ago that life was too short and the world too big to stay in Bradford until she keeled over, so she went travelling. Now she's even sold the house."

"You're northern?" Jack asked, his voice pitching up dramatically in surprise.

"I know, I don't have the accent. Blame Cara. Her posh accent dulled the edges of mine."

"It must be hard having your mum so far away," he said. "So when you go home, where do you go?"

"That's a great question. I'll let you know when Mum gets back, if she actually does come back."

"And no brothers or sisters? Grandparents? Wealthy, eccentric third cousins?"

I shook my head. "Not that I know of."

"Wow. That must be so lonely. Your mum's on the other side of the world, and now Cara's moved away?"

I didn't say anything at first, not sure how much of my recent loneliness to admit. It *had* been hard, but in an almost embarrassing way. The fact that my life had been so wrapped up in one other person that I felt lost without them? And not even a partner or family member, but a friend? It felt ... well, a bit pathetic.

I kept my eyes fixed on the crest of the hill still a long way ahead of us. Jack must have mistaken my consideration for offence though, as he jumped in to apologise.

"I'm sorry, that was insensitive to bring up."

"Not at all," I assured him. "You're not wrong. It's just a weird thing to admit. But hey, plus a hundred XP for paying attention."

He paused for a long moment, and all I could hear was the scuff of our shoes on the gravel, our laboured breathing, and the rush of wind. I was expecting something snarky about emotional XP in reply, but it never came.

"Has Chloe told you about my hermit months?" he finally asked.

"Yes, because Chloe and I get paid to sit around and talk about you all day," I said, smirking at him out of the corner of my eye. He laughed, just as his fingers brushed against mine again.

"Fair enough. Well, when Aria and I split up, I was in a pretty bad place. I came home and basically didn't leave the farm for six months other than to buy food or building supplies.

I built my house all on my own, and I fixed up the Defender, camping on site the whole time."

"Wow. Very *Bob the Builder* of you."

He shrugged. "I liked it. Designing the house, figuring out how to integrate it with such an aggressively altered landscape..." His voice turned wistful. "But the point is, I had a lot to process. I'd spent almost seven years as half of a pair, and I needed to get to know myself as a person without her. I had to do that in my own way. And Chloe and Phil respected that. They forced me to eat with them once a week, all of us together, but they put on a film so I didn't have to talk. They'd even come sit with me whilst I worked, and hand me tools and stuff. They never made me talk. They were just there for me."

I swallowed the feelings that were building listening to him talk about his built-in support network that I very much didn't have, despite what Chloe had said. "Is this supposed to make me feel less alone?"

"Sorry," he said. "I'm not saying this well. What I'm *trying* to say is, you'll work through it at your own pace. And in the meantime, no pressure to talk it out if you don't want to."

I smiled up at him. "That's really lovely, Jack. Thank you."

We came to a stop as we reached what looked to be the highest point on the ridge, where a small rock formation marked the summit. I made sure to get a good look at the view we'd worked so hard to reach. And it really was stunning.

A cloud passed in front of the sun, throwing us into shadow, which made all the colours around us come to life. Jack and I both pushed our sunglasses up onto our heads to see better.

"That's Wales," Jack said, pointing to the ridge on our left, and then to the right. "And that's England."

"Amazing," I said, in a way that probably sounded trite, but I was genuinely amazed. The hills to our right – England, apparently – formed a dramatic cliff, and sparse low-hanging clouds drifted along it, only about halfway up the cliff face. The wind rushed at us, even though it hadn't been a particularly breezy day back at the car, and I leaned into it. It felt like we were on top of the world. Like there was nothing I couldn't do.

"How do you feel?" Jack asked, and I turned to see him smiling, because he already knew the answer. I was sure it was written all over my face.

"I feel invincible."

The corners of his eyes crinkled slightly, the brilliant green of them glinting in the sunlight. He looked genuinely thrilled for me, and maybe something more. Something that I was sure I was reflecting right back at him.

I stepped off the rock and over to him, feeling emboldened both by the hike and the way he was looking at me. I don't know what came over me, but I reached out and put a hand on his forearm.

"Thank you, Jack. I really wouldn't have done this without you. And I would have been missing out."

"I'm just happy you got the chance," he said, his voice low and rough, and as I dropped my hand, he reached his out, our fingers brushed against one another. Looking up at him, his face was just inches from mine, and I got flashbacks to floating in front of him in the river. As if the current were still pushing me, I stepped forward slightly, and I saw him look down at my mouth as I did. I took the chance to admire his, too, and the slight golden stubble on his jawline, and the muscled line of his neck. His fingers pressed gently between mine so they were somewhat entwined. By the time my eyes made it back to his, I was certain this could only be headed in one direction, and I tilted my chin up just a bit more, waiting for him to close the gap between us.

But instead he took a big step back, his fingers dropping away from mine, and frowned.

"Sorry," he said firmly. But he didn't sound sorry. The shift in his tone so jarring, in fact, that it was like he'd become a completely different person.

"Sorry," he said again, "but I think you've got the wrong idea here."

CHAPTER 13
JACK

"I think you've got the wrong idea here," I said, setting my jaw in an attempt to make my voice come out strong and clear. My breathing was fast and shallow, but I tried my best to disguise it. I needed to seem calm. Unbothered. Unflustered. Despite the fact that I felt the exact opposite. The weight that had formed in my stomach felt like it would pull me to the ground, and it was everything I could do not to let it.

Morgan's face fell, and I nearly lost my nerve. I wanted to reverse the step I'd taken away from her; to rub my finger over the crease that had formed between her eyebrows. She was so confused, and I didn't blame her. It was my fault. I'd been gravitating closer to her – physically and otherwise – since we'd got out of the car. I couldn't keep my eyes off her poof of a ponytail and her sun-kissed shoulders. And I'd been the one to grab her hand just a moment ago.

But it was a bad idea. And if I'd been thinking about anything other than her, I would have known that, and I could have prevented this. But instead I'd let it come to this awkward crescendo, and now she was embarrassed. I mean, I was definitely embarrassed, too. But I could live with that.

I should have drawn the line hours ago. Or maybe even weeks ago, the first time we'd ever touched. And the fact that my resolve was softening so quickly after drawing the line was proof of how badly it was needed. I was doing the right thing.

"Sorry," she said at first, looking at the ground. But I wanted her to look up at me and take it back; it wasn't her fault, and I hoped she knew that.

"It's fine," I said, my voice cold. "I just ... I told you I don't date."

"Yeah, I know," she said, looking out over the cliffside and slipping her sunglasses back on. "It's whatever. Let's just go."

She turned to start walking back down the way we'd come, but I put out a hand to stop her, careful not to actually touch her. She looked at me pointedly, and I knew she was glaring, even if I couldn't see her eyes anymore.

"The route goes this way," I said. "Through the valley. We can get some shade." I also knew that the spot I'd picked out for our picnic was in that direction, though a picnic dinner now seemed possibly ill advised.

"Fine," she said. "After you, then."

I nodded and turned back in the direction we'd been headed, angling for a switchback that I knew descended the other side of the summit. I could hear Morgan following after me, but I forced myself to keep my eyes on the path ahead, not only because it was actually quite steep.

Once we got to the bottom of the switchback, the path met up with a small creek, which was bubbling away from the recent rain. Willow trees and purple loosestrife clustered around the water source, offering us a bit of respite from the midsummer sun, which was more than welcome, since it was still extremely warm.

I kept wanting to ask how Morgan was doing – offer her some water, maybe a refresh of her suncream – but she walked single file behind me, even when the path was big enough to accommodate us side by side. And I didn't blame her.

I spent most of the walk mentally chastising myself for letting it get that far. I wasn't stupid; I'd known there had been a flirty energy between us on the weekend away. Hell, I'd been admiring her on some level since the first time I'd seen her. And it felt nice, being attracted to someone again. Being interested.

I'd wanted it; participated willingly. Enthusiastically, even. But the moment she'd stepped in to let me kiss her – and there was no getting around it, that's what had been happening – something in me had closed up shop. Out of business. Caution: do not enter. I hadn't done it on purpose. But I also should have been able to see it coming.

I also, it turned out, really didn't like her being mad at me. I could practically feel a hole being burned into the back of my head as we hiked, and I couldn't bear the thought of enduring the drive home with her so hurt. So furious. And that would pale in comparison to the wrath I'd incur from Chloe if I didn't manage to patch things over before the next time we were all together.

So just before I knew the trail would meet up with the road back to the car park, I veered off the path to find the spot I'd picked for our picnic.

"What are we doing?" she asked, pushing her sunglasses back onto her head. "Shouldn't we get back? I don't need a break. Plus, it's almost eight, and I'm starving."

There was an edge to her voice, like she was trying to one-up me. To prove that she could hang. But I ignored her, finding a fallen tree that spanned the creek; it seemed dry and sturdy enough, so I covered it with the picnic blanket I had in my bag.

"I've got food," I said, extracting a baguette and holding it out to her. "It's chicken and blue cheese with mustard and honey."

She crossed her arms and narrowed her eyes. "Someone was paying attention the other week."

I shrugged. "Do you want it or not?"

She didn't move for a long moment, her lips pursed in thought. But she finally stepped towards me and took the sandwich from my hand, sitting next to me on the tree. I noticed she sat as far away as possible whilst still being on the blanket. She set the sandwich down between us and reached down to take off her trainers and socks, letting her feet dangle in the water instead of resting them on the rocks like I was doing. Then she picked up her baguette, unwrapped it from the paper, and took a massive bite.

"Look, Morgan," I said, determined to clear the air, but she put up her hand between us.

"Don't," she said, her mouth full. She put down all but one finger, gesturing for me to wait, chewing a few times before swallowing hard. "Let's just pretend it didn't happen. I'm mortified enough without rehashing it, okay?"

I nodded, but I wasn't convinced. I didn't love that she seemed to think this was her responsibility to fix. Still, I couldn't refuse the olive branch she was extending.

"If you say so," I said.

"It can be water under the tree," she said, gesturing at the stream below us, smiling even as she chewed. I couldn't help but laugh, half in relief. I leaned over to untie my shoes so I could splash alongside her.

"Water under the tree then."

It wasn't all water under the tree for me, though. It sure seemed to be for Morgan; from the moment we agreed to put it behind us, she was mostly back to her bubbly self. There were fewer daring glances and definitely less touching, accidental or otherwise, but anyone else would struggle to believe that an hour earlier I'd effectively dumped cold water all over our friendship.

But I couldn't stop thinking about it, and I surprised myself at how adamant I felt about taking her on more adventures and holding up my end of our bargain. She'd seemed to enjoy the hike, so maybe she'd like camping, too? Kayaking? Quad biking? Fishing? I hadn't been fishing since I was a kid, but I was sure I could brush up if I needed to.

And at night, as I stared out at my pond or up at my ceiling, my mind would make up alternate universes in which I hadn't stopped her. In which I'd taken her face in my hand and kissed her the way I wanted to. In which maybe she'd be next to me now, not on the other side of town thinking I wanted nothing to do with her.

But it was better for her to think that than for me to let it go any further. Because I knew what I was like in relationships, and what they brought to my life. And I wanted nothing to do that, for Morgan or for me.

Dad was not thrilled with my distraction levels, that much was clear. I was replaying that mountaintop moment yet again when I was supposed to be helping him with a site visit and quote for a conversion: turning one old house into two smaller semi-detached units. It was obvious I wasn't on top form when I asked what colour of grout they wanted for the tiles, after they'd already said they wanted tile-effect vinyl. Dad gave me a look that probably didn't even register to the client, but clearly communicated to me that he wanted to throttle me for my stupidity.

"You're meant to be the future of this business," he yelled on the drive home, "and you can't even pay attention when quoting for work? How am I meant to trust you?"

"I'm so sorry it's not my passion in life to keep flooring types straight," I said with a sigh. Arguing with Dad always made me revert to my stroppy teenage self.

"Well it should be!" he bellowed, his voice far too big for the van, like it was trying to break out. I rolled the window down to get a bit of air. "Or at least it should look that way to your clients. *My* clients. If you can't even bother to pay attention in a meeting, no one will ever hire you again."

"Then maybe I shouldn't be the one doing this," I muttered, my arm and head half hanging out the window.

"What was that, son?" Dad asked, in a tone that told me he'd heard me, but he was giving me a chance to revise what I'd said.

I sighed before I answered, speaking louder this time. "I said, I'll do better next time."

"Yeah, well, you'd better," he said, sounding pacified for now. He switched on the stereo, and Behemoth came blasting through the speakers, which I took as permission to put on my noise-cancelling headphones. But instead of pressing play on my audiobook, I took advantage of the lack of Polish death metal and parental lecture to think instead about when I would next get to see Morgan.

As I climbed out of the van at home and started the walk up the drive towards my house, my phone buzzed with a text from Amy. It was another horoscope, this one laughably accurate:

> Be a hot mess if you need to be a hot mess!

I smiled down at my phone as I tapped out a reply:

> This better mean you're on your way home for a visit?

But almost as soon as I'd pressed send, I crested the hill and looked down at my little house to find my sister Amy sitting on my front steps. She looked up from her phone and stood as my phone buzzed with her reply:

> Nope.

"Good to see you," she said, stepping towards me. She looked well; her golden hair was pulled back in a ponytail, but it looked longer than when I'd last seen her. Her denim cutoffs and cropped tee looked clean. She was wearing a bit of make-up. She certainly didn't look like a depressed, heartbroken shell of a person like Mum had implied.

"Get over here," I said, opening my arms as I closed the distance between us. She fell into them as I wrapped them around her.

Amy and I had always been close growing up, but then I'd moved away. I'd made a concerted effort to spend time with her when I'd come home, only for her to move to Manchester two years later. Now I hadn't seen her in ... three, four months maybe?

"How long are you here for?" I asked as she stepped back.

She shrugged. "Maybe a week?"

"You don't have to work?" I asked, frowning. She shook her head.

"I'm between jobs."

Now *that* was a bit worrying. I'd helped move Amy into her place, and I knew it wasn't cheap. I knew her first restaurant job hadn't worked out, but I'd thought she'd been at a shop since then.

"Well, I'm glad to have you home," I said, climbing the steps and unlocking the door. "You crashing with me or with Mum and Dad?"

She pulled a face. "Your sofa is horrible. I'll stay in the guest room where I'm treated like the princess I am, thank you very much."

"It is not! I spent good money on that sofa. It's made of one hundred percent recycled materials."

"Ooh, so comfy," she said sarcastically as I dropped my bag down in the entryway.

"Whatever. But you'll be wishing for that tencel fabric when Mum starts getting under your skin."

"I'll just come here then," she said.

"Not if I lock the doors." I filled the kettle up and flipped it on. No chamomile for me; if Amy was home, it would be a late one.

"Fine then. I'll just hang with Dad," she said, sitting down at my little two-seater dining table.

"Great, get him off my back."

"Prodigal son having issues with Dad? No way." She scoffed. "The two of you are hilarious. Just tell him you don't want to be a contractor!"

"Yes, because he'd be so thrilled to have that conversation," I said.

"Just tell him you're going back to uni. He was so furious when you dropped out."

"Deferred," I corrected, though it had officially been a decade since my supposed deferment, so I supposed that qualifier wasn't valid anymore.

"What about this?" she asked, and I turned around from dropping teabags into our mugs to see her holding up my RIBA Journal. It was open to the same page I'd been staring at for weeks since it had arrived.

"What about it?" I asked. "I just like the stuff they write about sustainability."

"Which is why the magazine lays completely flat to the page about certification programmes?"

I rolled my eyes. "Fine. So I've looked at the programmes. But there's no way I'd be able to do it. Dad would never forgive me. The deal we made when I moved back was that I would take over when he retires. If I go back on that, he's screwed. I'm the only one he's been training."

"He's not exactly about to keel over," Amy said. "He can find someone else."

I thought about Dad's "what was that, son?" when I'd even flippantly suggested not wanting to do his job. If I told him I was going back on my promise? He'd be furious. He might even kick me out.

No, I'd worked too hard to rebuild my life after Aria. Was it my dream to take over the family business? No. But it was a sacrifice I was willing to make if it meant I got to live and work with my family and be near my friends.

"It's a non-starter," I said, placing an Earl Grey down in front of her. "Plus, I'm not the one who's in between jobs. Why don't you just move home?"

"Because," she said, and if I'd thought I'd reverted back to my teenage self earlier, the defiance in that single word put me to shame. "How embarrassing would it be to move home at twenty-four?"

I narrowed my eyes at her, trying to figure out if she was being a dick or just forgetful. She cracked a smile, and my suspicions that she was just being a dick were confirmed. Man, was it good to have her back, even if just for a few days.

CHAPTER 14
MORGAN

I couldn't stop thinking about Jack fucking Evans.

I'd never felt more embarrassed than I had at the top of that stupid hill, and the worst part was that I still had no idea what had gone wrong. I was pretty sure it wasn't my fault; every time I replayed the moments leading up to his rejection, I became more convinced that he'd been giving off serious mixed signals.

Come to think of it, he'd been giving me mixed signals for weeks. On that stupid weekend away, he'd got close to me in the river only to proudly proclaim that he didn't date. And he'd been the one to ask me to go hiking ... well, sort of. It had at least been mutual, and I was certain that almost-kiss had been, too. Or maybe I was the only one who had felt something when we'd been floating face-to-face in that river; when our hands had brushed against one another as we walked.

But that was beside the point. "Water under the tree," as I'd so idiotically said. And he was clearly trying hard to prove a point that he still wanted to be my friend. He'd been texting me throughout each week, and he'd been way friendlier than usual at our Monday night games. So despite my persisting confusion, I was determined to move forward as if it hadn't happened. At least as far as he could tell, anyway.

All I wanted to do at work was go cuddle Pablo and plan my Ren Faire outfits; Phil wanted us to send him our ideas by the end of June at the latest so he could start sourcing materials.

But not only did I have actual work to do, I couldn't even use my lunch break today for puppy cuddles; I had lunch plans with Chloe, which had morphed into plans with Grey and Fatima, too, apparently.

We met up at a cafe a short walk from the office, Grey still in high-vis from their job as a train guard, and Fatima looking as polished as ever. When I asked why she wasn't at school, she muttered something about inset days and actually having a lunch break for once.

"I genuinely can't wait for October," Grey said as we tucked into our food. Their hair was now a sunshine yellow, and they'd added a new patch to their biker vest: a frazzled-looking possum with the words "even baddies get saddies" in lime green embroidery around it.

"I know, I'm so excited," Fatima said. "I told Jared about it and he tried to invite himself." Jared was Fatima's long-time boyfriend who lived in Manchester, where she spent most weekends.

"He could totally come."

"No way," she said, her mouth full of sweet potato hash. "He'd just get in the way of my flirting with all the tavern wenches."

"Yeah, having a loving partner around really fucks with your game," Chloe said sarcastically, and we all laughed.

"Seriously though, what are you all thinking for the character day?" Grey asked. "I can't even picture what I should be wearing."

We'd agreed in the Wench Please chat that, whilst Phil would be making us some more classic Ren Faire looks for one day, we wanted to dress like our D&D characters for the other.

"I feel like I've always pictured Gorlag in basically a loin cloth," I said. "Not that that should stand in your way."

"True. I should probably add an intense workout routine into my preparations," Grey said, flexing their biceps. Or, I could only assume that's what they were doing, given their pose; their arms looked no more muscular for the effort.

"Good luck with that," Chloe said, pointing her fork at Grey. "I'm definitely dressing like Calamity though, meaning lots of black leather." She wiggled her eyebrows up and down.

"You gonna paint yourself purple, too?"

She shrugged. "Maybe I will."

"What about you?" Fatima asked me. "What would Captain Morgana wear? A full suit of armour, I assume."

I nodded. "Yeah, but I doubt that's practical, so we'll see. I'll come up with something."

Grey's cutlery clattered against the table as they dropped it, looking up at me. "Wait a minute, sorry, just back up a minute. Morgan, you said you always pictured Gorlag in a loin cloth?"

I shrugged. "I mean, yeah?"

They winked at me. "I'll try not to let that get to my head." The rest of us laughed. "What might that loin cloth look like, exactly? I'm struggling to conceptualise this costume."

I was secretly glad they'd asked; I'd actually got to the point of feeling excited to show everyone the drawings I'd done. I pulled out my tablet, opened my gallery, and handed it over to Grey.

"Oh my god, Morgan, this is so cool!" they shrieked, spreading their fingers to zoom in.

"Thanks," I replied, beaming.

Grey passed the tablet around to Fatima and Chloe, who were equally full of praise for the drawing, before Grey snatched it back to study the outfit.

"Can I see more?" Fatima asked, pointing to the tablet in Grey's hand. When I nodded, Grey very reluctantly handed it over, literally growling in protest. I saw Fatima swipe several times, mentally indexing what I'd drawn in the last few weeks that she might see. It wasn't until she stopped and cocked her head to one side that I remembered what I'd drawn just after the images I'd shown them.

"This person looks familiar," she said, turning to show the table a drawing of a tall blonde man in a plaid shirt standing on an overlook, ridges rising up on both sides of the landscape. I felt my face go red, and I turned my attention to my plate as Fatima showed Chloe what she'd found. She wasn't mocking me; they seemed to actually be admiring the drawing. But when I'd drawn it, I'd been thinking about how embarrassed I'd been. And where they probably saw a slightly more chiselled jawline than was realistic for Jack, I knew I'd drawn it that way because I remembered the set of his face – the tensing of his muscles – as he rejected me.

I was glad I hadn't saved the one of us in the river to my image gallery.

"He told me it was great," Chloe said.

"Yeah, it was really beautiful. You could see for miles." My cheeks burned, but I forced myself to look at her as casually as possible.

"He's done that hike at least a dozen times," she said. "I don't think that's what he meant."

Okay, so, no eye contact with Chloe then. I looked at Fatima and Grey for support, but they were too busy giving each other a conspiratorial glance.

Blissfully, Fatima changed the subject, scrolling back to the drawings I'd done.

"Hey, one of Jared's friends is actually looking for a freelance illustrator for a project. Do you do that? Or know anyone who does?"

I shook my head. "I've never done any freelance work before, and no, I don't know anyone else who does it." But something in the back of my mind wouldn't let me leave it at that. Showing them what I'd done had been exciting until they'd found that drawing of Jack, hadn't it? And I could certainly do with the money. "Why? What's the job?"

"Apparently one of his coworkers he's quite close with is quitting to open a games shop in Manchester."

"Oh that's awesome!" Chloe said. "We'll have to take a trip up when they open."

"Well, I think he's a long way from that," Fatima said.

"You can give him my details," I said. "I don't have any experience, but if it's a gaming shop, maybe I'd actually enjoy it."

"Yeah, for sure," she said with a smile before pulling out her phone and taking a picture of the character drawing up on my tablet in front of her. She spent a few seconds looking down and typing before setting her phone face-down on the table. "Done."

The slight buzz of excitement mostly washed away the lingering embarrassment I'd felt. I'd only ever drawn for myself, so I'd be shocked if he wanted me for the job, and even more shocked if I could actually manage to do it. But at least it was something different – something that wasn't a spreadsheet or a cold call. Maybe it would even be worth some more XP.

By the time I got home that evening and sat down on the sofa with dinner – a poor attempt at a one-pot curry that had actually required a chopping board, a mixing bowl, and *two* pots, since the first one I chose ended up being way too small – I had three emails waiting in my personal inbox. Well, four if you counted the one from the cosplay shop that kept emailing me after I downloaded a PDF from them called "The Perfect Guide to Ren Faire Layering". But three that actually needed my attention.

The first was from Jared's colleague. *Damn, that was fast*, I said, opening it up.

Hey Morgan! I'm Greg, Jared's work mate.

Fatima sent the picture you drew, and I think it's really cool - exactly the style I'm going for. I'm looking for something cool like an axe, or a sword and shield, or something that conveys combat since a lot of the shop will be minis. Also would be cool to have a D20 involved somehow? The shop will be called "Game On!" which I know isn't that original, but it does what it says on the tin I guess.

The catch is that I don't have much of a budget for this - £500 max really. I know that's not a lot for a professional logo, so if you can't do it, I totally understand. But if you're interested, let me know and I can maybe send you a deposit? What do you think? However you would want to work. And if not, no worries, really.

Cheers,

Greg

I blinked at the email on my laptop. Five hundred British pounds? For drawing swords and axes, something I did for fun? Hell yes, I wanted to do it. I balanced my bowl of curry on the sofa – risky business, but my feet were occupying the free space on the coffee table – and was typing a reply almost immediately.

Hi Greg, nice to meet you!

I'm sure Fatima said, but I don't have freelance experience. That said, this project sounds great! I can make that budget work, and it sounds right up my alley. What's your timeline? Let me know and we can get started. Maybe you can send over some other images you like? And a deposit sounds good - let's say £100 up front and the rest when we're done? Let me know.

Speak soon,

Morgan

PS - I think Game On! is great! Like you said, does what it says on the tin. And I love a bit of friendly competition.

I wasn't sure if I was completely off base asking for twenty percent up front, but I didn't care; I would have done it for free as a creative exercise. So I hit send and did a little happy dance, almost sending my bowl of curry sliding to the floor, but I caught it in time with my free hand.

I let myself finish my dinner before turning my attention to the second email, which was from Mum. She sent them roughly once a month, letting me know where she'd been and where she was headed. She'd left Big Sur and was staying in San Luis Obispo, where she was taking a yoga instructor certification course for the next few weeks. I closed the email out without replying.

The last email was from Cara's mum. She'd attached the listing for the house, which had apparently gone live a couple of days ago. She also had a block of time over the weekend that the estate agent wanted to show some people around.

I sighed and looked around me; I'd thought I might have more time to figure things out, but it seemed things would move quite quickly. I shouldn't have been surprised, really; I'd been spending enough time browsing listings myself. I needed to make peace with the fact that I would have to give up my little home sooner rather than later.

Suddenly I was overwhelmed by a wave of nostalgia. I missed Cara. I missed when things were predictable, and safe, and I wasn't being kicked out of my house and rejected on mountaintops and forced to cook myself horrible dinners. I missed my friend, and I missed what life was like when she was with me.

I picked up the phone to ring her. We hadn't actually managed to catch up properly since she'd left, but was clear from her sporadic texts and her less sporadic Instagram stories that she was having the time of her life. I didn't want to be the needy friend. But I really did need her in that moment.

I tried not to be surprised when it rang through to voicemail. And even though I stared at my phone for a solid five minutes after hanging up, she didn't ring or text back. I thought about texting Chloe, or maybe even Jack, but instead I just grabbed a book I'd already read and let myself get sucked into the adventure there. At least I knew how it ended.

CHAPTER 15
MORGAN

A few days later, I was relieved that nothing seemed to have come of the viewings that had happened over the weekend. I also hadn't had a response from Cara at all, despite texting her the following day to see if she was doing okay, but I tried not to let that get to me. Because what I did have was a costume for the Ren Faire.

Or, well, a concept for one.

I'd messaged Phil separately to the rest of the group; my idea was a bit unorthodox for a Ren Faire, and I wasn't sure if he'd be up for it. But I'd been so inspired by an outfit the character had worn in the fantasy book I'd been reading that I couldn't help but draw it after I'd closed the book.

At least something good had come from my escapism.

> That looks sick! Are those ... chains??

> Yes! Really tiny ones. Is that ok??

> Yeah, I mean, I'll need to find the right materials to get that effect, but it looks too cool not to try. Let's do it.

On Monday, we all lined up in Fatima's lounge to get measured. It was the first time I'd seen Phil do his thing. I'd sent everyone their character portraits I'd done, and after a few tweaks, I had them ready to share with Phil so he knew what to measure. I went first, and then Grey, and then Jack, who smacked at Phil's hand as he got a bit cheeky measuring his inseam, and we all laughed.

"Is that really necessary?"

"Yes, it most definitely is," Chloe insisted. "Ignore him, Phil."

"Don't I always," Phil responded from behind Jack, now measuring from his shoulder to his waist.

Once Jack was done, he came over to where I sat on one end of the sofa, making Phil's requested tweaks to Yorick's armour. I cursed the traitorous butterflies in my stomach for taking flight when he came over, especially after how last time with Jack had panned out.

"Hey," he said, sitting down next to me, turning on the cushion so he was facing me.

"Hey," I said back, not looking up from my tablet.

"So," he said, "I was thinking, I know the hike was quite ... eventful. I'm thinking that's a solid three hundred XP."

"Three hundred," I said, nodding my head. "That's pretty good." I had no idea if that was pretty good, but I was willing to go along with it.

"Well, how would you like some more?" There went those cursed butterflies again.

"XP, or hiking?" *Or near misses?*

"XP," he said wryly, and I was almost sure he could tell what I'd been thinking. "I figure we could do something else. Something a bit more challenging."

I nodded slowly, not sure that I liked the sound of "challenging", but unwilling to admit that. "Sure," I said. "What did you have in mind?"

"I've got a couple of kayaks. I thought we could take them out on the river."

"Which river?" I asked, my face pulling into a grimace. Jack laughed.

"The Wye," he said, as if that should have been obvious. "The same one we went swimming in before."

I pulled a face. "Yeah, but that river looks very different in its kayakable sections than it did running through the back garden."

"Fair. But you said it yourself; you want to be a bit more adventurous, right?"

"What about the weather?" I asked. It had been raining all weekend.

"It should clear up by then. But even if it doesn't, we'll be wet already. Come on Morgan, what do you say?"

I pretended to consider it, but I knew I'd say yes; I really did want to put what happened behind us, if only so I could stop replaying the almost-kiss in my mind. He was offering me a clean slate I intended to accept. And an adorably endearing puppy dog face.

"Let's go for it," I said. "When?"

"Saturday morning?" he asked. "Ten am. Wear a swimsuit."

"Morgan!" Phil called from the lounge, where he was rolling up his measuring tape. "Let's talk about your text?"

"Coming!" I called, thankful for the distraction from Jack. I stood up and walked back around the table. "Looking forward to it," I said to him.

"Back at ya."

He was obnoxiously casual in light of how last time had gone, but I reminded myself that it was all *water under the tree*. He was clearly just better at embodying that than I was.

Chloe came back into the room just as I was leaving, clearly having caught the tail end of the conversation. She looked at me quizzically as she passed me, bouncing her eyebrows up and down. I rolled my eyes and shook my head, trying to communicate "there's nothing to see here" as best as possible.

"Let's take this chat to the bedroom, shall we?" Phil asked, faux-suggestively.

"At least buy me dinner first?"

"You'll have to settle for a custom Ren Faire outfit, I'm afraid."

Fatima's house had two guest rooms; apparently it was the designated party house. I'd yet to meet her partner Jared, but given my situation, I felt quite jealous of the space, and the stability.

Phil opened the door to the first room we came to, and we sat down side by side on the double bed. I turned on my tablet and flicked to the drawings I'd been working on.

"This is so cool," Phil said. "It's kind of like ornamental armour."

"Exactly!" That was how it had been described in the book I'd been reading, and precisely what I'd been going for.

"I'll have to bust out the embroidery kit for the flowers, I think," he said, zooming in on different parts of the outfit I'd drawn. "I'm not sure we'd be able to find a fabric that would replicate it like this."

I frowned. "That sounds complicated."

Phil shrugged. "It's not that bad. I can probably do it with the machine, actually, which will be a lot faster."

"If you're sure," I said, trying my best to give him an out, but I really, really wanted this outfit.

"I'm sure," he said, smiling, and I let out a little sigh of relief. "Now, what are you doing for your Captain Morgana outfit?"

He looked mischievously over at me.

"Oh, I'm not sure yet," I said. "She wears chain mail in the game, but that's just because we don't have enough money in-game for plate mail. And funny enough, I don't have enough money in real life for it either. So honestly I was leaning towards a crap costume version."

Phil's shoulders sank. "You don't want to try to make something?"

"I may be able to draw," I said, lifting the tablet slightly, "but I'm far from crafty."

"Well," he said, wiggling his shoulders as if he just couldn't contain his excitement, "how would you feel about some homemade chain mail?"

I balked at him. "I'm sorry, you know how to *make* chain mail?!"

"It's really not that hard," he said, shrugging. "Just time consuming. But I've got nothing but time on my hands." He said the last part quietly, as if it were an aside to himself.

"Well, I mean, I'd be up for it," I said tentatively. "What kind of cost are we looking at?"

Phil looked pensive as he did his mental calculations. "If I use some plastic rings instead of metal, which is better for weight anyway, maybe seventy-five? We'd have to spray paint it silver, but that should be fine."

Seventy-five pounds felt like a lot for a shirt, but the prices

I'd seen online had been much, much higher. I reminded myself that it was just for one day, but then another, louder part of me insisted that looking cool on that one day was worth the investment. And hey, who knew, maybe I'd discover a new passion for cosplay, and it wouldn't just be one day.

As I sketched it out on my tablet, Phil and I agreed on what the Morgana outfit would look like – we agreed that a surcoat or tunic may hide the chain mail a bit, but it would look more historically accurate, and keep me from getting fried alive by the sun – and then made a list of everything he'd need. I transferred him some money to start with the materials, making him promise to let me know if he spent more. Then we headed back downstairs, where the rest of the group was waiting for us. The tin of cookies Phil had bought was already down to just two, which had presumably been saved for us.

"Okay," Fatima said as we sat down. "I believe you were about to enter the glowing chamber, right?"

"Damn straight!" Grey said. "Let's do this."

"I still think we need to strategise first," Jack said, and everyone started arguing about what to do.

Without saying anything, Fatima slipped into teacher mode and brought everyone's focus to her. It was always like this when we played – the anticipation was like sitting in a theatre waiting for a stage show to start, and I swore the lights even dimmed around us as she opened her notebook and picked up a handful of 20-sided dice.

Everyone took a coordinated sharp breath in as the dice clattered to the table, holding it as we all leaned forward to see the results, even though we didn't know yet why she was rolling. Random dice rolls from the DM never bode well.

Fatima looked up and gave a sinister grin, and I felt a sense of dread settle over the table before she uttered the three words I knew she would.

"Roll for initiative."

CHAPTER 16
CAPTAIN MORGANA SILVERSWORD

"Holy shit," Calamity said. "Yorick, you did it!"

"Of course I did," he said, "and I'm offended that you ever doubted me."

Morgana stepped closer to the orb, her eyes flicking between it and her own feet, making sure she wasn't triggering any pressure plates or crossing any barriers. They'd encountered enough booby traps in the maze of passages and chambers, even having to fight off a small stone golem at the entrance to this very room, and she didn't relish the idea of triggering another. She stopped a couple of feet away, and she watched from the corners of her eyes as her companions did the same, forming a respectful circle around the artifact.

"What do we do now?" Yorick asked, looking up at the rest of them.

"Here, let me," Thrormir said. "I've been saving my magic for this." He spread his hands in front of him and contorted his fingers into different positions, muttering the spell under his breath. A frown appeared on his face.

"What is it?" Morgana asked, her voice low. Almost reverent.

"That's funny," he said, "I can't detect any magic. Not anywhere around it, anyway. Just the orb itself. Which is enchantment magic, by the way."

Gorlag reached their hand out. "Then let's just take it."

"Not so fast," Calamity said, swatting their hand away. "It could be a physical trigger."

"What do you mean?"

"Like in Indiana Jo— I mean, in a parchment I read one time? About having to replace the item with something of the same weight or the cave gets destroyed?"

They all eyed the cavern around them as she said that last part.

"Since when are you a reader?" Thrormir teased, and Calamity glared at him.

"Since it could save our lives, dumbass."

The group argued about how they should take the orb, or attempt to calculate its weight, whilst Morgana looked around her. She was certain there must be a clue somewhere, right? Otherwise they'd never be able to guess what to do.

Her eyes settled on the Sphere as she considered the options. The orb itself was translucent; it seemed to be the glow that was giving it any kind of colour at all. She held up her hand to cover the centre of it, which seemed to be the source of the light. And as soon as she did, she was able to see straight through the bottom of the Sphere to the top of the plinth that held it. There was a small symbol carved there: a twelve-pointed star. It looked familiar, but she couldn't place it.

Morgana looked around to give her eyes a rest as she wracked her brain for anything to do with a twelve-pointed star.

She would have to point it out to the rest of the group if they ever stopped arguing about what to do. But as her vision cleared, her eyes fixed on the floor, she realised that some of the stones that made up the floor had twelve-pointed stars carved into them, too. There were other symbols, but only one per stone.

"It's a path," Thrormir said under his breath when Morgana pointed this out, and Morgana followed his gaze to the door they'd come through; the only door in the room. Sure enough, she could draw a path from the door to the plinth using just stones with stars on them. The final one was the one on which she was currently standing.

Once the others agreed to the plan and were safely out of the room, Morgana took a deep breath – okay, lots of deep breaths – before reaching out and palming the orb. It weighed so little that she could barely even feel it in her hand. She tried to make her way through the room with it as quickly as possible, but she also took care to put weight on each subsequent starred tile before removing her foot from the previous one. She made it to the door, and as she came to the last tile, she could see the party watching her, surprised smiles on their faces. She tried not to take their surprise personally.

Just as she thought they'd got away with it, she took her foot off the last starred stone, and a screeching wail filled the air.

CHAPTER 17
MORGAN

"This feels like a bit of an escalation from swimming," I said to Jack as he unloaded the kayaks. I was looking at the murky water and trying to imagine myself getting anywhere near it. At least my cheap sunglasses gave it a bit of a blue tint, making it look less horrible than normal.

Jack dragged the kayaks down to the water, beached them on the pebbly bottom, and walked back over to me. "What are you afraid of, exactly?" he asked. I leaned back against the side of the Defender.

"Well, let's see," I said, holding up my hand and counting off my perfectly reasonable fears on my fingers. "There could be large debris in there, like a rusty old bicycle, and I could get scratched and contract tetanus. I could fall out and hit my head on said debris lurking under the surface. I could fall out and get dragged under by the river's current and drown. I could get swept out to sea because I can't make it to the side. I could knock myself out with an oar and drown. And look at that"—I wiggled my now-five raised fingers at him—"I'm all out of fingers."

He wasn't laughing at me, but there was definitely a hint of mockery in his mirthful smirk. "Why are you the only one meeting an untimely end in all of these scenarios?"

"Because you do shit like this all the time," I said, gesturing to the kayaks behind him. "I've got ineptitude on my side."

"I'll have you know, I haven't used this kind of kayak since I was a kid," he said.

"I'm sorry, is that supposed to make me feel better?!"

Now he was laughing at me, a full-bodied, head-back laugh that carried on the wind towards the river. I was certain people miles downstream could hear him.

"You'll be fine," Jack said, tentatively reaching out to place one hand on the car just above my shoulder. The proximity this created caught me off guard, and I swear my whole body responded to the way he was suddenly hulking over me. I desperately tried to regulate my breathing and tried to remember what I'd had for breakfast, and if my breath would smell.

"First of all," he said, "there probably is debris, but people swim and paddle in this river every day. It's likely at the bottom in the middle. Which you won't find, because it's a lot deeper than the one we were in before. And you won't get pulled down, because that's not how river currents work without white water, which you won't be encountering today. And you won't wash out to sea, because there's like a hundred miles of river between here and the Severn, and I promise I would rescue you at some point before then." He smiled endearingly at that last point, the epitome of believability. Dammit, I was going to get in that awful water, wasn't I?

I tried to maintain my pouty expression, but it was a real effort. I could feel the weight of Jack's presence as if he were pressed up against me. It wasn't so much claustrophobic as just close. Really close. Close enough, in fact, that if I just lifted slightly onto my toes, this outing might take a very different turn.

"Fine," I relented, and Jack smiled victoriously.

"Good, now, let's go," he said, pushing away suddenly.

We put our phones in the dry bag, grabbed the oars – sorry, *paddles*, he'd insisted – from the boot and waded into the water once more. I followed after him, stopping every couple of strides to shake pebbles from the riverbed out of my sandals. Jack waited for me to catch up, then pointed to the empty kayak. I gave him one last reluctant look, then obediently pulled myself into the hard green plastic, though not without some manoeuvring I was sure had been thoroughly unflattering. Once I was situated, Jack handed me the paddle, then flipped it for me since I was apparently holding it the wrong way around.

"Okay, now what?" I asked, looking around, finding Jack just staring at me from the back of my kayak. "Which way?"

He shook his head, a strange expression on his face as he pushed me further into the middle of the river, trailing his own kayak behind him. Was he annoyed with me for being so inept? No, that wouldn't have been like Jack. So why was he frowning? What was that look on his face? He looked at me almost ... almost apologetically.

"I'm so sorry, Morgan," he said, sounding almost tortured, as his hand reached under my kayak. "It's a safety thing. You need to know how. My dad did the same to me when he first taught me..."

The penny dropped when it was way too late.

"Jack, nonononoNO— Jack!!!"

By the time I shrieked his name the second time, I was already tipping into the water, flailing to hold onto the sides even as my arm and then face made contact with the surface.

Somehow my hand stayed gripped on the paddle as I spluttered quickly to the surface. It was actually helping me float a bit, thankfully. I used my free hand to clear my eyes, realising with horror that I was floating quite quickly down the river. I swivelled my head left and right and saw my kayak floating just a couple of feet behind me, upside down. I reached back and clung to its side. I was a perfectly fine swimmer, at least by local lido standards, but I didn't want to get separated from the kayak, and holding onto it allowed me to lift my legs, bringing my knees to my chest, avoiding all the hypothetical debris.

Out of the corner of my eye, I saw a flash of bright orange – Jack's kayak. I snapped my head to the side to see him paddling towards me, then overtaking me, then spinning around to face me so he was floating down the river backwards. He dipped his paddle expertly on either side, keeping himself perfectly aligned with me.

"What the actual fuck, Jack!" I spluttered.

"I'm so sorry," he said again, and from what I could see of his face through my hair, which had matted down across my field of vision, he did look rather guilty, or at least concerned.

"Fat lot of good that's doing me," I said. "A little help here?"

"You've gotta be able to get yourself back up," he said. "Flip the kayak first."

I actually screamed out loud in frustration, but I did what he told me, shifting the paddle into the hand holding the side of the kayak so I could reach the other one over, grasping for the other side. I had to haul myself up a couple of times, which was difficult whilst managing the paddle, but eventually my hand caught the opposite edge, and I cried out "Yes!" as my momentum pulled the kayak over easily. I nearly lost hold of the paddle, but I managed to grab it and haul it up into the seat.

"What now?" I shouted to Jack as I examined the kayak,

wondering how I would get back into it without any leverage. It had been hard enough when I'd had the riverbed to launch myself from.

"Really good, Morgan!" He sounded a bit like a summer camp counsellor looking after idiot children, and I vowed to exact vengeance just as soon as I got back up on the damned thing. "Just place your hands like you did to flip it, one on this side and one over the top onto the other. Then launch yourself kicking, and pull down with both hands at the same time so that your bottom arm goes straight and you're laying stomach-down on the kayak."

I tried to picture what he was telling me to do, and it took a moment for me to understand logistically how that was going to work. He started to talk again, but I held up a hand to shush him, and he complied. The least he could do was let me think. After all, apparently we had a hundred miles to deal with this.

Eventually it clicked in my mind, and it only took one try to salmon-flop up onto my kayak. Jack was yelling out instructions again, but I didn't listen, instead just rolling backwards on the kayak so my bum was in the well, then sitting up with my feet hanging on either side until I could scoot into the right position. The paddle went briefly overboard, but helpfully it floated down the river at the same speed as me, so it was easy enough to rescue. I held it up the wrong way around again at first, but I remembered Jack telling me to make sure I could read the logo, so I flipped it before he could correct me.

"Well fucking done!" Jack called, and I looked up to see him pumping his paddle in the air excitedly.

"Fuck you!" I said, burying my paddles in the water over and over to try to catch him. He saw me coming and did the same, only he was paddling upstream towards me, so I overshot him and had to spin myself around, which took an embarrassingly long moment that resulted in a bit of an anticlimax to my charge.

"Wrong way," he said over his shoulder as he passed me, giving me a taunting grin and raising his eyebrows repeatedly. So I dug deep and paddled after him, every ounce of me intending to send him overboard as soon as I got to him.

But by the time I caught up, which he'd clearly allowed me to do based on the virtually nonexistent paddling effort on his part, I was too tired to bother. We'd not only passed the spot where we'd put in, but we'd gone just as far on the other side. And kayaking, it turned out, was fucking *hard*. My shoulders felt like they were on fire, and not just from the hot sun beating down overhead.

"Can we please slow down?" I called, panting.

"Sure," he called back, sounded much less strained than I did. "I want to make it to the island before we stop, so let's pace ourselves."

I rolled my eyes, understanding that he expressly meant that *I* should pace myself, but it actually was much easier when I let myself slow down.

And as my breathing eased and I started to feel less like I was dying, I was able to look around me properly and see just how much there was to enjoy. Yes, there was algae, and there were mosquitos, but there were also late-blooming rhododendron hanging over the water, as Jack informed me, and we even saw a pair of river otters bathing on the bank at one point. Jack even risked pulling his phone out of the dry bag for that one, saying it was rare to spot them during the day, and I didn't blame him; I'd never seen one in person before, and they were even cuter than I'd imagined, flicking at their faces and at each other with their little paws.

After about forty minutes of paddling, just as my shoulders

felt like they might give out, we passed through some old viaduct pillars before coming up to what looked like a narrow island in the middle of the river. Jack pulled ahead and paddled straight up onto an exposed bit of riverbed connecting the island to the bank on the right, and I copied the manoeuvre. I imagined it would normally be underwater, but with the dry weather we'd had it had been left exposed, making the island more of a weirdly shaped peninsula.

Satisfied the kayaks weren't going anywhere, Jack marched over to the island and spread out the towel he'd brought, pulling two sandwiches out of the drybag. I dropped down next to him and accepted one as he held it out, but it was much heavier than the chicken and blue cheese baguette he'd made me last time.

"What is this monstrosity?" I asked, holding it up to Jack, who had already bitten into his.

"Ifainshub," he said, his mouth full. I must have looked as clueless as I felt, as he made a big show of chewing and swallowing before answering again. "Italian sub."

I opened the sandwich, which seemed to be a whole charcuterie board's worth of meat, slices of pale white cheese, shredded lettuce, tomatoes, and some green pepper-looking things. I smelled it, and a sharp vinagery scent hit my nostrils, so strong that I reeled back. I thought about clarifying all the ingredients with Jack, but he looked so enamoured with his own sandwich that I couldn't bring myself to question it. So I opened my mouth as wide as possible to take a bite – so wide that my jaw clicked – a necessary effort given the size of the sandwich.

At first, all I tasted was the tang of the vinaigrette and the peppers, and the crunch of the lettuce, and I began to question Jack's sanity. But on the second bite, the meat and cheese joined the party, and it was a totally different story. It was sensational.

"Well you can't get that in a meal deal," I said, and I looked up at Jack, realising from the way his eyes were creased with laughter that I'd spoken with my own mouth full just like he had a moment ago. I mimicked his exaggerated chew-and-swallow routine and repeated myself.

"No you cannot," he agreed. "I haven't had one in years."

"Why not?" I asked. "When did you last have it?"

"I don't know," he said, his grin drooping, looking down at the sandwich in his hands. "When I was in New York with Aria, I guess."

Of course. I shook my head and laughed. "Stop trying to sound casual. We both know that breakup is why you haven't had one since then."

"Okay, fine," he said. "So I haven't had my favourite sandwich in years. Are you telling me there's nothing from your friendship with Cara you won't be able to do or have anymore because it's too painful?"

"Of course there is," I said. "But that's because I miss her, and I wish she were here. If I were over her, if I didn't want her in my life anymore, I don't think there would be anything, no. Not after four years."

It was all speculation; I'd never been in a proper relationship before, and I knew having a friend move away and breaking up with a long-term partner were worlds apart. But I could see him actually thinking about this.

"Do you want her back?"

He shook his head and grimaced; it didn't look put on. "Hell no," he said. "I don't even really think about her anymore."

I nodded. "So why don't you eat Italian subs anymore? Why don't you date? Or travel?"

"Because those things *do* make me think of her," he admitted, looking away from me, "and I don't like doing that."

"Because you feel..." I prompted.

"I don't know," he groaned, crumpling his now-empty sandwich paper and dropping it on the ground between his legs. "I try not to look too closely at it."

"Well, try now," I insisted, half because he clearly needed this and half as payback for earlier. "Picture someone you really like asks you on a date. How does that make you feel?"

He looked back at me, and even though he was wearing his sunglasses, I felt like he was looking straight into my eyes, and my face went red in response.

"Anxious," he said quietly.

"And what emotion makes us feel anxious?"

"Fear?"

"Bingo," I said, touching one finger to my nose and pointing at him with the other hand.

He nodded as he processed what I'd said. "So you think I've lost my ability to do the things I want to do because I'm letting the fear stop me."

I almost fell backwards with relief. Playing therapist was fucking exhausting. "Well done, Jack. Plus one thousand emotional XP for you."

"You're incorrigible," he said as I laughed. I ate in silence for a moment.

"You know what the next step is, right?" I asked as I finished my own sandwich. He looked at me again, and I saw his shoulders drop.

"I'm not sure I want to know."

"Exposure therapy, baby," I said, admittedly a bit smug. "You've gotta do your version of what you're making me do."

"I'm hardly making you do this," he said.

"You literally pushed me into the river," I countered.

"Fair."

"So, you and your ex," I started, "you guys broke up what, four years ago? Where were you? Some far-flung tropical beach? Chucking coconuts at each other?"

"We were home, actually," Jack said, looking down at his lap. "Or, at least, I was. We hadn't been back in like a year, but we came for her dad's birthday. I travelled home after the party, and she stayed in Kent where she's from. We'd planned to spend the week with our separate families before flying out to Singapore. But once I was back, I couldn't bring myself to leave."

"Why not?" I knew I was being nosy, maybe pushing him a bit, but I couldn't help myself.

He shrugged. "I mean, we both knew for ages that it was over. It just took us being apart for a millisecond to acknowledge it."

He sat forward a bit and exhaled deeply. This was definitely the most open he'd been with me so far. It turned out we were actually pretty good at the talking stuff, as long as we stayed away from the touching stuff.

"When my family were asking me about my travels – I was super bad at keeping in touch, so they didn't know anything we'd been doing – I realised that every single story I had to tell was about her. Not about me. Not about us. She'd been having all the cool experiences, and I'd just ... been there. On the sidelines. And even though I'd had lots of fun travelling, it was like I was always secondary to her needs. Her career. Her agenda."

I wanted to say something trite like *Oh Jack, I'm so sorry*, but I knew it wouldn't help, so I stayed quiet.

"And when I was driving to see Chloe and Phil, a song came

on, and I just started crying. Like, full-on weeping. I had to pull onto the verge and everything."

I took a punt; the track change when he'd picked me up for our hike. "No Room In Frame?"

He nodded. "Yeah, sorry about that. It's literally the one song I still can't handle. There are others that remind me of Aria, but the problem is that one reminds me of myself too much. The version of me that got lost in her world."

"It's a good song," I said, "but not a great one to find relatable."

Jack laughed. "Yep. I even got a tattoo to remind me never to let another person push me out of my own life like that again." He pulled up his t-shirt on the side closest to me, all the way over his shoulder, turning away from me so I could see his back. Across his left shoulder blade was a fine line tattoo of a camera, with a silhouette inside the lens. Not just any silhouette; I could tell just from the shape that it was meant to be Jack himself.

"That's amazing," I said, resisting the urge to reach out and touch it.

"I got it the day I was supposed to fly out," he said, dropping his t-shirt and turning back to me.

"So you broke up before the trip?"

Jack cringed slightly. "Not exactly."

"Go on..." I prompted.

"I sort of ... told her I'd meet her in Singapore. And then just ... didn't."

My mouth fell open. "That's horrible!"

He raised his hands in front of his shoulders in surrender. "To be fair, I didn't consciously know I wasn't going when I said that. But I did know I wanted to break up, so it wasn't a fair thing to promise, you're right."

"I'm just imagining her wandering sadly around Singapore

waiting for you. Taking sad, lonely outfit-of-the-day pics at the Marina Bay Sands rooftop pool because her Instagram boyfriend wasn't there to take them for her."

"Don't feel bad for her," he said with a scoff. "By the time she got there, she already had plans to meet up with some other influencer. They're together now, I'm pretty sure."

"Oh my god, the GigaChad pop star wannabe she's still with?? I didn't know they'd been together that long."

He nodded. "As far as I know. But to be fair, I haven't checked in a while. Here, give me your phone and I can see." He reached out his hand, but I shook my head.

"Can't. I blocked her. Both of them, actually."

He squinted at me, his head cocked to the side. "Why would you do that?"

"I'm team Jack," I said, smiling softly.

"There's no teams," he said, but his grin grew, and I knew I'd done the right thing. "But thank you."

He was opening up, *finally*, and I wanted to see how far I could push it. "Who have you dated since then?" I asked. "I know you said you don't date, but I assume there have been at least some encounters?"

"Oh you do, do you?"

"Um, absolutely," I said. "You don't go around looking like that"—I gestured vaguely at him—"without drumming up at least a little interest."

"Well, it's been a pretty uneventful few years in that department," he said with a shrug.

"No girlfriends? Or boyfriends?"

He shook his head. "It would be girlfriends, but even if I'd wanted to date, it's pretty slim pickings around these parts."

"What, you're not on the apps?"

He looked at me pointedly. "Why, are you on the apps?"

"Ew, no," I said, curling my lip in disgust. "Tried that."

"And why did you stop?"

"Because it was mostly students and creeps. But I can't imagine it's anywhere near as bad for men as it is for women. Cara always told me men had much better options."

"There just aren't many options to begin with," he said. "It's like seventy per cent men on those apps. And when you take the rest, remove anyone who's too young or too old, and anyone I've known since I was a kid, you're not left with much."

"You don't want to give a second chance to some primary school outcast? See the glow-ups for yourself?" It felt weird, essentially pushing him to date, after what had happened on the hike. But I figured it sent a strong message that I wasn't holding out hope that something would happen between us.

"I did try for a while, actually," he admitted, and I cocked my head, my eyes going wide, like I couldn't believe he'd been holding out on me. "I went on dozens of first dates from those apps once I'd finished my house. But there was never anyone I was interested in spending more time with."

He cleared his throat, signalling that we were done talking about him, and turned his attention to me.

"What about you?" he asked.

"I haven't been on since right after uni," I said.

"Fair enough. But surely you've dated?"

I shook my head. "I never went out with anyone from the apps. It was a war zone on there. Cara tried to set me up a few times, but usually just with the friend of whatever guy she was dating so she wouldn't feel bad for me all alone. But they never made it past one night."

I didn't tell Jack about how hard those nights had been – to always feel like nights out with Cara or the house parties she threw were acute reminders of the fact that she was the only real friend I'd had. She'd be bouncing around between friends, and I'd be dawdling along behind her like a lost duckling. And when she got sick of babysitting me, she'd try to fob me off on whatever single guy passed her very lax screening. As long as he was single, into women, and not an incel, she would make me his problem until I either gave up and went home or settled for a sub-par hookup to keep things ticking over. I'd never seen a single one of them past the first night.

"I find that so hard to believe," Jack said. "Not about the war zone apps; even the way Phil behaves on those is morally reprehensible. But that no one has scooped you up."

"Oh lovely, I see we're doing the 'I can't believe you're still single' thing," I said, rolling my eyes. He laughed and dropped the line of questioning, which was a relief. I didn't really want to think about how much I'd missed out on all these years; how different my life might have been if I'd lived somewhere else, or worked somewhere else, or anything that wasn't just doodling and clinging to my best friend.

"Do you get lonely?" I asked Jack, chancing one last probe into this landmine-laden topic.

"Sometimes," he said, and I was surprised at how quickly – and honestly – he answered. "I mean, I really enjoy my own company. I'm actually quite happy on my own. But I do remember what it's like to have someone to share the small joys with. The intimacy of waking up together; planning your day together. I miss that."

I didn't know what that felt like; I'd never had it, except maybe with Cara. But it spoke to something I'd always felt was missing when I'd tried getting to know people. Something I'd been beginning to feel with this new group of friends. And to an extent with Jack, as infuriating as he was.

After a digestion break, we took a relieving dip in the river, the hot sun having turned our shoulders a pale pink. And was I imagining things, or did Jack's gaze linger on me a little longer and more openly than usual? We dried off and reapplied our suncream; Jack decided to go shirtless for the rest of the afternoon and asked me to do the skin he couldn't reach. I was so cautious of being overly intimate that I had to apply twice because I'd missed so many spots, of course just prolonging my contact with his muscled back. Then we were back in the kayaks and headed downstream, side by side this time, admiring the world around us whilst we enjoyed a more relaxed return trip now that we were travelling with the current. Jack pointed out the willow trees and the pink balsam blooms, and I felt like we'd rounded a corner in our friendship. Like maybe what had happened before actually could be "water under the tree".

As we rounded a bend in the river and the put-in came into sight, I sidled up next to Jack, one more thing I really wanted to say to him.

"Today has been great," I said. "I mean, it's hard, and I'll need a shoulder replacement after this, but thanks again for bringing me. And for teaching me how to do it. Sorry I was such a wuss."

"Don't be silly," he said, smiling and holding my gaze for a long moment. But he must have spotted the mischief in my eyes, because his expression turned, and it was his turn to panic.

He couldn't even get my name out of his mouth before I tipped him unceremoniously into the river.

CHAPTER 18
JACK

I spent most of the next two weeks replaying that day on the water with Morgan. Yes, partly because she'd read me like a picture book. And despite how hard I'd tried to tow the line of friendly but not too friendly, I'd opened up like that book had a long-ago-cracked spine. I hadn't talked about my breakup in that much detail in years, and only two other people knew about my tattoo and why I'd got it: Phil and Chloe.

A fortnight later I was still shocked at how Morgan had taken a sledgehammer to my meticulously constructed walls, despite everything. Why did she care so much? And why was I glad she did?

But I wasn't just thinking about me, and the revelations I'd had. I was thinking about Morgan, too: the curves of her body as she splashed around after lunch, the tentative touch of her hands on my back as she applied and then reapplied my sunscreen, the cackle she'd unleashed as she'd ruthlessly tipped me into the water. I'd set a firm boundary on our hike, and she'd respected it, but all of a sudden I was the one who was beginning to regret that it was there. I knew it was for the best, but I couldn't help but imagine what our most recent adventure would have looked like if I hadn't stopped her from kissing me on that mountaintop.

I thought about her – about that day – whilst I worked, when we were sat across from one another at Faṭima's and the pub, and at night when I was trying to quiet my mind. A montage of Morgan played on repeat, and I couldn't press pause. I also wasn't sure I wanted to.

Which was why, when I texted her a few days after kayaking to see if she'd be free for a day trip away in a couple weeks' time, I'd basically held my breath for the three minutes it took her to reply and say yes.

I TOOK the scenic route to Manchester later that week; it only added about twenty minutes to the three-hour drive, but it meant that I got to admire rolling hills and charming villages rather than the monotony of the motorway. My phone showed the M6 in deep red, so I did my best to bypass as much of the traffic as possible. I rode with the windows down and the music up, trying to turn off my mind, where the Morgan Montage played incessantly.

I was on my way to collect Amy from her flat. She'd only stayed home for a few days before heading back, but then she'd messaged to say that she needed to move out suddenly, and apparently she didn't have enough money for a train ticket. She'd texted me, I imagine because she was too embarrassed to admit to Mum and Dad how broke she was. She would have known that they'd have sent her money in a heartbeat.

Which was how I found myself cancelling my standard

Friday night plans with Chloe and Phil to drive to Manchester instead. If my little sister needed me, I'd be there. In person.

The red lines leading into the city thankfully turned green as I got closer, so I pulled up in front of Amy's building about fifteen minutes earlier than the ETA I'd sent her. I leaned over to read the parking sign to make sure I'd be okay whilst I waited, and then looked around. Despite all the cities I'd travelled to all those years ago – even living in them for a month or two at a time – I'd never been a city guy. I'd enjoyed being in New York for a few weeks when I was twenty, but seeing how busy everything was around me on a Friday afternoon in the middle of summer, I was already tired. I felt like an old man. I saw people spilling out of a stopped bus, huddling around standing tables outside packed pubs, walking their dogs in the tiny park across the street ... none of it appealed. If I were questioning everything about my life all of a sudden, at least I could definitively say that I was a country mouse through and through.

I looked up across the street at the building that I knew Amy lived in, wondering what it was like to share a flat with people she didn't particularly know, surrounded by identical units of people she didn't know at all. I counted the windows up to the sixth floor where I knew she lived, and then my heart dropped.

I could see her looking out the window, and gone was the confident smile and pulled-together impression she'd given me a few weeks ago. She looked as awful as Mum had been insisting she was. In fact, she was too far away to say for sure, but she kind of looked like she'd been crying.

I decided to let her know I'd arrived, pulling out my phone to shoot her a quick message. I watched her as she looked away from the window and down, then back up to scan the street. I pressed myself into the back of my seat so she wouldn't see me watching her when she spotted the Defender. A moment later she texted back to say that she could see me, and she'd be down in a minute or two.

When she did come down, she only had a single box, a suitcase, a duffel bag, and Dad's toolbox with her. I took the box and toolbox from her, gave her a hug and helped her load her things into the car, which I'd prepared for the drive by putting the back seats down and lining the floor with an old blanket.

"Shall we go get the rest?" I asked, cracking my knuckles. Amy just blinked at me, confusion etched across her face.

"The rest of what?"

"Your stuff..."

"This is all my stuff, Jack," she said, gesturing to the three things we'd already loaded into the boot. I tried not to balk at the fact that years of living here had amounted to just two bags and a box; I considered myself quite a minimalist, but even I would have needed more than that for my things, even without furniture.

"Okay," I said, trying to save face. Not to embarrass her when I knew she was already on the edge. She was trying to act casual, happy even, but I'd seen her before, and I knew now it was just an act. So I had to be peppy enough for both of us, I supposed. "But you and I both know that box is full of crystals, so excuse me for assuming you had at least a few things."

Amy flipped her middle finger at me, and I smiled. I handed her a twenty-pound note to go grab us some dinner for the drive home, and as soon as she was out of sight, I put the back seats back up so that her things wouldn't slide around or fall over. Then I texted Chloe and Phil with a change of plans.

By the time we got home, Phil and Chloe were ready for us. I'd cancelled our Friday night plans when Amy had texted, but when I'd un-cancelled them before the drive home, they'd pulled through big time. Phil handed us both ice-cold beers as soon as we walked in, where we found a spread of hot pizzas waiting on the kitchen island and a rom-com queued up on the TV.

"Good to see you Ames," Chloe said, wrapping her in a hug. "Important question first: meat lovers or veggie?"

"Veggie, please," Amy said, cupping her hands in front of her and jutting out her lower lip, looking like Oliver Twist. Chloe plopped a plate with two slices of veggie lovers pizza into her hands.

When we'd been growing up, I'd hated how Amy tried to wriggle her way into my little friend group. She and I had been close, but it had always annoyed me when she'd tried to hang out with my friends. But the older I'd got, the more I'd appreciated that they were close, too. And when I got back from travelling and realised that they'd been keeping up with her just as much whilst I'd been away, it had given me a newfound appreciation for them. All three of them.

Still though, there were times when I began to regret how integrated they were. Like when we were done with our pizza and halfway through the crappy Netflix rom-com, the four of us squished together on the sofa, and Chloe started pestering me about Morgan.

"I hear kayaking went well," Chloe said, her voice suggestive.

"Yeah, it did," I said, trying to be as matter-of-fact, nothing-to-see-here as possible. "Wait, how do you know about that?"

Chloe shrugged. "I may have seen a sketch of a kayak over her shoulder on our lunch break on Monday. So I asked her."

"You took her *kayaking*?" Amy asking, balking at me. "You wouldn't even teach *me* to kayak!"

"That's not true!" I countered. "I'm the one who did teach you!"

"Only because Dad made you," she said. "You said it was your happy time, and teaching a newbie would just ruin it for you."

I cringed. I had actually said that; I remembered it perfectly. And I had meant it, too.

"I don't know," I said, trying to come up with an explanation for the three sets of prying eyes staring at me. "I just felt like she needed to experience it. She's trying to be more adventurous this summer."

Not one, not two, but *all three* of them smirked suggestively at that.

"Fuck all of you," I said, sitting back and taking a long swig of my beer.

"Now that would be adventurous," Phil said, "but sadly illegal in Amy's case. So let's keep it family-friendly, shall we?"

I rolled my eyes, a million other expletives running through my mind, but I was sure any of them could be twisted against me, so I kept my mouth shut.

"It's nice that the two of you are spending so much time together," Chloe continued. "I don't think she's got any local friends other than us since Cara left."

"We've hung out literally twice," I said, clearly too defensively, because Amy tilted her chin down to look up at me sceptically.

"Who is this Morgan person? Why haven't I met her if she's so important that you've hung out with her *twice*?"

"Just someone from our D&D game," I said, wracking my

brain for a change of subject, but not coming up with one quickly enough.

"Someone *hot* from our D&D game," Chloe said. "But tragically straight, otherwise she would have succumbed to my charms first."

"Definitely cute," Phil agreed. "And I'm making her chain mail armour, which is awesome."

Amy looked at me as if for confirmation of Morgan's attractiveness, but even as I pictured just how true that claim was, I just shrugged. I wouldn't give Chloe the satisfaction. Though I'd spent far too much time these past weeks admiring and imagining Morgan to deny it if pressed.

"What are her big three?" Amy asked, wisely directing that question to Chloe.

"I dunno about moon and rising," she said, "but she's definitely a Sagittarius. Her birthday was the same day as the work Christmas party last year."

"Oooooh, a Sag. Interesting choice for a Pisces."

"Yes, because we're nothing more than our birth charts," I said, rolling my eyes, "and everything is preordained. Tell me, oh wise one, when are my stars next aligned with hers?"

"Well I'd like to meet this Morgan," Amy said, completely ignoring me. "If she can worm her way under the surface enough for Jack to take her kayaking, I suspect she's worth getting to know."

"You can come to one of our games," Chloe offered. "I'm sure Fatima wouldn't mind."

Amy pulled a face. "I still don't get what you guys do in those games. It sounds kinky, all those dungeons and chains."

"It's chain *mail*," Phil said. "And honestly, we've spent tragically little time in dungeons."

"We literally just escaped a dungeon," Chloe said, but Phil waved her off.

"That was the catacombs," he said dismissively. "Just a glorified basement. Hardly a classic dungeoneering opportunity."

"Nerds," Amy said through a poorly-faked cough, then turned back to me. "So tell me about you and Morgan. When are you seeing her again?"

Chloe and Phil looked over at me, too; I never talked about Morgan with them, so they were getting this hot off the press, too.

"Next weekend," I said. *Really,* anything *for an appropriate change of subject!*

"And what are you doing next weekend...?" Amy asked, drawing out her words like she was trying to draw the information out of me.

"I don't actually know yet," I said. It was sort of a lie; I had an idea. But I hadn't fully decided yet.

"I'm sorry, you know you're seeing her, but you don't know what your plans are?" Amy asked. "That sounds like a date if I've ever heard one."

I scoffed. "How can it sound like a date if we don't actually have anything planned yet?"

Amy sighed and turned towards me, explaining as if I were a child. "When you have friends, you say 'hey, do you want to do this thing?' and you make plans around the activity. But when you're seeing someone, you say 'I'd like to see you again', and then you make plans around the timing."

"Yes!" Chloe said. "That's absolutely right."

"I don't know," Phil said, "I feel like sometimes we just pick days and then make plans around it."

"Exactly," I said. "Especially because I'm trying to help her try all these new things."

"Oh, we don't count," Chloe said, waving Phil off. "We're basically family. Amy's right." She turned her attention fully to me. "When you asked her to hang out for the day – and I'm assuming you asked her, because I heard you ask her to go kayaking, too – were you asking her because you were thinking, 'we need to do more of these silly adventures, and I'm free at this time', or were you thinking, 'I want to see Morgan again'?"

I scowled at her, then took a deep breath and leaned my head back against the sofa. I thought about how I could answer that would contradict what she'd said, but I couldn't. Because not only would I have sounded hella defensive, but she was right.

"Fine," I said, sitting up suddenly enough that I spilled a bit of beer on my leg. "I wanted to spend more time with her. Can we not make a big deal out of it? I'm freaked out enough about it on my own as it is."

I looked up at the three of them, who were all staring at me wide-eyed.

"Sure," Phil said. "Sorry, mate."

"Yeah, no big deal," Amy agreed. Chloe just nodded.

"Thank you," I said, grabbing the remote from the coffee table and turning up the volume on the TV. "Now can we please just watch Meg Ryan flirt with Tom Hanks?"

But as the little boy in the film spelled out F-O-X over and over, I descended into a spiral over whether Morgan thought next weekend was a date, too. And if she did, how she felt about that.

CHAPTER 19
JACK

The idea I'd alluded to that night with Chloe, Amy, and Phil had built out over the next week, and before I knew it, I'd compiled a mini itinerary in the Notes app on my phone. I'd heard Morgan swap book recommendations with Grey, so I was pretty sure it would be a hit, even if she'd been before. Still though, I was questioning the plans up until the moment I arrived at Morgan's house to pick her up.

I saw the "For Sale" sign hanging out the front and grimaced. She'd mentioned on a Monday a few weeks ago that her house was being sold, but I hadn't noticed the sign before. I wondered how long she had before she'd have to move.

The green front door swung open, and out came Morgan, looking like the vision of summer in denim shorts and a strappy, flowing top. She smiled at me as she got into the car, then looked at the stereo, clearly expecting me to turn it up like I usually did. But today, I wasn't looking to avoid conversation with Morgan. We'd opened up Pandora's box the last time we'd hung out, and this time I was actually looking forward to the conversation part of the day.

During the drive, we talked about work – the block of flats in town that I'd been working on for the last few weeks, and the gala planning and fundraising for her. By the time we were close to our destination, I felt like I knew everything about her job. But I was surprised to hear that she'd been working on a freelance project, too.

"I don't know, I'm nervous," she said, bringing her fists to her face in embarrassment. "I've never drawn for anyone but myself before."

"I mean, you drew everyone's characters for them, didn't you?"

"Yeah, but that's a bit different."

"Is it? What are the concepts so far?"

"Well I've got a few that look promising," she said, and though my eyes were on the road in front of us, I heard her voice perk up, changing from anxious and weary when she'd been talking about her day job to wistful and excited, and I could picture the glimmer in her eye when talking about the project. "He wants it to evoke combat, but I'm trying to avoid the obvious imagery like a sword and shield, so I'm thinking maybe an axe, or even an anvil? He sells lots of crafty stuff, like minis and paint and materials for 3D printers. So an anvil feels fitting to me. I just hope he likes it, too."

"That sounds like a lot of work though," I said. "On top of everything going on with your house? Have you found a new place yet?"

"Ew, no," she said, and I could hear the frown in her voice even without looking over at her. "Honestly I'm avoiding it at the moment. It's a lot easier to focus on the illustrations."

"Sorry," I said as I turned into a lay-by and parked along the verge behind a few other cars. "I won't make you talk about it. Today's meant to be an escape from all that."

I looked over at her to see her smiling softly at me. "Thanks, Jack. I really appreciate it." Then she looked around. "But, um ... where exactly are we escaping to?"

"Are you up for a little bit of a walk?" I asked. "That way you won't know where we're going until we get there."

"Ooh, fun," she said, clapping her hands together. "Definitely."

We started down a drive coming off the lay-by, which gave way to a path that cut across fields and along borders before joining up with the River Wye. As we walked, Morgan told me about a rescue dog she'd fallen in love with at work; how she'd been walking him at least twice a week, sometimes more, and how even the rescue was shocked by how few enquiries they'd had. Sure, he was a senior dog, but he was a fairly sought-after breed apparently.

By the time we arrived, I'd had a full run-down of the dog-friendly vs no-pets-allowed options on the current housing market, and I had a new appreciation for what it was like to not know where you would be able to lay your head in a few months' time. I offered to help her look, but she brushed me off, and I got the impression that she just didn't want to think about it.

We reached the end of the path and followed the signpost towards the town centre. We crossed a bridge over the river and came into town, and she started staring at the signs pointing to various destinations – the toilets, the castle, the car park, and more – first in Welsh, and then in English.

"I'm sorry, did we cross into Wales? I totally missed that!" she said, pointing at the signs.

I nodded. "Just before we parked the car."

She looked at me confused, and then pensive as she puzzled

through it. Her gaze landed on a sign for the Globe at Hay Art Institute, and then her face lit up.

"Oh my god, are we in Hay-on-Wye?!"

I smiled at her reaction and nodded. *Nailed it.*

She squealed and did a little shimmying motion, which I took to be a kind of happy dance. I was excited, too – I'd never actually been, either. I wasn't as much of a reader as Morgan, but the concept of a "book town" still appealed to me, if just for the vibes. Apparently there was a bookshop for every hundred people who lived there, which had sounded unbelievable until I'd looked at the map and realised just how many there were. There was a big literary festival there every year and everything.

"You've heard of it then?"

"Of course I've heard of it," she said. "It's a bookworm's dream." She looked up and down the high street, mesmerised. "Okay well, very well done," she said. "Cara and I always talked about coming here, but we never made it happen."

"Okay, well, I've got a plan, if that's okay," I said. She nodded, so I continued, checking the time on my phone. "It's just after ten, so most if not all of the bookshops are open now. If you're up for it, I thought we could wander on our own until about half past twelve, and then meet up for lunch."

Morgan's smile faltered. "You don't want to walk around together?"

My heart did a weird little skip at knowing she wanted to spend the day together, even when I'd given her an out. But I wasn't done. "We will after lunch," I assured her. "But I had an idea. Before lunch, we each have to find the other a book. So we can't be together, or it would spoil the surprise."

I didn't want it to feel too much like a school trip with an assignment, and I didn't want worrying about shopping for me to get in the way of her enjoying the day. But I also thought it could be fun. And part of me was curious to see what she would choose for me after the last time we'd hung out.

She thought about it for a moment and then nodded. "I like it," she said. "Do you know where you want to eat for lunch?"

I nodded and sent her a pin to the place I'd picked out. She checked her phone, and I saw the text go from "delivered" to "read" in my messages.

"Then let the game begin," she said, sticking her hand out in front of her. I grabbed it, and she shook her hand exaggeratedly before turning an about-face and striding away from me. She was going in the opposite direction of most of the bookshops, but I figured she'd realise that soon enough. And plus, you couldn't go a hundred metres without stumbling into a bookshop around here, so she'd make her way.

As I watched her walk away, my admiration for the way the sunlight kissed her shoulders was suddenly overshadowed by a sinking realisation: that as much thought as I'd given to today's plans, I'd not thought for a single moment about what book I would get her. I had a lot of ground to cover.

CHAPTER 20
MORGAN

Every small child's dream upon seeing *Beauty and the Beast* was to have a library like the one the Beast gives Belle, and I couldn't be convinced otherwise. That's why Cara and I had filled our home with books; having them around us made both of us feel like the world was right at our fingertips.

So whilst I had never been to Hay-on-Wye, the moment I had seen it mentioned for the first time – on social media, of course – I'd been hooked.

And now, as I walked into my *fifth* book store (!!) in the last two hours, a used bookseller with books stacked so high they were wedged against the ceiling, I couldn't help but feel like I was a tiny step closer to living that bookish dream. And I had a Gay on Wye tote bag already half full of books to prove it, including two books I'd picked out for Grey. I took a picture of my reflection in a window I passed, in theory to send to Cara, though I already knew she wouldn't respond.

As I ran my fingers along the spines of the books on one of the shelves, I spotted *the* book. I hadn't known what exactly I'd been looking for, but I knew instantly this was it. I pulled it out from the shelf; it was packed in so tightly I had to use my other hand to keep its neighbouring books in place.

Every time we'd hung out, Jack had obsessively told me about the trees and rocks and whatever else around us. He knew every bird species, every flower, all of it. As much shit as I gave him for obsessively bedding in at home after all his travels, this was the most beautiful result of that bedding in: he knew everything there was to know about the landscape and life around him.

And so when I saw the deep forest green spine with a gold foil tree running up the side, roots and branches and thick, knotted trunk adorning every inch, when I felt the uneven deckled edges of the pages, I almost didn't need to see the title to know that I'd found what I was looking for. But when I saw that it was an illustrated guide to the flora and fauna of the Wye Valley in the late 1800s? The book could have cost a month's wages and I couldn't have put it back.

I had a moment of panic when I did think about how much it might be, especially when I couldn't see a price scribbled inside like in the rest of the books. But it was surprisingly affordable, so I bought a bookmark for good measure before walking back out into the summer sun.

But in the back of my mind – okay, pretty much front and centre in my mind – I was worrying about this little challenge. I'd never been a particularly good gift-giver; it was always way too much pressure trying to find the right tone, somewhere on the spectrum of silly to sentimental, and I felt like I always missed the mark.

For Cara's twenty-first, I'd given her a necklace I knew she'd been admiring. We'd walked past a shop with jewellery on display, and she'd told me one of the necklaces looked sort of like one she'd been pining after that she saw one of her favourite influencers wear. It had cost me what felt like a fortune back then, but I'd thought it was worth it for a big birthday.

But when I gave it to her at her party, right in the middle of joke gifts from her friends like nipple tassels and offensive t-shirts, I could tell straight away that it had killed the vibe. And even though she wore it constantly, and had even posted a picture wearing it the other day, I had seen a brief flicker of embarrassment on her face that night that I'd taken things too seriously.

The book I'd found for Jack wasn't particularly sentimental, but it wasn't exactly funny, either. What if this was all meant to be a funny thing? And what if giving him something sentimental made him throw up his guard like he had after our near-miss the first time we'd hung out? I figured I needed a backup plan, and fast; I only had thirty minutes until I was meant to meet him for lunch.

As I turned onto Lion Street, I actually passed Jack coming out of one of the bookshops. I saw him before he saw me, and seeing him like this, unaware that he was being noticed, I could admire him properly. He really was handsome. I mean, objectively I had known that, but amidst the other people bustling around him, he looked like a celebrity, or the prince of some tiny European nation no one has ever heard of. His honey-blonde hair shone in the sunlight, and the stubble currently adorning his jawline made it look even sharper than usual. The sleeves of the white t-shirt he was wearing hit his arms at exactly the right spot to show off his biceps, which I knew weren't from long gym sessions but from years of paddling and manual labour. Why was that such an attractive detail?

But most of all I loved how his resting expression was a

smile. The corners of his mouth were turned up by default as he walked along the street. There was an intangible aura of warmth radiating off him, and I didn't know how everyone wasn't stopping to stare like I was.

Until he saw me watching him, that is, and his eyes went wide. He clutched a brown paper bag to his chest to hide it from me.

"I didn't see it, don't worry," I said as I came close, though I did try – unsuccessfully – to get a peek at the logo on the bag.

"Have you gotten mine yet?" he asked, looking down at my hands. Helpfully I'd stashed his book in the tote alongside all the ones I'd picked out for myself and Grey.

I shrugged. "You'll find out in half an hour, Evans. Now get out of my way." I brushed past him with a wink, and his smile back to me, his green eyes crinkling at the corners, nearly made me go weak in the knees.

The shop he'd just come out of was one that sold new books, and I scanned the shelves for a second option for Jack. I was hoping he'd give me his gift first, and I could choose the most appropriate one in return. Eventually I found a book in the humour section about how to become a "grouchy old hermit"; it made me laugh, mostly because the first step was building a house with one's own two hands. It was a throwaway, but it would be a good backup in case I'd missed the mark, so I paid for it at the till – along with a new fantasy release for me – and headed towards the pub Jack had sent me, which was up the hill at the south end of town.

Of course, he was already there when I arrived, sitting in the beer garden out back with his sunglasses on. Once I was settled we ordered from the menu on our phones, but from the way Jack was practically bouncing up and down by the time we'd paid, I could tell that we wouldn't be waiting until after lunch to exchange books.

"Did you want to give each other the books now?" I offered, and he grabbed his paper bag before I'd even finished the question.

"I'm excited," he said. "This was actually really funny."

My excitement deflated slightly at this – clearly he'd gone the jokey route – but at least I had grabbed a backup.

"Actually," he said, pausing with his hand in the bag, his face dropping suddenly, "you go first."

I squinted at him. "Why?"

He shrugged. "I don't know. I got nervous all of a sudden."

"Okay..." I said, digging in my rucksack for the joke book. I had to move the nicer one out of the way to get to it, and for a moment I considered just giving him that one, but he'd said he went funny, so I pushed it aside and grabbed the hermit book instead.

I took a deep breath, tried to stop my leg from bouncing with nerves, and put the book on the table between us, facing Jack. "Here you go," I said, and watched his reaction carefully. I watched his eyes scan the title, and he smiled, but it wasn't the crinkly-eyed one he'd been wearing before. *Shit.*

"It's funny because the first step is about building your own house," I said, but dammit, I knew I had missed. Did he not find it funny?

Jack laughed brightly enough to fool most people, and he flipped through the book, showing me other funny bits I hadn't even noticed myself. But I knew he wasn't as into it as he was trying to appear.

Then it was his turn, and he hesitated before pulling the book out of the bag.

"I'm afraid I didn't go for the humorous angle," he said,

which of course confused the hell out of me given his previous comment. But I didn't have long to contemplate it, because he placed the most perfect book ever on the table in front of me.

I ran my hands over the green spine, the circular illustration in the middle surrounded by runes, the gold foil printed signature from J. R. R. Tolkien. It was an illustrated version of *The Hobbit*, and a beautiful one at that. Thumbing through it, I was captivated by Tolkien's illustrations – paintings, maps, sketches.

"What was funny about this?" I asked, a bit breathless, unable to take my eyes off the pages as I flipped through them.

"Sorry?"

"Before. You said it was actually really funny."

"Ah, yeah, sorry. This is a used copy, and the previous owner wrote their name inside the back cover. Check it out."

I flipped the book over and opened the back cover, and there, in childish, unsteady handwriting, was a message:

> *This is my very favourite book. My granny bought me a new one, and I'm too old for picture books, so I don't need this one anymore. I hope you love it as much as I do.*
> *Sinceerly,*
> *Morgan, aged 9*

I gasped in delight when I saw the name. I looked up at Jack, so excited that I had tears in my eyes. He looked more pleased than I'd ever seen him.

"Thank you, Jack," I said, my voice dripping with sincerity. There was no room for sarcasm or emotional distance or stoicism right now. This was a magnificent gift. I grabbed his hand on the table between us and gave it a squeeze. His smile faltered slightly as he stared down at it, so I pulled my hand back, but I didn't even have the mental capacity to be worried or embarrassed.

Until I remembered the actual joke of a book I'd given him, and then suddenly embarrassment was the only thing I could feel.

"Jack, I'm so sorry," I said, my eyes going wide and my shoulders drooping forward. "I wasn't sure if you were going more for a joke or something genuine. I only gave you the grumpy old hermit book as a joke."

"I know," he said, his smile a bit halfhearted. "It's okay. I'm just glad you like yours."

"I *love* it," I said, "but I also have another one for you."

He frowned. "Why did you get me two?"

"Like I said, I didn't know which direction you'd go," I said as I went rummaging in my rucksack once more. "It's nowhere near as amazing as the book you got me, but this one should be a bit more up your alley." I placed the gold foiled book directly into his hand.

It took a moment for him to look away from me and down to what I'd given him, but when he did, I finally got the expression I'd been after all along. That crinkly-eyed grin, and a bit of astonishment for good measure. He pulled the book closer to inspect it, running his finger along the deckled edges just as I had.

"Amazing," he said, flipping through the book and pausing on key pages; I, too, had chosen one with sketches. Perhaps all adult readers came full circle to liking illustrated books again. I wished I could tell nine-year-old Morgan that one was never too old for picture books, but then she might ask for her book back, and that would be a tragedy.

"Better?" I asked, but I hardly needed to based on his reaction.

"Definitely," he said, still combing through the book, but then he looked up at me suddenly. "Not that I didn't appreciate the other one, of course. It's funny in its—"

I shook my head and held up a hand to interrupt him. "It was a joke that was funny for exactly five seconds when I gave it to you. I'm sure you'll get lots more enjoyment out of this one."

"Definitely," he said again with a nod, and he was right back into the book. I stared flipping through mine, too, and we both stayed like that, admiring our gifts, until our food arrived.

AFTER LUNCH, we wandered through the town together, dipping into the shops we hadn't been in earlier. It turned out we'd gone into almost all the same ones before lunch, and even bought each other's books – the real gifts, not the joke one – in the same place. We bought each other books again at the outdoor honesty bookshop just inside the castle walls, with the brief of finding the most ridiculous, unhinged novels possible for each other. He found a copy of a famously deranged science fiction novel, but I found him what appeared to be a why-choose, enemies-to-lovers erotic romance between Mothman and two World War II deserters from opposing sides. We both agreed that, whilst his find might have been iconic, I'd definitely won on novelty.

Once we'd been into all the shops, we circled the castle again and then stopped at a sweet shop for fudge, which we ate on the riverbank as we watched people in canoes and kayaks paddle around. My shoulders and cheeks were pinking up in the sun yet again, like they seemed to every time I was with Jack, as if it was his presence giving off light. But I didn't care about a slight sunburn. Sitting next to him, filling up on fudge and sweating in the sun somehow felt like heaven. My favourite flavour was the Irish cream; Jack's was the maple nut. And when I was so full I thought I might be sick if I took one more bite, Jack suggested we walk back to the car.

Partially from our full bellies and partially from how tired we were, it took us twice as long to walk back to the car as it had to walk down into town, but that was okay; despite any gastric discomfort, it was one of the best days I'd had in a long time. And as we walked in a companionable silence completely devoid of awkwardness, I knew why: because there was no more posturing here. I wasn't wearing any of the masks I'd always had to bust out around new people. I groaned when my belly ached instead of sucking it in, and asked the random questions that popped into my mind.

And whilst I couldn't speak for Jack, it seemed to me that the panic that had set in for him that first time we'd gone on one of these adventures was long gone. He seemed ... comfortable. And that made me feel happier than it probably should have.

CHAPTER 21
CAPTAIN MORGANA SILVERSWORD

"No way," Clover said, looking over the bedraggled party. It had taken them three days to make their way out of the catacombs, being pursued by the city guard the entire time. The alarm they'd triggered had not only called in the full force of Thelanoris's security measures, but also put them at the top of the most wanted list. The Thieves Guild had been the sentinels' first stop, so it wasn't safe for them there. They needed Clover's help.

"Please," Thrormir pleaded. "We can't get out of here on our own. The city walls are impenetrable."

The dwarf and the halfling were the only ones who could stand comfortably in Clover's cottage; the rest of the party hunched over, Gorlag especially, as they took refuge.

"You haven't even paid me what you owe," Clover said, and Morgana noticed that her hand tightly grasped the hilt of her dagger.

"The deal was in and out," Calamity said. "And as long as we're here, we're not safely out. You owe us."

"Safe never came into it," Clover snapped, baring her pointy faerie teeth as she flitted closer to Calamity.

"Please," Thrormir said, holding his hands out between them to keep them apart. "Clover, we'll get you the money. Half of what we owe you now, half when we're safe."

"Outside the city walls," Clover offered. "That's the best I can do."

Yorick shook his head. "We'll be sitting ducks if you drop us there. No way. We said *safe*."

"And what's safe?" Clover asked. "When you're back in your own precious city on your own plane of existence? No, you'll pay now."

"We won't," Morgana said, moving onto her knees so she could grasp at her own sword. Clover looked her over and clearly decided that she wasn't worth the fight, backing off a bit.

"Mummy?" a somehow even smaller voice called from the corner of the room, and the party looked over to see a tiny faerie child poking its head down through a hole in the ceiling.

Clover flitted over to the hole so quickly Morgana couldn't even see her wings moving.

"Go to bed, sweetie," she said.

"I can't sleep though."

"Mummy will be up soon, as soon as my friends are gone." She turned a pointed look to the party, who all waved awkwardly at the little one.

Once Clover had managed to convince her child to go back to bed, she looked back over at her guests.

"I have a lot at stake, too," she said, "as you can see. So tell me what you want, but I'm not doing it if it puts my family on the line."

"We respect that," Morgana said. "We just want to go somewhere we can find sanctuary."

"Tell me where," Clover insisted. "Because all I know is inside this city, and that does you no good."

Morgana shared a look with Thrormir, who shrugged. They'd all agreed that telling the Thieves Guild exactly where the portal was could be a bad idea, so that was off the table. But they needed to go somewhere.

When Yorick stepped forward, Morgana preemptively cringed. He had a tendency to try to seduce his way out of situations.

"I have an idea," he said, and they all braced for what he was going to say, not expecting it to be the best idea any of them had had yet. "Take us to the Bards College."

CHAPTER 22
MORGAN

A few days later Cara's mum messaged to let me know that we were going to have to change tack on the sale. With how quickly properties in the area were selling, they'd expected to offload it by now, and they blamed my decor aesthetic for the lack of interest. Apparently this was backed up by listing engagement data from the estate agent, who would be coming around again in less than a week. And my to-do list from Cara's mum to have done before then was unreasonably long:

- *Contain books to actual bookshelves only, no double-stacking (looks cluttered)*
- *Remove all but one living room rug (keep the beige one)*
- *Reduce cushions by half*
- *Remove all stick-on kitchen items (backsplash, worktops, and floors)*
- *Re-dress Cara's bedroom with forthcoming supplies*
- *Remove all string lights and LED lights from the second bedroom*

- *Repaint front door (same colour, please)*
- *Clear rear courtyard of all weeds and moss*

I abstained from emailing her back to ask where I was meant to put all the stuff I had to remove, or to remind her that her daughter had purchased most of it. I also didn't suggest, as much as I wanted to, that they were responsible for improvements; I wasn't technically on a lease, and I wasn't paying market rates, so I knew helping out was sort of assumed. Instead I did what I did best: ignored her message until the latest I could possibly leave it so that I could rely on the pressure of a deadline to motivate me.

I threw myself into my design project; Greg had loved the anvil idea I'd sent him, so I was refining it and trying out some different overlays for the text. I'd had to teach myself so much in order to design a logo – Could I use graphic brushes in the app I used without copyright infringement? What was the difference between a logo and a logotype? Not to mention the fact that I hadn't worked with text design since uni – but I was loving every second. It was the first time I'd ever really *challenged* myself with my art, at least since I'd finished my degree. When I was designing, or drawing, or even just watching the YouTube videos I was learning from, I felt like the best version of myself. Like I could do anything. *Make* anything. It was a feeling I'd only ever got secondhand when playing D&D or reading a book, except now the sense of achievement was mine. Not some other main character's, and not Captain Morgana's. Mine.

Unfortunately, things were decidedly less dreamy at my day job. Aaron was so set on "training me up" that I was basically doing all the work myself, on top of my normal job. There was no way I was going to hit my (newly increased) quota for the quarter, so I had to make sure the gala was as incredible as possible to make up the numbers. But Aaron seemed to be doing his best to make that impossible.

For starters, he'd blown the budget right out of the gate. He'd neglected a whole tab on the spreadsheet, which meant we were left unable to pay the design agency we'd contracted for the invites, the place cards, the name badges, and all the signage at the event itself.

I was escaping the problem over my lunch break by going to play with Pablo. It was tipping it down with rain outside, so we had to content ourselves with playing in his pen, which was fine; he just seemed happy to see me, which melted me and put me back together again all at once. I hung my dripping jacket and tote bag up on a hook, then sat down next to him and started playing. Only he seemed to want nothing to do with that, curling up in my lap instead.

"Oh, how cute!" Lauren said as she walked by. "There was a big group of school-age kids here earlier, so they must have tired him out."

"That's great," I said. "Hey, can you hand me my bag?"

Lauren grabbed the tote bag when I pointed to it and handed it to me over the half wall. "Here you go."

I thanked her, and then took advantage of the quiet moment to open up my tablet and work on the Game On! logo some more.

But then I noticed that Pablo was doing an adorable snarl as he slept, and after I took a video on my phone and sent it to Chloe, I decided to try to draw him. It was another new effort for me; most of what I'd drawn in the past had been more of a cartoon-style fantasy art. It took me a few minutes to figure out how I wanted to approach it, but once I did, I was actually quite pleased with how the picture was coming out. I was sketching fast, but it was a fairly minimalist illustration style, and it came together quickly once I knew what I wanted to do.

Once I'd finished his face, I decided to try drawing the sausage dogs that had been recently adopted, and then I moved on to the cat I'd had growing up, and then the otters Jack and I had seen when we were kayaking. That one was harder, and I had to look at a reference image, but I was happy with it by the time I was done. And by the end of my lunch break, I had a file full of almost a dozen animal faces, lined up like they were at a party. I'd even added little party hats on their heads to add to the effect.

That's when the idea came to me.

I got up quickly, displacing Pablo, who gave me a very disgruntled, "how dare you" kind of glare.

"I'm so sorry Pabs," I said. "But I've had an idea, and I need to go back to work. I'll see you tomorrow."

I practically sprinted through the rain back to the office, where I didn't even stop at my desk before barging into Simone's office, dripping all over her floor. I only realised what I must look like when she glanced up at me with a passable Miranda Priestly impression (read: unimpressed).

"I had an idea," I said, quickly hiding the layer with the party hats, "but it's a bit of a departure."

"What's that?" she asked, gesturing for me to sit down. I perched as far on the edge of the seat as possible, not wanting to get her chair wet.

"Well, like I told you earlier, we don't have budget for the design agency," I said. "And I already checked with the internal team, and their pipeline is packed. They wouldn't get to us in time."

Simone gave me an impatient look. "These sound like problems, not solutions."

I took a deep breath, all the urgency and enthusiasm I'd felt before suddenly evaporating out of me. But I'd come this far, and it would be much more embarrassing to leave now without showing her what I'd done than for her to reject the idea. So I handed the tablet to her and watched as she squinted at it, pinching her fingers together and apart several times to see the drawings better.

"Tell me what I'm looking at here," she said.

"They're animals from the rescue," I said. "Well, some of them. But I drew them. And I think we should use them for the gala. Give everyone a different animal. Use it on their place card, their name badge, their invite, all of it."

Simone was quiet for a long moment before she spoke, and I had to remind myself to breathe. "It's not exactly on theme."

"Well, to be fair, without the signage, there really isn't a theme. There will be bunting and lights, but that's hardly a creative direction. So this would, I guess, *inform* the theme."

She nodded as she considered this. Then she nodded some more, and considered some more. She was quiet long enough this time that I was sure she'd forgotten I was sitting there.

"There's no way," she finally said, and I felt myself deflate, sitting back in the chair, wet spots be damned.

"Oh," I muttered. "Sorry, I just thought—"

"You couldn't possibly get this done on top of all your fundraising work. I'll have to reassign your call list."

I sat back up again. "You would do that?"

She handed me the tablet back. "Well, we can't very well have no signage, can we? And no one else has brought me a better idea. So let's try it."

I smiled as I turned off the screen and stood. "Thank you, Simone."

"But you have to promise me that you'll tell me the moment you get stuck."

"I promise," I said, turning to leave.

"And Morgan?" she said as I reached the door. I stopped and turned back to her.

"Yes?"

"This is good," she said. "Really good. Well done."

I GOT HOME a few hours later and instantly collapsed on the sofa, breaking my "don't sit down" rule. Now that my feet were up, I'd be unlikely to get anything productive done for the rest of the evening. And by the time I'd finished a takeaway that only required me to be standing for about twenty seconds whilst I opened the door, it was clear I wasn't going to be tackling anything but my Watch Later playlist on YouTube.

Which was a problem, because I only had a few days until the new pictures were being taken, and I'd done exactly zero things from Cara's mum's list. I did have a large box from her that had arrived a couple of days ago, which I assumed was the "forthcoming supplies" for Cara's room that she'd mentioned in her note. I'd yet to open the box.

I started making a mental schedule; I'd have to fit everything into just two days, including a trip to the shop to get some paint. It didn't leave me much wiggle room for Monday's slot with the estate agent. Really I needed to get myself going now so that I could gain a day, but the idea of that sounded horrible when all I wanted to do was be as cosy as possible.

Or maybe there was a way I could get it all done *and* stay put this evening...

No, bad idea, I told myself. I'd only just hung out with Jack over the weekend – this would be the shortest time yet between seeing each other, outside of Monday nights, anyway.

As I debated texting him, my eyes scanned the room, looking at everything I needed to do. I would probably have to donate a few books, which broke my heart, and it would be good to have a car, right? What if we needed supplies suddenly? I couldn't walk to the big hardware store from here. And plus, he'd apparently built his whole house on his own. And he was an absolute nerd about plants; I didn't even know what in the neglected back garden was plant and what was weed. *He would certainly be useful...*

My eyes landed on the book he'd bought me in Hay over the weekend, which stood propped up against the bookshelf. On paper, it was a pretty safe choice – we'd watched *The Lord of the Rings* together on the group weekend away, he knew I liked illustration, and my name was in the front of the book – but there was something about the idea of him combing the shelves for something I'd like, actually taking the time to open the books and run his hands across them, that made me feel all fluttery. It was how I'd felt shopping for him, too. And as I looked at the gorgeous cover and remembered his crinkly-eyed smile coming out of that bookshop, I admitted to myself that I also just wanted to see him. And not just because I knew he'd look good with a tool belt on; because I actually craved his company, weirdly enough.

I knew nothing would come of it; he'd made that much clear. But with everything that was going on – work, the house, Pablo, all of it – being around him made me feel grounded. Excited. Brave. And that wasn't nothing.

Still, it took me a solid ten minutes to talk myself into texting him, despite the fact that we exchanged casual texts all the time, and another five to craft a message that I thought sounded casual enough that he could easily say no if he didn't want to come. As soon as I was done, I chucked my phone across the room onto the window seat as if it were about to explode, attempting to distract myself with my tablet.

Less than a minute later, it lit up, and I practically sprinted over to it to read Jack's response. Then I did a highly embarrassing happy dance into the kitchen, where I cracked open a bottle of beer. Tonight I could be cosy. And tomorrow ... well, tomorrow I'd get to be grounded and excited and brave.

CHAPTER 23
JACK

By Friday night, I was completely shattered. I'd spent the day with Phil and a few old school friends doing something called "canyoning" for Adam's stag do, which essentially involved jumping off cliff after cliff into the cold water of the Irish Sea on the North Wales coast. I'd enjoyed it, but it was nothing short of exhausting; with all the time I'd been spending with Morgan, I'd gone on way fewer solo adventures than usual, and I was feeling it in my lack of stamina.

I wasn't the only one who had struggled; Adam himself was terrified of every single jump, and his best man Freddie who had planned the weekend was karmically rewarded for the choice of activity with a too-small wetsuit. Whilst none of us had enjoyed looking at the effect that had created, the waddle it had caused had us all in stitches for the entirety of the hiking portion.

Now we were back at the big house Freddie had rented, eating a massive takeaway order, the leftovers from which were supposed to be our lunch the next day, too. I didn't relish the idea of leftover Chinese, nor was I keen on the next day's loose agenda; Freddie was trying to rally everyone to go to a strip club, but he seemed to be the only one interested. Which was saying something, because he was also the only married guy on the trip.

I wasn't used to quite so much laddish socialisation – I wasn't sure how I was going to make it through another day and a half – so instead of playing drinking games, I was off in a corner, sitting in an armchair in a little bay window, holding a beer in one hand and scrolling on my phone with the other.

Naturally I'd found myself on Morgan's profile. I hadn't used my account in years until Morgan and I had started hanging out, but I'd reactivated it recently, checking out her profile every now and then without actually following her. I was scrolling through a carousel of images she'd posted after our trip to Hay that I'd now seen about a dozen times; there was nothing of me, or even her for that matter, but rather just artful shots of the books and shops, and of a box of fudge next to the river. I could almost taste the chocolate and feel it melting on my fingers when I saw it, and I wished, not for the first time, that I were doing something with Morgan this weekend instead of listening to a bunch of drunk guys try to one-up each other with how well they knew the groom. Three nights was a long time, and not for the first time today, I asked myself if the two days of holiday I'd had to use had been worth it.

"Whatcha doin?" Phil asked, staggering over – he'd clearly had a few beers himself – and sinking down into the chair opposite me. I pocketed my phone as quickly as I could. "Insta-stalking Morgan?" he asked, pointing to my shorts where my phone was still peeking out of my pocket.

"Don't be ridiculous."

Phil laughed. "You're in so fuckin' deep, man."

I shook my head and rolled my eyes, but he wasn't wrong. I'd spent most of the week reminiscing about last weekend, or looking at the book she'd bought me, or thinking about the Ren Faire. It was getting closer – we were about two and a half months out, and I knew Phil had been sewing his little fingers off to get us ready.

"How's it going with you?" I asked, partially because I cared, but mostly to get the spotlight off of me.

"Living the dream, man," he said, but there was a bit of sadness in his eyes that I hadn't noticed. I instantly panicked – had I missed something going on with Phil? Had something happened? If he wasn't okay and I'd missed it because I'd been running around with Morgan too much, I'd never forgive myself.

"Is everything okay?" I asked, and he must have heard the heightened tone of my voice, because he instantly smiled, and it was like the sadness just evaporated.

"Oh yeah, all good," he said, waving his hands. "I'm just getting sick of being unemployed. I know Ethel needs someone around, but she doesn't actually like being looked after. So when I'm not doing the three things a day she actually needs me for, I'm either working on a project or watching *EastEnders* reruns with her. That's why I was so excited to have the costumes to work on. I've gone through so many audiobooks making Morgan's chain mail..."

I smiled, but it didn't escape me how he'd brought the conversation back around to Morgan already.

"How is she?" Phil asked, taking a sip of his beer, looking pointedly at me over the glass.

I rolled my eyes. "We're just friends, Philip."

He pointed at my pocket again. "Jack, you've barely been on social media of any kind since you and Aria broke up. If you're casually scrolling through her profile, that's a big deal."

"What makes you think I was on her profile?" I asked, but he just pointed to the window behind me. It was dark outside, so the reflection was crystal clear. He'd actually seen me on Morgan's profile, which meant he'd known I was deflecting. Which, of course, made me look even guiltier.

"Okay, fine," I admitted. "She posted some pictures from our trip to Hay over the weekend. I just wanted to see them."

He nodded slowly. "Sure you did."

"That's all I was doing," I insisted.

"I believe you," he said, in a way that told me he very much did not believe me. I wouldn't have, either. "But you know, it would be okay if you *did* like her."

"What does that mean?" I didn't like his tone; it was the way he talked to his nan when he was trying to help her remember something. Like he needed to beat around the bush so she could figure it out for herself.

"It doesn't *mean* anything," he said. "But it's been a while. And if she makes you happy, you should go for it."

I took a deep breath and closed my eyes for a moment. It was exhausting, trying to make sense of things with Morgan. I couldn't even figure out my side of the equation, much less how she felt – and even *less* how to go about articulating that to someone else.

A roar of "Wheyey!" erupted from the other room, causing us both to jump slightly.

"Beer pong," Phil said in explanation, and I sighed. It was like a frat house out of some American comedy film.

I was about to suggest I might go for a walk, or at least find a spot even further from the noise, maybe somewhere I could put my headphones on without seeming antisocial. I'd actually brought the bloody book with me, just in case I had time to actually read it – maybe I could flick through it in my room. But before I could suggest it, my phone buzzed.

I took it out of my pocket and tried to control my facial expression as best as I could when I saw the message was from Morgan, but I could feel the corners of my mouth wanting to tug upward.

> Hey! I've got an obnoxiously long to-do list from Cara's mum that I have to get done before Monday. If you're around at all, can I buy you pizza in exchange for doing my work for me? I know you said you're seeing friends this weekend though, so I'll text Chloe as backup. No worries.

I'd typed my reply before I could even think twice:

> I'm away tonight, but I can be there by 1pm tomorrow. If we don't get it done then, I can come back on Sunday. That work?

Her reply came almost as quickly as I'd sent mine:

> Perfect! See you tomorrow x

I smiled at that little x for longer than I should have, picturing the lips that might form that kiss. Then I realised how pathetic I was being and looked up, where I saw Phil squinting at the window behind me.

"There's no way you could make that out," I said, squinting at him sceptically.

"I've got incredible eyesight," he said with an obnoxious wink. "By the way, mate, you're not looking too well ... maybe we should head home in the morning?"

I sighed at him, but I was biting back a smile. "Yeah, I think you're right," I said. "I'd better turn in."

"Good for you," he said as we both stood up. He put a hand

on my shoulder for a moment and squeezed, then dropped it. "Yeah. Good for you."

～

BY THE TIME I dropped Phil off and pulled up to Morgan's house the next day, my duffel bag still in the back seat, it was a quarter to one. I was planning to sit in my car for five or ten minutes before showing up helpfully early, but a minute or so after I parked, I got a text:

> You can just come in now. I've been at the window for like twenty minutes.

I couldn't help but laugh – we were actually quite alike sometimes, weren't we? I hadn't been past the gate before, and as I came through it, I saw the curtains in the bay window twitch slightly.

As I walked up the front path, I admired some of the species that had taken over the front garden. Mum would have loved it. There was red clover, Yorkshire fog, and even some spotted orchids, one of which was currently hosting a marbled white butterfly. Sure, there was some burdock, which would be a nightmare to pick out of Pablo's fur if Morgan ever got to bring him home. But it was a pollinator's dream, and it had an unkempt beauty about it.

As I reached the door – a sage green Edwardian with leaded glass insets – I saw a patch of colour on the step. I bent down and picked it up; it was a postcard from Los Angeles, a stylised print of the Hollywood sign. It must have missed the letterbox.

Before I could read the message on the back, Morgan opened the door dressed in a pair of denim cutoff shorts and a retro Charlie's Angels t-shirt. Her curly hair was piled on top of her head, and I could tell she'd put on a small amount of make-up. Something tensed in me, not unpleasantly, at the thought of her putting in effort for me. The sun shone in on her through the door, making her skin, which was tanned from our summer adventures and dewy from the heat, shimmer slightly. I had the overwhelming urge to hug her: to wrap my arms around her waist and pull her in close to me.

But I didn't get the chance, because she hugged me instead, opting for the single-armed side hug, which created painfully little contact.

"This was on the step," I said as she stepped back, handing her the postcard. She took it from me and frowned down at it.

"Thanks," she said, setting it down behind her without reading it.

She invited me inside and thanked me for coming, then started rambling about everything we needed to do, but I wasn't listening, because I was too busy looking around at the inside of Morgan's mind. At least, that was the impression I got from looking at her home; it was a bit chaotic, with books and knick-knacks everywhere, and it had a pitiful amount of light coming through the big front window; the whole street was appallingly positioned. But it was also warm, and cosy, and vibrant, and full. It made me feel exactly the way she made me feel – like I wanted to stay a while. Settle in. Look around and see what I could discover.

As my eyes scanned the room, I saw a window seat, where I imagined from the indent in the cushion she spent a lot of time. It looked like a great place to draw, or to read. And I pictured her sitting there last night, texting me, whilst I sat in a different bay window over a hundred miles away.

Then I saw the bookshelves, which looked to be double-stacked with books, some of which I recognised from her Hay-on-Wye haul. I'd known she liked to read, but I hadn't realised just how much. And as my eyes passed over the fireplace and to the other set of bookshelves, I saw the book I'd bought her only a week ago turned outward, different to any other book. Like she'd been looking at it, the way I'd been looking at the one she got for me. Like it meant as much to her as it apparently did to me.

I felt a weight form in my stomach, and I recognised it instantly; it was the same thing that had happened when we'd been hiking. The thing that had made me shut down; made me lash out. And after all the time I'd spent with Morgan, after she'd played riverside therapist, I could finally tell what it was. It was fear.

But there's nothing to be afraid of, I told myself. *It's just Morgan.* And when that didn't work, when my breathing started to get shallower and faster, I decided to try a different approach. *Just take it one step at a time*, I thought. *You're just doing a bit of DIY. That's all. You can panic later if you need to.*

Surprisingly, that seemed to work, and I was able to calm myself down. Morgan was now over by the shelf, clearly having realised that she'd left the book on display, apologising.

"It's fine," I said. "I've been reading mine, too."

I didn't know why I'd told her that, but it seemed to appease her, or even thrill her; she grinned, and her cheeks went even more pink.

Her phone buzzed on the coffee table, and she bent down to grab it. She clearly enjoyed what she saw, smiling as she stared down at it.

"Good news?" I asked.

"Oh yeah," she said, turning it towards me. "Phil and I have been texting about my second Ren Faire look. He's just sent a picture of the progress."

I scoffed; he'd been home for all of twenty minutes, and he was already back into the projects. Then I processed what she'd said.

"Sorry, he's making both of your costumes?"

She smiled innocently, putting a hand under her chin to add to the cherubic image. "Yeah, but honestly the chain mail is so expensive I'm beginning to regret it."

I beckoned for her phone. "Show me what you've got."

She started to give it to me, then thought twice about it and yanked it back before it could settle in my hand. "Actually, I want it to be a surprise," she said. "We're doing something a bit different."

I narrowed my eyes. "A surprise?"

She nodded. "At least until it's ready for me to try on, I guess."

An image flashed into my mind unbidden of Morgan in a classic Ren Faire get-up, like the tavern wenches in the videos I'd seen online. I didn't hate the idea of it. But I needed to stop thinking about it, otherwise I'd be useless for getting anything done.

"Okay fine, what's on the list for today?" I asked. And when she smirked, I realised my mistake. "Sorry, yes, I know you were telling me a minute ago. But I wasn't listening. I was too busy being nosy."

"Fine," she said, then walked me into the kitchen – equally cosy, though the stick-on vinyl everywhere was definitely a choice – and showed me the to-do list she'd written up on a tiny whiteboard. Funny enough, removing all the offending vinyl was on the list. Only one item was checked off so far – "get rid of mood lighting". I chuckled and wondered if that was a landlord-mandated task or a precaution for me. Either way, it was probably for the best.

"Okay," I said with a big exhale, taking in everything we still needed to do. "This is a lot for one day, but it's possibly doable. Do you have the paint?"

I looked down at her, and she shook her head, baring her teeth in a not-quite-smile.

"Okay, then that's job one. It also depends on how easily this stuff comes up," I said, rapping my knuckles against the worktop. "Did you keep any of the instructions from when you put it on?"

"I'll give you one guess," she said, and I sighed. This would be a long day.

"Okay, then we'd better get started," I said. "Why don't you start on some of the easier stuff, like boxing up the books that need to move? I'll go get paint."

She frowned. "I don't know what colour it is."

"That's okay," I said. "Here, let me show you."

I grabbed a knife from the small pile of dishes in the sink and led her to the front door. I opened it and then held up the knife, working slowly and carefully to remove as big a piece of paint as possible from the door. It wasn't easy; most of it was weather-beaten, and it had clearly been years since it had been painted. But it was a nice wooden door, not a modern PVC one, and so I managed to get roughly a square inch, which I held carefully in my hand.

"Can they really match it that way?" she asked. I nodded.

"It's usually pretty good. It may not be exact, but I'm sure your landlord wouldn't notice. If they knew the exact colour, I'm sure they would have told you."

"Thank you," she said, and she sounded genuinely relieved. "I mean, I could have figured out the paint matching. But thank you for being here. I've been dreading all of it."

"Happy to help," I said, trying to sound as casual as possible.

"Now, I should go get some paint. You take this" – I handed her the knife handle-first – "and make sure you wash it before you use it again. Really well."

"Aye aye, captain," she said, saluting me. I rolled my eyes and then headed back to the car.

A moment later, right as I got in, she ran out after me, thankfully no longer wielding the knife. "Wait," she said, leaning in through the passenger window. "I need to give you money for the paint."

"I don't mind helping out," I said. "You can pay me back later."

"It's fine," she said. "I took out some cash specifically for it. Take it." She reached over to hand me two folded-up twenties, which I was confident was more than enough for what we needed.

Just as the notes transferred from her hand to mine, her eyes panned to the duffel bag in the front seat, and she frowned. Then she looked back up at me and narrowed her eyes.

"What's that for?" she asked, and I had the sudden realisation that it might look like I planned to stay the night.

"Oh god, not that," I said, and she instantly softened, and something that maybe looked like disappointment flashed across her face. I tried to ignore how that disappointment made me feel. "I was away with some friends."

"Oh really?" she asked. "What for?"

"A stag do."

"Fun," she said, then leaned back out of the window. "See you in a bit then!"

"Yeah, see you," I said, waving as I put the car in gear and drove off, desperately hoping she hadn't seen the book-shaped protrusion on the side of the bag.

CHAPTER 24
JACK

By the time the sun went down, we'd made significant progress on the list. Or rather, *I* had – Morgan had spent most of the day holding a hairdryer to the various forms of vinyl she and Cara had installed in the kitchen. Between that and the August heat, it got to be almost unbearable inside, so we opened all the windows and got all three of the fans Morgan owned circulating fresh air. I taught her a bit about air circulation and how to design for it, and she suggested that might have been more helpful in the early twentieth century when the house had been built, which was fair enough.

The only helpful feature it did have was a cellar. I imagined most of the houses on the row had finished them over the years, but Morgan's was still dingy and dirt-floored, which I discovered when carrying the boxes and boxes of books down for storage.

I'd made quick work of the door once I was back, but the back garden had taken some time, and I'd ended up making another trip out to the garden centre to get some mulch. There were too many tiny weeds, and I made the executive decision that it shouldn't be Morgan's problem, so I did a little cover-up job around the border. The stuff coming up between the stones was dealt with easily by my power washer. Part of me hated getting rid of the plants that had persevered enough to reclaim the space, but it was paved over anyway, so I decided to just be glad we weren't having to touch the front garden. As I worked, I told Morgan about the treasure trove of native species she had out there, and she seemed genuinely interested, which made me feel like less of a nerd for knowing the difference between the various types of clover native to the area.

And finally, just as my stomach grumbled in protest of the fact that it was 8pm and I hadn't eaten anything but a meal deal from the services, Morgan scraped away the last of the vinyl covering the worktop.

"That took fucking forever," she groaned from the stool she was perched on, hunched over the worktop. "I'm sorry I'm so slow."

I resisted the urge to rub my hand over her back, which I imagined was sore from hours of repetitive activity; to tell her that I wanted to be here. That I was hoping there was more for me to do. That as long as she needed help, I was her guy.

"Hey, better that than damage the worktop," I said instead.

"True that," she said, punctuating her words with a wave of the hairdryer. "In which case, I vote we order some pizza."

"Seconded!" I said, waving my scraper in response.

We ordered from the nice local pizza place instead of the cheaper chain; Morgan insisted that it barely covered the petrol I'd expended, let alone the labour. I mentioned that, in that case, she probably owed me a beer, too, and she pulled two six-packs of my favourite IPA from the fridge. It seemed she'd been paying attention.

Morgan didn't have a dining table, so we put the pizza box and beer on the coffee table and sat on the floor. We were both a full beer down by the time we started eating, so we got very chatty very quickly, and she asked me about what it was like growing up with Chloe and Phil. I told her about the time Chloe and I had broken into Phil's house to try to decorate for his fourteenth birthday, only he had somehow figured out we were coming, and Ethel had pretended to be unconscious on the ground.

"We genuinely thought she was dead," I said through laughter. Morgan was giggling, too, as if she were remembering it right along with me. "I mean, now I know that she wasn't *that* old at the time. But back then, she felt ancient to us."

"I wish I had stories like that," she said. "I never really had friends that close growing up."

"No one?" I asked. "Not even from school?"

She shook her head, her smile dropping slightly. "No. I mean, I had friends; I wasn't a total loner. But I don't think I was anyone's best friend. Not until Cara, anyway."

"How did you meet?"

She sighed wistfully. "A random housing ad, actually. She was a bit of a spoiled posh girl; she'd be the first to tell you that. So her parents didn't want her slumming it in the halls. That's why they bought this place."

"What a life, eh?" I asked. "Must be nice to have parents who will just buy you a place if you need it."

"Says the guy that lives on his family's land and works for the family business?"

I barked out a laugh. "Fair enough."

She chuckled, too. "Well, it worked out well for me, because I didn't really fancy the halls either. And this place was cheaper."

"Cheaper than the uni accommodation?" I asked, incredulous.

"Cara's parents didn't actually know she was letting out the extra bedroom," she said. "She was just doing it so she had someone to live with. So it was dirt cheap. Mum had saved a bit for uni, but not enough for somewhere to live, and I wanted to keep my loans to a minimum."

Morgan's mum wasn't exactly a loaded subject, but it also wasn't her favourite one. But unexpectedly I sensed warmth in her voice when she mentioned her now, so I took my chance to dig a bit deeper.

"Do you miss her?"

"Mum?" Morgan asked, then, when I nodded, "Yeah, sometimes. It really sucked when she left. She gave me a whole speech about how life had passed her by, but given how close we were when I was growing up, it kind of felt like she was saying that *I* hadn't been enough. Which was bullshit, considering how much trouble she went through to have me."

Her lower lip wobbled slightly on that last part, and it was everything I could do not to catch it with my own and try to make her forget that anyone had ever made her feel like she wasn't enough. But instead I settled for the only thing anyone could say in that situation; words that are never enough.

"I'm so sorry, Morgan."

"It's okay," she said. "Now I get postcards every month or so. Last year I got one from a nudist colony in the Pacific Northwest, so I get to have those nightmares every now and then. Thanks, Mum."

I laughed, probably a bit too loud, but I was officially three drinks in and feeling very merry.

"That's amazing," I said. "How long did it take Cara's parents to figure out that you were living here?"

"More than a year," she whispered, almost conspiratorially. "They retired to the French Riviera when they were like forty-five. They're pretty rich."

I was becoming very aware of how close Morgan was sat to me, our shoulders just an inch or two from one another. We had slouched down so that our heads were leaning back against the seat of the sofa, the cushions pulled down and stuffed under our backs, the coffee table pushed out with our feet. We were almost lying down.

She seemed to be a bit tipsy, too, and an image flashed into my mind of her on the bank holiday trip, drunk enough to come in for a hug after learning about Aria. I felt my breathing go shallow again, but I reminded myself, *Just one step at a time.* I'd been repeating it to myself every time I got a bit flustered – like when it got too hot in the kitchen and Morgan stripped out of her t-shirt into just her sports bra, which is how she was still dressed next to me – and so far I'd been able to keep the anxiety at bay. I pulled in a deep breath and held it, willing myself to calm the fuck down. It was harder this time than it had been before, but I managed it.

"It's incredible," she said, "how much of my life was defined by that friendship."

"What do you mean?"

"I mean, I didn't try very hard to make other friends because I'd finally found my best friend. I didn't try for design jobs after uni because it would have meant moving away, and I didn't think I would find another friend like her. And when Cara joked that I was the square one, the cautious one, I sort of took on that persona, even though I don't think it was particularly true when we first met. I just liked finally fitting together with someone."

"I get that," I said. "It's nice to feel like you understand your place in the world." I adjusted the cushions beneath my back, and inadvertently ended up a smidge closer to Morgan, which I didn't mind. I braced myself for the anxiety to kick in, but it didn't.

"Yeah, I knew you'd get it," she said, which made me smile. I liked being the person who "got" her. She turned her head to face me, and I did the same. "I just sometimes wish I'd made different decisions. Like, I love the design work I've been doing so much. And now I'm even getting to do some at work. Did I tell you that already?"

I shook my head. "No, what for?"

"For this big gala. All the design budget was blown, but I came up with an idea to do illustrations of all the animals on the signs and stationery and stuff."

"That's brilliant," I said, grinning wide. "Can I see?"

She sat up to reach for her tablet, which was in a bag at the end of the sofa. I mourned the sudden lack of proximity, but when she sat back down cross-legged, was I making things up, or did she end up a couple of inches closer to me?

She tapped a few times on the tablet and handed it to me, and I sat up to take it. My suspicion that she'd closed some of the distance between us was confirmed when my knee knocked against hers, and I had to turn slightly towards her to sit up.

I looked at what she'd pulled up on the screen: a large file with dozens of drawings of dogs and cats and – wait, were those otters? Did her rescue do otters? I'd have to find out later. These drawings were incredible. They were cute, but they were also beautifully done. She'd used a layered watercolour effect that made them look like they might jump straight off the page.

"I love these," I said, my voice low. "Where are they being used?"

"All over the place," she said. "It's kind of driving the concept now."

"That's amazing," I said, scrolling to see more. Instead of more animals though, I found the logo she'd been working on for the gaming shop. It was an anvil, just like she'd said last weekend, and I knew I was biased since I knew about the project, but I was sure I would have known immediately what kind of business it was for. "Are these final?"

"I think so," she said, taking the tablet back and looking down at the logo. I hoped she could see how great it was. How talented she was.

"Do you know how talented you are?" I asked, surprised that the thought had made it through my mental filter. Morgan looked at me like I'd just suggested she had Martian lineage.

"Don't be stupid," she said. "It's literally the first logo I've ever made."

"Exactly," I said. "And it's amazing. Better than most logos for small businesses that I see. You're really, really good. The fact that this isn't your job is fucking wild to me."

She looked at me sceptically for a moment, her eyes locked on mine, and I could tell she was internally debating whether to accept the compliment or laugh it off.

"You really think it's good?" she asked, and I could tell she was hanging a lot on my answer. Luckily it was the answer she was hoping for, and it was the truth.

"Yes," I said with as much conviction as I could muster.

"Thank you," she said quietly, and I could tell it meant a lot to her. But she looked away and turned off the tablet, chucking it back across to the end of the sofa.

It took her a moment longer than it should have to turn back around, and when she did, she fixed me with an intense gaze. She was facing me fully now, her legs crossed like mine were, her knees resting on mine, her feet grazing mine.

"Hey, Jack?" she asked, and I could tell her question was

going to be a big one. I felt the weight start to form a bit, but I managed to suppress it, or at least to stop it from growing, by reminding myself to take it one step at a time. A question was just one step.

"Yeah?" I asked, as light-hearted as I could, but I felt my voice wobble as I said her name.

"Why didn't the stag do carry on until tomorrow?"

I blinked hard – I wasn't sure what I'd been expecting her to ask, but it wasn't that. I also had no idea how I wanted to answer her. My mouth went dry as if in protest; it was shutting up shop so that I could save face. But I had to answer her, so I took the last swig of my third beer, partially for courage and partially to make it so I physically *could* answer.

"The stag do *is* carrying on until tomorrow." There we go. That was an answer.

"And why aren't you carrying on with it?" she asked. *Well, shit.*

"Because I decided I'd rather be here than there," I said before I could filter out the truth, and then I leaned back a bit, astonished at my own honesty. And maybe a bit on the other side of buzzed.

"Gotcha," she said, not dropping my gaze, squinting at me as if I were a puzzle she was trying to solve. It was almost disconcerting how long she spent looking at me, not only because it forced me to stare directly into her eyes in return. Otherwise my own eyes might have wandered to her shoulders, or the delicate jut of her collarbone, or the lower lip she was biting the corner of. Otherwise I might accidentally start to lean in, like a magnet had been turned on inside her and I couldn't help but gravitate forward.

Oh wait, I was actually doing all of those things.

By the time I realised that and looked back into her eyes, her expression had changed. Her brow was pinched together, and the corners of her lips were turned down. I'd seen this before, on the mountaintop. She was angry. But had I given her something to be angry about?

"I think you should go," she said, all the friendliness gone from her voice.

That snapped me back into reality instantly. "Wait, what? Sorry, did I say something?"

"No, you're fine," she said, but she was standing up, clearing the pizza box and empty beer cans. I noticed that we'd finished off both six-packs between us.

"Morgan, hang on," I said, standing up, too, but I was a bit wobbly, and I had to sit back down on the couch for a moment as an interim step.

Finally I was on my feet, and I walked over to the kitchen where she stood rinsing out the recycling. I put a hand on her forearm, and she turned in place to face me, her lower body pinned in place by mine. But none of the softness and warmth from before was there. Instead it was just pure heat. Intense, mind-numbing, *angry* heat.

"What do you want?" she asked, looking up at me.

"I just want to know what's wro—"

"No," she interrupted, shaking her head. "What do you want from being here?"

I frowned. "I wanted to help you."

Her eyes went wide, and she raised a single eyebrow. I wished I could do that; she looked so admonishing. "Really? You wanted to *help* me?"

"Yes," I said, and I knew that was the truth. "I did. And..."

She nodded, as if she'd known there would be more. "And what?" she asked, impatient.

"And I wanted to see you," I said quietly.

She narrowed her eyes again – that wasn't quite what she'd been looking for. And I understood what she was getting at. I just wasn't sure I could offer her more of an explanation when I hadn't managed to articulate it to myself.

She crossed her arms, her elbows jutting into my abs, but I didn't move.

"Morgan, I'm sorry," I said. "I didn't mean to make you uncomfortable."

"I'm not the one that's uncomfortable, Jack!" Her voice was raised now, and I could feel myself getting emotional for some reason. She looked like she was, too, her face going blotchy and her voice shaking. "You're the one that can't stand to get close to me."

She pushed past me to the centre of the kitchen, and I spun around, desperate to have her back. To prove a point, I followed her, holding her by the elbows and pulling her back into my space.

"Do I look uncomfortable, Morgan?" I asked, and she looked back and forth disbelievingly from my hands to my eyes. I dropped my hands away, but she didn't move again.

"No," she said quietly. "No, I guess you don't."

I took the step back this time, leaning against the now-stripped worktop. "I get it," I said, matching her quieter tone. "A lot has happened. But it's all water under the tree, right?"

"Right," she said tentatively, crossing her arms tighter across her. "Water under the tree." I got the sense she meant it differently than I did, but I didn't have the faculties at present to analyse it too closely.

I closed my eyes and leaned my head back against the upper cabinets, taking a deep breath. This had escalated *so* quickly. Maybe I should have let that weight pool when it had wanted to. It had been protecting me from exactly this situation. I'd taken things one step at a time, and they'd landed me right here. With Morgan angry with me, and with me too tipsy to make heads or tails of whatever the hell I was feeling.

"Okay," I said, "can we put a pin in this?" I opened my eyes and saw her leaning against the back door on the opposite side of the kitchen.

"A pin in what?" she asked.

"The conversation," I said. "Because I do think we should have it."

"And what conversation is that?" she asked, but I gave her a slight scowl, and she backed off. "Okay, okay, I get it. To define the conversation is to have the conversation. I can live with that."

"Tomorrow," I said. "We can talk tomorrow."

"Tomorrow," she echoed.

"I'll pick you up," I said. "I'll have to come back for my car."

"Oh god," she said, standing straight up suddenly, her voice worried. "How are you going to get home? I didn't even think about it with the beers. I'm so used to walking everywhere."

"It'll be fine," I said, closing the gap between us and putting my hands on her arms again, this time in what I hoped was a calming gesture. "Phil will almost certainly be orchestrating the end of an awkward Hinge date right about now."

"Are you sure?" she asked. "You can stay on the sofa if you need to." I sighed and levelled my gaze at her until I saw the realisation click. "Oh, yeah. Okay. Maybe not."

"I'll see you tomorrow," I said. "Put the second coat of paint on the door in the morning, and I'll see you at, say, four?"

"Okay," she said, nodding.

I took a single step towards the door and then paused. A

little voice inside my head was yelling *Keep going, Jack!* but my body didn't listen. I turned around, pressed a kiss to Morgan's cheek, and then strode away as quickly as possible, catching her shocked expression in the reflection in the window as I left.

CHAPTER 25
MORGAN

Jack had kissed me.

It took me a solid hour after waking up the next morning to convince myself it hadn't been a dream. That I hadn't imagined him staring at my mouth, and telling me he'd left a weekend away and driven hours to spend time doing manual labour with me, and *kissing me*. On the cheek, sure, but given how panicked he'd been when I'd merely *implied* a kiss, it still felt like a big deal. If I'd been able to tell the version of myself who had just got done with that hike that this would happen a mere two months later, past me would have laughed in my own face. It was absurd.

Or was it?

After all, there had been something between us on that hike. And before that, in the river. And probably before that, when I'd been tipsy and told him he was a good guy who didn't deserve what had happened.

(And hell, probably before that; I'd always found him attractive, and maybe – though the idea seemed, again, *absurd* – he'd been attracted to me, too.)

But it didn't change the fact that last night had felt like it came out of nowhere, especially when he'd been the one to draw that hard boundary between us. It was emotional whiplash. I'd cut off any and all hope I'd felt of something happening with Jack, but now, suddenly, it was all I could feel.

I distracted myself throughout the morning with work stuff, refining a few of the gala signage options I'd started in the week. Then I got an email from Greg, letting me know he was thrilled with the brand packet I'd sent over. I'd gone a bit overboard in the end; he'd only paid me for a logo, but I'd seen someone on social media design a brand pack with colours and patterns and everything, and I'd decided to go all in. He loved all of it, and he'd sent me the rest of the money for the job. *At least that'll cover the Ren Faire outfits*, I thought.

I looked over the designs, proud again of what I'd done. So I decided to share it. I opened Instagram on my tablet, tapped to create a new post, and selected all the image files I'd used for the brand board, sharing them as a carousel. On a whim, I changed my bio so it said "DM me for design enquiries!"

I knew I should spend some time at some point thinking about how I felt about ... you know ... *everything* before Jack picked me up later, so naturally I did the opposite of that: I put on a cosy mystery audiobook and tackled re-dressing Cara's room, which consisted of unboxing and laying out a collection of boring, vacuum-packed soft furnishings.

I'd barely finished fluffing the new cushions when Jack texted me that he was on his way. He said it would take him a bit longer than usual, and that I should wear full-length trousers. I replied asking if I'd forgotten about an activity we'd planned, but he didn't respond.

Half an hour later though, I got my answer when he pulled

up outside on the back of a quad bike, which was being driven by a stunning blonde.

They both dismounted, and Jack tossed a set of keys to the blonde – Amy, I assumed, or at least hoped – who strode over to his car and climbed into the driver's seat. Jack put both helmets down just inside the gate and headed towards the door. I backed away from the window, not wanting him to see that I'd been watching him.

When I heard his knock on the door, I took a deep breath before opening it. He was looking at his feet when I did, so I got a split second to admire him, taking in his baggy jeans, his muddy boots, and the flannel shirt he'd worn on our hike, open over a white t-shirt. The breeze funnelling along the row of houses was pulling at both tops, so I could see the lines of his body beneath, and I remembered what he looked like in the sun, in the water, with no shirt to cling to him like it did now.

And then I met his eyes, and I could tell the same appraisal I'd been undertaking had been done to me, too.

"Hey," I said, sounding breathier than I had any right to, given that I'd just been standing there.

"Hey," he said back, sounding the same as me.

"New wheels?" I asked, pointing to the quad bike.

"Well, you nicked my car," he said. "Very rude."

"Seems a leggy blonde just nicked it, not me."

He smiled. "That's Amy. She's just taking it home. You up for a ride?"

A small part of me was disappointed that we wouldn't be jumping straight into our conversation, but then again, adventuring together was what we did best. So I swallowed the part of me that wished he would come inside instead and smiled.

"Let's do it."

Jack trotted ahead to pull the gate open for me, handing me

a helmet as he did. I slid it on and watched as Jack swung his leg over the seat, starting the engine. He pointed to a little step I could use to get on the back, offering me his hand to help, and I accepted it.

Once I was on, it became clear I'd be holding onto him the entire time. *Crafty man*, I thought. But I wasn't complaining.

Jack put his helmet on, too, and suddenly I could hear his breathing just behind me and to the left. It was strangely intimate, and disorienting, as if he were whispering in my ear from behind. I wrapped my arms around his torso without even thinking about it, feeling the hard lines of his muscular form beneath my fingers.

"Shall we?" he asked, and I nodded before I realised he couldn't see me.

"Ready," I said, and the quad bike lurched forward slightly; not enough to knock me off balance, but enough to make me tighten my grip around him. I couldn't look straight ahead with the helmet, so I turned my head to the side and rested it against his back.

He drove slowly along the roads, but as soon as we passed the football club and joined the path to the river, he opened it up. Suddenly we were flying, slowing only occasionally to pass people.

As we rode, Jack asked me about my day, and I told him about Greg's response to the designs I'd sent. He was thrilled for me, congratulating me so enthusiastically that it was actually a bit much coming through the helmet speaker.

We were on the river path for several minutes before we turned off up towards the closest village, and then off into some farmland.

"Are you allowed to ride here?" I asked as we manoeuvred around a closed gate to get into a field.

"Oh yeah, this is Uncle John's land. This field's fallow this year."

We followed a farm track for a couple of minutes before suddenly taking off like a rocket into the field of tall grass to our left.

I'd thought we'd been going fast before, but that had been nothing. We were going so fast that I couldn't hear Jack's breathing anymore. So fast that he had to tell me to lean into the turns, and it was only because I was clung so tightly to his body and could feel his muscles moving that I had any idea what I was actually supposed to do and when. It was terrifying at first, but once I let myself cling tightly enough to Jack that we felt like one mass, I was able to relax into it a bit. Before long I was laughing as we caught air going over bumps and drifted around corners.

Then Jack stopped and asked if I wanted to drive, and I'd never said yes to anything more quickly. We swapped places – which involved him getting up and me awkwardly shuffling forward on the seat so he could re-mount behind me – and then he talked me through what the different buttons and levers and rotating handlebars did. He had to go through it twice; I hoped he thought it was because I was just confused, and not because of the real reason, which is how I was concentrating too hard on ignoring the feeling of him pressed against my back, knowing that he'd be able to hear every hitch in my breath.

Once I finally grasped the basics, I was able to get us going, slowly at first but then faster and faster. I found that it felt even more controlled when I was the one doing the steering, and I let myself really open up, then fought the urge to pull the brake when I felt him tighten his grip around me, his hands low around my stomach, his hands brushing the zip of my jeans. He whooped and cheered as I took hard turns and found where he'd managed to get a bit of air, managing at least a couple of inches myself.

When I slowed to turn again, he took the chance to move his hands from their position clasped in front of me to the crease between my hips and thighs, and I couldn't help but arch my back in response. I realised what I'd done when I heard a sharp intake of breath through the speaker in my helmet, and I accidentally released the throttle, effectively causing us to do the quad biking version of slamming on the brakes.

Flustered, I got off the bike immediately and let Jack take back over. He asked if I was okay and I said yes, that I just got a bit excited about the jump and was ready for him to take over again. He agreed and offered me his hand to climb on again, but I declined this time, using his shoulders instead.

"So I was thinking," he said, "if you want, we could have dinner at my place? I got some really nice stuff from the farm shop today, and I thought I could make us dinner."

"Uh, sure," I said, not sure what I'd been expecting. When I'd seen the quad bike, I'd just assumed that was the activity. The adventure. Going to Jack's house? That was something else entirely.

But I wasn't opposed to it. If anything, it made the butterflies I'd already felt whirling around my stomach flap their wings even harder. If he wanted me to come to his, what did that mean for this conversation we were having? My mind raced to the obvious conclusion, which probably only felt obvious because I was pressed up against Jack in that moment, and the butterflies threatened to start a whole-ass tornado.

We pulled back onto the farm track and followed it for a while, almost reaching the road before we came to an old stone farmhouse. I thought I saw Amy disappear from one of the windows.

Then we turned up the drive and carried on past the house, passing between more fields, these ones full of what looked like actual crops. We were going vaguely uphill, but then we came to the top, and a tiny little hollow appeared in front of us, a lush pond pooled in the bottom and a small wooden cabin perched half over it.

We parked the quad bike out front, and I stood and admired Jack's handiwork. When he'd said he'd built his own house, I hadn't really known what to expect; at times I'd imagined it as some super modern shipping container conversion, and sometimes as a glorified shed. But if there had been a spectrum between those two, Jack's house wouldn't have been anywhere on it. It fit perfectly within the landscape, like it was a natural part of it, yet looked so purposefully crafted. The wooden exterior didn't look cheap or rough but intentional, like an extension of the fields around us.

Walking through the front door, which he held open for me as he watched me take it all in, I was surprised at how spacious the vaulted ceilings made it feel. It was also nice and cool, which didn't surprise me after the "designing for air flow" conversation we'd had yesterday. It also got much better light than my house, despite the fact that I couldn't see any actual lights on. Clearly he'd designed for that, too.

A door off to the right was halfway open, and I saw a small slice of a very stylish bathroom beyond. The door opposite was closed, but I suspected it led to his bedroom (cue those damn butterflies again). The open kitchen was made of finished plywood with poured concrete worktops, including waterfall edges on the giant island that housed the sink and three barstools. A small table with three chairs sat just off to the side of the island against the windows, and a comfortable-but-sparse-looking lounge lay beyond with a tiny wood-burning stove in one corner and a desk in the other, piled high with file folders.

But the main focal point was the huge wall of glass that made up the back of the house. Big French doors opened up onto a wooden deck, which seemed to lead straight out over the pond. There was a single rocking chair and side table there, perfect for watching the ducks I could see paddling around the pond.

Of all of the times I'd pictured Jack's day-to-day life, this house fit that life perfectly. It was so meticulously made. So practical. So considered. So *Jack*. From what he'd told me about his relationship with Aria, he'd spent years bending himself around someone else and her idea of what their life should look like. With this house, for the first time, he'd been able to create out of his grief a home that was exactly what he needed; nothing more, nothing less. And from his body language as he moved around, grabbing dishes and ingredients from various cabinets and drawers, I could tell he was instantly more at ease just being here. It was how I felt at home, too, and I was glad to see him visibly relax a bit.

Jack poured me a glass of wine and recommended I go sit on the deck whilst he made dinner. But I was feeling nosy, so instead I wandered over to his desk, where a stack of folders sat next to an ancient-looking laptop.

I looked over my shoulder to make sure he wasn't watching me, and then I pulled open the top drawer. Inside were several sketches on scrap pieces of paper, all of buildings. There was one that seemed to be almost carved into the side of what looked like a quarry. There were old farm buildings converted into modern houses, the materials blending seamlessly together. There were floorplans, too, dozens of them, from tiny cabins like the one we were in to sprawling family homes. There even seemed to be one for a restaurant.

"Did you do these?" I asked, turning around and holding up some of the sketches. Jack looked up from the pomegranate in his hand and squinted across the room at me. When he realised what I was holding, his eyes went wide.

"Nosy, much?" he asked, and I could tell he was trying to sound casual.

"Answer the question," I said, walking over to the island with one of the sketches still in my hand.

"Yeah, I guess," he said, looking down at the pomegranate as he opened it with a knife. Red juice flowed out over his hands, and for a moment I thought he'd cut himself.

"They're really good," I said, wondering why he was so intent on ignoring me.

"Thanks," he said. "Will you pass me a towel? I don't want to drip everywhere."

I walked around the island and grabbed a kitchen towel, placing it next to his chopping board as he knocked the seeds out and pulled chunks away.

"So is that what you want to do?" I asked. "Architecture?"

Jack shook his head. "I'm taking over the family business," he said. "Contracting. So not designing, building."

I frowned; not that he saw it, with how focused he was on his hands and the pomegranate he was holding.

"Come on, Jack," I said. "Clearly you're really good at this."

"Like I said, thank you." He sounded much more dismissive this time. "Now please, just go out onto the deck for a bit so I can focus."

I narrowed my eyes at him until he looked up at me, a pleading look in his eyes.

"Fine," I said, rolling my eyes and turning around, back

towards the desk. I replaced the sketches and plans in the drawer and shut it.

As I headed towards the back door, I saw a magazine open on the dining table. It was open to a full spread about an introductory course for aspiring architects. It certainly made the sketches and plans and perfect house make a lot more sense, but his insistence that he was planning to take over the family business did not.

After I'd stepped onto the deck and pulled the door shut behind me, not wanting to disrupt his precious air flow pathways, I settled down in the rocking chair that he had there; it was the only piece of furniture. Not a pair, just the one.

Actually, looking back through the window, there seemed to be little about his home that suggested he had any intention of housing anyone but himself. There were no chairs, just a three-seater sofa; the perfect size for him, Chloe, and Phil. There were three chairs at the tiny dining table. Three barstools. I'd only seen one sink in the bathroom. And I'd have bet that his bed was pushed up against one wall.

But those were decisions made years ago, deep in the throes of his heartbreak, I told myself. They weren't a reflection of who he was now. At least I hoped they weren't.

I sat back and looked out over the pond, rocking myself. I relaxed so quickly and to such an extent that I started to zone out for minutes at a time, only to be brought back by the sound of a duck quacking or a bird twittering nearby. *This* was the nature people were always trying to "get back to". I was jealous that Jack got to experience this level of Zen every day, but then again, it explained a lot about how laid back he was.

Until one of his triggers was pulled, of course, but that was all of us, wasn't it?

I was just pulling out my phone to take a photo when I saw

that I had several notifications – two Instagram messages, and one email from Greg with the subject line "Whoops!"

I sighed, wondering what he'd decided he wanted to change about the logo, and tapped to open the email:

I told them you charge twice what I paid you – hope that's okay! And before you thank me, it was partially to save face for myself over my atrociously low budget.

Greg
Sent from my iPhone

I frowned as I wondered what he was on about, scrolling back to see if I'd missed another message from him, but no; I didn't have any other unread emails.

I opened up the DMs instead, and Greg's message quickly made sense. Two different people had messaged me, asking for information about my brand design packages. Apparently Greg had shared his new logo in a Facebook group for aspiring small business owners, and they were interested in my services because they'd liked his logo so much.

I practically jumped out of the rocking chair, which was more difficult than one might think, and which almost resulted in my phone flying into the pond. But I managed to avoid disaster and ran inside, desperate to tell Jack the good news. After everything he'd said about my art last night, I knew he'd be over the moon for me.

But when I ran inside, Jack was just setting the table with two plates full of food.

"Voilà," he said, doing a little hand flourish around the steaming spread, putting on a terrible French accent. "Dinner is served."

I sat down at the table, deciding to let Jack show off his surprisingly fancy creation – a dish of "pan-fried wood pigeon in an orange glaze" – before accosting him with my design news. I took a bite and practically sank into my chair; the bitter chicory and vibrant pomegranate seeds he'd paired it with added just the right touch. And the white wine, which he'd topped up when I'd sat down, went perfectly with it.

"I didn't know you were such a chef," I said. "But this is incredible."

"Can I admit something?" he asked.

"There's a little rat hiding in your hair who actually made this dinner?"

Jack laughed, and I smiled at how satisfied I was to have caused it.

"No, but that would be better. Rather than a rat, it's Phil."

"Phil is hiding in your hair?" I asked, squinting and moving my head around as if to get a better look. "I know he's not a tall guy, but that feels like quite the feat."

Jack laughed some more, and I chuckled along with him. It was such a far cry from the stoicism he'd shown months ago. I wouldn't have wanted to go back to that for anything, now that I'd seen how silly and joyful he could be.

"No," he said again, "Phil is the cook."

"Oh, well I knew that," I said. "But really, is he hiding here somewhere? Because if not, it feels like you did this."

"Well, I was on the phone to him pretty much the whole time. He sent me the recipe, told me where to shop, and talked me through it. Why do you think I sent you out to the deck?" I smiled at him, and he held my gaze for a moment as he took a bite. He was clearly enjoying making me smile as much as I was enjoying making him laugh.

Well, if he wanted to see me smile, I could help him out.

After I'd taken enough bites of my food that I could stand to part with my fork for a moment, I unlocked my phone and pulled up one of the messages I'd got.

"Look at this," I said, handing him the phone. "I've gotten two enquiries since I sent Greg his logo. People love it! People want to pay me for design!"

"Of course they do!" he said, matching my enthusiasm. He handed me my phone back. "You're so talented! They'd be idiots not to want to work with you."

"And I was thinking you were right," I continued. "Maybe I want to do this as my job."

Jack's fork paused slightly on the way to his mouth, but then he carried on as if it had just been a glitch. "I mean, yeah! You should probably build your client base up a bit before you go full-time, especially with your house situation, but that sounds great. I'm really proud of you."

"Thank you," I said. "I'm really proud of me, too. Though I'm not sure I'm cut out for the whole freelance thing full-time."

Now his fork stopped all the way, and he set it down on his plate and looked up at me. "What do you mean? Like, you want it as a side hustle?"

I shook my head, my smile faltering slowly. Hadn't this been his idea? "No, I mean, maybe I want to apply to some design jobs. Like, at companies."

"Oh," he said, the enthusiasm dropping like a lead balloon. I stayed quiet for a moment to let him continue, but he didn't. And the lack of excitement was riling me up.

"Sorry, Jack, but just to clarify, this is a good thing. You helped me have this big revelation last night that I may actually be good at this, now I'm choosing to pursue my passion, yada yada. Why aren't you more excited?"

He stayed frozen for a long moment, his eyes fixed on his

plate before he spoke. "This is not the direction I thought this conversation would go," he said, his voice low.

"Yeah, well, me either," I said, *my* voice definitely *not* low. "Given how effusive you were last night, I sort of expected you to be happier for me."

"You expected me to be happy that you want to leave?" He asked, his voice rising in volume to match mine. He looked up from his plate finally, and I could see that there was hurt in his eyes.

Suddenly I was very, very confused.

"Sorry, when did I say I wanted to leave?"

"Last night," he said. "You told me that you didn't apply for design jobs after uni because it would have meant moving away."

The memory hit me right as he reminded me. Of course. My heart sank as I realised what he must be thinking. That me telling him this was my way of saying I wasn't interested. I could have cried with relief; that was the whole point of the conversation we needed to have, right?

"That was years ago, Jack," I said, putting out a hand to touch his forearm. "The town is bigger now. And there are other towns nearby. Hell, I didn't even go to uni here, but I lived here."

But he went rigid beneath my fingers, so I pulled them back and folded my hands in my lap instead. The wall had gone up.

He looked back up at me, his jaw set but his eyes searching. He didn't soften, or speak. He just sat there, staring at me. I remembered the first time I'd seen his jaw set like this. When *he* had rejected *me*. Was that what was happening now? He'd been the one to set that boundary to begin with, I supposed.

But then, why did he care so much if I left? I couldn't sit here and guess anymore. I couldn't read him when he made himself so unknowable like this. It wasn't fair to me, and I wasn't going to let him feel entitled to certain intimations if he was going to play his own cards so close to the chest.

"But Jack," I said, sitting up a bit straighter, a new sense of daring coursing through me. I tried to pull all emotion out of my voice. "Even if I did want to leave..."

His eyes narrowed ever so slightly, and I locked my gaze with his as I asked him what we'd both come here to ask, really.

"What's it to you?"

He sighed, and I could see how his eyes glazed over that I'd lost him once and for all. But I couldn't bring myself to care.

He wanted to put up walls? He wanted to push me away every chance I got? Fine. Two could play at that game.

CHAPTER 26
CAPTAIN MORGANA SILVERSWORD

Taking refuge at the Bards College had been a stroke of genius on Yorick's part. Not only was Clover able to get the party there fairly easily – all they'd had to do was hide in barrels and pose as a shipment of wine – but they also suddenly had access to a vast library of knowledge.

It was there that Thrormir and Morgana's teamwork began to shine. Within days, they'd uncovered almost everything they might need to know about the Supremacy Sphere. It had been forged by a lich, an ultra-powerful undead wizard, seeking – of course – world domination. If activated, which required sacrificing an unwilling creature under a full moon, the Sphere would release an aura that would bend the will of anyone nearby to the wielder. It required a very complex attunement ritual to wield, but once it was activated, it would remain in effect indefinitely.

"Well shit," Calamity said as Morgana relayed this knowledge to the group in their chambers one night. "Human sacrifice *and* mind control? Kinky."

"Delightful," Yorick said, rolling his eyes. "And how do we destroy this apocalyptically dangerous artefact?"

"That's the catch," Thrormir said, exchanging glances with Morgana.

"An unwilling sacrifice activates it," Morgana said. "But a willing sacrifice destroys it."

The group blinked back at her.

Calamity sighed. "Can't we just bury it?"

"That's what they tried to do before," Gorlag said. "That's why we spent days wandering around those catacombs."

"Then let's have someone good wield it! Someone who won't do evil shit with it!"

Thrormir shook his head. "Absolute power corrupts absolutely."

"And besides," Morgana said, "good or not, people would still be under their control. They'd have no agency in the situation. That's still wrong."

"Well fuck that," Calamity said. "I don't intend to lose my life for this thing. And if that makes me a bad person, so be it."

"Well, you are half demon," Yorick muttered, and Calamity slapped him on the back of the head. "Hey!"

"Enough," Thrormir said firmly. "Helpfully, there are a lot of people wiser and more equipped to handle this decision than we are."

Morgana turned to frown at him. "Do you really think that's wise? Giving this to people in power?"

"It's not our decision to make," he said softly back to her. "Your Queen asked for this, remember?"

Morgana did remember. She had never disobeyed a direct order in her life, and she didn't intend to start now. But it also didn't sit well with her that she would be handing over power over everyone she knew – including, maybe, herself – to someone else.

"Fine," she said. "Let's go home."

CHAPTER 27
JACK

Over the next thirteen days, I felt more anxious than I had in years. Analysing every word Morgan had said to me, and how everything I said could have been taken. Every sigh and glance during the silent dinner that had followed, and the silent car ride back to hers after that. *This is why I don't bother with dating*, I said to myself on multiple occasions when I found myself dissecting the events of that dumbfounding evening yet again. *Except you're not dating*, I said back to myself almost as often. *And you only have yourself to blame for that.*

The only way I could think to make things better – because a tiny, persistent part of me refused to believe I'd blown it completely – was to show her how sorry I was.

I tried to say it after our game the next evening, but she barely gave me the time of day. She was frosty all evening, and then she didn't come to the pub with us after, saying she had too much work to do. I wondered if it was the freelance work she'd been telling me about, or work on the gala; either way, I wasn't given the chance to ask her.

The only good thing about not being alone with her was that I was able to actually process what she'd said, and I took a much-needed solo road trip along the Pembrokeshire coast on a rare weekday off.

As the mineral scent of the sea air cleared my mind, I realised just how poorly I'd handled the situation. Of course Morgan could work anywhere. Hell, there were loads of fully remote jobs now that hadn't existed four years ago. There were more and more businesses opening offices nearby. And even if she had to move, it didn't necessarily mean anything for us, assuming there might still be an *us*. Jared and Fatima had been living apart for months, and as far as I could tell, they were doing great.

The next time I talked to Morgan, I wanted to have something to say. Something to show her that I knew I'd fumbled. The campsite didn't have any signal at all, so I hiked out to the clifftop and sat above the sea on my phone, the wind whipping me as I researched my peace offering.

THE NEXT WEEK after our game, she seemed to be in a better mood, and she came along to the pub like she now usually did. It was strange to me to think of a time when she played with us but didn't come along; she fit into the group so seamlessly, and it felt more complete when she was there. But then again, maybe that was just my own interests talking.

Still, I was able to get her alone for a moment as we were waiting for our drinks. I'd been trying to find a quiet moment with her since she'd arrived at Fatima's; I had a speech prepared and everything. But in the end I had to hold her back when she tried to head to the table with her drink, causing Chloe to glare at me as she walked away.

"Listen," I said to Morgan once I had her alone, setting my drink down on the bar. I was relieved when Morgan did the same, despite the sceptical expression on her face. "I'm so sorry about what happened at mine. You were excited, and I was a jerk."

"Yeah, you kind of were," she said, eyeing me warily, but then she sighed, like it had been weighing heavily on her, too. That didn't make me *glad*, per se, but it did make me feel less alone in my angst. "I just don't understand what you want from me, Jack. Sometimes you seem to reward me for being open with you, but then when I try to be even more open, you shut down. Help me out here."

"I know," I said. "It wasn't about you being open. I just got scared, like you said. That you wanted to leave."

"Of course I don't want to leave," she said softly. "And I won't if I can help it. But you're the one who helped me see what I want to be doing to begin with. And it really sucked when you threw that back in my face less than twenty-four hours later."

"I hate that I did that," I said, chancing a half-step towards her. She didn't move; in fact, her expression softened even more. "That's why I made you something."

She looked around me, at my hands and pockets, like I was going to pull out a present. But instead I just pulled out my phone, copied the text from my notes, and sent it to her. She pulled out her own phone when it buzzed a short moment later, scowling as she scrolled through the message.

"What is this?" she asked.

"About three dozen different design jobs," I said. "A lot of them are here, or close to here. But there's some as far as Scotland, and even one in London."

Morgan looked up at me, and it seemed like she felt conflicted. Her brow was creased, and she bit her lower lip. But the corners of her mouth turned up reluctantly.

"I don't want to move away," she said. "I hope you know that's not what this is about. It was about the fact that you clearly didn't want me to either, but you wouldn't just say it."

I shook my head. "I'll say it again: I don't want you to leave. But I also want you to be happy. And I think you would be really fucking good at any of these jobs."

She smiled again, but it looked slightly sad. I held her gaze for a long moment, until someone at the bar shoved into me slightly, breaking the moment.

"Sorry," the person said.

"S'fine," I said back over my shoulder, but when I turned back, Morgan had her drink in her hand again.

"Thank you for this," she said, holding up her phone. "You've given me a lot to think about."

We walked out to the beer garden together, where Fatima was showing different models of air-con units to the group, debating which one to get installed. We were all thrilled that we wouldn't have to sweat anymore during our sessions, though of course it would have been even more helpful had she got it at the beginning of the summer instead of towards the end.

"Not to meta-game," Phil said, leaning forward onto the table conspiratorially, "but can we talk about what we're gonna do next in-game? Because I felt like last week we had what we needed, and then this week we're still not dealing with the threat at hand, because *someone* wanted to explore the library. And I don't really want to split up."

"Plus one for not splitting up," Fatima said. "It's a pain in the ass to run, especially when you lot use it as a chance to socialise when I'm not on your group."

"Right," Morgan said, "but do we actually have what we need? Because I know we got information about the Sphere, but we still don't know how to get back to our realm."

"And we're still being hunted by those soldiers," Grey said.

Phil argued that those were much smaller problems, whilst Chloe insisted that the top priority was taking out the people following us so we could have more time to problem-solve. The two of them started bickering, with Grey backing Chloe and Morgan backing Phil. Fatima just sat back, watching them go at it, with a smug look on her face like it was all part of some dastardly plan.

"Okay, okay," I said, holding up my hands. "Everyone here has a point. But I think what you're *both* saying is that we can't do anything in a considered way whilst we're being hunted. And we can get to a point of not being hunted by either leaving the fae realm, where we know the soldiers won't follow, or dispatching of those soldiers. Right?"

"Right," Phil said. "Well said."

"Good," I said, then pointed at the empty glasses that had already accumulated. "Another round whilst we figure this out?"

"Good ol' Jack," Chloe said, patting my shoulder. "Our real-life support character."

Something about the way she said that made me bristle. Like my only purpose in life – or at least in this friend group – was to mediate. To help out. To get the next round and give people lifts.

"I mean, I do have an opinion," I said.

"Okay," she said, taking her hand away, her eyes wide like she realised she'd touched a nerve. "And what's your opinion?"

I met her gaze and saw that she thought she knew what I was going to say. Because Jack would never suggest doing anything brash, would he? I didn't like being seen as so one-dimensional.

But I also didn't want to derail the entire campaign. So I swallowed my pride and acted the part of the good little cleric.

CHAPTER 28
JACK

I didn't see or speak to Morgan again for the rest of the week, but I spent all of it fretting about seeing her on the Saturday. I had to get past that though, because it was Chloe's birthday, which was a massive deal to her, meaning it was a massive deal to me. And to Phil, who pulled up to Fatima's just after me. I hung back so I could go in with him, watching as he hauled a massive plastic storage bin out of his boot.

"What the hell is that?" I asked as he struggled up the path to the front door. The August heat was no joke, and I saw beads of sweat forming on his forehead.

"Surprise," he grunted.

"That's not for tonight, is it?" I asked, confused; we'd agreed that I would do the shopping since he was doing the cooking, and the six Bags for Life digging into my fingers showed that I'd done my part.

"Not strictly," he said. "Just a little activity for later."

I narrowed my eyes at him, but we were interrupted before I could question him further.

"Get in here!" someone – probably Chloe – shouted from inside, so I swung the door open and smiled at the cool air that rushed over me. The air-con had finally been installed.

Everyone else was already there – including Jared, whom I hadn't seen in months – sat in a circle playing SushiGo.

"Watch out, she always goes for the nigiri multipliers," I said from over Chloe's shoulder, giving her a gentle kick.

"Hey, fuck off!" she said, swatting my knee.

I locked eyes with Morgan across the circle, and I felt myself freeze – I'd been wondering what it would be like to see her tonight – but I needn't have worried. She smiled up at me with the same cheerful smile I'd come to know and love.

"Okay, no, actually fuck off," Chloe said, shooing me away, so I absconded to the kitchen. I had a lot of prep work to do, and a lot of anxious thoughts to rewrite based on that smile.

I put the bags down on the worktop, then pulled out my phone when it buzzed in my pocket.

> New information received today will change the course of your life forever!!

Normally I dismissed Amy's messages as hokey, but every time I saw Morgan these days, I had high hopes of getting some new information. My brain went instantly into a spiral of speculation, and I had to actively close down that part of it so I could focus on the task at hand.

Over the last couple of years, Chloe had got really into mead. She'd become a bit of a snob about it, actually. So when Phil and I had started planning her birthday, he'd immediately suggested a mead tasting to put her snobbery to the test. Now I had meads from all over the UK, from the country's largest meadery to an obscure small-batch producer in Scotland who only produced a few dozen bottles a year.

Jared came into the kitchen as I was unloading them. I braced myself for the conversation; Jared was a good guy, but he was *such* a lad, and I'd had enough of that on the stag do a couple of weeks ago. He and Fatima had been sixteen when they'd got together, and apparently she'd had teacher vibes even then, so I always wondered what had attracted her to him.

"It's really good to see you, man," I said, trying to remember the last time I'd seen him. He'd moved to Manchester a while ago for work, and he didn't make it back very often except to see Fatima.

"Yeah, you too," he said. "I really miss it around here."

I grabbed the paper cups I'd bought and started lining them up behind the meads – seven cups for each of the twelve kinds. Without being asked, Jared started writing numbers on the bottom of each one so we could remember what they were.

"This is so cool of you guys," Jared said, "making such a big deal of each other's birthdays. I wish I were around more, but work is so busy. I'm glad Fatima has you all."

"The shiny new job not so shiny anymore?"

"Not so new, either," he said. "I've been up there almost a year now."

"Yikes. And no sign of getting to come home?"

Jared shook his head as he started to pour out sips of the first mead into the paper cups behind it. "Nope. Gotta make manager for that. I thought I was closer to that promotion than I am. It feels so out of reach sometimes."

I nodded in understanding, even if I didn't, in fact, understand. "How's it going with Fatima then?"

Jared sighed, and I heard the weight of a thousand sleepless nights in it. "Mate, long distance is fucking *hard*. Honestly, between you and me, I've been thinking about just coming back. Getting a new job. I miss my friends. I miss my house. And damn if I don't miss Fatima all the time."

I could empathise; I was worried I'd just handed myself the same fate by pointing Morgan towards jobs further afield.

"But I fucking love work, actually. It's weird, because I know it's the thing keeping me from Fatima. But when I'm there, I really love it. I sort of lose myself in it, you know?"

I nodded, but I did not, in fact, know. I certainly didn't love my job enough to get lost in it. So I offered him the only advice I could think of; the only part of his plight I felt I could relate to.

"I think that if you care about someone, you want them to have that. Something they love doing. Even if that means you don't get as much of them as a result."

Jared stood up from the pour he was in the middle of and nodded, staring at me for a moment.

"Damn if that's not the most sentimental shit I've ever heard you say."

I gave a weak laugh as I felt my face go red, looking down at the cup in my hand. "Yeah, sorry."

"No," he said, reaching a hand out, not quite touching me but grabbing my attention. "I meant that in a good way. Everyone else is all, 'go get that bag, Jared'. Or even 'love comes and goes'. But I like that perspective."

I laughed again, pouring out the last bottle of mead in the cups marked with the number twelve. "Yeah, well, it's hard being so wise."

"You've got it bad yourself, haven't you," he said more quietly.

I looked up at him and tried my best to look confused. "I don't know what you're talking about."

"Fatima told me you and Morgan have been hanging out a lot. I don't know her, but she seems cool."

"She is," I said, almost defensively, even though it was a painfully oversimplified way to describe her. "Like, really cool."

The rest of the group broke into shouts and gasps, and I looked over to see Morgan doing her ridiculous victory dance in the middle of the group. She looked so happy. So comfortable. It made me smile.

Jared must have caught me staring. "Yep, real bad," he said.

Fatima and Grey came into the kitchen, arms linked. Grey was wearing their rainbow cloud-pattern biker vest, which they always busted out for birthdays. They'd even dyed their hair pastel pink to match.

"What are you fellas talking about in here?" Fatima asked, reaching for one of the bottles, but Jared shooed her hand away.

"Just work," I said.

"Jared's favourite topic," Fatima said, helping us start to carry the cups to the table. "If I had a pound for every time he geeked out over a spreadsheet, we could pay off this house."

We set the mead out, making sure there was one of each number in front of each seat. Then we called in the others for the tasting.

I was surprised to discover I actually liked some mead. I'd always turned my nose up at what Chloe ordered, but apparently that was because she liked sweet and semi-sweet meads, whereas I preferred dry ones. Most importantly, Phil begrudgingly had to admit that he could, in fact, taste the difference.

Morgan seemed to be enjoying herself, though I tried to force myself not to just stare at her the whole time – half because I didn't want to freak her out, and half because I could feel Jared's gaze bouncing between us like he was watching a Wimbledon match.

After the tasting, everyone pulled out their presents for Chloe, and she did a terrible job of pretending like she hadn't been expecting anything. Grey got her some new dice, naturally, not that either of them needed any more. Fatima (and, nominally, Jared) got her some fancy stationery with her initials on it. Morgan got her a plant pot with illustrated boobs on the side, tiny gold hearts forming the nipples. Phil and I had got all the mead and food, but I had something for her from Mum and Amy: a pair of dangling earrings made of silver wire wrapped around red-and-white-banded stones.

"I was instructed to tell you," I said, pulling out my phone, "that not only is sardonyx your true birthstone, but that if you"—I cleared my throat as I got to the part she would know for sure hadn't come from me—"charge it under the full moon, it will help protect you from any and all toxicity that would threaten to come into your life."

"Thank you, Amy and Patricia," Chloe said, slipping her existing earrings out so she could put the new ones in. I took a picture and sent it to Mum and Amy.

Just as everyone started to get up from their seats so Phil could start dinner, mutterings of giant Jenga in the garden making their way around the table, Phil cleared his throat.

"Just a minute," he said, gesturing for everyone to sit back down, which they did obediently. He left the room and came back with the giant storage bin, setting it down heavy in the middle of the table.

"Is that for me?!" Chloe asked with a gasp.

"Part of it," he said. "I know I said I wouldn't have them ready until closer to the trip," he said, and Fatima and Grey, clearly seeing where this was heading, squealed quietly and leaned towards one another in glee. Phil continued. "I've got your costumes ready for your first fitting. If you could please try them on, I can pin them and see if anything needs to be altered."

He took the lid off the box, and everyone leaned forward to

see inside, but there were just brown parcels with each person's name scrawled across them. He took them out one by one and handed them to us.

Since we were all sleeping over, per Chloe's request, everyone dashed off to the rooms they'd be sharing. Phil and I always bunked in the twin guest room together when we stayed over, but when he didn't follow me, I went alone to our room upstairs, shutting the door behind me.

I untied the twine holding the parcel together and unwrapped the costume, running my fingers over the fabric. I could already tell it was beyond anything I would have expected or hoped. There was what looked like a white shirt, and a folded brown garment I suspected was trousers, and the hero piece: the jacket. I'd known roughly what it would look like from the drawings Morgan had done, but I hadn't been prepared for how well it would translate to real life.

I set the pile down on the bed and pulled on the trousers and shirt, then slipped the jacket on over my shoulders, doing up the buckles at the front. One of the shoulder ties was undone, and I tried to contort myself to tie it, to no avail. I'd just decided to take it off when I heard a knock at the door, which I assumed was Phil there to check the outfit.

"I need to tie the shoulders," I said as I swung the door open, but when I looked up, it wasn't Phil standing there.

It was Morgan, and she looked fucking incredible.

I was surprised at first; I knew she'd wanted to keep her outfit a surprise, but I'd thought Phil had been working on chain mail for her. But this was as far from a suit of armour as possible – almost. The blue strapless dress was tight around Morgan's torso, then flared out at her hips to brush the ground. Small ivory and gold flowers were stitched into the fabric every several inches of the dress. Her hair was behind her shoulders, showing off a piece of blue lace that wrapped around her neck like a choker, gold stitching following the lines and bringing out the pattern. The lace gave way to dozens of delicate gold chains, all interconnected, draping across her chest and around her shoulders. It gave the illusion of armour, despite the sweetness of the dress.

"What happened to the chain mail?" I asked, unable to hide my awe.

"That's for my Morgana outfit," she said. "This is the idea I had for the second day. I know it's a little unconventional for a Ren Faire—"

"It's perfect," I said, my eyes still roaming. If I'd thought I'd admired the lines of her body before, this gown was another story entirely. It looked so light, like I could rip it with the slightest touch; and that thought, of course, brought lots of mental images rushing in that I could have done without.

Phil was a fucking genius.

I tried to form words, but none seemed to come, and I gulped instead. Morgan smiled at the floor, her face pink.

"It's pretty great, isn't it," she admitted. "And it already fits perfectly."

"Beautiful," I said, and it came out all choked.

"I saw Chloe's before I came in," she said, "and it's suitably slutty. She's thrilled. This came out really cool, too." She reached out to run her pinched fingers along the edge of my jacket, her knuckles brushing against me through my shirt.

"The shoulders aren't tied up properly," I said, turning to show her.

"Here, let me," she said, pushing past me into the room. I hesitated for a moment before closing the door again behind her.

I turned towards her, and she was already reaching towards

my shoulder. I ducked slightly to help her, watching in the mirror as she tied the small strings into pretty little bows, tweaking until she stepped back and patted them, seeming happy.

I turned to look at my full reflection, shocked at how badass I looked. With a pair of high boots and a fake weapon of some sort, maybe a bit of stubble along my chin, I'd look right at home.

I'd never understood cosplay before. I loved gaming as much as the next nerd, but part of the fun was it being in your imagination, right? But standing here in these clothes, I felt like a completely different person. One who might do things differently. Be a little wiser; a little bolder, even.

"Not bad," Morgan said. I turned back to face her and was struck yet again by how amazing she looked.

"Thanks," I said. "We make quite a pair."

I didn't mean it as a loaded comment – I just meant that we both looked so different than usual, and like we came from the same storybook – but as soon as the words left my mouth, I knew they held weight.

"Jack," Morgan said, stepping towards me so she was just a few inches away, "I know we talked about this already, but I really hated how everything went down at yours. I wasn't trying to reveal some escape plan I had, and I'm sorry that I didn't realise how you might take that."

"Well, like I said on Monday, I don't want you to go. But that's no excuse for me overreacting."

Morgan smirked. "You did kind of overreact," she said. "But it's okay. And thank you for the list. There were some good options on there."

"You're welcome," I muttered, meeting her gaze. I didn't

want to think about the list right now; not with how close she was to me, or how heavy her gaze was.

"Also, I have to admit..." she trailed off, and I could tell that whatever was going to come next was going to be important. New information that could change the course of my life forever, even. A pregnant pause hung between us, and it felt like we were about to step around a corner. Through a doorway that would lock behind us.

"What?" I urged, ready to step through.

"I ... I had very different hopes for that night than what happened."

My heart dropped out of my body. Was this it? Was this really – finally – happening? Morgan dropped my gaze and looked at the ground again. Without thinking, I put a finger under her chin and angled her back to me, catching her eye again, holding the side of her face. I wanted her looking at me for this. I needed to see her eyes when she said it; to know that she meant it. To finally put an end to all the wondering; all the wishing; all the *want*.

"What did you want?" I asked, my voice a low rasp now. "What did you hope?"

She didn't look away this time, not that I would have let her. She let out a sharp breath through her nose, her shoulders falling. I felt her chin lift slightly away from my finger. She was steeling herself.

And then she raised herself up on her tiptoes and closed the distance between us, her mouth crashing into mine.

My lips parted in response, and my body took over immediately, one hand finding the small of her back to pull her closer, the other sliding through her curls and tugging at them at the base of her neck, tilting her head up further to deepen the kiss. Our breaths were hot and fast against one another's faces, and almost immediately I started to go a bit lightheaded.

I dipped down to wrap an arm around her back, pulling her towards me as I backed up, stepping until the hard wood of something – the door, I was pretty sure – hit my back. I slumped down slightly against it so I was closer to her height. She leaned into me, bending one leg to bring her hips closer in to mine. Fragile fabric be damned, I bunched up the skirt of her dress, desperate to find that leg, that hip; to run my hands over it. Finally I found the bottom of the dress with one fist, pulling it up until my knuckles brushed against the bare skin of her thigh, making her shudder and push her hips fully against mine. I was already rock hard, which I was almost certain she could feel, even with so many layers of tulle between us. I moved my mouth along her jaw to her ear, clawing at her thigh as I sucked gently on her ear, and she let out a soft moan.

Morgan's hands began to roam, too, tracing my jaw with her fingers as I kissed down her neck, smoothing along my chest with her palms, slipping under the thick fabric of the jacket to unbutton the top of my shirt. She grabbed me by the lapels and pulled away, making me groan at the lack of her, but she pulled me with her back across the room. As she did, she unbuckled my jacket and then pushed it off over my shoulders.

Holy shit, was this really happening? Five minutes ago I'd been desperate to get a moment alone with her, and now she was in my arms in a fucking ballgown, biting at my lip and pressing herself against me. I thought I might pass out from happiness already, but then she pushed me back to sit on the edge of the bed, and when she planted a knee on either side of my hips and straddled me, I knew for sure this would be the end of me. And I'd die a very, very happy man.

"Should we stop?" I asked, my mouth pressed against hers

again, sharing hot breaths between us. I was begging her in my mind not to take the out I was giving her, but I forced myself to pause before lifting her gown any further.

She smiled against me, and I thought I might melt. But before she could answer, another voice interrupted.

"Yes you should!" Phil stage-whispered from the doorway, and Morgan practically jumped off me, backing up until she knocked into the chest of drawers, her hand over her mouth. I quickly grabbed a pillow from behind me and placed it over my lap, certain the tight trousers would give away just how hot and heavy things had got.

"What were you thinking?" Phil asked, still in a whisper, pulling the door shut behind him and walking over to Morgan. He smoothed out the skirt of the dress and checked it over as Morgan stood frozen in horror.

Seemingly satisfied that I hadn't actually ripped the dress, Phil stood and turned to face me. "You know that I am a fan of this," he said, gesturing back and forth between Morgan and me. "But please, for the love of all things holy, not in the costumes, yeah?"

Morgan burst out laughing, and I couldn't help but join her.

"I'm serious! Those flowers took me a full week on their own," he said, his best angry face on, though I could tell he was trying to hold back a smile. "Don't make me take it back," he added, turning to Morgan.

Morgan's face went suddenly deadpan as she clutched the skirt of her dress in her fists. "Please don't."

"Then no more funny business in the dress. After the Ren Faire, you can get railed in a ballgown all you want. But until then, get naked first like normal people. And *gently*, please."

"Deal," I said, then waited until Phil looked at me so I could give him a stern look. "Now get out."

"No way," he said. "You two can't be trusted."

"It's fine," Morgan said as I opened my mouth to tell Phil off. "We can continue our ... um ... conversation later."

"Suuuuuure," Phil said, waving her towards the door. "Now let's go."

She glanced at me apologetically as she obeyed, letting herself be shooed out of the room. But there was still laughter in her eyes, and that heat that I'd seen there just before she'd kissed me, and I knew she meant it when she said we'd be continuing this later. I strained against the pillow once more just at the idea of it.

Phil shut the door behind Morgan and turned back to me. His stern expression split into the most laddish grin I'd ever seen, even on him.

"Fucking finally, mate!" he said, coming over to grab my shoulders and shake me. "Well done."

In the mirror I saw my face turn a bright beet red. "Don't be an idiot," I said, but I was smiling, too.

"How long has that been going on?"

Morgan had actually pushed me onto Phil's bed, so he sat down on mine, facing me.

"About sixty seconds longer than you've known about it."

"Score one for the costumes."

"Hey, I'd like to think I had something to do with it."

We both laughed, but my mind was still with Morgan, and what she was doing now. Would she go back to her room and debrief with Chloe about our own near-debriefing? Or would she play it cool? I had no idea – it had happened so suddenly, and we'd had no time to talk about what it meant.

"Hey, could you please not say anything to the others?" I asked. "I mean, obviously if she tells the others then that's fine, but I want to follow her lead."

"Yeah, totally," Phil agreed. "Now get dressed, please; I need to see if that costume fits."

He waved for me to stand up, but I shook my head and pointed at the pillow. "I'm gonna need a few minutes."

"Riiiiiight," he said in understanding, backing towards the door. "Let's do that later then. And I suppose that can be your bed now. Oh, and just remember, no funny business in the costumes, and that goes for solo play, too."

I threw the pillow at him as he dashed through the door, but he was gone before it got there.

CHAPTER 29
MORGAN

Dinner was a literal feast. We were all squished onto a picnic table in Fatima's garden, fairy lights strung overhead, having just devoured the four-course meal Phil had painstakingly created to pair with Chloe's favourite meads. There was even a honey-flavoured birthday cake. We all sang a delightfully off-key round of "Happy Birthday", after which we drunkenly polished off the cake in one sitting, digging straight into it with forks. It was all delicious, and Phil looked equal parts pleased and exhausted after his whirlwind effort in the kitchen. After he'd cockblocked Jack and me, of course.

It was both the best and worst thing that Jack and I were sat across from each other and not next to each other. Worst, because I was certain the secret smiles and lingering eye contact were giving us away. Best, because those same gazes had me wanting to pick right up where we left off, which wasn't exactly dinner table appropriate.

Okay, so maybe that was the worst, too.

I'd been spending the last two weeks oscillating between feeling confused by Jack's reaction and indignant over the fact that he couldn't just tell me how he felt. So when he'd cornered me at the pub and handed me a laundry list of proof points that he did actually care about me, it had left me with just confused. He'd seemed finally ready for something to happen between us, only to then tell me he was okay with me leaving? Even when I hadn't been planning to leave in the first place? I realised in the throes of that frustration that if I waited for Jack to be clear about what he wanted, I might be waiting forever, so I'd started applying, fairly indiscriminately, to the jobs he'd sent me.

So since Monday, I'd been steeling myself for tonight. All I'd been hoping for was to clear the air. I certainly hadn't expected to see him looking like Arthur Pendragon in his Ren Faire look, or for him to do the finger-under-chin thing I'd only ever read about in books.

Everything that had happened from that point on was a blur, but I had distinct memories of his fingers running through the hair at the nape of my neck, tugging gently as he kissed me. I even wore my hair up to dinner just so I could appreciate the tingly flashback I got when the breeze caught my curls. Looking at his hair matted against his forehead from the heat, thinking about his hot breath on me, I felt almost pained at the distance between us.

But he didn't look pained. Despite how stuffed we all were from dinner, as he kept his green eyes locked on mine, he looked somehow ... hungry. I'd never seen him look anything but cheerful or brooding, and the raw desire was an exciting change of pace. Heat spread through my core every time we locked eyes, and I felt the ghost of a sensation against every part of my skin he'd touched.

It took an agonisingly long time after we'd finished dinner

and then games for everyone to decide they were ready for bed, but after a couple of hours, Fatima and Jared were the first to peel off. Grey and then Phil were the next to go, and thankfully Chloe could always read a room, because despite it being her birthday, she excused herself to bed shortly after.

Finally it was just Jack and me, locking eyes across the picnic table, no spectators for whom we needed to be subtle. In fact, subtlety was so absent from the look he was giving me that I wondered how I'd ever questioned his feelings. How had it not been obvious every time we'd spoken that he wanted me just as much as I wanted him? How had I never noticed the mind-melting mix of affection and desperation in his gaze? Had I been so blinded by my own confusion that I couldn't see what was right in front of me?

It didn't matter, because I wasn't blind anymore. I could see clearly what Jack wanted, and I wanted the same thing.

We didn't say a word to each other for a full five minutes, and as intoxicating as the eye contact was, I was looking at the windows in the house, watching as they turned off one by one – first Phil and Jack's room, then Grey's, and then Chloe and mine. I took the briefest of moments to lament the fact that I wouldn't be finishing the book I'd brought with me as planned, but I wasn't mad; my plans were definitely looking up. Finally Fatima and Jared's ground floor bedroom light went off, and it took almost no time at all for me to step around the picnic table and climb onto Jack's lap, my dress bunching up around my thighs as I pressed my mouth to his. I wedged myself between him and the table, using the tight fit as leverage to press myself against him. I'd been watching him eye-fuck me all dinner, and now I was ready for the real thing.

And clearly Jack was, too. Almost immediately, one hand slipped up under my dress to palm my ass, whilst the other teased up my back until it found my hair, dispensing with the claw clip so my curls fell around both our faces. He bit my lower lip softly and then plunged his tongue against mine. The hand in my hair found its way down towards my shoulder, his thumb rubbing up and down my windpipe and along my collarbone, his other hand on my back, pulling me so tightly into him that I could barely breathe.

This man was starving, and frankly so was I.

He broke our kiss, and I gasped for air as he moved his mouth to my ear just like earlier, kissing along it and behind it and doing something with his tongue that was so effective I couldn't even decipher what it was exactly, only that it was working. I moved my hips against him, and I felt him harden in response.

"I want you so badly," he said, his voice so low and gravelly that it could only be described as a growl. The romance girlies were right – growling was fucking hot. I felt a throbbing between my legs telling me all the blood-flow was there right now. That was okay, who needed cognitive function anyway when months of slow burn were finally coming to fruition? In that moment, all that mattered was whatever the fuck Jack was doing with his other hand, which was no longer palming my ass and was instead on the bottom of my thigh, reaching up between my legs, kneading the flesh there so it spread me apart, bringing me closer into him, his fingertips brushing against the lacy underwear I'd put on after changing out of my gown. Now I was cursing the fact that I'd worn any at all, angling myself further into his touch with each breath.

"I want you, too," I said, my own voice more growly than I would have expected. Clearly Jack found it just as hot as I did though, based on how he hardened noticeably more when I spoke. Or maybe it was what I was saying. "I've wanted this for so long."

Then I cursed myself for saying anything, as Jack's hand came away from where it was brushing against me, and his tongue stopped doing the thing. Instead he brought both hands to my cheeks to cradle my face, resting my forehead against his.

"You have no fucking idea," he said. "I think part of me has wanted you since the moment I saw you. If you want me, I'm yours."

Then he dropped one hand and brought it between us, this time in the front. *Oh, thank god.*

"Is this okay?" he asked, his hand held in midair just in front of my belly.

I nodded eagerly in response, swallowing hard, and his hand passed through the slit in my dress and underneath the lace that had been so in the way before. The heel of his hand pressed almost uncomfortably hard into my pelvis, but I didn't even care, because his fingers were now moving slowly through my wetness, just enough pressure where I wanted it, but not too focused. Not yet.

"You walked into Fatima's that day in January," he said as he stroked, and I started to tip my head back in pleasure, but he stopped me with his free hand, bringing my forehead back to his, locking eyes with me. "Your cute little dungarees and your single set of dice. You had no idea what you were in for. I didn't, either. But it only took five minutes alone with you to know that if you wanted me, I was yours."

As he talked, he zeroed in on the spot that was now throbbing so hard I felt like he must have been able to feel my heartbeat through his fingers. And just as I felt like he was getting too close, too concentrated, he plunged two fingers inside me and pressed his palm against the spot he'd just been circling, the friction building as he stroked inside me.

"Fuck," I said, tilting my head back again, bracing myself against the table with my hands, and he let me go that time, his free hand holding me up by the neck, a bit of light pressure around my throat. "J-jack, that f-feels s-so good," I croaked out. "P-please..."

"Please what?" he growled again into my ear, and I felt myself right on the precipice. But I wasn't ready to go over yet.

"D-don't you w-want to be ins-side me? W-when I c-come?"

But Jack didn't relent. "I'm already inside you. There's plenty of time for that later," he said, and the way he said "later" sent images flashing through my mind of all the times we could have been doing this – in the guest room earlier, in his car, under the stars on our very first outing... How did we go so long without this??

"Come for me, Morgan."

That sent me toppling straight over the edge, and I clenched around him in ecstasy. He released my throat as I gasped in huge mouthfuls of air. His fingers kept their pace, drawing out my orgasm as long as possible, and I ground against his hand until I was fully sated.

I collapsed back so I was sitting on the table, and he buried his face against my chest, his hair flopping into my mouth. I clutched his head to me like I was holding onto it for dear life; I felt so weightless that part of me thought I might float away if I didn't.

It was a long moment before either of us moved, despite the beads of sweat I could feel running down my back and between my breasts. I was sure Jack was getting the worst of it with his head buried there, though maybe it was worth it to him for a face full of tits.

After a couple of minutes, though, once my breathing had abated and his hands had moved to my back, we finally leaned apart.

"You said you had other hopes for that night two weeks ago," he said. "Was that a bit closer to what you had in mind?"

Between the heat, the mead, and what had just happened, my throat was parched enough that I couldn't muster any words, so I just nodded my head. Jack must have noticed the slight dehydrated smack of my lips, because he lifted his glass of water to offer me a sip. I tipped it greedily backwards.

"Better?"

I nodded. "Much better. Thank you."

It took another minute for us to finally move apart and stand up in a way that didn't feel jarring, and I noticed with satisfaction that he was still hard. We stacked the plates and glasses and carried them inside, not wanting to leave too much mess for the morning. Then Jack laced his fingers in mine, and something about our interlocked fingers and the casual intimacy they conveyed made me feel flutters all over again.

Jack stopped me in the hallway and pressed a kiss to my lips, backing me against the kitchen door, a reverse of our position from earlier when we'd kissed for the first time. And almost surprisingly, this one was no less urgent. Clearly we'd be working out this tension for a long time to come, but I didn't mind that one bit.

Once we were done snogging in the hallway like a couple of school kids, we turned into the lounge at the front of the house, thinking we'd be able to be alone together, only to find Phil asleep on the sofa, a tiny woven throw wrapped around him as he rested his head on a decorative lumbar pillow. He was snoring lightly – I was surprised we hadn't woken him up.

Jack and I shared a look, and I wondered if I looked as

hopeful and excited as he did. We practically sprinted up the stairs to his room, where we found a note on Phil's bed:

GO FOR IT YOU ABSOLUTE SLUTS xx

I smirked at Jack, fanning myself with Phil's note, and a devious grin broke out on his face.

"I believe you mentioned 'later'?"

CHAPTER 30
CAPTAIN MORGANA SILVERSWORD

The journey back to the Capital was much trickier than the party had bargained for. The bards at the college were able to open a portal back to their home realm – again, for a cost; they were really burning through the stipend Lord Arnault had given them – but it transported them not to the Capital, or even to the grove through which they'd entered the fae realm, but to a random forest in the opposite direction.

Three days into their estimated ten day journey back to the Capital, assisted by a horse-pulled wagon they'd bartered for in the last town they'd passed through, Morgana called the party to a halt. They were on a quieter portion of the Queen's Road, and they hadn't seen anyone for several hours. But when she saw a twitch in the trees up ahead and heard a clicking noise carried on the strong breeze, something in her recognised trouble. Thrormir, who was sat next to her as she drove the wagon, looked over at her with confusion in his eyes, and she pointed to the trees.

"Take the Sphere and go," she whispered to Calamity, who was lying down inside the wagon with their belongings.

Calamity nodded and whispered her newest spell. Still lying down, she grabbed the Sphere and started to fade out of sight, fully invisible in under a second.

The back step of the wagon creaked slightly, and Morgana knew Calamity was out. She clicked her tongue, urging the horses forward, though even they were tentative in their movements, picking up on her nerves. Morgana brought her hand to the hilt of her sword just as they passed under the trees where she'd seen the movement, prepared to strike whenever someone charged or jumped them.

Sure enough, almost as soon as they'd passed under the trees, two figures dropped onto the wagon. Morgana didn't even hesitate to suss out what was happening; anyone who dropped onto someone's wagon from above uninvited was an enemy. She reacted instantly, slicing through one of them with as much force as she could muster, and realised, as she felt her blade clatter against bone with little resistance, that it was a skeleton. It fell to pieces in the footwell.

"Undead!" she called, just as four more figures ran out into the road. She and Thrormir jumped down from the wagon, and Gorlag and Yorick emerged from the wagon. The other undead was still up on the wagon, where it started tearing through their belongings. Morgana hoped that Calamity was well clear of the skirmish.

Morgana, Thrormir, Gorlag, and Yorick dispatched of the remaining undead, then turned their attention to the one still ransacking the wagon.

"Allow me," Thrormir said, holding up his amulet with the symbol of Chaius.

"I need healing though," Gorlag said, motioning to a tiny gash in their arm.

"Me too," Yorick said; Morgana couldn't see a single wound.

"Just let me do this first," Thormir said with a sigh, "and I promise I'll heal you after."

He held out his amulet and started muttering under his breath. They all watched as the cloaked skeleton continued tearing through their packs, pulling open Morgana's bag of rations, and then suddenly exploded into a cloud of dust. The cloak blew away on the wind, and when they leaned over the side, there was no sign the undead had ever been there other than the mess it had made of their belongings.

"That's a cool trick," Calamity said to Thrormir, appearing in the middle of the road with the Sphere in her hand.

Morgana began to look over the body – if it could be called that – that was still crumpled in the footwell; it had no other possessions except for a small, standard dagger. The cloak, however, was of interest. Because on the outside of the hood, stitched in blue, was a twelve-pointed star.

CHAPTER 31
MORGAN

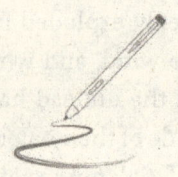

I was well and truly in my Lover era.

As concerned as I'd been that the novelty and heat would wear off and we'd be left with nothing to say, a month later we were still just as comfortable in each other's company as ever. Except maybe more now, because we could jump each other's bones whenever we wanted instead of just letting the tension eat at us. Instead of throwing up our walls left and right. After months of mounting tension, Jack and I were now ... well, just mounting. Constantly. At mine, at his, anywhere we could. We were both completely unburdened, and often undressed.

The best part about finally being together was that we could finally call our little adventures what they actually were: dates. Our trip to the botanical garden was romantic enough to put *Bridgerton* to shame. Our wild swimming plans became skinny dipping in the moonlight. He'd come along to walk Pablo a few times, and they'd got on so well it was like they already knew each other. We'd even exchanged spare keys.

I had a date to the gala, too; Jack wanted to be there for me, and whilst I knew I wouldn't have a ton of time for him, I liked the idea that he'd be a safe place to crash amidst the madness.

We still hadn't told the rest of the group, though; we'd talked about it, and we both felt that we wanted to just be *us* for a while. Not complicate it with other people's hopes or expectations. But I knew it would cause a splash when we did fess up, especially for Chloe, who had been asking me more and more pointed questions about how busy I was.

In the meantime, it had me feeling even more conflicted about my search for the perfect career, and the perfect place to live, and everything else. I'd been really enjoying my freelance work thanks to Greg's word of mouth, but I knew I wasn't ready to try to freelance full-time, so I was still planning to get a new job. Now that Jack and I were together, was there an expectation that I wouldn't move? He'd said it was fine, that Jared and Fatima could be the blueprint for making it work, but how serious had he been?

I was afraid to ask, because part of me suspected the answer was yes, that things had changed. But the reality was that I had already been invited to a couple of interviews from the jobs I'd applied to.

One was for an agency in London that used cringey language like "design rockstar" and "disruptive innovation", so I'd checked out about halfway through the call. I'd never heard back from them afterwards.

The second one, a remote role for a software company, had been promising though; the woman on the call was much nicer than the previous interviewer about my lack of experience, focusing instead on what I liked about design and what kinds of projects I'd tried. I knew by the end of the call that they were moving me onto the next stage, and she gave me a small design assignment to complete. Did I like designing fake social posts as much as I liked drawing D&D characters or illustrating a logo? No, of course not. But did I like it better than planning events and cold calling donors? Hell yes.

I sent off the designs just three days after my interview – I'd finished them on the same day, but I didn't want it to seem like I hadn't put time into them, even though I hadn't really – and within a couple of hours, I'd been invited back for another video interview.

I promised myself that I would tell Jack about it before I spoke to them again, but I kept putting it off. Every time I thought it might be a good moment, I flashed back to the night I'd told him I wanted to find a design job, and how he'd shut down. It wasn't fair to keep it from him; he'd apologised, and he'd been the one to send me the listings to begin with. There was no reason for him to be upset, right?

But for some reason, the second interview came and went, and I kept it to myself.

CHAPTER 32
JACK

Making Morgan Matthews come was my new life's purpose.

I'd never been a particularly horny boyfriend with Aria. We'd been teenagers when we'd got together, so of course we'd had sex a lot, but it was always quick and singularly focused. Even as we got older and I had to work harder to make things good for her, it was always about a release of tension.

But with Morgan, even after four years of not being with anyone, I could have spent all my time with my tongue between her legs and never got bored. I'd done it enough over the last month that I knew exactly what to do to bring her to the edge, but that was only half the fun. The other half was just exploring her, and that exploration inevitably brought the first half with it, too.

For example, if I hadn't taken the time to explore, I wouldn't have been feeling her squirm around me as I rotated my fingers inside her and stroked her from a new angle, the rhythm of my tongue steady the whole time. Well, almost steady – it broke slightly as I couldn't help but grin.

"Fuck, Jack," she said, her legs pressing against the sides of my head as she tensed.

"That's the idea," I said, and she moaned as I stopped to speak.

I pressed my tongue flat to her clit and closed my mouth around it, creating suction and friction at once, and she writhed for me again, squeezing her legs harder this time, sitting up off the bed to run her fingers through my hair. Fuck, I loved how she tugged at it. But I used my free hand to press her firmly back down, and she let out a groan as she hit the mattress.

"Please, Jack," she said, then gasped as I changed the angle of my fingers again to stroke where I knew, from careful study of course, her G spot was. Her panting grew harder, as did I.

"Please," she moaned again.

"Hmmm?" I asked, not daring to actually speak and break the suction I'd created over her, instead looking up her body to meet her hungry, desperate gaze. Not that she was making it easy, her hips starting to buck slightly as she sought more.

So I gave her more. I pressed up slightly so I could increase the pace of my fingers inside her – not too fast, but upping the friction just enough.

"F-fuck!" she yelled, and I could tell she was close again; I supposed it was time for me to let her come. So I used the tip of my tongue to flick at her clit, almost directly this time, keeping my rhythm steady. She sat up slightly as she arrived at the edge, then collapsed backwards as I felt her tighten again and again around my fingers.

I kept stroking her for a moment, and then, even once I'd removed my fingers, I kissed gently at her swollen vulva, bringing her down from her climax gently.

"Was that good?" I asked, crawling to the top of the bed whilst she lay there, breathing hard. I scooped her up against me, resting her head on my chest, smelling her citrusy shampoo as I kissed her curls.

She batted at me weakly. "Shut up. I think we both know it was. You don't need a gold star from me."

I laughed. Post-orgasm Morgan could be feisty, but I loved it.

In fact, I was beginning to think I loved *her*. It was still way too early to say it, but I'd been feeling it more and more.

As she slunk off to my bathroom and I heard the shower start, I lay back and immediately came down from the high. I had a long workday ahead of me – Dad had been making me do all the paperwork for a new job so I could learn the admin ropes, and I hated it with every fibre of my being – but being with Morgan made everything better. Genuinely. Even the idea of taking over the family business was less of a drag when I realised it would be a solid foundation on which we could build a life together.

I'd even been thinking we could build a literal house together at some point. Whether it was how much time she spent drawing or talking about design, or the fact that she just brought out that side of me, I'd been spending more time than ever on my own sketches. Lately I'd been drawing the same thing in different iterations: a family home, with a sun-filled art studio for Morgan, and plenty of space for a dog. We could find a south-facing hill, and maybe build a home into the side of it. There were plenty of farmers looking to sell up these days; hell, Uncle John was probably only a few years off it himself.

I pulled out the notebook I kept in my bedside table and opened to the next blank page, sketching roughly the same home as I had yesterday, but this time on a specific hill on the other side of Uncle John's land. I knew the contours like the back of my hand from having grown up on them, and it was amazing how just a slight curve this way or that way completely changed the optimal layout of the house. And if we incorporated some local birch into the materials, maybe the flooring, it would feel like we were sat outside when the sun filtered through the windows...

The shower turned off, and I stashed the journal away. I wasn't embarrassed of the sketches, but it felt a bit intense to tell her I'd been drawing our future home, and I knew she would have loads of questions. She was always so curious; I loved that about her.

I knew I'd show them to her someday. I just wanted to double- and triple-check that we were on the same page before I did.

Morgan and I hadn't yet "burst the bubble", as we'd been saying. In other words, our friends still didn't know we were dating. Phil obviously knew we'd hooked up, but given that Morgan had snuck back to her own room in the early hours of the morning at Chloe's party, we were pretty sure Phil was the only one who suspected anything. This meant all the hand-holding, the calling each other "babe", and the copious snogging was just between the two of us. When we were at game night, or out with our friends, we acted as we always had.

Unless we could get a moment alone, that was. And on Monday, as Fatima gave us a five-minute warning before starting, Morgan and I stole away, each purportedly needing bathroom breaks, so we could conduct a re-enactment of our make-out session in the guest bedroom. When Fatima called for the two of us a few minutes later, just as I was beginning to think we'd be re-enacting more than just a make-out, we had to strategically time our egress so we wouldn't raise suspicions.

When I came down the stairs a minute or so after Morgan, Fatima was waiting for me at the bottom, her arms crossed and her foot tapping. My face flushed red, as if she'd actually walked in on us, and I wondered if this was how her students felt all the time.

"You wanted to talk?" she asked, and I breathed a huge sigh of relief. I'd almost forgotten that I'd asked her to pull me aside for a character chat. I'd been thinking about what she'd offered us on our weekend away at the start of the summer, and about what Chloe had said about me being a permanent support character. And I'd been thinking about making a change.

Once I'd told her what I was thinking, Fatima closed her eyes for a moment, moving her finger around, as if she were rearranging things in her mind.

"Do you want to make a big deal of it?" she asked. "Like, close the door for good? Or just quietly change over?"

"Let's go big," I said, and she smiled; that was a good sign. She had an idea.

"I mean, I could do it next week," she said. "It would fit well with what I think will happen, assuming you all don't go completely off-piste."

"So in other words," I said, "it could be months from now."

"Absolutely," she agreed with a laugh. "But I'll try to make it happen sooner. Does anyone else know?"

I shook my head. "Nope, I thought it could be a surprise."

"Well yeah," she said, "we haven't had this happen yet in this campaign. Morgan will be shocked, I'm sure."

It took me a moment to realise that she meant because it was Morgan's first campaign, not because I should have told her. And I had considered it; I knew she would be surprised. But it was just a game ... right?

Morgan's lunch breaks had been slowly disappearing as the gala drew nearer, so I'd been taking her to see Pablo every weekend. Going on walks together, we felt like a little family, and it broke my heart that Morgan couldn't take him home permanently. I'd thought more than once about adopting him myself, but the house wasn't super dog friendly, what with the wildlife pond and the farm machinery. So instead I'd just been planning to make a large donation (large for me, anyway) to the rescue in hopes that it would help.

This weekend, we'd got special permission to borrow Pablo for longer than his usual half-hour walk.

"Thanks again for this," I said to Lauren.

"Of course," she said, smiling warmly and running her fingers through her short hair. I could totally see how she was Chloe's type. "Just please have him back by three. I need to close up a bit early today."

I narrowed my eyes. Chloe had said she had plans tonight, too. But it was probably a coincidence, and even if it wasn't, it certainly wasn't my place to say anything.

"Will do," Morgan said, oblivious, walking back out into the lobby with Pablo. I hooked his lead to the back of his harness as Morgan put him down. He stood next to me, looking up at me expectantly as if to ask, *where are we going, Dad?*

The weather felt properly autumnal for the first time all year. Some of the maples were even starting to change colour, which was rare for mid-September, so we walked hand-in-hand up the riverside path through a patchwork of colours, Pablo trotting just ahead of us at the end of his lead. There were fewer kayakers and paddle boarders on the river than there had been when we'd gone out on it, and we even saw people in hats and scarves. It was probably a Fool's Autumn, and we'd have another heatwave soon enough, but I for one was appreciating it whilst we had it.

As we walked, we talked about the Ren Faire. I wanted to keep Morgan's mind off the gala, at least for the weekend, and we were getting tantalisingly close to the trip. Phil had finished her chain mail for her second outfit, and she'd even bought a few foam swords to choose from that we could share between us, her for her Morgana outfit and me for my generic outfit. We talked about other places we may want to visit, and things we might want to experience together. It was the first time I'd really thought about travelling since Aria, but with Morgan it didn't scare me like I would have thought. We talked about other Ren Faires we might want to visit, and seeing Hobbiton in New Zealand, and even taking a trip up to the Isle of Skye next summer. I tried not to let myself get carried away with excitement at hearing her talk about next summer as if it were a given.

We took a break on a bench under the trees at the top of the path and chanced letting Pablo off lead to play with a terrier that kept coming up to him. He was beautifully behaved, and he came back every time we called.

I was finally getting to experience all the small, intimate joys I'd been yearning for whilst I'd been alone, and they were made all the better by the fact that it was Morgan I was sharing them with. Sitting next to her on the bench, watching the dog that felt like ours play in the grass, I almost blurted out to her that I loved her right then and there. She looked up at me, the human equivalent of the heart-eyes emoji, and I knew we were on the same page. I knew we had only been together for a few weeks, which was really no time at all in the grand scheme of things, and a drop in the ocean of what I hoped we'd have together. But the more time I spent with her, the more I felt certain that I was in love with her. And I suspected, or at least hoped, that she felt the same about me. That she saw a future with me like I saw a future with her. We looked out at the water, both of us, I hoped, imagining all the adventures we could have together.

I was also admiring the foliage in a nearby grove of neatly spaced beech trees, which had already started to turn for the autumn, the golden leaves on the outside blending perfectly to the verdant green at the heart. I mentally started sketching a low-lying house in the middle, no taller than the shortest of the trees, made of hard-wearing maple to match the less durable beech trees, picture windows reflecting the grove so it appeared unbroken from the river.

"Hey, question for you," I asked Morgan. She looked up from Pablo and over at me, expectant. "What drawing programme do you use on your tablet?"

She squinted her eyes at me and then smiled; I wondered if she knew why I was asking.

She pulled her tablet out of her tote and walked me through what she was using. It seemed easy enough, and she could even download special "brushes" to create different effects and graphics. My mind ran wild with the possibilities.

Once she'd finished showing me, and I'd promised to let her give me a proper tutorial, we stood up, said goodbye to the terrier, and headed back to the rescue. The way she said goodbye to Pablo, telling him that she loved him and that she hoped he got to go home soon, made my heart break all over again that I couldn't make him hers.

After we left, I dropped Morgan at home so she could do some freelance work, and so I could have dinner with my parents and Amy.

"Hello my love," Mum said as I walked through the front door. She pressed a kiss to my cheek. "I saw a new outcrop of anemone by the supermarket earlier and thought of you."

"Oh amazing," I said, "the one in town?"

"No, is there some there, too?"

Mum and I discussed autumn wildflowers for a few minutes whilst we waited for Dad and Amy, who came in together from outside. I'd thought I'd heard tinkering around in the workshop, but I was surprised to see Amy had been part of it.

Dinner was Mum's classic lasagna, which, from the smell of garlic and red wine wafting through the house, I could tell she'd been working on all day. I knew from experience being the designated stirrer that the ragu alone took a solid four hours to cook. Phil tried to recreate it sometimes, but he was almost never patient enough to let it cook that long, and I could always tell.

"So darling," Mum said as we tucked in, "when are you going to let us meet your girlfriend?"

I immediately turned to glare at Amy next to me, but she just shrugged. "Wasn't me."

"Aha!" Mum said, jabbing her fork in my direction. "I knew it."

I sighed. "It's still really new, Mum. I don't know if we're there yet."

Mum frowned. "Have you not been hanging out with this girl since summer started?"

I dropped my cutlery noisily on my plate and turned to Amy again. She did the same and threw up her hands.

"Still not me!"

"Oh please," Mum said, "do you really think I don't know when you're seeing someone?"

"Honestly?" I asked. "No, I don't. It's never happened since I've lived at home, anyway."

"Exactly," she said. "You've been holed up in that house by yourself for the last four years. Of course I was going to notice the head of brown curls always in your passenger seat."

I rolled my eyes. Mum could be so *nosy*. So deep in other people's business. But I guess that was her job, after all. At least she was here, noticing things, instead of halfway around the world like Morgan's mum.

"It's like you forget we share a driveway," she said, resuming her dinner. "Anyway, you'll bring her round next week."

I looked around, as if searching for the version of me that had agreed to this. "Will I?"

"You will," Mum said, locking eyes with me and nodding so aggressively that I couldn't help but nod along. Satisfied, she took a massive bite of lasagna, humming happily as she chewed.

CHAPTER 33
MORGAN

Jack and I woke up together in my house on a Friday morning a few days before the gala.

"You should meet my family," Jack said against my temple. We were tangled in my bed, my leg flung over his hip, his face squished between mine and the pillow, our arms wrapped around each other. I could see the edge of the tattoo on his back, and I was tracing the lines over and over with the tip of my finger, tickling his skin with my fingernail. It was chilly – we'd yet to experience the second summer that inevitably came every year – but the body heat we were sharing was still just a side benefit to the proximity. Either way, wild horses couldn't have dragged me even an inch away from Jack until the moment I had to leave for work. I wished desperately I could call in sick again. We could make love, I could read a book, we could just never leave the house ... but Jack had to leave for work soon. They were scoping a new job – the biggest one they'd ever taken on, apparently – and Jack's dad had decided to foist all of the admin onto his unwitting son.

"We haven't even told our friends," I said instead.

"Mmmm," he groaned. "Maybe we should do that, too."

"Nooooo, not the bubble," I said. "You know Chloe is going to be insufferable once we tell her."

"It's been four weeks, babe." My heart clinched at the casual "babe" – he said it constantly, my actual name apparently lost to him, but I got butterflies every time.

"Exactly. Weeks. That's nothing."

"Your call," he said, but he sounded grumpy. "But we can't hide this whilst we're in America."

The Ren Faire was just a month away, and I'd been thinking every single day about how magical it would be to walk hand-in-hand with Jack through the festival.

"No, you're right," I said. "Plus, Chloe needs to know before the gala." The gala, on the other hand, was now only a week away, and Chloe would definitely be there. If Jack were to be my safe harbour in the hurricane of my job, it would be pretty obvious.

"You should come to film night tonight," he said. And though part of me felt a little weird about intruding on their years-long tradition, it actually made me really happy to think about their little threesome becoming a foursome. I smiled and nodded.

"Yeah, okay."

Jack smiled back, and leaned in to kiss me. My alarm went off right as our lips met, and he groaned into my mouth.

"I don't want to go," he said, pulling back from me and covering his face with a pillow. I frowned at his sudden distance, despite the fact that we were still basically one person from the hips down, and so I burrowed under the pillow to get close to him again.

"You can't make me go," he said to me, his breath hot under the pillow.

"I wouldn't dream of it," I said. "But that means I have to go, too. It's crunch time."

"My kingdom for a lazy day in bed with you," he said, pulling me close and kissing the tip of my nose. I giggled in response.

"You get those every weekend."

"But I want it *now*," he insisted, throwing the pillow off our faces and onto the floor.

"You just want to avoid this walk-through with your dad."

"Both can be true," he said. "But you're right, I really don't want to do this."

"Better get used to it," I said, sitting up and running a finger down his chest. "You're the future face of Evans Contractors!"

I meant it in a joking sort of way, but I saw his face fall in exhaustion.

"Don't remind me."

I hated seeing him like this. Every time he had to do anything for work other than build – every quote visit, every "finance day", every little whiff of management – he deflated. He obviously hated it. Why wouldn't he at least admit it to me?

"Hey, question for you," I said, laying my head down on his arm, continuing drawing on his chest with my finger. I could feel it rising and falling with his breath.

"Answer for you," he said, planting a kiss on the top of my head.

"If you *weren't* taking over the business, what would you want to do?"

He chuckled. "I don't know. I don't really think about it, because that's what's happening."

"Right," I said, "but if it weren't."

The laughter disappeared from his voice. "But I am," he said. "So there's no point in getting carried away with what-ifs."

"But surely there is a point, if you don't actually like it?"

Jack's body tensed, and his chest went still, as if he were holding his breath.

"What are you talking about?" he asked, all the warmth and grogginess gone from his voice. It was almost disconcerting. "I didn't say that."

"Well, I mean, it's obvious from how you react every time you have to do his job instead of yours."

Jack stretched a bit and then wiggled out from under me, sitting up on the edge of the bed. My hand fell to the sheet as he moved away.

"I think you're reading too much into it," he said. "I'm perfectly happy, I promise. Plus, it's really nice to feel like I get to help my family out."

"Whatever you say," I said with a sigh. Work was yet another landmine in the landscape of Jack Evans, it seemed. "But can you humour me for a moment?" I reached up and poked his arm, pawing at him until he turned to face me.

"Sure," he said, softening again. "Go on then." He smiled at me, but it wasn't the deep smile he'd been wearing when we woke up together.

"If you could have any job ever, what would it be?"

His smile widened. "Okay fine, that's easy," he said, and I sat up, anticipating some unexpected insight into him. But then his smile tightened into a smirk. "I'd be a naked butler with exactly one customer."

"Hmmmm," I said, playing into his joke even though it hadn't been what I was after. I could keep it light. "I could think of a few uses for a naked butler." I reached up and grabbed the back of his neck, pulling him to me. We kissed once, twice, three times, his tongue running gently along my bottom lip in a way that made it tingle. Then he broke away and winked at me.

"Oh, I didn't mean you," he said, and I rolled away from him in mock anger. I pressed myself up on my elbows and glared at him.

"Sorry, who is it that's managed to monopolise my man?"

"Chloe, obviously," he said, running a finger down my spine like I had run mine down his chest just moments ago. "She's said she would pay me to clean her flat in the buff once a month."

"Just once a month? That doesn't sound like enough to live off."

"It's a filthy flat," he said. "Takes ages."

"That sounds painfully inefficient." I arched my back as he walked his fingers back up towards my neck, nuzzling at my ear. "Seems you should take a 'little and often' approach if you ask me."

Jack leaned in to whisper in my ear, his voice dropping into a low rumble that I could feel in my belly. "Oh, is it efficiency you value? Because I can be efficient."

"I mean, efficiency isn't everything," I said, my voice breathy as he hovered over me from behind, pressing a tantalisingly gentle kiss first to the nape of my neck, and then below that, and then below that.

"No, you're right," he said, dropping a knee between my legs, then suddenly using it to spread me apart. I audibly gasped as the cold air hit my wetness.

Over the last four weeks, Jack had learned exactly what buttons to press to make me lose myself almost right away. I was almost cross over how easy it was for him, when I'd had to work hard for it my entire adult life.

But as Jack nibbled at my ear, and then my neck, and then my shoulder, I was the furthest from cross. If I'd thought his attention to detail only extended as far as my preferred sandwich, I'd been painfully wrong. No, *deliciously* wrong.

And as Jack positioned himself at my entrance, one hand on my hip and the other wrapped in my hair, and pulled me back onto him, I couldn't remember a single reason I'd ever had to be cross in my entire life.

Less than an hour later, I was sat at my desk, looking even less put together than my already quite casual standards for work attire. My getting ready time had been ... eaten into, so to speak. But I was far too busy to worry about what I looked like.

I scanned my to-do list, which was laughably long; there was actually, literally, no chance of me getting through all of it by the end of the day. And if the past week had been anything to go by, it would be twice as long by the time I went home. I'd even had to push my second interview with the software company to after the gala; there was just no way I would be able to make it happen before.

Aaron came up and set a tea down on my desk. For the person who was, in theory, running the event, he seemed significantly less stressed than me. But he always brought me caffeine, so I didn't get too angry.

"Simone wants to see us in her office," he said, and I audibly groaned; Simone was a bit of a micro-manager, and I spent so much time answering to her about what I was doing that it made it difficult to actually, you know, *do it*. But I shut my laptop and carried it with me after Aaron, not forgetting the mug of tea as I went.

Simone got straight to the point, which I loved about her. "Aaron's parental leave is starting next week, and he's just handed in his notice. So that means he won't be coming back, as we discussed might happen."

"I see," I said, nodding along. No wonder he'd been so checked out recently; I hadn't realised he would be gone so immediately after the event.

"He tells me you've been managing the gala pretty much solo," she said, and I tried not to be shocked at actually being recognised for how hard I'd been working. "So, assuming next week goes well, and we hit our fundraising goal..."

Part of me knew what she was going to say, and I braced myself for it.

"... the promotion we talked about is yours."

Simone talked me through the next steps she'd initiate the next week, and I tried to look appreciative, but it was all I could do to nod along without checking out. On the way back to my desk, Aaron talked my ear off about all the things I'd need to brush up on. It sounded exhausting. I thanked him again and told him I needed to get to work, and he nodded at me conspiratorially before walking away.

"What was that about?" Chloe stage-whispered.

"Ugh, nothing," I said. I felt a little bit bad, but then again, there was a lot I hadn't told her about at the moment. Hell, she didn't even know I was crashing film night later.

But also, telling Chloe meant telling Jack. Not because she would mention it, though that was a genuine risk. But because he was my boyfriend. My partner, even. He deserved to know. But I was dragging my feet, because part of me knew that if I told him about that job opportunity, I also needed to tell him about the others I'd been going after. And deep down I knew how that conversation would go.

∼

Jack texted me at about five, asking if I could be ready by six fifteen instead of six thirty. I knew Chloe wouldn't be arriving until seven, so I figured he must have finished work sooner than expected, and I knew exactly why he wanted me early. I rushed through my tasks for the rest of the day, more than willing to make them Monday Morgan's problem so that I could steal away to my boyfriend's house for a quickie.

I mean, he *was* my boyfriend, right? We hadn't used those words, but something about "If you want me, I'm yours" and spending every night together gave off serious boyfriend vibes. I made a mental note to clarify the terminology with him, just as soon as I'd had my second orgasm of the day.

Jack and I had to prioritise the efficiency we'd joked about earlier, but we *just* managed to get each other off again before Phil knocked on the door. Helpfully we were already on the sofa, so I hurried to pull my pants back on as Jack buttoned his trousers and walked to the entry.

"Why was your door locked?" Phil asked as he walked in with a bag of food in one hand and a tray of takeaway cups in the other.

When he came around the corner to see me sitting on the sofa, no doubt looking extremely guilty, he froze for a moment, his eyes darting back and forth between Jack and me as he worked through the clues: two people moving apart suddenly, one with mussed hair, the other with the top of her dungarees undone, throw cushions cast onto the floor.

When it all clicked into place, he threw his hands in the air like his football team had scored, and several chips launched out of the bag; miraculously the cups stayed securely in the tray.

"Finally!" he yelled, just as the door clicked open again.

"I'm here!" came Chloe's voice, and she rounded the corner

to see Jack standing over me at the sofa, and Phil looking like he'd just scored a goal.

I watched Chloe's face carefully – I wasn't worried about her reaction, per se, but I was interested to see just how she'd react – and I was disappointed when, instead of smiling or squealing as she was wont to do, she frowned.

"Ah, shit," she said, walking over to Phil. She dug through her bag, producing a five- pound note and handing it to him. "I've been keeping that on me since my birthday, you know. I really thought they'd hold out on telling us until the Ren Faire."

"Nah," Phil said, napping the bank note in front of him before pocketing it. "No way they were keeping that secret for more than a month. You guys only made my deadline by a couple of days, so thank you."

"I'm sorry," Jack said, and I looked up to see him staring at them with his mouth agape. "You *both* knew about this?"

Chloe laughed. "Please, you two have been making googly eyes at each other for months. This was an inevitability."

"I would have known even if I hadn't been there," Phil said, setting the food down on the coffee table.

Chloe punched him on the arm. "I'm sorry, you were *there*? You didn't tell me that!"

"It was even at your birthday," Phil said tauntingly, and Chloe groaned.

"Nobody tells me anything," she said.

Jack and I looked at each other disbelievingly. If there had been any part of us that had been nervous about this, it was long gone.

"Well, we're telling you now," Jack said.

"Fat lot of good that does," Chloe replied, rolling her eyes. She slumped down on the sofa next to me and put her head on my shoulder, where Jack patted it. "Congrats, I guess."

"Thanks," I said, leaning my head on hers. "Very touching."

"Listen," Phil said, coming to sit on the other side of me, leaving Jack without a seat. His house had been designed for three at a time. "Since you're here, I've actually got some Ren Faire stuff to show you."

"Ooh, yes please," I said as Phil pulled out his phone.

"Here's the chain mail," he said, pulling up a picture of what finally looked like a shirt. "We'll have to spray paint it like I said, but we're getting there."

"That's incredible," I said, thankful that I wouldn't have to lug around a fully metal shirt all day. I was sure I was more capable now than ever, with the adventure-packed summer I'd had, but I didn't relish the idea.

"So are you two like, boyfriend-girlfriend now?" Chloe asked.

"I mean…" I started, tilting my chin back to look at Jack.

"You okay with that?" he asked. He held my gaze softly, like he was just asking me if I wanted a cup of tea.

"Yes," I said. "I am." He smiled gently, his eyes wrinkling in the corners like I loved, and he pressed an upside down, Spider-man-style kiss to my lips.

"This is all very sweet," Phil said, "but if you're going to be a part of film night, you have to take a turn on food. I can't keep buying these stupid expensive burgers every three weeks."

"Then don't buy the stupid expensive burgers," Jack said. "No one makes you go to Five Guys every time it's your turn."

Phil grimaced, like Jack's reply was pure blasphemy.

Jack sat in front of me on the floor, and I leaned forward to drape my arms over his shoulders, pressing the side of my face to his. He scrolled through the app on the TV to find the film we'd picked out: some obscure sci-fi release he'd had his eye on. They'd agreed to watch *It*, but with me joining, horror was off the table. I'd have to make sure I didn't crash every single film night so they could still get their spooky fix.

As the opening credits started, I finally let myself settle into the sofa and into the moment. If this was my new normal, I was more than happy with that. I only hoped it would go as well with his family the next day.

But I wasn't left to revel in my satisfaction for long.

"So, what was that at work earlier?" Chloe asked. "With Aaron?"

My stomach dropped.

"Everything okay with the gala?" Jack asked from the other side of me. "Aaron being unhelpful again?"

Over the last few weeks, Jack had become intimately familiar with the logistics for the gala. He knew about every drawing, every spreadsheet, and every vendor conversation; venting to him had, I was pretty sure, been the only thing keeping me sane.

"Yeah, he's fine," I said. "I mean, well, no, he's still hugely unhelpful. But that's not what was happening." I pleaded with Chloe with my gaze to change the subject, but we'd always been terrible at telepathy.

"Then what was?" Chloe asked. "He seemed excited about something, and I haven't heard him willingly talk about anything but his unborn child in months."

I had my back resting against Jack, but I felt him look down at me. There was no good reason not to tell him. It was weird that I hadn't told him already, even. But something in the back of my mind knew that it was a can of worms.

"Well..." I started, grateful I only had to look at Chloe. "He's leaving, actually. And Simone says I can have his job if we hit our goal next week."

Chloe shrieked and clapped for the second time this

evening; she almost spilled her drink down me in the process. "That's so great!" she said. "That's a killer promotion!"

"I know," I said, trying to sound more enthusiastic than I felt, "but nothing's official yet."

"Still," she said. "That's amazing you're being considered. I'm so jealous. And only mildly annoyed that I'll have to keep covering part of your call list."

I finally mustered the courage to look up at Jack, who was smiling; of course he was. Because he thought this meant more than it did.

Suddenly I was grateful we had a film to watch so I couldn't find out why.

CHAPTER 34
CAPTAIN MORGANA SILVERSWORD

It took some persuading, but Lord Arnault finally agreed to see them in his chambers. They waited for hours at the palace gates – Morgana had never had to wait for admittance, and she was frustrated at being waylaid – before he sent for them to be brought to his study.

Lord Arnault was a slight man, with a chin puff beard long enough to touch his chest. His face was gaunt, implying an age beyond his actual years, and Morgana had always wondered if that added to his air of authority. He'd certainly curried favour with the Queen unusually quickly, ousting several other advisors in the process.

"I take it you have succeeded on your mission?" Arnault asked as the party walked into the room. He didn't gesture for them to sit opposite him at the large desk, nor did he offer them any refreshments after their travels and their long wait.

"We have," Yorick said, "but we have some questions for you."

"Very well." Arnault smiled wide, and the expression looked unnatural on his face. "What are your questions?"

Yorick looked back at Thrormir, and Morgana could see him readying the spell. But when he went to cast it, he just frowned. He exchanged glances with Morgana and with Yorick, shrugging, a confused look on his face.

"That won't work in here," Arnault said, standing up. He was almost as tall as Gorlag, and he moved around the desk with an otherworldly ease. He rapped his knuckles on the wood-panelled walls. "I have very specific protections in place. But if you'd like to ask me a question, you may."

"Great," Calamity said, breaking from the plan. "We wanna know what you're gonna do with it."

Yorick smacked her leg and jutted his chin out at her; he was usually the one to do the talking, and for good reason. But Calamity could be persuasive when she wanted to.

"Great question," Arnault said, perching on the edge of the desk closest to the party, who all took a half-step back unconsciously. "I take it that means you've learned what the Sphere does?"

When the party didn't answer, Arnault cleared his throat.

"That's very good. And it's so touching that you're asking that question. You really are heroes, you know? The exact right people for the job."

"Then tell us what it's for," Thrormir said, and Morgana could hear a slight tremble in his voice. Whatever he could sense in Arnault, it wasn't good. She moved her hand to the hilt of her sword, only for Arnault to snap his eyes to hers.

"Uh-uh," he tutted her, and waved a finger. "There will be none of that. I've just had the place cleaned."

Morgana narrowed her eyes at him and looked him over, her eyes landing on the lapel of his tunic. Stitched into it, the same colour as the fabric, was a twelve-pointed star.

Arnault snapped his fingers, and suddenly cloaked figures

stepped into existence all around them. In an instant they found themselves outnumbered two to one. The figures were all completely faceless, as if magic were distorting their appearance. One held a knife to Morgana's throat, and she could see that her companions were equally indisposed. She held her hands up in surrender, then reached out a foot to kick Gorlag when they were the only one who didn't immediately follow suit.

"You'll never find it," Calamity said, struggling against her captor. The party had had the foresight not to bring the Sphere with them, instead lowering it into a disused well a mile out of town.

Arnault stepped closer and locked eyes with Calamity, and she stilled.

"It's in the well on the old Biltreb farm east of the city," he said to a cloaked figure next to him, who nodded and strode out of the room. The others produced shackles, moving to restrain the party.

"You won't get away with this," Morgana spat, daring Arnault to look at her. She was working out a move to make, but there didn't seem to be a way to get at her captor or Arnault without putting her friends' lives at risk.

"Take them to the dungeon," Arnault commanded, then looked Morgana dead in the eye. "The full moon is tomorrow."

CHAPTER 35
JACK

Mum insisted that we all sit in the garden for a glass of wine, despite the fact that Fool's Autumn was still in full swing. All of us but Dad were draped in blankets and bundled in multiple layers; I knew Morgan was wearing her own socks under the pair of mine I could see peeking out of her boots. I'd also had to be the one to get the garden ready, including pruning some of the plants encroaching on the patio, and, as Chloe predicted, clearing masses of spiderwebs off the bug hotel.

"So darling," Mum said as she refilled Morgan's wine without asking, "tell us, what are your parents like?"

I winced; I hadn't remembered to prep Mum on the fact that Morgan didn't have a dad. I looked apologetically at her, but she just smiled at me. She was fine, and she had Mum eating out of the palm of her hand. She pressed her knee to mine under the table, and even after weeks of having basically unlimited contact, this small form still sent a heat wave through me.

"Mum used a donor to have me, so I don't know my dad," Morgan said, as if her history was run-of-the-mill. Which, I supposed, it was for her. "Mum was a librarian, but she retired when I went to uni."

"Oh lovely," Mum said, thankfully skipping past the part about Morgan's mum using a donor. "That sounds so nice, being retired. Does she do a lot of gardening? Maybe a touch of writing?"

"You should know, Mum," Amy said from across the table. "You haven't worked since I was born."

Mum's mouth fell open and she reeled back. "You know very well that's not true, young lady. I stay very busy."

"Yeah, chucking bee bombs onto the sides of the motorway."

"It's much more involved than that," Mum insisted to Morgan. "I'm the chair of multiple committees, I'll have you know."

I'd told Morgan before that Mum volunteered for the local rewilding trust; she nodded back at Mum dutifully.

"And what was the latest committee decision you made?" Amy asked. "Something about what kind of lamps to get in the office?"

Mum sighed. "It was assessing grow lamps for environmental impact," she said. "So we can make sure the native species we're cultivating are grown as sustainably as possible."

"Your mother's work is very important," Dad said, the first time he'd spoken since introducing himself to Morgan. "Now let's move on, please." Amy sat back and rolled her eyes, but she didn't push; Dad had a way of squashing the squabbles that inevitably arose between them. And when he said something was done, it was done.

"Thank you dear," Mum said, then turned back to Morgan, waiting for an answer as if the conversation hadn't halted long enough for a whole argument to unfold.

"Oh, um, she's actually travelling," Morgan explained. "Sold the house as soon as I moved out, and she's been abroad ever since. I'm pretty sure she's in Southern California at the moment, road-tripping the West Coast in a camper van. But she's been all over. Southeast Asia, North Africa, the Canadian Rockies..."

Mum's face pinched together in confusion.

"But where does she go when she comes back for Christmas? Your birthday?"

Morgan shook her head. "She doesn't. I haven't actually seen her in person in about two years. The last time was when she came back for a family funeral."

"Oh, so you must speak on the phone all the time," Mum said, concocting an explanation that made the idea of being permanently away from one's children even slightly more tolerable. But Morgan shook her head again.

"She sends postcards," she said. "And emails. And we talk every few months or so. On my birthday, as you said. And hers, and Mother's Day."

Mum just blinked at Morgan, as if waiting for her to laugh and say she'd been joking. But when she didn't, Mum visibly shivered and went back to pointlessly swirling her wine in her glass.

"Jack's been telling me about the new project you've got coming up," Morgan said, and it took me a moment to realise she was talking to Dad. It took him a moment, too, to the point that we were all looking at him before he looked up from his glass.

"Oh, yeah, biggest we've done," Dad said. "Should put us on the map with some of the bigger developers investing in the area."

It was almost the exact same spiel he'd given me when we'd first taken the job.

"Is that important?" Morgan asked. "Is there a lot of competition for the smaller jobs?"

Dad sort of half-chuckled, looking at me as if I would intervene. But I just shrugged. I didn't know where she was going with this any better than he did.

"Not really," he said, setting his fork down and leaning forward onto his elbows, "but the bigger jobs have much better profit margins. We can work a lot more efficiently."

"Interesting," Morgan said, taking a sip. "Seems like it creates an awful lot of admin, right? That's what Jack has been dealing with?"

Dad nodded. "A bit more than we're used to, but what's a bit more admin for that kind of profit margin increase?"

Morgan shrugged. "Well, a lot if you hate admin, I suppose."

Dad laughed – a big hearty laugh that echoed, even outside – and pointed at Morgan. "You're funny, Morgan. She's funny, Jack."

"Sure is," I said, but I wasn't laughing. I glared down at Morgan, fully aware of what she was doing. She looked up at me and smiled, but her smile faltered when she saw that I wasn't impressed.

"Well, I'm glad to have you here," Mum said, her voice strained with emotion. Was she seriously on the verge of tears? "Our Jackie here hasn't always been so lucky in love."

"Mum!" I said, begging her with my eyes to stop – or, better yet, to rewind time and not be embarrassing as fuck – but she just shrugged at me.

"What?" she asked, oblivious.

"Maybe not the best time to bring up Aria?" Amy offered, but that wasn't much better, so I glared at her, too.

"It's fine," Morgan said quietly to me. "It's not like I didn't know."

"Still," I said, "it's a bit pointed, isn't it?"

"Well, fine then," Mum said. "I suppose I'll never say anything lovely or sentimental again, how's that?"

"Great, Mum," I said, sitting back and downing the last of my glass of wine. "Perfect, actually."

THE REST of the evening went as well as it could have: Dad was more talkative, Mum managed to avoid asking any overly embarrassing questions, and Amy gave Morgan a chunk of rose quartz, apparently to help with "bourgeoning love". As we left to go back to mine for some food, a walk of shame made no less awkward by Amy whistling after us, Morgan snaked an arm around my waist and leaned into me. I draped my arm over her shoulder, but she must have sensed that my heart wasn't in it, because she looked up at me in concern and, when she saw the frown on my face, clearly decided she would wait until we were inside my house to talk about it, dropping her arm away from me.

"That wasn't funny," I said quietly as soon as the door was shut. "That comment about the admin?"

Morgan rolled her eyes and threw her hands out to the sides as she walked ahead of me into the kitchen. "Your dad seemed to think it was."

I pulled two beers out of the fridge and slid one across to her.

"Yeah, well, my dad doesn't know why you were asking. If he'd had all the context, I can assure you he wouldn't have been laughing."

"Well, maybe he should have the context," she said as she sat down at the island, and I shot her a look I knew probably rivalled the glare Dad often used with me. But it didn't work on her. "Seriously," she continued. "Does he even know you don't like doing that part of the job?"

"No," I said, "because that's not true." My voice was slightly raised now.

"Don't bullshit me," Morgan said, matching my tone. "You fucking hate this stuff." She flicked at a stack of papers on the end of the island, weighted down by my laptop.

"Well yeah," I said, "but everyone hates paperwork. I like knowing that Dad can retire when he wants, and know that his business is in good hands."

"Is it actually in good hands if those hands don't want it?" Morgan asked, very quietly, and I narrowed my eyes at her. She narrowed hers back, and we just glared at each other for a moment. She was hamming it up: the oppositional posture, pointing her two fingers at her eyes and then at me, baring her teeth at me. She was trying to defuse the tension, and it was up to me whether I let her.

"Whatever," I said, deciding that I didn't want to fight with her.

Part of me wanted to dig my heels in. Because it wasn't just this thing with my dad, was it? We still hadn't talked about the revelation last night that she'd apparently got a promotion at work. And we definitely hadn't caught up about what that meant for the other jobs I knew she'd been applying to. At least, I was pretty sure she had been, because why else would she be putting off looking for a place to live?

But if that meant a fight, I wasn't ready to be the one to cause it. We'd bickered plenty when we were just friends, but we hadn't had a proper fight since we'd got together. Probably because we hadn't burst the bubble until now. I wondered if, now that our relationship was out in the open, this kind of spat would happen more often.

But I didn't want to spat with Morgan. Not now, and not ever if I could help it.

I walked around the island towards her so we could kiss and make up, but she was looking down at her phone, her face completely slack save for a crease between her eyebrows. Something was wrong. A dozen possible tragedies flashed through my mind – her mum was in some horrible parasailing accident, or her house had burned down, or her house had sold, or Pablo had got sick, or Pablo had been adopted – but I refused to let myself panic until she filled me in.

"What is it?" I asked. She finally looked up at me, and her face drooped in sadness.

"Don't have that," she said, pointing at my beer. "We need to leave."

"Why?" I asked, the panic creeping in anyway. "What's happened?"

She pressed her mouth together in a line and sighed, and I braced myself against the worktop for the worst.

"It's Fatima."

CHAPTER 36
JACK

The intensity with which girls rallied around each other had always made me a little jealous. Morgan hadn't even known Fatima for a year, but the way she'd glued herself to Fatima's side, one might have thought they'd shared a womb.

After eleven years together, Fatima and Jared had broken up. Or, if Morgan's secondhand account were anything to go by, Jared had dumped Fatima out of the blue. When I'd questioned that – I'd been friends with Jared after all – the ferocity with which Morgan insisted that's how it was had me backing down instantly.

I was glad that Fatima had the others, but I was worried about Jared, too. He'd seemed so tired when I'd seen him at Chloe's party; if I hadn't been so distracted, I might have followed up. I felt I owed it to him to give him the benefit of the doubt. So whilst Morgan worked on gala prep from Fatima's a couple of days after it happened, I took advantage of a few minutes alone on my deck and called Jared.

"Hey, man," he said as he answered, and if I'd thought he

looked tired at Chloe's party, he sounded like he had one foot in the grave.

"Hey, mate," I said, sitting forward in my seat. "You don't sound so great."

"I don't feel so great," he said, punctuating with a sad chuckle. "It's been a shit few days. Few months, really."

"Was it the long distance?" I asked, beelining straight to the point. I knew I should have been a bit more subtle, maybe worked up to it, but the moment I'd heard the news, I'd made it about Morgan and me. About her job hunt, and the fact that we might soon be in the same position.

"Um, sort of," he said. "I mean, it's not been great. I really don't recommend it."

My shoulders sank, and I sat back against the rocking chair. "I can imagine."

"I got the job I wanted," he said. "Manager."

"That's great!" I said, but then I remembered what he'd told me at Chloe's birthday. "Wait, wasn't that the promotion that was supposed to bring you back? Did you leave the company?"

I heard him sigh on the other end of the line. "Not the company, mate. The country."

It turned out that manager roles at smaller regional offices were super competitive; not only was he competing against other people from that office, but from others who wanted to move out of the city. His only hope of getting it would have been to commute to Birmingham and go for the role there, or to move to a different city. And when the opportunity had presented itself for him to transfer to America, he'd taken it. San Francisco, to be specific.

"Jesus, man," I said, trying to sound supportive.

"I know. It's been so wild."

"I'm kind of surprised, actually," I said, deciding to be

honest. "When I talked to you a few weeks ago, you guys seemed fine. You were even talking about moving back here to be with her. What changed?"

Jared was quiet for a long time, and I was on tenterhooks waiting for his reply as if it was a portent for my own future.

"I guess I just got honest with myself," he said. "I loved Fatima. I still do, obviously. But I didn't want to live in a small town. That was her thing. I just wanted to be with her. And when I asked myself if I was okay giving up everything else I wanted for her, the answer was no. And I can't be mad at myself about that."

Well I can, I thought, but helpfully I kept that to myself, settling for "fair enough" instead. And it was fair enough, I supposed. If he didn't love her enough that she made up for everything else, it was better that he was gone.

"How's she doing?" he asked, quietly enough that I almost didn't hear him.

"I don't know, really," I said. "Morgan's been over there a lot, but she hasn't told me much. Says Fatima's being pretty stoic about it."

"Hey, you two finally got together!" he said, and he sounded genuinely happy for a moment. "Good for you, man."

"Thanks," I said. "It happened the night I saw you, actually."

"That's awesome," he said. "You really deserve it, man."

We talked a bit more about where he'd be in San Francisco, and I told him that the next time he was around, we should get a drink. That he had a friend in me still. And he did; I didn't like the idea that he was public enemy number one because of a decision he'd made for what, from the sound of it, was a perfectly valid reason.

But as I hung up the call, I didn't feel better. I felt so much worse. Because as well as I understood Jared's decision, I knew that, if Morgan and I went the same way, I was going to be the one heartbroken at home.

For the first time since Morgan and I had got together, I felt terrified. The weight began to pool in my stomach like it had every time she'd tried to get close to me. And no matter how hard I tried, I couldn't shake the thought that Morgan and I might just have an expiry date.

No one was surprised when Fatima cancelled our session on Monday. We talked about going to the pub still, but Chloe thought it would be better to just pretend that Monday didn't exist, and to come back swinging the next week. Fatima insisted she'd be okay by then, though I knew she wouldn't actually be okay for a long time. I didn't suspect it was possible to get over an eleven year relationship in a week.

We were only three days out from the gala, and I knew Morgan had freelance work to do, too, but she insisted she'd accounted for the game in her planning. She wanted to go on another little adventure – "get some last-minute XP before our trip", she said – so I picked out a spot for us to do some stargazing. But come Monday, the classic British weather made an appearance.

"If you wanted to have the river to ourselves," I said as we both looked out her front window at the rain, "this would actually be the perfect weather for some kayaking."

"I think I'll pass," she said, screwing her face up, but not looking up from her phone, where I could see her posting some of her recent freelance work on her social media. It was my turn to pull a face; maybe it was my post-Aria prejudice, but it bothered me how obsessively she would check her "post performance" each day.

"Oh come on," I said. "You've never done it before. That's worth at least five hundred XP for sure."

Morgan shook her head. "Nope, no thanks. You go for it, though."

I frowned when I saw her open up a new post and start editing one of her recent designs for it. Was she really going to stay home and post promotional material when she'd been the one to ask me to plan an adventure? Sure, it wasn't the one I'd initially thought of, but it wasn't like I was asking to go skydiving. And honestly, I really liked the sound of the idea. I hadn't been on a solo adventure in months; Morgan and I had been practically attached at the hip, certainly since getting together, and realistically before that, too. So the idea of having the river to myself wasn't the worst sounding way to spend the evening.

"Yeah, okay," I said, talking myself into it. "I think I will."

"Wait, what?" Morgan snapped her gaze to me. "Seriously?"

"Yeah." I shrugged. "Why not?"

"Um, let's see, because it's raining? Because it's not safe?"

I laughed softly. "I'll be fine," I said, reaching out a hand to squeeze her shoulder, but she dodged it, sliding out of her seat instead.

"Fine," she said as she put her phone face-down on the seat, "but I don't like being manipulated like this, Jack."

It took me a moment to realise what she meant. "I wasn't trying to manipulate you into coming," I insisted. "I just wanted to push you, because you're the one who said you wanted to do something interesting."

"Well excuse me for having my own ideas about what I do and don't want that to look like," she snapped.

Unlike our little spat over the weekend after she'd met my

family, there was a real bite to her words now. It sucked the air out of the room. I was trying to decide how to respond when she sighed and plopped back down onto the seat.

"I'm sorry," she said. "That was a bit intense."

"Yeah, a bit," I said. "You okay?"

She snapped her gaze up to look at me. "Why, because I must not be okay if I disagree with you about something?" Almost immediately, the intensity drained from her eyes, and she brought her hand to her forehead. "Sorry, I did it again."

I'd learned my lesson; I stayed quiet this time. I just sat down next to her and put a hand on her knee, stroking it with my thumb.

"I'm just so stressed about the gala, and about work in general..."

"What else is going on?" I asked.

"Well, this promotion," she said. "If everything goes well on Thursday, I'll get Aaron's job. But the problem is, I kind of hate his job."

"Yeah, but didn't you hate your job before, too?"

"That's kind of the point," she said, shrugging. "That's why I've been trying to find a new one."

So she had been actively applying. Maybe even interviewing. Even since we got together, from the sound of it.

"How far have you gotten with that?" I asked, trying to sound as casual as possible, but I was no longer breathing.

Morgan looked up at me, her eyebrows pressed together. I wasn't fooling her. "Pretty far, actually," she said. "I've got a final interview booked with one in a week."

"One of the ones I sent you?" I asked, looking down at my hand on her knee to try to keep from giving myself away, but my voice was starting to shake.

Morgan nodded.

"Which one?"

It took her several seconds to answer, during which she swallowed hard and looked down as well, placing her hand over mine, lacing our fingers together.

"The software company," she said. "The one in York."

Whoomp, there it is.

"You're thinking about moving to York?" I asked, and I didn't even try to hide the disbelief in my voice. I felt my hand tense on her knee, so I yanked it away before she could feel it.

"You sent it to me," she said, still calm, but not really answering my question. Which I guessed was a question in and of itself.

"Yeah, I know I did," I said. I sort of hated Past Jack for basically giving her the green light to leave me, but I also knew we probably wouldn't have got together had I not extended that olive branch. But knowing that didn't make it sting any less.

"This doesn't change anything between us," she said, reaching out for my hand, but I moved it away. I wouldn't hold her hand whilst she explained how it was okay that she was possibly moving hundreds of miles away.

"How can you say that?" I asked, running my fingers through my hair, holding my head in my hands. "Of course things will change. We've spent almost every night together for over a month."

"That's not fair," she said, and I still didn't look at her, but I could hear the scowl in her voice, all hard consonants and over-enunciation.

"You know what's not fair? You not telling me about this until now."

"I didn't want to freak you out if it wasn't going to happen," she said, her voice cracking slightly.

"Oh, so you admit that you knew it would freak me out," I

said. "Which means some part of you knows that things *have* changed. Or at least they have for me. Have I been deluding myself about what this is?" I gestured back and forth between us.

She shook her head. "You're the one that sent me the listing to begin with. I'm not letting you make me feel bad for following the course you laid out for me."

"That's not what I was doing," I said, but she held up a hand to stop me.

"I can't do this right now," she said. "It's a moot point until I know if I've even gotten the job."

Morgan moved to the sofa and opened her laptop; clearly the conversation was over. I didn't want it to be, and I knew I could push it, and the spat could turn into an all-out fight. I could feel it brewing and knew it would happen eventually, one way or another.

But as I watched her instantly lock into whatever she was doing on her laptop – probably more gala prep, or freelance work – I could tell how overloaded she felt. How one more straw might break her back in two. And as strongly as I felt about the conversation we needed to have, I didn't want to be that straw. To risk pushing her further away. I could press pause instead.

CHAPTER 37
MORGAN

About two-thirds of the way through the most stressful night of my life so far, I finally got a chance to take a deep breath. I pulled myself off the path to lean against the castle wall, narrowly dodging a caterer carrying a tray of champagne. I closed my eyes and tried to focus my breathing, feeling the rough stone on the back of my shoulders. Another niggle popped up telling me it was probably snagging my dress, but the night was over anyway, so I batted it away.

The past four hours had been like playing a logistical game of whack-a-mole; I'd had to deal with everything from last-minute guests to an interpersonal conflict between three members of the string quartet. It seemed two of the violin players were both sleeping with the cellist, and shit was hitting the fan. I'd had to threaten them with withholding the rest of their fee to get them to play nicely, and even then I'd heard what sounded like some competitive violin playing during the silent auction.

But the gala was past the point of no return – the logistics were done, and guests were officially just mingling – and months and months of stress could finally be put behind me.

I'd been told countless times how lovely the event was, both by guests and employees. And looking around at the crumbling castle around me, I had to admit it was definitely an upgrade from last year's boring hotel ballroom. The bunting and string lights looked genuinely magical zig-zagging across the courtyard formed by the ruined walls, offering a glimpse of what I hoped the Ren Faire would be like. We hadn't even had to use the marquee or two hundred umbrellas we'd hired, because the rain had held off. I'd have to make sure everything came down in a couple of hours, but whilst there were still guests dancing and drinking, I could pretend that was further off than it was.

Plus, it had been pretty thrilling to see my designs come to life everywhere. I'd been staring at the printed materials for weeks, but seeing the seating chart on the easel and the signs hung from the historic stone walls, I felt a pride that buoyed me all night.

Jack had been my anchor in the storm. Despite how shell-shocked I knew he was from finding out about the York job – despite how close we'd come to an actual fall-out the other night – he'd stayed by my side with a cup of tea at the ready since then, and he'd been a quiet shelter for me several times throughout the night.

The cynical part of me did wonder if it was him trying to ingratiate me; to manipulate me into feeling bad about exploring all my options. I could tell from the look in his eyes when I caught him staring at me that there was a lot on his mind, and I didn't blame him. I'd been thinking a lot about it, too. Still, though, I was grateful for the support, regardless of the motives.

Chloe looked gorgeous, of course, her burgundy strapless gown with a thigh-high slit somehow complementing rather than clashing with her red hair. She looked like Jessica Rabbit, actually. I'd opted for comfort myself – a simple black sheath dress with a shawl, and black flats I could scurry around in easily – but Jack had told me I looked beautiful in it anyway.

For me, the highlight of the night had been Pablo. Lauren had brought some of the dogs to play with the guests, and Pablo had whined for Jack and me the moment he'd spotted us. I'd been able to steal just a couple of minutes with him, especially whilst Lauren was distracted by Chloe putting the moves on her, and though I'd had to take a lint roller to my dress afterwards, it had calmed me enough after managing the dinner service to tackle the silent auction.

The night had been a smashing success from a fundraising perspective. The silent auction alone had met our target, and the call for donations at the end had almost matched the contributions again. Whether Aaron had been conservative in his estimates, or the event had just been that much of a hit, I wasn't sure; I wanted to think it was the latter, despite how much I'd hated being the one to orchestrate it. On some level, it would make it all feel worth it.

But the bittersweet side of raising so much money was that I knew Simone would be offering me the promotion officially. And just like when she'd first mentioned the possibility, I knew I should be grateful. Jumping for joy, even. But I couldn't bring myself to feel excited.

"Well done," Jack said, appearing suddenly beside me, making me jump. The blue light caught his blonde hair, making him look like a fae prince or something. I arched away from the wall so he could wrap his arm around my back, and I leaned my head against his chest as we watched Chloe flirting with Lauren on the other side of the courtyard.

I let my eyes shut for just a moment. I couldn't wait to get into bed later, especially next to Jack. "Did you have a nice time?"

"Yeah, really nice," he said, "though I could have done without Chloe's running commentary about which couples she thought she could break up if she wanted to."

"I'm glad she waited until *after* they gave us their money," I said. "That was kind of her."

"Speaking of which," Jack said, shifting against me as he used the hand around my waist to reach into his jacket pocket. "I have a last-minute donation."

I looked down at the pledge card he'd filled out. The amount line read "£500.00."

I squinted at him, trying to figure out why he wanted to donate so much. Part of me wondered if he was trying to do what he could to help us hit the goal so that I'd be offered the promotion. I didn't like that it was my first thought when he was being really generous, but that didn't change the fact that it felt like a loaded gesture.

"Jack, that's really unnecessary," I said, smiling up at him as thankfully as I could. "We brought in almost twice what we expected to. But I really appreciate the sentiment."

He shook his head. "It's not for you. Presumably they could always do with a bit more for the animals."

"Well, yeah, but—"

"No buts about it," Jack said. "I can't adopt one of them, so this is the next best thing. I want to help."

"Okay..." I said, not sure what to say to convince him to keep his money, and even less sure why I wanted to. He was right;

every little bit helped. But after he'd learned about my likely promotion, and about the other jobs I'd applied to, it was hard not to read into it.

"Do you not want me to give the money?" he asked, a slight edge of annoyance in his voice.

"It's not that," I said with a sigh. "It just feels really pointed after our conversation on Monday, doesn't it?"

Jack pulled his arm out from behind me and ran his hand over his face. As if he were the one who felt dead on his feet, not me. "Morgan, not everything is about you, okay?"

The comment was so unexpectedly condescending that I physically reeled back. It seemed my news had got to him more than he'd let on, after all.

"Then what is it about?" I asked, trying not to raise my voice; the last of the guests were still filtering out. "Walk me through your decision making."

"If you must know," he said, still condescending, as if he were dealing not with his girlfriend but with a petulant child, "it was about Pablo. Because I've grown to love the little guy, and I feel bad that I couldn't adopt him because of my house and my job. So I tallied up how much I thought it would cost to adopt him, and this is the number I came up with." He flicked the pledge card with his free hand. "There, happy?"

I closed my eyes and exhaled slowly. "I'm sorry," I said, keeping my tone measured. "But my first thought was that my boyfriend's generosity came from an ulterior motive, and his first response was to tell me it wasn't all about me, and to treat me like an idiot. So how could I be happy?" I opened my eyes to meet his gaze, expecting to find him looking sad, or even apologetic. But his eyes looked dead. Cold. Unfeeling. Just the way they had every time he'd put up his walls with me in the past.

"Well, I'm so sorry you're so unhappy," he said, keeping his tone low, too, but practically spitting his words out. "Maybe you should pull a Jared and just bow out."

The suggestion hit me like a slap, and I actually gasped.

But I didn't get a chance to react, because Chloe wandered over, Lauren having abandoned her to get the dogs back to the rescue. I willed her to look at me so I could just shake my head and get her to go away, but she was too busy looking at the grass, making sure her heels didn't sink into it, and my attempts at telepathy failed again.

"You ready to go?" she asked Jack, but the moment she looked up and saw our faces, she stopped in her tracks. "Woah, what the hell did I just walk into?"

"Nothing," Jack spat, not looking away from me.

"Hey," I said, admonishing him. "It's Chloe. Don't be a dick."

He sighed deeply and clenched his jaw. "Sorry, Chlo. Please just give us a minute."

Chloe lifted the skirt of her dress and opened her mouth as if to speak, but I interrupted her.

"It's fine," I said to him. "I think *you* should go."

He balked at me, as if the suggestion hurt him, but what did he expect? We were at my *job*. I didn't want to have it out with him on an already-stressful day in front of my colleagues. I'd thought he'd understood that, which was why he hadn't brought all this up again since our fight on Monday. But clearly it had been *my* restraint, not his, that had kept this at bay.

"Fine," he said, looking away from me at last. "Come on, Chloe." He started walking towards the exit, quickly enough that there was no way Chloe would have been able to keep up.

"Are you sure you don't need me?" she asked me. "You okay?"

"Those are two different questions," I said, looking up at the sky so I wouldn't start crying. "Yes, I'll be fine. I need to get back to work." I stepped over to her and wrapped her in a hug. "But no, Chloe. I don't think Jack and I are okay."

∼

The rest of the evening was uneventful, which was good for everyone. I was finally able to go home at about one in the morning, where I proceeded to crash so immediately that I discovered the next morning I hadn't taken off the tights I'd been wearing, leaving them on under my pyjamas instead.

Waking up in pyjamas was weird enough; I'd woken up naked next to Jack most mornings since we'd got together. So when I opened my eyes and felt the clothes touching my skin, it was an instant reminder of what had happened.

But there was no rest for the wicked, because it was Friday, and despite the fact that I had been up until the wee hours, I still had to go to work. Even Chloe had had the foresight to take the day as holiday, but I was saving mine up, hoping for a payout when I managed to finally get a job somewhere else. Speaking of which, I'd actually taken Monday off to go to York for my final interview with the software company.

I let myself wander into the office around ten, and when I got to my desk, I saw an envelope with my name written across it sitting on my desk. My first thought was that it was somehow the pledge card from Jack that I'd never handed in, but no, it wasn't his handwriting on the front.

I looked over my shoulder to see Simone watching me from her office. I smiled, and she nodded at me and mouthed the word "congrats" before stepping back through the door. *Well, shit.*

I opened the envelope and unfolded the A4 sheet of paper inside with the charity's letterhead across the top.

Dear Morgan,

We are delighted to offer you the role of Events Coordinator, Full-Time. This promotion will be effective immediately...

CHAPTER 38
MORGAN

Early Monday afternoon, I walked out of the software company's headquarters and breathed in the misty Yorkshire air. It was colder here, and the slight nip made me feel awake and alive in a way I never did back home. There were trendy cafes, cute bookshops, and photogenic corners galore. As I sat in the window of a little hole-in-the-wall cafe for lunch, I couldn't help but pull out my tablet and draw the streets and alleyways whilst I waited for my food.

The interview had gone really well. The Head of Design had shown me around the office, giving me a chance to meet the rest of the team. One of the other designers had shown me the tools they used, and I'd even seen their design pipeline with all of the projects coming up. It was no wonder they needed someone; the queue was even longer than what I'd seen at the charity. And importantly, they seemed like nice people. Easy to get along with.

I pulled out my phone without even thinking about it, pulling up my messages with Jack as if to tell him about the interview. I hadn't spoken to him since the gala; it was the longest we'd gone without seeing each other since we got together, and the longest we'd gone without so much as a text since months before that. I stared at the last message between us – him letting me know he was on his way to the gala, and me reacting with a thumbs up – and wondered if he was just giving me space, or if he was waiting for me to make the first move. He'd sent a meme yesterday in the Wench Please chat, but nothing to me directly. I thought about messaging him to see how things were going, but then my food arrived, and I tucked into my soup and sandwich instead.

As I ate my lunch, I pulled up a quick search of flats in the area. Where the pickings back home had been slim at best, there was a lot more on offer here, and for a lot less money. I even found a charming little one-bedroom with exposed brick and an arched window, mentally furnishing it as I scrolled through the pictures. It was even pet friendly, and I pictured Pablo curled up in front of the giant window, basking in the sun.

I was only up for the day, so after lunch I started my walk back to the train station. At least I'd be back in time for D&D; after missing last week's session, I was craving it. That was one thing I'd need to figure out if I moved here; maybe there was a local gaming club or something? Or maybe, like Jared, I'd find someone at work who played. That was how I'd found my current game, after all.

As I got closer to the travel interchange, I saw signs and adverts for some of the local attractions: a deer park, ghost tours, the minster, and even day trips out to Whitby and the Yorkshire coast. I started to imagine what kind of person I'd be if I lived here: the kind to go on weekend excursions, and shop at places like Seasalt instead of Next, and appreciate the world around her a little bit more. I immediately felt a pang of sadness at the idea of living far away from my friends – from our

Monday night games, especially – but surely being on my own would motivate me to spread my wings, right? I would finally be in a place in life where I wouldn't be living according to someone else's agenda. My own place, a job I chose for myself because I wanted it, in a new, exciting city. It sounded ideal.

Except I wouldn't have Jack. I might still "have" him, if he didn't break up with me over the fights we'd already had. But he wouldn't be with me. I wouldn't get to wake up next to him. Go for Pablo walks with him. We'd spend all our spare time on trains back and forth to see one another, and trying to catch up on one another's lives, and none of it actually *being* together.

Five weeks didn't seem like a lot; I knew that. It sounded brand new. If someone else had told me they had been dating someone for five weeks, I would have mentally filed that under "barely together". But it hadn't felt that way with Jack and me. Five weeks – after months of dancing around each other, anyway – had felt like the first steps into something big. Something life-changing. Maybe even something permanent. And to roll back all of that time, all of that progress, because our friend's boyfriend dumped her? It felt unfair.

But I knew it wasn't just the breakup; it was their whole situation. I'd never found their arrangement particularly appealing, even when we'd thought everything was fine.

As I sat down at a table on my train home, my vision of who I could be started to unravel. After all, I was only the brave, adventurous version of myself because of Jack, right? Because he'd pushed me? So who would I be if I pushed him away? And would that make things worse, or possibly be for the best?

For a moment I thought about texting Cara, but she'd missed so much context over the last few months that I knew she wouldn't understand. I thought I'd grieved that friendship already, but I felt a fresh sting as I realised I had no one to speak to about this other than the friends I shared with Jack. I'd have to muscle through it on my own.

I put on my headphones and pulled up my Daylist, and just as I pressed play, a notification appeared at the top of the screen. It was a message from Jack:

> Can we talk after the game tonight?

I was so relieved he'd been the one to break the seal, and I texted back before I could even think about my response:

> Yes. I'll be there.

And as soon as I finished sending it, another notification popped up, this one from my email. Just above a still-unread update from my mum was one from the software company. *Already?*

Attached was the second job offer letter I'd received in as many business days.

Suddenly York Morgan was nowhere to be seen. If she'd been the one reading the offer, surely I would have been over the moon, right? Ready to go on a brand new adventure; carpe the diem and all that jazz. But it was Real Life Morgan reading the letter, and all she wanted was to go hide away in her house with her dog and her lover.

But none of those things were *mine*. Certainly not the house and the dog, and the lover was tenuous at best. And as scared as Real Life Morgan felt, she needed to grow up. She needed to refuse to stay stuck in Jack's little world of safety, and focus on building a life she could actually call her own, whether that included him or not.

I GOT BACK with just enough time to change before heading to Fatima's; I didn't really fancy answering questions about why I was dressed like I was cosplaying as a girlboss. But as I came up the road, I saw a group of three people huddled at the front door to the house. At first I wondered if maybe it was my friends, or even Cara's parents, but then I remembered that there was supposed to be a viewing today. It should have been over hours ago, but maybe, since I'd told Cara's mum I'd be out all day, they'd rescheduled it.

I slowed as I got closer, not sure whether to try to go inside with them standing there or just keep going. In the end I decided to loiter out by the street, sitting down on the kerb as if I were waiting for someone to pick me up. I was definitely going to be late now.

I glanced over my shoulder to see if I could get away with watching them, but the middle-aged woman dressed – well, like I was, actually – was looking almost directly at me. I recognised her as the estate agent from the online listing, and from the emails Cara's mum had forwarded; Paula, I was pretty sure her name was. She was speaking to a young couple, who looked not much older than Jack and me. The fact that anyone my age was in a position to buy the house I'd been renting made me feel a bit sick.

"I mean, I think we'd want to do quite a bit to it," the man said. "It desperately needs a cellar conversion, and we'd want to apply for a drop kerb for a driveway."

I imagined the overgrown front garden being paved over for this guy's car, and I almost turned around to tell them about the red clover and spotted orchids they'd have to kill to do it. But I bit my tongue and continued to listen to all the apparent shortcomings of my beloved house.

"I reckon we go in twenty below asking," the man's partner said. "It's been on the market long enough to warrant that, I'd say."

Good, I thought. *Let them low-ball and get turned down. They don't deserve it.* But as I watched them leave and walk hand-in-hand down the street, I had a sinking feeling in my gut.

The estate agent didn't leave right away though, so I stayed still on the pavement whilst I waited for her to go. Instead, she seemed to make a phone call.

"Oh hi, it's Pauline," she said.

Oh right, Pauline.

"Well, I've got an offer for you... It's not quite at asking, no, it's actually twenty below... Yes, well, we knew this was a risk with it having been on the market for so long with no price drops... I can't advise you on that of course, but I was pleased to receive it, yes... Do you need some more time?... Oh, that's great! I'll get the ball rolling as soon as I'm back to the office. Congratulations from all of us."

I sat frozen as I heard the tap-tap of low heels come down the front path and then out the gate, which clicked shut. But even once Pauline was around the corner and out of sight, I couldn't quite bring myself to move.

CHAPTER 39
CAPTAIN MORGANA SILVERSWORD

A day and a half after their imprisonment, the party was dragged into a huge open chamber, not unlike the one where they'd found the Sphere. Their hands and feet were chained, and they were each led in by a faceless captor. Morgana tried to get a good look at them, but despite noticing differences in their attire – Yorick's captor had a crystal amulet around his neck, and Gorlag's was wearing skirts instead of trousers – they were still indistinguishable.

Arnault stood in the middle of the room clutching a crooked dagger in his hands. Next to him was a familiar sight: a pedestal, on top of which floated the Supremacy Sphere. Moonlight filtered down over it through a skylight directly above it.

Morgana had spent most of her imprisonment trying to sleep; she knew she'd need to be on top form for a fight if there were to be one. Calamity, Yorick and Thrormir had whispered all through the night, but all Morgana had heard was that their cells were blocking their magic. She wondered if that were true in here, too.

"Welcome," Arnault said. "You're just in time." As the light coming through the ceiling brightened, so did the Sphere. Morgana figured it must be close to midnight.

"Let us go," Calamity shouted, her voice on the verge of breaking.

"I can't do that, I'm afraid." Arnault stepped over to Calamity and lifted her chin with a long, bony finger. She set her jaw and glared down her nose at him.

"Then just fucking kill me already," she snarled.

Arnault sighed and rolled his eyes. "Well, that just won't do." He went down the line to each of us, looking us in the eyes. "I need someone who's desperately clinging to life." He walked down the line of them, poking his dagger out at each of them, until he reached Morgana on the end. "You," he said. "You just might do."

Morgana's chest went cold. She was a soldier; she would do what needed to be done to get the job done, even putting her own life on the line if needed. But Arnault was right. She didn't want to die.

Just when Morgana thought the Sphere couldn't possibly get any brighter, the cloaked figures, led by Arnault, began to chant. The light of the Sphere began to change, turning from blue to a more purple colour, and then from purple to red. Thankfully Arnault dropped his knife from Morgana and walked away, consulting a tome on the far side of the room.

The Sphere was almost the colour of blood when she heard Yorick muttering.

At first, Morgana thought he was chanting along with the cloaked figures, but then she saw Thrormir's shackles drop to the ground, and before his captor knew what had happened, he was racing across the chamber.

The chanting turned chaotic around them as the others – both the captors and the members of the chorus – realised what had happened. Arnault had his back to the party, but he turned around as he saw Thrormir try to knock the Sphere from the pedestal, only to be burned by its touch.

"Do mine next!" Morgana called to Yorick, but he just shook his head.

"I need my magic! Don't worry, we've got a plan."

Morgana looked back over to Arnault, who had descended upon Thrormir, his dagger drawn. There was a struggle, and with Arnault's cloak swirling around them both, Morgana struggled to make out who was winning.

The other cloaked figures moved to intervene, but suddenly a strange swirl of patterns and colours appeared in the air, and the figures began fighting each other instead. Morgana looked over at Yorick to see him grasping the crystal amulet around his captor's neck and a piece of his tunic to power the spell. The captor hung there, looking up at the swirls as if mesmerised by them.

Thrormir emerged from the fray with the knife, and Morgana whooped along with the rest of the party; it was clear from Yorick's reaction that this was the plan. But the whooping turned to gasping as, instead of attacking Arnault with the blade, Thrormir ran back over to the pedestal. He locked eyes with Morgana and mouthed the word "sorry".

Morgana frowned, and then realisation dawned, but she couldn't get free of her shackles to stop him. Instead she could just watch as he dragged the dagger across his own throat, his blood trickling down onto the Sphere.

Then the Sphere shattered, and everything went dark for Morgana.

CHAPTER 40
JACK

Morgan had been late to the game, which hadn't surprised me; I knew she'd been to York and back today for her interview. But that hadn't stopped me from watching the clock on my phone as I'd waited for her to arrive.

I hated feeling this way again. The last time I'd felt so anxious and insecure had been at the end of my relationship with Aria, where every single decision we made – where to live, what to do, what income we made – was based on her. Her opinions, her desires. I was just a support character in her life, too; maybe that was why Chloe had triggered me so badly when she suggested that was what I was in the group. But it had certainly been true in that relationship. And being a support character, it had been my job to pay attention to everything about her: her moods, her needs, the things she wanted, the hints she dropped... Making Aria happy and keeping her in business had literally been my full-time job for years.

So now, feeling that way about Morgan was awful. Not only had I been actually supporting her in the lead-up to the gala, but she was making decisions as if I would just fall into line no matter what she chose. Hell, I'd spent the weekend on my own paddling up and down the river like I'd wanted to last week, and I hadn't been able to stop myself from obsessing the whole time. Even being on the water couldn't quiet my mind like it usually did.

And I'd meant what I'd said; I did love her. But I had also promised myself that I would never let anyone else make me feel that way. I'd never allow myself to be in a life where there was no room in the frame for me.

So when Fatima surprised me by remembering to kill off Thrormir, it meant more to me than just a character change in our D&D game. It was symbolic of the fact that I didn't exist just as a refuge for the people in my life. I wanted to have my own moments; my own glory, so to speak. As long as Thrormir existed, that wouldn't have happened in-game. And as long as I let Morgan treat me like a support character in her life, it wouldn't happen in reality, either.

"Did you know he was gonna do that?" I heard Chloe ask Morgan after the game as we were clearing up. Everyone seemed a little bit shellshocked.

"No," Morgan said, looking over at me. "I certainly did not."

Her disbelief made it more plausible that we weren't up for the pub, and Fatima looked like she probably just needed to crawl into bed anyway. So Morgan and I headed out as the group dispersed post-session for the first time in months.

Once we were in the car and at the end of Fatima's road, I put on my indicator to signal right, towards my house.

"Let's go to mine," Morgan said. Instantly I knew why she wanted to go to hers. If we went to mine and she wanted to leave, she'd have to let me drive her home. But if I went to hers? Easy out.

I'd been thinking a lot about what I wanted to say to her during our weekend of no contact. It was almost painful, going that long without speaking. Every stray thought I had that I normally would have texted her – or even said out loud because she would have been with me – just fizzled out instead. But I also knew this wouldn't be a fun conversation.

I didn't want Morgan to move to York. That wasn't a new revelation; I would have said the same thing months ago, even at the start of our friendship. But I knew from last week that she wouldn't like being asked to stay, no matter what motivation I had. So I was prepared to lay down an ultimatum.

Yes, I knew that an ultimatum was the quickest way to piss her off. But it was also the only way I knew of to communicate how important this was to me more than I already had. And if I wasn't just as important to her as the other things in her life, then I wanted to know that now. I didn't want to be like Fatima, and realise eleven years down the line that I wasn't as much of a priority as I'd thought.

By the time we walked through her green front door and sat down on her green sofa, we hadn't said a word to one another. Maybe it was just me, but it felt like we both knew what the other was going to say, and we were trying to postpone the inevitable as long as possible. We were soaking wet from the rain, but neither of us seemed to care enough to dry ourselves off.

I grabbed her hand as it lay between us, squeezing her tight. I really did love her, and despite what I knew in my gut was about to happen, I wanted just one last moment with her. She squeezed my hand back, like she was holding onto this last moment before the bomb went off, too.

"I got the job," she said, and I felt the blood drain out of my body as she did. Her hand slipped out of mine as it slackened.

"Of course you did," I said. "They would have been stupid not to hire you."

"Jack..." She sounded so tired. I wasn't surprised, with everything she was juggling.

But I was tired, too, and I didn't have the stamina to beat around the bush.

"I can't do that kind of long distance," I said, my eyes fixed on my feet. "I'm sorry, because I know I'm the one that pushed you down this path. But I don't feel it's unreasonable to think that things should have changed when we got together."

"Of course things changed," she said, standing up and moving across the room, leaning against the bookshelf. "Don't you know how hard this decision has been?"

"Not hard enough," I said under my breath.

"Excuse me?" she asked, but I knew from the irritation in her voice that she'd heard me.

"Don't you realise that I love you?" I asked, looking up at her. It was the first time either of us had said those words to each other. And yeah, part of me wanted her to melt then and there, say it back, and ride off into the sunset with me.

But that didn't happen.

Instead, her back was straight, her arms were crossed, and her gaze was levelled at me. She was *pissed*.

"How dare you," she said. "That's such a cheap shot, trying to use those words to change my mind."

"Maybe they *should* change your mind!" I said, standing too. I paced over to the window seat and back again. "If you loved me, and knew I loved you, wouldn't you want to stay?"

"Not if it meant giving up what I finally know I want," she said. "Not if it meant handing over my agency to someone who can't even admit to himself what he wants for his own life."

My mouth fell open. "What the fuck does that mean?"

"You know what it means," she said, unmoving. Unblinking. But I could see the heat simmering beneath the surface. "You can't even figure out your own bullshit, let alone mine. If you had it your way, nothing would ever change."

"What are you *talking* about?" I asked, holding out my arms as if to show her everything that had changed. "There's been nothing *but* change lately. You and me, Amy moving home, Fatima and Jared breaking up—"

"There it is," she said, rolling her eyes. "I knew that had spooked you. I'm not Jared, Jack. I don't want to break up with you and move to a different continent. And if I could pick up that job and move it here, I would. But I can't do that."

"But you *do* have a perfectly good job here," I said, but I could tell from looking at her that I'd lost her. She'd made up her mind. She looked ... resigned.

"I want so much for myself, Jack. And you of all people should be proud that I feel bold enough to go after it. To boldly commit to new experiences."

I felt myself starting to clam up – to turn to stone like I had so many times before, with Morgan and otherwise – but I fought against it. This was too important. I didn't want to push her away any more than I apparently already had. So I forced myself to breathe, and to stay in the room, and to not freeze over.

"Of course I'm proud," I said, stepping towards her, and as I reached for her hands, I half expected her to move them out of reach. But she didn't, letting me grasp them between us.

"I wasn't being manipulative when I said I loved you. And it wasn't sarcasm when I said of course they gave you the job. You're brilliant, and you're so talented. I want you to have everything you want.

"But I want you to want me, too. Like I want you. Like you want all those other things for yourself."

"You want me so bad?" she asked, fire in her eyes. "Ring your dad right now. Tell him you don't want to be a contractor. Apply to that course. Apply to literally anything. Anything but the stupid family business that you hate."

"How is that fair?" I asked, dropping her hands. "I told you, *you're* what I want. I don't need the rest of that."

"But you do," she said. "You may not realise it, but— Actually, no, I think you do realise it. But you're too scared to admit it."

"Not everyone wants to go on some epic quest of self-discovery," I said. "Some of us are happy with the little, everyday adventures. Maybe if you'd bothered to embrace that, you wouldn't feel the need to move to the other side of the country to prove a point."

Her scowl deepened, and I saw her fists ball up at her sides. "This isn't about proving a point, and you know it," she said. "We've both been living our lives on other people's terms, whether you'll admit it or not. You're so desperate to keep yourself safe, you ended up shoving *yourself* out of the frame in the process. But I won't let that happen to me. At least I'm willing to do something for myself."

"Do literally anything else!" I cried, throwing my arms out to the side. "I don't want to lose you."

"Why?" she asked, her voice disconcertingly calm. "Because you're afraid of what your life will be like without me?"

"Yes," I said, stepping back towards her. "Exactly."

But before I could reach her, she stepped away.

"Exactly," she echoed. "You're so scared. Your entire life is a shrine to your fear of getting hurt. But I won't be a part of it.

And I'm tired of having to play therapist to try and get you to realise it. Level up on your own."

Her words sounded so final, and something in me realised that there was nothing I could say or do to change her mind. She was so hell bent on the fact that this was her only choice, and there was nothing that would convince her otherwise. Not my logic. Not my love. Nothing.

But I couldn't do *nothing*.

I closed the distance between us faster than she could step away, gathering her to me, wrapping my arms around her in a hug. Her hair clouded my face, and I took a deep breath in, smelling her familiar scent whilst I still could.

"Please," I said, fresh tears wetting my cheeks. "If you want to be bold, stay. I know I have a lot to figure out. But please, Morgan. Stay anyway."

"Jack..." she muttered into my shoulder, her arms limp at her sides.

"Hey, bold commitment, right?" I said, pleading. "Boldly commit to me, Morgan, please. I love you so much. I promise I won't let you down."

I begged her in my thoughts to give in; desperately hoped and imagined that I would feel her arms around me, too, and she'd relent. But she didn't, and I had to drop away. It hurt too much to hold on when she wouldn't even lift an arm to me.

As I took a step back, I saw that she, too, was crying. But they didn't look like desperate tears, like I was sure mine did. They were tears of grief.

"How can I boldly commit to someone," she said, "who won't even boldly commit to himself?"

Then she pushed past me and out of the room. I listened to her footsteps on the stairs and the click of her bedroom door, then the squeaks of her mattress springs as she sat down on the bed.

I stood there for a long time, listening for other sounds – her crying, ringing someone, anything – but the house was silent. It felt empty, like she'd already left and taken all the soul with it.

So I pulled my keys out of my trousers and removed the one to the front door, placed it on the mantle, and left through the front door, into the miserable night.

CHAPTER 41
MORGAN

When it rained, it motherfucking poured, and it had been raining since the gala – both literally and figuratively. Some of the rainfall I experienced over the following week included:

- Getting a tentative move-out date. Sure, I'd known this was coming for a while now, and I'd done very little to prepare for it. Shockingly, that didn't make it any easier.
- The dye Phil had used for my tunic/surcoat thing hadn't worked as planned, turning it bright Barbie pink. There wasn't time to make a new one, so I was mentally adjusting to being a knight in girlypop armour.
- Since I was officially promoted, I now had to start work on the Festive Fundraiser happening in December. And because Aaron had known he was leaving, he'd done exactly zero prep, so I was starting from scratch.

- I was so busy with work and freelance jobs that I hadn't drawn anything for myself in weeks, maybe longer, and as much as I wanted to, it just made me think of Jack now.
- And, oh yeah, I was single again. Fan-fucking-tastic.
- Not to mention the fact that I had to see Jack, who was now my ex-boyfriend, at our Monday night games sessions, where I apparently was incapable of making eye contact with him.
- I'd got so overwhelmed with all the above that I'd tried to ring Cara, who, like the last several times I'd tried to ring her, didn't even acknowledge my attempt. I hadn't bothered to send a follow-up text this time.

But to top it all off, the cherry on the shit sandwich that was my life at present, I got a text from Lauren; I was already on edge, and the message nearly brought me to my knees in the middle of the office.

> I just got the notification that Pablo's getting moved to Leeds. The move won't happen for another two weeks, but I wanted to let you know. Sorry xx

"Fuck," I said, slightly louder than I'd meant to, and Chloe looked up from her desk in concern.

"What's wrong?" she asked.

"Pablo," I said. "He's getting moved in two weeks. To Leeds." Not that the location mattered – Chloe knew as well as I did that after this move there would be maybe one more, and if they still couldn't find a home for him...

As I followed the thought to its obvious conclusion, the

reality we all knew about working here but hated more than anything, I felt my breathing start to go shallow. I sat down in the closest seat and put my head between my legs. The guilt hit me like a freight train: could I have done more? Had I been so caught up in my own drama that this little dog, who trusted me and loved me, was going to suffer?

And all I wanted to do was talk to Jack. For him to wrap me in his arms, and kiss the top of my head, and tell me everything would be okay. But of course I'd managed to fuck that up, too, and remembering that made the heat pooling on my face ten times worse.

"Hey, it's okay," Chloe said, and I felt a firm hand on my back. The weight of her touch brought me back into the room, and as I lifted my head and felt warm wet streaks form on my cheeks, I realised I was crying. She pulled me to my feet and supported me by the arm as she led me to the bathroom; we only got a few stares on the way, and I was beyond caring.

"It's all my fault," I said as Chloe locked the door behind us, the tears coming hot and fast. "I've known he needed a home for *months*. I've known I needed to move for *months*. I talk such a big game about finally doing things, finally taking initiative in my own life, but here we are four months later, and I'm still sitting here letting things happen around me!"

"That is not fair," she said. "You've had a lot going on."

"No more than most people," I said, wiping at my cheeks, but they were filling up as quickly as I could clear them. "I just can't handle it. It's too much."

I felt myself getting worked up and tried to rein it in at first, swallowing my gasps and pinching my eyes shut hard, willing myself to stop making such a scene. But when it was clear it was all going to come out one way or another, I shut the lid on the toilet and sat down on it, burying my face in my hands, collapsing into tears.

I cried for Pablo. Of course I did. His fuzzy little face was front and centre in my mind, and I mourned all the ways I'd failed him; all the times I'd been with him and could have stayed just two minutes longer.

I also cried for Jack, and the desperation in his eyes when he'd asked me to choose him. Not to leave him. I didn't want to; walking out of that room had been maybe the hardest thing I'd ever done.

But every time I felt him tugging on me, the part of me that had been tethered to others my whole life yanked back. I didn't want to wake up in a year, or five years, and be just as stuck as he was. No matter how much he said he didn't want that either, how could I trust him not to do that when he couldn't even see that he'd done it to himself?

And then I cried for me, because I was just so fucking tired. As much as I loved working for the charity, and making it so that as few animals as possible met Pablo's fate, I didn't love what I was doing.

But doing what I wanted to do meant leaving this place. And leaving my friends, like the one who was squatting in front of me in the bathroom, gathering toilet roll for me to use to dry my tears.

I looked up at Chloe as the waterworks ebbed. "I'm sorry," I said, accepting the toilet tissue she held out to me, using it to wipe at my face. Black flecks from my mascara came away on the paper. "I haven't actually had my breakdown yet."

"It was only a matter of time," she said. "I was worried you'd been doing this alone at home every night. I'm just glad I could be here."

I offered a feeble laugh, but the truth was that I'd reverted to numbing myself in every way possible at home. I'd been bingeing shit YouTube videos and reality TV. I hadn't read a book or drawn anything since the gala. I'd been in complete burnout, and I'd been doing it alone. By choice, too; I'd had plans with Chloe twice since then, and I'd cancelled both times. We were supposed to be getting sushi after work now, actually, to make up for it.

"About tonight..." I started, but she shook her head vehemently.

"Absolutely not," she said. "I'm not letting you cancel on me for the third time. This girls' night is happening, whether you want it or not."

I narrowed my eyes at her, but part of me was grateful that I wouldn't have to spend another night wallowing alone, and that part won out. I smiled.

"Okay, fine," I said, "as long as I'm aloud to be sad."

"Perfect," she said. "I can invite Fatima, too. It can be Sad Girl Autumn."

AND THAT WAS how I ended up sandwiched between Fatima and Chloe on my sofa several hours later, a smorgasbord of sushi and wine spread out on the coffee table, *Legally Blonde* queued up on the TV. It felt like the perfect option to fuel our current hatred of men.

The weather outside matched our moods, too; not only was it still raining, but it had started thundering as well just as Fatima had arrived. The delivery driver with the sushi had looked positively terrified, so we'd tipped him a bit extra to make up for the fact that he'd brought us our food on what was basically a moving lightning rod.

We were just getting to the iconic "What, like it's hard?" moment when the power cut out. We all froze for a moment, hoping it would just be a flicker, but when it didn't immediately come back on, we simultaneously checked our phones.

"I'm at twenty percent," I said.

"I'm at twelve," Chloe said.

"Ugh, you're both so unprepared," Fatima sighed, turning on her torch. "I'm on fifty, and I've got my portable charger in my bag."

"Sorry we're not all preppers," Chloe scoffed as I got up to find the actual torch in the kitchen.

"I'm not a prepper," Fatima said, slipping fully into teacher mode. "I'm a responsible adult."

I found the torch, but it seemed to be dead. So I rifled around in the junk drawer for batteries, not finding any.

"Here," Fatima said, "use the batteries from this." I turned around to see her extending the TV remote towards me. "We don't need it if we can't use the TV, right?"

Once Fatima and I were both equipped with torches, we started trying to fix the lighting situation. The fireplace was operational, but I'd never learned to use it, always having left that to Cara, and there wasn't any fuel for it anyway. So instead we started gathering candles from around the house. I had a shocking number of them for someone who didn't actually like burning candles, which I told Fatima when she gave me her fire hazard lecture after seeing how many there were on the bookshelves.

There were so many in the end that, when we lined them all up on the hearth and lit them, it was almost as bright as the lamps had been.

"What now?" Chloe asked.

"I don't know," Fatima said. "Seance?"

Chloe laughed. "You joke, but you know I'd be well up for that."

"And I decidedly would not," I said.

"I'm just sad we won't get to finish the film," Fatima said, slumping back down on the sofa. "We hadn't even made it to the best part."

"The part where Ali Larter shouts 'liposuction' in the prison?" Chloe asked, sitting next to her.

I scoffed as I brought another bottle of wine out. "Um, I'm pretty sure she means 'Don't stomp your little last season Prada shoes at me, honey'," I said, putting on my best Enrique impression, waving my finger around and everything.

"Oh my god," Fatima said, clapping, "that was brilliant! Do another."

I set the bottle down on the coffee table and thumbed through my mental repository of *Legally Blonde* quotes. "Um, let's see, how about..." I cleared my throat and pitched my voice up to a register worthy of Elle Woods, donning what was probably quite an offensive American accent. "'Isn't it the first cardinal rule of perm maintenance that you're forbidden to wet your hair for the first twenty-four hours at the risk of deactivating the ammonium thioglycalate?'"

Fatima squealed in delight, but Chloe just sat up and donned a nervous expression.

"'Y-yes?'" she asked, giving me the next line. I stood in front of the fireplace and postured towards the window seat as if speaking to an imaginary jury.

"'And wouldn't someone who's had, say, thirty perms before in their life be well aware of this rule?'"

Chloe continued her impression of a panicked Chutney, and Fatima sat back with her glass of wine, watching us as if she were watching the film for the first time. And by the time Chloe yelled "'I thought it was *you* walking through the door!'" Fatima was sideways on the couch in a fit of giggles.

Within a few minutes, we'd re-enacted most of what we could remember of the film, and right as Chloe finished rattling off the where-are-they-now updates from the end, the lights flickered back on.

"What do you say?" I asked, swapping the head torch batteries back into the TV remote. "Watch the rest of the film for real?"

"Hell no," Fatima said, snuggling up next to Chloe. I sat on the other side of her, and she grabbed my hand, lacing my fingers with hers. "That was definitely my preferred rendition."

CHAPTER 42
JACK

"You have to do this," Dad said over the workbench as I remeasured the batten I was about to cut for a stud wall. It was an odd height because of the roofline, and I forgot what the measurement was supposed to be by the time I'd extended the tape, so I glared at him before going back to the wall.

The big job was kicking off, and we'd had a change order come in for the flooring. So instead of getting to focus on the job I was actually supposed to be finishing, I would have to spend the afternoon doing *his* job.

"Dad, you know I hate paperwork." *Ninety-three. Got it.* "Can't we get someone else to do it? God knows I'll be hiring someone to handle it when I do have to take over." *Ninety-three, ninety-three, ninety-three.* "A lot of contractors don't do their own paperwork. Or emailing, or scheduling, any of the admin stuff." I lined up the measuring tape and made sure it was straight, then readied my pencil for the mark. *Ninety— Fuck.*

"Ninety-three," Dad said, his voice deep and sharp.

"I know," I said, too sharp in return. The glare he levelled at me made sure I recognised that. "Sorry," I muttered as I marked the cut.

"I know you can hire someone," he said, following me as I lowered the saw onto the batten. "But if you don't know how to do it, you won't know how to manage it."

I rolled my eyes, but he was right. I just didn't know how to articulate that I wasn't particularly interested in managing it, either. I'd never fought Dad on the stuff he'd asked me to do, and maybe it was just that Morgan had got in my head a bit. But I had to admit the work was getting to me.

"I'm on it," I promised, and as thanks, Dad dropped a new folder on the workbench to add to the ones I already had back at home.

I WRAPPED up work a couple of hours early so I could go home and start on the cursed paperwork Dad was on my case about. I had to drive past Morgan's on the way, and it took a Herculean amount of effort to keep my eyes on the road, even in the rain. I held my breath without even thinking, as if she might pop out into the road in the middle of a workday. I let it out as I turned onto the main road at the end, almost disappointed that I *hadn't* caught a glimpse of her.

But I did see someone I wasn't expecting on my journey; Phil's car was parked out front as I pulled up to my house, the sides splashed with mud from my driveway. I could hear shouting as I approached the house, and as I opened the front door and shed my raincoat and my now-muddy boots, the shouting formed into words.

"The man had been baking for all of five seconds," Amy said, quite passionately. "And yet he was still a finalist."

"But he couldn't make it happen when it counted, which is all that mattered!" Phil sat on a barstool opposite Amy, who was standing at the sink. An untouched pan of brownies sat between them.

"If you gave Chigs a time machine and quadrupled his experience, he'd be way better than Giuseppe. So proportionately he's the best."

"And yet," Phil taunted, leaning across the kitchen island, a smile on his face, "Giuseppe took home the win. You can't argue with that."

"That's not even what we were arguing about. You said Giuseppe was the best, not that he won."

"Don't be pedantic," Phil said. "That's obviously what I meant."

Amy threw her hands up. "Obviously it wasn't obvious!"

"Hello, you two," I interjected, and they both turned to look at me like I was the least welcome interruption ever. "Phil, what the hell are you doing in my house?"

"Just educating your sister on *Bake Off* royalty, apparently." When I didn't respond, just holding his gaze until I got a real answer, he sighed. "I was dropping off your outfit so you could pack it. I was just gonna leave it outside, but the kid here was out by your pond." He jabbed his thumb in Amy's direction.

"I'm not 'the kid', dickhead," she said, swatting at him from across the island.

"You are until I decide otherwise," Phil retorted, sticking his tongue out.

"Who's the kid now?" I asked, risking life and limb to reach between them for a brownie. "Also, as thrilled as I am to see you, I've got loads of paperwork to do. Dad will end my life if I don't get it done today."

Phil held his hands up as if I'd pulled a gun on him. "Definitely don't wanna be pissing off Papa Evans," he said, standing up and grabbing his car keys off the worktop.

I watched in amusement as Amy said goodbye by flipping him the bird. He blew her a kiss, which made her even more furious, glaring at him until he shut the front door behind him.

"You realise you're the one letting him wind you up like that," I said, taking his place at the island. I took a bite of the brownie, which was heavenly, of course.

"I know," Amy said, hanging her head in her hands with her elbows propped up on the edge of the sink. "I don't know why he gets under my skin so badly."

"I can think of a reason," I said under my breath, but she heard me anyway, snapping her head up to scowl at me.

"What the hell is that supposed to mean?"

"Listen," I said, shoving the last of the brownie into my mouth. "I'm not gonna be that classic, overprotective big brother. That's not me. You're a grown-ass woman, and he's a good bloke."

"Ew," she said, twisting her face in disgust. "Both to him being a 'good bloke'" – she curled her fingers into speech marks – "and to what you're implying to begin with."

"Whatever you say," I said, smiling smugly at her. I could tell I'd hit a nerve, and I wasn't sure what it said about my brotherly instincts that I was more amused than annoyed or concerned.

Amy grabbed the folder Dad had given me. "What's he got you doing this time?"

"Change order for the flooring," I said, trying to banish the thoughts of Morgan that were suddenly front and centre. "They want to do the vinyl instead of the wood to save money."

"Well that's fine," she said. "You just need to make sure you calculate any labour cost changes and flag any timeline dependencies."

I looked at her in confusion long enough that she groaned and came around to sit next to me, muttering something about "weaponised incompetence". She leaned over the change order and entered the details for the new flooring into her phone, pulling up the trade listing. "See how it says delivery date of the thirtieth?" she asked, pointing to the date on her screen. I nodded. "You need to put that into the schedule and move things around to accommodate it," she said. "I'm betting Dad wants you to be able to communicate how that impacts the schedule?"

I nodded again.

"Okay, show it to me."

I stood up and went over to the little desk in the corner, where I had several folders now piled up, and an A3 paper with the schedule written on it pinned to the wall. I took it down and brought it over to Amy, spreading it out across the surface. She looked down at it and then back up at me, her mouth wide.

"You're using a paper schedule?" she asked.

"Yeah," I said, "that's what Dad showed me."

"Jesus Christ," she said, grabbing my laptop off the sofa and typing in my password.

"How do you know that?" I asked, gesturing at the computer.

"Please," she said dismissively, "you've had the same password since you were a teenager. MrJackMichelleGellar?"

I felt my face go red, dropping the subject as immediately as possible.

"Here," she said, turning the screen to show me what looked to be the website for some project management software. "This is the one Chris used. You put in all the pieces of the project and the dependencies, so when you move one thing, it moves all the other things, too. It's called a Gantt chart."

"That's cool," I said, pulling it towards me. It definitely sounded better than the paper version, which I'd already had to Tipp-ex half to death as things had changed. "Why doesn't Dad use this?"

"Because he's old," she said. "Set in his ways."

"How much does it cost?" I asked, scrolling down the page. I saw an option for "pricing", so I clicked it, my mouth falling open when I saw that there was a free plan available. "I'm sorry, *free*?"

"Probably," she said. "You'll miss out on some features with the free plan, but it'll still be better than paper."

"Anything's better than this, honestly," I said, running my finger along a crease in the paper schedule, trying to smooth it out.

Over the next hour, Amy helped me set up the upcoming project in the software. The good news was that it was immensely better than the paper version; processing the flooring change took about twenty seconds, and I could even export the new timeline to send to Dad. All of the documents were easily scanned in and stored against the project, too.

The bad news was that, despite the novelty of the new system and how easy everything was, I still found it exceedingly boring.

"Can't you just do this?" I asked Amy as we finished, multiple hours before when I thought I'd be done. "You're so good at it."

"Hey, you pay me, and I'm in," she said, sounding surprisingly keen on the idea. I squinted at her sceptically.

"You don't think that sounds horrible?" I asked. "Working for Dad? Managing all those projects?"

"Not really," she said. "It actually sounds kind of ... dare I say fun?"

My eyes went wide as I closed my laptop. "You may dare, but I sure as hell don't. Guess I'd better get used to it, though."

I stood to start putting everything away, ferrying it all back to my desk before sinking down on the sofa. I'd assumed Amy would follow, but when I looked up, she was still stood in the exact same position, her face wearing the same expression.

"Yeah, about that," she said. "I think you really need to talk to Dad about this whole family business thing."

I felt myself go cold all over. It was like déjà vu; a flashback to my fight with Morgan. Maybe a bit more tender, a bit less loaded, but the same damn thing over again.

"What are you talking about?" I asked, giving her the opportunity to say *anything* except what I knew she would. What Morgan had tried saying to me, too.

"Your heart's clearly not in it," she said, moving to sit next to me, "and I really think you need to consider bailing out."

I swallowed hard, my mouth going dry. "Amy, I don't wanna—"

"I know," she said, putting her hands up. "But honestly, I'm really worried about you. Your horoscopes have been terrifying for weeks. And every time something bothers you, you just gaslight yourself into being okay with it. It's disconcerting."

I shook my head, desperate for her to drop it. "You don't have to worry about me."

"And yet I do anyway," she said. "Because you're never going to be happy doing this. Even once Dad retires, do you think he's gonna leave you alone? Do you think you'll ever be able to change things to the point that you don't hate it anymore?"

I opened my mouth to disagree, but we both knew she was

right. I'd imagined it before: taking over the business in name only, Dad still calling all the shots from behind the scenes.

"You'd just be his puppet," Amy said.

"His support character," I said quietly.

"Sure," she said, confusion passing briefly across her face. "Whatever that means. But either way, it's not fair to either of you. You'll end up resenting him, and he'll be bitter with you. And Mum and I will be stuck in the middle as always."

I sighed again, resting my head back against the cushion. "You've always been so much better with him than I am," I said. "Why couldn't you be the joiner in the family?"

She laughed. "You say that as if *you're* the joiner in the family."

I narrowed my eyes at her.

"You're not," she insisted. "You never have been. You're good at it, yes. Of course you are. Just look at this place." She held out her hands, gesturing to the house. "But we both know it's not what you want to be doing."

Again I opened my mouth to protest, and again she cut me off.

"Don't make me get that damn magazine."

The moment she mentioned the magazine, the thoughts of Morgan I'd been holding back all day came flooding in like a dam had burst. I remembered her standing over by the table, looking at the advert. How terrified she'd looked when we heard about Fatima and Jared, as if she knew what it would mean. Her gasping at me at the gala, like I'd just slapped her. Her asking me in her lounge how I could expect her to commit to me if I couldn't even commit to myself.

"Just fuck off, Amy," I said, standing suddenly. She startled backward in surprise, pressing herself to the back of the sofa as I stormed past her and to the back door. I flung it open, my steps splashing as I walked to the edge of the deck, my t-shirt almost instantly soaking through. I felt like I was about to explode; like the pressure inside me was reaching a bursting point, and I needed to do something. Anything.

"Fuck!" I yelled at nothing in particular, causing two ducks and a pigeon to take flight.

I looked down at the raindrops on the water, which for some reason made me think of Morgan, too, because it seemed everything did these days. I thought of all the times I'd been on the river with her: that first swim on our weekend away, her first time kayaking, a nighttime swim in the nearby forest that had turned into skinny dipping, and then to making love against a tree ... it all felt so real, so tangibly close, and yet so far away. And the space between here and there – between what I had and what I'd lost – felt like a screaming chasm in my chest.

My breath grew fast and shallow, and before I knew it I was crying, despite my best efforts to keep it at bay.

How had I let it all slip through my fingers so easily? I'd had exactly what I'd wanted, and she'd been *mine*. She hadn't chosen to leave *me*, just to leave *here*. I'd been the one to draw the line, to give the ultimatum, despite having told her all those weeks ago that she should do whatever would make her the happiest. I was the villain in my own fucking story, and I hated myself for it.

"Jack?" came a quiet voice from behind me.

But I didn't turn around, instead sinking to the deck right where I stood, rain be damned, wrapping my arms around my legs, drawing them to me. I buried my head there so my little sister wouldn't see my tears, but she came up behind me anyway. Instead of trying to hug me, or shush me, or anything like that, she just sat on the deck, her back to mine, holding me up whilst I held her up in return. She leaned her head against me, her cheek resting on my shoulder blade, whilst I cried quietly into my knees.

"I really fucked up," I said after a while.

"Phil told me you guys broke up," she said. "Do you wanna tell me what happened?"

I sighed. "She's taking a job in York, apparently."

"Wow," Amy muttered. "There must be something in the water."

I shook my head, though I know she couldn't see it. "It wasn't the same as Jared," I said. "I knew she was applying. Hell, I sent her the job listing."

I couldn't see Amy's face, but I could hear the frown in her voice as she responded. "Why the hell would you do that?"

I shrugged. "It was before she and I ... well, I'd hoped she would change her mind once we got together."

"Did you say that to her?" Amy asked, and I didn't blame her for implying that maybe I hadn't. I didn't have the best track record of sticking up for myself.

"Yes. But then..." I hesitated to admit the next part, because I wasn't proud of it, even if I'd felt it was the only way. "I may have given her an ultimatum."

"Yikes," Amy said. "Because ultimatums are always such a good idea."

I sighed. "If you're trying to make me feel better, try harder maybe?"

Amy moved to sit next to me so we were shoulder-to-shoulder, dangling her feet off the edge of the deck.

"I'm not trying to make you feel better," she said. "I don't think I can do that. But tell me what you said, and what she said back."

I wasn't sure what reliving it would achieve, but I took a deep breath, not having to dig very hard to find the memory. I'd been replaying it enough over the last two weeks that it was pretty top-of-mind.

I told Amy what Morgan had said about the job. About how she wasn't Jared, but that I was stuck, and she wouldn't let me keep her stuck with me.

"Ouch," Amy said. "I imagine you didn't take that well?"

"Not exactly," I admitted. "I told her if she wanted to be with me so badly, she should be willing to do it even if I didn't have my shit together."

Her sharp intake of breath told me Amy didn't love this.

"You know you're both the bad guys here, right?"

"I *know*." I buried my face in my knees again. "I've been replaying it in my mind constantly since it happened."

Amy was silent for a long moment, but then she shook her head. "But like, do you know actually?"

"Excuse me?" I sat up straight.

"I mean, prove that you know what you did wrong. Because I can tell you for free, it wasn't just the ultimatum."

I frowned at her. "What are you on about?"

She stood up without saying anything and walked back into the house, and I just gawked after her. Then she walked back out again with the RIBA Journal. I groaned.

"Not the fucking magazine *again*, Amy!" I said, then gasped as she chucked it as hard as she could into the pond.

I leaned over the edge to watch as it stayed open to the spread I'd had it on for months now, the page changing colour as it saturated with water, then sank further and further from the surface until I couldn't see it anymore.

Once it was out of sight, I whirled around to face Amy.

"What the hell was that about?!" I shouted.

"How did that make you feel?" she asked. "Seeing it sink away like that?"

"Fucking fuming!" I said, looking back over to the spot where the magazine had been. I hoped it hadn't pinned one of the fish or something.

"Good," Amy said. "Anger. I can work with that. Now what else? Tell me what you feel."

I felt my jaw tense; she was talking to me like I was a child. But I bit my tongue, quite literally, and exhaled slowly, trying to give her the benefit of the doubt. I closed my eyes and held the image of the magazine hitting the water in my mind.

"Not good," I said.

"'Not good' is not an emotion," she said. I huffed, but then wracked my mind for what I was feeling.

"Angry," I tried.

"You already said that," she said. "Go deeper. Why were you angry?"

"I was sad?" I tried again, straight away.

"*No*," she said insistently. "Jack, just fucking try please. What did you *feel*?"

I forced myself to try to give her an answer, but I felt like an idiot. It was eerily like when Morgan had got me to admit that it was fear driving my lifestyle. Except now it was Amy having to play therapist. She'd already watched her big brother have a meltdown, and now I couldn't even answer a simple question. What was wrong with me?

I focused in on my breathing and tried to calm down, but it was futile, like I was trying to fill that chasm inside me. The chasm that appeared whenever I thought about Morgan.

The same chasm that had spread even further open when I'd watched a future I'd once dreamed for myself sink away in front of me.

Oh. *Oh*. Was it really that simple?

"I feel grief," I whispered, more to myself than to Amy. But I knew she heard me, because she pressed her shoulder to me again.

"That's good," she said. "Tell me more."

"Like I've lost something that didn't feel like it was mine to begin with," I said, and I felt her nod. "Something I wanted so badly, but felt like it was part of a different life. One I don't get to live. One I said goodbye to a long time ago."

Amy turned me towards her and put her hands on my arms, ducking her head down and forcing me to catch her gaze. "Jack, listen to me," she said. "When you and Aria broke up, you were devastated. I get that. It changed who you were as a person."

Talking about grief, and Morgan, and my future, I felt the mention of Aria in my chest like I hadn't in years. I felt more tears well up inside me.

"But the decisions you made back then? No one's holding you to them. You can do whatever the hell you want with your life."

I shook my head. "It's a bit late for that," I said. Amy dropped her hands and flung her arms out to the side, gesturing around her.

"Why?" she asked. "I don't see anyone holding a gun to your head, making you do anything."

"But people count on me!" I said, my voice hoarse.

"They do," Amy said, smiling and nodding. "But only because you've made it that way. You've put yourself in the position to be as helpful as possible to everyone else, and that's so lovely. But you need to understand that they would survive without you. And maybe they should."

On an intellectual level, everything she was saying made sense. I'd embedded myself so that I felt safe, and that became the new status quo. But in becoming embedded, I'd also become ... yes, stuck.

"Fuck," I said, rubbing my hands over my face, which was burning hot despite how cold it was outside. "I've really fucked this up, haven't I? All of it."

"It's fine," Amy said, clearly trying to sound as casual as possible. "Nothing's permanent. Everything is changeable."

"I am the master of my fate; I am the captain of my soul," I said jokingly, but Amy just stared up at me. "'Invictus?'" She shook her head. "Never mind."

"No, no," she said, shrugging, "whatever makes you feel better."

I let out a laugh, which clearly surprised her, because she started nervously laughing, too.

"It does, clearly," I said, then pulled Amy in for a hug. "Thank you," I said. "I'm supposed to be the one doling out the wisdom, though. Could you try to be a little less mature?"

"Sorry," she said, pulling away from me and stepping back towards the door to inside. "You're being enough of a baby for the both of us."

"Oh fuck no," I said as I charged after her. I grabbed her by the arm and pulled her back along the deck; she tried to wriggle away, but she was no match for me. I wrapped an arm around her hips and hoisted her over my shoulder in a fireman's carry.

"Put me down!" she yelled through laughter, banging on my back with her fist. I carried her over to the edge of the deck.

"Not until you bring back the magazine you threw," I said, eliciting a blood-curdling scream from her as I dropped her into the pond. "I'm gonna need it."

CHAPTER 43
MORGAN

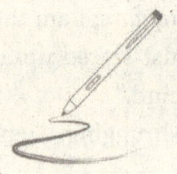

I was so fucking done with work.

We were still two months from our Christmas event, but I was already being asked to share daily updates with the leadership team, and it was all the very last thing I wanted to be doing. I was so over it that I'd actually taken a break to read Mum's latest email, all about her yoga certification and how she was starting to offer classes on her travels. That explained her latest postcard, which had been a beach with old-fashioned lifeguard hut on it, with the words "Nama-stay in Malibu" written in the sky.

I took solace each evening in my freelance work. I had finished the other projects Greg had referred to me, and I was now working on design mock-ups for a website for someone else in their Facebook group who was opening a used bookshop. I'd had to learn a lot about web design – accessibility, coding limitations, responsiveness – but just like when I'd been doing the Game On! Branding, I was enjoying learning about it.

I was only four days away from leaving for the Ren Faire, and two away from having to give the software company a decision. I'd managed to buy myself some time by negotiating the salary; my promotion at the rescue had definitely helped give me some leverage. They hadn't quite been able to match it, but they'd closed the gap enough that it wasn't a dealbreaker, especially given how much cheaper housing was in York.

That was a problem, too. Now that the house had sold, I needed to look in earnest for a place to live. And ideally it needed to be pet friendly; Pablo was just a week away from being moved, and I had every intention of taking him with me. So I needed to make a decision *now* about where I was going to live, which meant making a decision once and for all about where I wanted to work. I'd broken up with Jack over the fact that I was thinking about moving to York, so why was it taking me so long to pull the trigger?

Okay, that wasn't fair. I hadn't broken up with Jack because I wanted to move to York. I hadn't been planning to break up with him at all, actually. But the moment he gave me an ultimatum, I was right back to feeling tied to another person like I had with Cara all those years. And given how much freedom I'd found, how much I loved being the one calling the shots in my own life, I couldn't give it up. Wouldn't, even.

I'd been all but ready to accept the job before my girls night with Chloe and Fatima. I'd even drafted an email. But that night had reminded me that life here wasn't just about Jack, which made saying goodbye to it feel infinitely more complicated. So the email continued to sit in my drafts.

I WAS SITTING at the manspread desk – despite the promotion, I still hadn't been moved out of the Fundraising Corner – when someone I recognised from around the office walked over, a laptop tucked under her arm, her locs just tickling the tops of her shoulders. I caught her eye, and she waved in confirmation that she was coming to talk to me.

"Hey, you're Morgan, right?" she asked.

"Yeah, hi," I said, holding out my hand as I stood.

"Kim," she said, her handshake firm yet brief. "I work in design."

I stood up a bit straighter – I'd spoken to design over email, but I'd never actually met anyone from the team.

"How can I help?" I asked, trying not to sound too interested.

She pulled her laptop out from under her arm and opened it, setting it on the desk next to mine. There was a mock-up of a web page – the home page of the Rescue website, from the look of it – with low-resolution versions of my illustrations for the gala dotted around.

"We loved what you did for the gala," she said, "and we want to use it for the website. But as you can see, we've just used the screen grabs we could access for these mock-ups. Do you think you could send us the vectors?"

I felt a swell of pride at seeing my work on the website, even if it was low-res. But my creative wheels started turning immediately, seeing how the illustrations we had weren't going to be quite right. We needed way more versions of the animals, and maybe some other illustrations. Otherwise it would look like polka dots of animal faces.

"I mean, I can," I said, "but I feel like you need some variation, right?"

"Yeah," Kim said, squinting down at the screen. "I was thinking the same thing. I can try to match your illustration style, I guess."

I cringed – hopefully just inwardly – at the idea of someone else using those illustrations; trying to emulate them.

"Or I could just help with it?" I asked.

"I mean, that would be great," she said with a smile, her voice high and hopeful. "If you've got bandwidth for that?"

Aaaaaaaand there was the catch. Of course I didn't have *bandwidth*. Because I was too busy planning the Christmas event, which I hated.

"Let me double check," I said; I couldn't bring myself to say no without at least speaking to Simone. "I'll let you know by tomorrow?"

"Oh that's fine," Kim said, closing the laptop and tucking it back under her arm. "We're so underwater right now, it'll probably be a few weeks until we get to work on this."

I might not have a few weeks, I thought, but I just smiled and promised her I'd email her with either the vector files or confirmation that I could work on it myself.

Almost as soon as she was out of sight, I tiptoed over to Simone's office, peeking through the window to see if she was inside. She was leaning forward over the desk, her head in her hands. It didn't look like the best time, but I knocked on the door anyway.

"Come in," she said, sitting up straight and putting on what, for her anyway, passed as a welcoming expression. "Oh hi, Morgan, how's the leadership update for today coming along?"

"Uh, yeah, fine," I said as I shut the door behind me. "It'll be out by four as usual."

She gestured for me to sit, and I did. She tried to ask me another question about the Christmas event, but I cut her off; if I let this turn into a logistical catch-up, I knew I'd lose my nerve.

"So, Kim from design came to see me," I said. "She wanted to use my illustrations from the gala for the website."

Simone nodded. She was only half paying attention, looking down her nose at her screen rather than at me, scrolling through something. "They were very good. I'm not surprised."

"Thank you," I said. "The thing is ... well, they need more of them."

Simone flicked her wrist dismissively. "Oh, I'm sure they can handle it," she said. "Don't let them worry you."

I took a deep breath in. "Actually, I want to help them."

Simone stopped scrolling and slowly turned her head, looking over her glasses at me. She looked me over for a long moment, narrowing her eyes as she took me in. I tried to look as calm and collected as possible, but I couldn't quite control my shallow breathing.

"You know how busy we are with Christmas," she said. "I don't see how it would be possible to do both."

I didn't say anything yet; I could tell she was thinking.

"This is exactly what happened with the gala," she said, probably remembering, as I was, how I'd burst into her office with my tablet in hand to ask if I could work on those designs. I felt even more passionately about it now than I had then, but I knew Simone, and I knew she wouldn't appreciate another outburst. So I held my nerve.

"That's right," I said. "I really love the design projects."

"More than the events themselves?"

She was so incredibly straight to the point. And whether it was because I had another offer to fall back on, or just knew what I wanted, I decided I would be direct, too.

I nodded. And mentally shat my pants, but she didn't need to know that. I kept my face looking as unbothered as possible.

"Do you ... want to work in design?"

"Ideally, at some point, in the long term ... yes."

"I see," she said, sitting back in her chair and taking her glasses off. "I didn't know that about you."

I shrugged. "I didn't either, really. Not until recently."

She tapped one arm of her glasses to her lips, which were pursed in thought. She stayed that way for what felt like minutes, before she started nodding.

"Well, I can't lose you until after the Christmas event," she said. "You're too far down that road. But if we can hire someone quickly enough to start working on the next event before then, I can make it work. I'll put you in touch with the Design Manager so you can start interviewing in the meantime, though I suspect it'll be more of a formality."

My eyes went wide. *Wait, what??*

"Sorry," I said, struggling to comprehend whilst my brain was busy doing pirouettes, "you're just going to give me a design job? You're not firing me?"

Simone laughed. "Fire you? Absolutely not. I'm gutted to lose you, in fact."

"You are?"

"And no, I'm not giving you a job. But based on the fact that they want to use your designs for the website, I can't imagine you'll have a hard time getting it. I'd say that's pretty good leverage, in fact."

I stared at Simone for a long moment, appreciating her more than I ever had. This was the second time she'd done me what felt like a massive favour. I'd always been a little bit terrified of her, but it turned out she was my greatest ally in this place.

"I don't relish the idea of having to hire your replacement," she said, and I offered her a suggestion almost before she'd even finished the sentence.

"Chloe Barlow," I said. "She'd be brilliant at it." I didn't even know if that was true, but based on how jealous she'd been of my promotion, I knew she should have the chance to try.

"Great," Simone said with a huff, "so I'd just have to find a replacement for her instead. You know I still haven't filled Cara's role, and I haven't even touched your backfill yet. That would be half my fundraising team gone."

I shrugged. "Just an idea."

"Okay, well, you're giving me *more* work to do," Simone said, waving me away. "Now get out, and keep an eye on your email."

THE DECISION SHOULD HAVE BEEN easy now; Simone had teed it up for me, and all I had to do was close the deal. I knew I could, too. For once in my life, confidence wasn't the problem.

But when I thought about turning down the York job, staying at the Rescue, I couldn't help but picture myself crawling back to Jack. I'd still be here, in his hometown. We'd still see each other every Monday night. And I'd still be madly in love with him.

And I was in love with him. I hadn't said it back, because in the middle of our breakup had felt like the worst possible time to roll out that sentiment. But of course I loved him back. I'd been in love with him for months; since long before he had come to love me. Which is what made all of this so horrible.

As I sat on my window seat on Saturday morning sorting books into keep and donate piles – I was trying to get ahead of the monumental task I knew was ahead of me whenever the sale eventually went through – I thought about the concept of the fork in the road, and how many different places this decision could lead to. If I stayed, maybe Jack and I would get back together. Or maybe it would be too hard to be around each other, and we'd have another fall-out, this time in front of our friends. Or maybe he'd find someone else, and I'd be forced to watch their love unfold in front of me.

Or, if I moved to York, maybe I'd find someone else. Maybe I'd watch from afar or hear through friends when Jack eventually moved on. Or maybe I'd spend the rest of my life regretting leaving the one person I'd ever truly loved.

And that was just Jack. There were multiverses of possibilities, all of them laid out in front of me like the books I was combing through. I wondered in how many of them I was the one sending the postcards, and in how many I was still receiving them. I wondered in how many I was truly happy.

I picked up my phone, and it took me until my finger was over her name that I realised I was about to text Cara. She had always been the one I talked to about things like this. About everything, actually. But I hadn't heard from her in months now. And I realised, as I put my phone down again, that I didn't actually care anymore what she thought. She didn't know Jack, and she didn't know me. Not this version of me; the version who was taking things into her own hands for once.

No, I was the only one who could figure this out. I just wasn't sure how to go about it.

The next book I picked up was the copy of *The Hobbit* Jack had bought me, because of course it was. The book that, more than any other for me, symbolised both my yearning for adventure and my ache for the man I loved.

The clouds shifted, and sunlight poured in over my face; the bad weather had broken, and it felt like we were going to get a bit of proper autumn for the next week or so. Not that I'd get outside at all to enjoy it; realistically, I'd be working, preparing for the move, packing for the Ren Faire, or just generally moping. Plus, I didn't have Jack to drive me to whatever little adventures I wanted to have; he'd really been the catalyst for all the exploration I'd done over the summer.

But I realised, putting the book down, that that was bullshit. The whole reason I'd broken things off with Jack was because he was keeping me from getting to go on the adventure I wanted, right? So why was I letting his absence keep me from anything at all? Anything we'd done together, I should have been able to do by myself. And not just able, but willing.

I started by making myself my favourite chicken and blue cheese sandwich, eating it in the back courtyard that Jack had helped me clear. As I ate, I pulled out my phone and started making a list of everything we'd done together, seeing how hard it would be to do it myself. There was kayaking on the Wye ... but the kayak rental place in town had shut for the season a couple of weeks ago. We'd been wild swimming ... but I couldn't actually figure out where we'd gone. We'd gone quad biking ... but that had been his quad bike, and all the hire sites I found had a minimum party size. Then there was the hike...

Just when I thought I wouldn't be able to figure out where we'd gone hiking, I had an idea. I opened up my photo gallery and found the picture I'd taken from the top; my phone had recorded the location. I pulled open my maps app and found the spot the photo was pinned, then used satellite and street views to find the car park.

But it was nearly forty minutes away, and in the middle of nowhere. There was no bus route that would get me within even a thirty-minute walk of the base of the trail.

I spent a short moment annoyed with myself for not knowing how to drive, but I was determined to do something – anything – for myself, so I picked the phone back up and rang the local taxi company. It took me five minutes to get the guy who answered to take me seriously.

"Fifty quid," he said finally. "Each way."

I was almost certain he was trying to talk me out of going, but I was nothing if not stubborn, so I booked the cab for ten minutes later and rushed upstairs to change. I had a point to prove.

~

AN HOUR LATER, I was at the base of the hike Jack and I had taken all those months ago, forking over even more money to the taxi driver so he would wait for me. If I went out and back instead of doing the loop, I figured I'd be okay with the cash I had taken out for the Ren Faire.

As soon as I left the car park, I knew I'd be saying goodbye to my trainers after I was done; the entrance to the trail was basically a mud pit. But I kept my eyes fixed on the ridgeline, and over the next hour, I made it to the rock pile at the summit. My legs were on fire, and I could feel my face going pink in the sun, making me even more nostalgic for those summer adventures. I sat on the edge of the rock, overlooking two separate countries, and let myself feel the way I'd felt the first time I'd been here: invincible.

I'd wanted to hike this hill by myself, and I'd made it happen, at no small cost, literal and physical. *This* was what I wanted. *This* was the feeling I was chasing. This pride? I'd felt it secondhand in games, or in books. But I'd only felt it a few times in my real life, all within the last few months, and I wanted as much of it as I could get.

There was the first time we'd climbed this hill. The first time I'd gone swimming with Jack. The moment I'd sent Greg the Game On! logo. The night that I'd finally got over my own fear of how he'd react and kissed Jack. That was what I wanted.

And I realised, sitting there with my feet dangling off the edge of the world, that neither job, neither path in the fork, would get me any closer to that. No single decision would make or break the ability I'd found to chase what I wanted. To lean into the euphoria of living life on my own terms. I felt sure, for the first time ever, that I could find this feeling no matter where I was; no matter where I lived; no matter what I did for a living.

Like Jack had said on that rock by the river, and when he was pleading with me to stay, it wasn't about some big quest. It was about approaching life with a spirit of adventure. And somehow, somewhere along the way, I'd acquired that spirit. I didn't need anyone or anything else to help me find it: not work, not Cara, and not even Jack. For the first time, maybe ever, I understood what independence actually meant. And what it *didn't* mean.

I pulled my phone out and snapped a selfie, and then a panorama; I knew I'd want to draw this moment later. Because as soon as I realised that I already had everything I needed inside me, I knew exactly what I wanted to do.

CHAPTER 44
CAPTAIN MORGANA SILVERSWORD

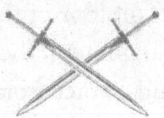

"Get up!" Calamity shouted, her hands on Morgana's shoulders. "We have to go, *now*!"

"Thrormir?" Morgana asked quietly.

"He's dead," Calamity spat. "Gone. You can't bring him back. Now let's *go*!"

As she shouted, a hunk of stone fell from the ceiling just a few feet in front of Morgana, blocking her view of Thrormir. She looked around and realised that the whole chamber was rumbling, and debris was falling all over the place. Her shackles were also loose on the floor. She was free.

"Where are the others? What's happening?"

"They're already gone," Calamity said, reaching for Morgana's hand. She let her take it this time, allowing herself to be dragged up and across the room. It was pure chaos, with fallen cloaked figures everywhere. Arnault was nowhere to be seen.

Morgana gave Thrormir's body one last glance – one last apology – before she was dragged out of the room.

Calamity shoved the door closed behind them, and then

they took off running down the passageway. When they reached the end, they had two choices: left or right. Morgana looked from side to side, searching for any clue of which way they went. But then a familiar figure stepped out into the hallway and waved.

"Morgana!" Gorlag called. Yorick stepped out, too, and Morgana and Calamity ran to meet them. They all embraced, and Morgana noticed that all four of them were shaking. They would have a lot to grieve together if they got out of this alive.

"There you all are," said a voice from further down the hall, and they all jumped; Morgana worried at first that Arnault had caught up with them. But it wasn't him; it was another cloaked figure.

A cloaked figure who had all of their armour and weapons with him, weirdly enough.

"Who are you?" Morgana called, standing in front of her friends.

"A friend," the man said as he dropped his hood. "From the Adventurers Guild. My name's Ser Liam Prize."

"Sorry," Yorick said, tittering, "your name is 'Ser Prize'? As in, surprise?"

"So you've heard of me?" Ser Prize asked, beaming.

"How did you know to find us?" Calamity asked from behind Morgana's shoulder.

Ser Prize set the gear down on the ground and took a couple steps back, his own hands in the air, but Morgana didn't miss the shape of a shield hidden beneath his cloak, or what looked like a javelin poking out.

"We've been tracking the Order of the Twelve for a long time. It wasn't until you were sent on your mission that we suspected they were after the Supremacy Sphere."

The Order of the Twelve. That must have been why the symbol was the twelve-pointed star. But twelve who? Or what?

"Where is the Sphere?" Ser Prize asked.

"Destroyed."

Ser Prize's face fell; he must have known what that meant.

"Then it's best to get you out of here and regroup. Arnault is likely to retaliate."

The others moved forward and began donning their armour and equipping their gear, but Morgana stayed put.

"We need to go back for his body," she said.

"We can't," Yorick said. "You saw what was happening in there. And if we get killed, he died for nothing."

Morgana scoffed. "He died to destroy the Sphere. He was protecting everyone."

"He was protecting *us*," Yorick said, staring up at her. "Don't negate that choice."

Morgana looked down at her little friend, who was clearly hurting, too. Then she looked back up at Ser Prize, who was beckoning them back the way he had come. She had a choice to make.

Yorick was right. If Thormir had died protecting these people, the people he loved, the best thing she could do to honour him would be to make sure that sacrifice wasn't in vain. So she bent down and picked up her armour and great sword, then nodded at Ser Prize.

"Lead the way."

CHAPTER 45
JACK

I'd been hyping myself up for this conversation so much that I was actually shocked when I walked in on my parents snogging in the kitchen.

"Please you two," I said, and they jumped apart, Mum wiping her mouth whilst Dad just strode directly out of the room. He was clearly as uncomfortable with me having witnessed it as I was. I wasn't exactly surprised – it certainly wasn't the first time – but I was possibly a *bit* sensitive to displays of affection, even from Mum and Dad.

"Jack," Mum said, smoothing her top, "so good to see you."

"Is it?" I asked, raising an eyebrow to her. "Seems like I may have interrupted."

"Never," she said, walking over to me and leaning in for a kiss on the cheek, but I dodged it.

"No thank you," I said. "Given the circumstances."

Mum shrugged. I leaned against the counter as she put the kettle on.

"Dad?" I called, angling my head as if that would help me see around the corner in the hallway he'd disappeared down.

"Yes, son?" he called back; he'd got all the way upstairs.

"You got a minute?"

"Just a sec." I heard his heavy tread on the stairs, clearly exaggerated, and a moment later, he was back in the kitchen, opening the fridge for a beer as if he hadn't just been in here.

"Alrighty then," I said, clutching my course booklet between my hands. Now that they were both here, it was showtime.

But I couldn't quite manage to start.

"What do you need, son?" Dad asked, cracking open a can. "I've got some emails to send, as you well know."

I nodded. I did know, though I was pretty sure his little make-out session hadn't been helping, either. "Yes, well, sorry," I said, "but this is a tough conversation to have."

That got his attention. And Mum's; she immediately waved both Dad and me into the lounge. I sat down on the armchair, whilst they settled on the sofa. Though settled was a strong word; they were perched on the edge clinging onto one another as if I were telling them I was dying. Hell, for all they knew, that was what I was going to say. *And I still might*, I thought, *depending on Dad's reaction*.

"So I've been thinking about my future," I said, and I saw Dad's eyes narrow. But I took a deep breath and pushed forward. Technically I'd already done what I was telling them about, so avoiding the conversation really wasn't really an option.

"What's this about?" Dad asked, using his boss voice.

"It's about work, Dad." I leaned forward and put the booklet I'd been clutching down on the coffee table, then spun it around so it would face them.

"What's this?" he asked, picking it up and bringing it close to his face, as if he didn't have better than twenty-twenty vision.

"It's a course catalogue," Mum said, looking up at me, confused. "For Oxford?"

I shook my head. "Oxford Brookes. It's where the RIBA certification courses are."

"RIBA?" Dad looked up at me. As a contractor, he didn't just know who RIBA were. He interacted with them all the time. Hell, our building contracts were a RIBA template.

"Yeah, Dad."

"The architecture dickheads."

"One and the same," I said, pressing my mouth into a line as I watched him grasp at understanding. "I want to be one of them, actually."

Dad sighed. "Look, Jackie. I know you like this stuff. But it's not just drawing all the time. It's a lot of admin still. You never get away from that."

"Do you not think I know that?" I asked. "It's not about the admin. It's about wanting something different."

I saw the moment Dad went from exasperated to offended. "What, my business not good enough for you?"

"Darling," Mum said, putting her hand on his arm, but he shook it off angrily.

"You think you're better than me? Is this your little girlfriend's work? Telling you you're better than a hard day's work?"

My hands curled into fists hearing him mention Morgan like that. "This has nothing to do with Morgan. We're not even together anymore."

"Like hell it's not," he said, standing up.

"Alan!" Mum shouted, standing up with him. "Don't be like this."

"I'll be like this if I want," Dad said, turning on Mum. I'd never seen him raise his voice to her before. "I've worked hard to build a business, so I'll say what I like. You talk to your ungrateful son about this if you've got a problem with it."

"I'm not ungrateful, Dad," I said, standing as well, but he just pushed past me to the front door.

"Please don't leave," Mum said, but Dad was out the door before she could get it out, and she sank back onto the sofa. I stepped over to sit down with her, putting an arm around her. A few seconds later, I could hear death metal coming from the direction of his workshop.

"I'm sorry, Mum," I said. "I'm not trying to be ungrateful. I'm just trying to do what I think is best for me. For my future."

She turned to me and smiled sadly, putting her hands on my cheeks. "Of course you are, darling."

"I've thought a lot about this," I said. "And it really wasn't Morgan's idea." Sure, Morgan had pushed me, but so had Amy. And really, that magazine had been lying open for months before either of them had found it. It wasn't their doing. It was mine. And that made me proud.

"I'm proud of you," Mum said, echoing my own thoughts, and I frowned.

"You are?" I asked. "But what about Dad?"

Mum dropped her hands and sighed. "Did I ever tell you that your dad didn't want you to work for him?"

I remembered the day he'd asked me to join the business; when he'd offered me the deal I'd been holding myself to for years now. "What are you talking about? It was his idea."

Mum shook her head. "No, dear, it wasn't. It was mine. Your dad was afraid that if you started working for him, you'd never leave."

I balked. "But isn't that what the deal was designed to do?"

Mum chuckled softly. "Well, I can see why you'd think that. But no, he just wanted to know that you were taking things seriously. That if he put the time and energy into training you, you'd stick around."

"But you just said he was afraid I'd never leave."

"Not stick around in the business, silly boy," Mum said. "He wanted to know you weren't going to run off to be with that horrid girl again."

I sighed. "Not this again," I said. "I broke up with Aria, remember?"

"Oh, we remember," Mum said, her eyes going wide as she patted my knee. "We remember all of it. You really scared us for a while there."

"Scared you?"

Mum nodded. "Building that house with no idea what you were doing, never leaving the property, not talking to anyone but Chloe and Phil ... honestly, thank god for them, because I thought we'd lost you."

Maybe for the first time ever, I realised what it must have been like for them when I came home. I could understand why they would have been concerned. Why they were worried I would run off again.

"So why offer me the job then?" I asked.

"Because," she said, "you were our son. And we wanted you to be well. And you seemed to be better here than you had in years. So we did what we needed to do to keep an eye on you. We never expected you'd still be working for your dad all these years later." She looked out the window as if looking at Dad over in his workshop. "And I think maybe he hoped you'd come to love it like he does."

I thought about all the times I'd come home after a day of hard work, and how my whole body would feel alive. Just like it did when I was climbing a mountain, or paddling a river.

"I think I did," I said. "Just not the part he wanted me to."

"And that's okay," Mum said. "I think he's just disappointed. But he'll come around. We've always known you'd want to do something creative. So this is no surprise really."

Mum smiled, and I could tell that she really believed that. I wasn't so sure; Dad had seemed really set on retiring soon. But I decided to just take her word for it, and Dad could sort himself out. It didn't have to be my problem.

"But I'll tell you what is a surprise," she said.

"What's that?"

"That you and Morgan broke up," she said. "We really liked her, Jackie."

"Yeah," I said sadly. "Me too."

"You wanna tell me what happened?"

I found that I did, actually; I did want to tell Mum what had happened. But I wasn't sure if I'd be able to without crying. I could already feel the tears pricking at my eyes – they were probably only half from being asked about Morgan, and half from the relief of having told my parents about RIBA – and I looked up at the light coming through the window to try to stop them coming. It didn't work, and I felt them drip down my cheeks as I blinked.

"Oh, darling," Mum said, wiping them away, but I quickly replenished them. I looked down at my lap, where she'd taken my hands in hers.

"She's so talented," I said, trying my best to distil everything into something easy for Mum to understand. "She had this job opportunity in York, and I gave her an ultimatum."

"Oh, love."

"I know," I said, nodding. "She said that she didn't want to leave, but that she couldn't be with me if I couldn't be honest with myself and with her about what I wanted."

Mum nodded, trying to follow along. "Which was..."

I shrugged. "Well, her, obviously. But also this." I nodded at the booklet, which Dad had dropped on the sofa when he left. "Just ... more. For myself."

"She's a smart woman," Mum said, rubbing circles on my shoulder.

"She really is," I said. "But I messed it up so badly."

Mum shook her head. "I'm so sorry, darling."

"I don't know what to do," I said, the tears coming faster now, and I bent forward to rest my forehead on her shoulder.

"I think you're doing everything you can do," Mum said.

"But what if it's not enough?" I asked, sitting up again, searching her eyes for reassurance.

"For what?" she asked. "Because if you're doing all this to get her back" – she gestured to the booklet – "it doesn't mean anything. But I don't think that's true."

"Enough to be happy," I said. I didn't tell her that I wasn't completely convinced I *could* be happy without Morgan.

"You'll find happiness no matter what," Mum said. "It's not about one thing that will make you happy, remember? It's about how you approach life. And it seems like you're finally starting to get that."

I THOUGHT about Mum's advice all through the next twenty-four hours, as I packed for the Ren Faire. It was almost verbatim what I'd said to Morgan all those months ago on the riverside on our weekend away. But then I'd been talking about adventure. Maybe what I meant then and what she meant now were the same thing.

The time had finally come. My costumes were expertly packed by Chloe, and the Defender was full of petrol. I'd been bracing myself to be around Morgan for the weekend, but I still had a few hours until I'd need to confront that. In the meantime, I was sharing a lift to the airport with my two favourite people. And if I were ever going to find happiness amidst my grief and anxiety, it was going to be with them.

I picked Phil up first, and I laughed out loud when I saw him come down the drive with a cardboard lute in his hand.

"How the hell are you gonna get that on the plane?" I asked as he actually buckled it into the back seat to keep it from moving around.

"That's the definition of a personal item, mate," he said.

"I really don't think that's true."

I backed out of the drive, careful not to hit the other car there besides Phil's; presumably it belonged to the nurse he had staying with Ethel whilst we were on our trip.

"How's Ethel doing?" I asked, and Phil told me all about her physical therapy and her memory specialist appointments. He looked exhausted just talking about it.

"How are *you* doing?" I asked, and this time he just scoffed.

"Oh me? Better than ever," he said. "I'm perfect."

"You didn't seem so perfect the last time we talked."

"Yeah, well, that was a while ago," he mumbled. I wracked my brain, but I realised he was right.

"Shit," I said, "is Adam's stag really the last time we had a proper chat?" That had been almost two months ago.

"Well, you've been a bit busy," Phil said. "You've fit in a whole relationship cycle in that time."

"Oh fuck off," I said, rolling my eyes. But I knew it was just a defence mechanism.

"Sorry," he said. "Honestly, I've been better. I'm just tired, you know? My whole life is medication schedules and therapy rotations. That's why I was so glad for the costumes as a distraction. And now that they're done..."

It sounded like Phil was dealing with the same thing I had been, when I'd been dreading all the admin Dad was chucking at me. But Ethel wasn't a job. He couldn't just quit. She was everything to him.

"You should talk to Amy," I said, thinking about how she'd helped me. "She's only working part-time at the moment, and she's pretty good with that kind of thing." She'd recently started working as a virtual assistant, which made me happy; if she was getting a job, maybe it meant she was planning to stick around.

Phil turned to me and grimaced. "I sort of already have," he said. "And I've got a whole windowsill full of crystals at home for Ethel to show for it."

I chuckled at how unsurprised I was. Part of me was even ... relieved?

"I'm not gonna pry," I said, "but just be nice to her, okay?"

"Ew, Jack," Phil said, then slumped down in his seat and pulled out his phone.

I didn't know how the weekend would go with Morgan. I really did want things to be okay there, and if I could have snapped my fingers and had her back, I would have. But for the first time since the breakup, driving from Phil's to Chloe's, on my way to have a new adventure with my friends, I knew that I would be okay without her. It may only come in crumbs for a while, but I'd find happiness again. And that was enough to keep me going.

CHAPTER 46
MORGAN

I grunted as I lifted my bag from the carousel at Charlotte Douglas International Airport a few days later; I was surprised it hadn't been overweight when they weighed it at Heathrow with my chain mail knocking around inside. We'd all talked a big game about packing carry-on only, but it turned out two costumes each meant a checked bag each, too. And an extra one for Phil, who had constructed a lute out of cardboard and had to carry it on as his personal item so it wouldn't get crushed in his bag.

Given that it had been my first ever flight, I'd felt significantly less anxious than I'd expected to. I was nervous about seeing Jack; we were three weeks post-breakup and had yet to actually speak out of character. There was also a bit of bumpy air over Nova Scotia that had me gripping the armrest. But despite those hiccups, the frenzy of the past week won out, and I'd actually spent most of the flight conked out next to Grey, who read the book I'd brought for myself.

"Our car pickup was supposed to be an hour ago," Grey

whined, tugging at the short strands of their green buzz cut. Fatima shushed them for the tenth time since we'd got off the plane and knocked their hand away.

"I told you," she said, "they have our flight info. They know the flight was late. It'll be fine."

But despite her reassurances, the moment we all had our bags, Grey started speed walking towards customs. They shouldered past an old couple clearly on holiday and practically stepped over a toddler who wandered out in front of them, on a mission to make sure our "large SUV" wasn't given away to someone else.

As we walked, I gravitated towards Chloe whenever I could, avoiding falling into step with Jack. Not that I didn't want to know how he was, or tell him how I was. With everything that had been going on, everything I'd decided, all I wanted was to tell him. I wanted him to be proud of the fact that I'd managed that hike all on my own. I wanted to tell him all about my plans for the move, and to have him help me pick out furniture. I wanted to tell him that his opinions mattered to me, and they weren't an imposition.

But I hadn't had the chance. And if I knew what was good for me, I wouldn't manufacture one.

"I'm so tired," Chloe said with a yawn. "It's like ten at night back home."

"Says the girl who plays video games until two am every night?"

"Fair point."

The large SUV had not, in fact, been saved for us, so we were given what was apparently the next best thing: a minivan. At least it fit all of us, though with the level of chatter going on in the back seats, it did feel like a car full of kids. And with Jack and me at the front – I'd tried to avoid sitting next to him, but the other seats had been occupied by the time I'd loaded my bags into the boot – it felt like a mum and dad on the school run. I tried to focus on the autumn foliage instead of my ex-boyfriend, but I couldn't help but look over at him every now and then, taking advantage of the fact that he was concentrating too hard on driving on the right-hand side of the road to notice me staring.

THE HOUSE we'd hired was next-level. We'd opted for what we considered the ultimate American experience: a McMansion. Huge features, way out of proportion to the size of the garden, and way too close to the houses around it. The neighbourhood we drove into must have had hundreds of homes, all from the same four or five plans from the look of it, just the colours and materials on the outside differentiating them from one another.

As we pulled into a circular driveway and climbed out of the car, we all looked up at the hulking "Classic American Family Home", as the listing had claimed. Inside was just as gargantuan; everything was massive and so spaced out that we could have parked a car in the centre of every room. We all had our own bedrooms – thankfully we'd booked long before Jack and I had got together – and it was a challenge just finding all of them. Some were on the ground floor, including the giant primary suite Chloe had claimed for the trouble of managing the booking, and Jack's was even in the basement.

My room was upstairs, with a big window overlooking the driveway, and a shared bathroom with Phil. I laid out my chain mail and bright pink tunic on the chair by the window and hung my dress on the curtain rod; the rail in the closet was too low, causing the dress to pool on the ground, and though I knew it would get filthy when I wore it to the Ren Faire in a couple of days, I couldn't stand the thought of just *letting* it get wrinkled.

Once I'd freshened up, I wandered out to the back deck with the others. It was much warmer here in North Carolina than back home, even in October, and even though the sun was setting, the humidity was still palpable in the air, making the hot tub in the corner of the deck look a lot more appealing. There was a massive barbecue on the raised deck as well. Beyond that there was a rolling pitch of grass, bordered by a laughably small privacy fence; laughable because of how close the neighbouring houses were. But the back of the property bordered the edge of the neighbourhood where, beyond a wide strip of grass and then a cluster of trees, we could see the colourful signs and bunting of the Ren Faire.

"Wow," I said, my voice breathy, "we're really here, aren't we?"

We all lined up against the railing, looking out over the manicured lawn and the festival grounds beyond. Jack was at the opposite end of the group, and I took advantage of the distance to watch him without getting caught.

There was something different about him, I could tell. He'd always done a brilliant job of blending into the group, but he seemed even more at ease than usual. Like that ease was less put on. And try as I might, I couldn't help but feel hurt. Was he that much happier now that we weren't together anymore? Had he been right all along, and he was actually happier and better off without a relationship?

A cool breeze blew across the back of the house, making the hair on the back of my neck stand up. I was determined to have a nice, drama-free time at the Ren Faire. I'd been looking forward to it for so long, and I didn't want what had happened between Jack and me to ruin it. Not for me, not for anyone. But based on the knot that formed in my stomach as I watched him joke with Chloe about something that I couldn't hear, I knew that was going to be easier said than done.

CHAPTER 47
JACK

All summer, even with all the costumes and the planning and the excitement from the others, I'd never really understood why this was so irresistible to them. I was mostly along for the ride.

But as we stepped through the gates, the trumpets ushering us into a wooded glade lined with colourful medieval-style shopfronts, the morning light overhead creating dappled shadows on the face of performers dressed as faeries and jesters, the smell of cinnamon roasted almonds and kettle corn floating on the gentle breeze ... I finally got it. It was fucking magical.

And it only got more magical as we went on and saw just how committed to the bit this festival was. There was a smith, a dungeon, and signs for "privies". There were callers advertising shows, and bards playing lutes and lyres. There were faeries on mats every hundred metres or so, blowing bubbles for the kids. We even saw a procession for the Festival Queen, who would be presiding over the jousts later.

We'd opted for our character outfits for the first day; the

weather was meant to be a bit cooler, so we thought we'd get the metal and leather out of the way. Morgan was wearing her chain mail, of course, along with our foam sword sheathed at her side. And despite the fact that Thrormir was dead and gone, I was still dressed as him, in my cheap plastic armour I'd bought online. I looked like the Wish version of Thor in the cheap blond wig, carrying my warhammer.

Other than Morgan, Chloe had definitely gone in the hardest on her costume; she'd worked black leather into a bodysuit that looked somehow both slutty and practical, which shouldn't have been possible, if her rants over the years about female characters in video games had been anything to go by. But she'd managed it, and with horns glued to her forehead, a very realistic purple wig, purple body paint, and a really cool flame effect painted on the palms of her hands, she looked like the Calamity of Morgan's drawings come to life.

Phil had gone in pretty hard on his own outfit, too, which was similar to my outfit for the next day, except with a huge leather pauldron on one shoulder and his cardboard lute strapped to his back.

Grey wore a tattered brown garment around their waist, and a leather breastplate and gauntlets. They had a faux animal skull of some sort attached to their shoulder, and pointy teeth poked up out of their mouth. Their skin was painted green from head to toe, their green buzz cut blending in perfectly. They carried a huge foam battle-axe, which, along with Morgan's sword, had to be peace-tied in red string at the gate. I noticed they didn't bother making me do that for my cheap cardboard warhammer.

Fatima was the closest to me in terms of cosplay quality – or lack thereof – in an outfit that I was pretty sure had been a pre-assembled Halloween costume with some faux leather armour on top. To our group, she was clearly Clover, the Thieves Guild faerie we'd encountered in the fae realm. But to everyone else, she probably looked like a battle-ready brunette Tinkerbell.

Either way, she was attracting a lot of attention, as was Chloe; they skipped along arm-in-arm, encouraging rather than ignoring the leering looks they got. *More power to 'em*, I thought, as Chloe blew a kiss at a caller staring directly at her chest.

By the time we'd made it just a couple hundred metres into the festival grounds, we must have stopped for half a dozen photo ops, standing in front of things like the "Flying DaVinci Machine" kids' ride and the sign for "Turkey Leggs". People also wanted pictures with *us*, and not just people that weren't dressed up; it quickly became clear that other groups would want to meet us and take photos with us, too. It was "Heroes and Villains Weekend" apparently, so the Renaissance theme was applied more loosely than I would have expected. A group of people dressed as Vikings stopped for one, and when I asked if they were heroes or villains, one of the girls smiled at me as she walked away, calling "That's the centuries-old question, my man!" as she went.

But mostly, I couldn't keep my eyes off Morgan. She looked incredible in her outfit. Powerful. And the joy in her eyes as she walked around and took in the faire, the desire she'd had for months and shared with all of us, the dream she'd made reality ... it made everything that had happened since then feel worthwhile. Even if I couldn't reach out and take her hand like I wanted to.

We walked all the way to the end of the fairground, passing the jousting arena, countless food stalls, the smith, loads of artisan shops and stands, at least ten performance stages – "fourteen, actually", Grey said, consulting the illustrated map they'd picked up at the entrance – and even a mermaid exhibit.

We queued at a food stall called the Cappuccino Inn, desperate for caffeine, whilst Chloe held a picnic table for us so we could strategise the day.

As I stood in line behind Morgan, I watched her laugh and joke with Grey and Phil about a group that had walked by, all seemingly dressed as different famous dragons; as far as they could tell, there was Puff the Magic Dragon, Mushu from *Milan*, the dragon from *Shrek*, what seemed to be Smaug, and two people attached as the two-headed dragon from *Quest for Camelot*. Morgan gasped in delight as she clocked Puff's bowtie, and something inside me ached as she reached out to grab Phil's arm; I wished I were the one getting her whispered jokes and amused smiles. But I was at least glad she was having fun.

We made our way to the picnic table, where Grey spread their map out across the surface. Fatima dug through her waist pouch and pulled out a pen, handing it to them.

"So," they said, clicking the pen, "there are three jousts throughout the day, so we need to catch at least one of them..."

It was no surprise that Grey and Chloe both had lots of opinions on what was can't-miss and what could be saved for the next day. But what surprised me – and honestly delighted me – was that Morgan steered the conversation as much as either of them. And rightfully so; coming to the Ren Faire had been her idea to begin with. It was nice to see her asserting herself so confidently, especially in contrast to when she'd first joined the group, and I couldn't help but watch admiringly over the next ten minutes as she helped shape the plan.

This staring and gazing and admiring was going to get me in trouble though, so I was glad when someone suggested we split up until lunch so we could see more shows between us. Even though Morgan, Fatima and Grey were going to see an acrobatics show I wanted to see, I figured it would be better to tag along with Chloe and Phil so I could stay out of trouble. And if I noticed a slight frown flash across Morgan's face as I shared that decision, I determined not to notice it, and certainly not to read anything into it.

I let myself have one last longing look for the day as Morgan and the others walked off towards the acrobatics show, whispering under my breath, "look back, look back". And then I tried not to let myself be too disappointed when she didn't.

Two shows later we had a message waiting for us in the group chat as we started looking for them: they had spotted how busy the joust already was, with people sat in the bleachers hours before the event, so they wanted us to find some food and meet them there. Grey had added a desperate plea to save the turkey legs for later when we could eat them together, so we opted for a smorgasbord of options from a variety of stalls, heading towards the arena with everything from barbecue mac and cheese to a "charcuterie cup".

As soon as we got to the arena, we could tell why they had been so desperate to grab seats: half the arena was in full sun, with the other half in full shade. Whoever was sat in the full sun would be squinting the whole time; as far as I knew, none of us had thought to bring sunglasses. And based on the way the shaded side was filling up, I suspected we would have had to endure it had we not had people saving seats for us.

It took us a couple minutes of scanning, but I saw the glint of sunlight off Morgan's chain mail, and then spotted Fatima waving to us. We apologetically climbed over the others sitting in the row until we reached the empty space in front of our friends, handing out food as we scooted past them, Grey leaning over to move the bags they'd used to hold our place.

"Thanks for lunch," Morgan said, looking directly at me and smiling. I'd taken care to hand her the mac and cheese, knowing that would be her preference.

"No worries," I said, holding up my slice of pizza in a "cheers" motion. Morgan followed suit and laughed. She seemed to be in a good mood, and I wanted desperately to talk to her normally – to ask her how their shows were, and how she was doing; really anything to get to talk to her properly for the first time in weeks – but something was starting in the arena, and it would have been too obvious to turn around for a chat. So instead I focused my attention on my pizza and on the person coming through the gate at the end of the field to my left. They began checking the field and the tilt rail, getting ready for the joust.

There was a large, two-level structure over the gate, with a viewing platform with three thrones in the middle running along the top. Musicians climbed a set of stairs at the back, placing their music on stands to the left of the thrones. Other guests filed into the space on the right, and below.

"I wonder how you get those seats," Fatima said behind me, pointing to the cushy, covered seating on the lower level, just below the balcony where I was pretty sure the Festival Queen would shortly appear.

"It's for the wedding guests," Grey answered. "The couple get to sit up there with the Queen." They pointed at the upper level, and I noticed that indeed two of the thrones seemed to be one double throne, as if for a couple.

The guests finished filing in, and I wondered why those were the coveted seats; surely they weren't a better view of the joust. But they were at least shaded, unlike the seats across the arena from us, where people were shielding their eyes and fanning their faces with their maps.

Eventually the gates opened, and three horses cantered out, each with a rider, followed by two more cast members on foot. Two of the riders were knights in shining plate armour, and one was an elegant-looking host in a long dress draped over either side of the horse.

"Welcome!" the host called, bringing things to order. The crowd was clearly ready for the show, and everyone else seemed to know exactly when to cheer and where to insert a hearty "huzzah", or at least were good at pretending like they did. The atmosphere was one huge, sustained crescendo, like we were all perched on horseback like the knights.

One after the other, the knights performed "feats of strength and accuracy", as the host dubbed them, spearing hoops on their lances and smashing through wooden targets. It was clearly a build-up to the main event, but it was entertaining to watch. The knights were performers like everyone else, each initiating taunts of their opponent and doing victory dances and poses from atop their horses when they succeeded. The one assigned to our side of the arena – Sir Maximus, as he was announced – was in elegant black and gold regalia. A few merchants roamed through the crowd on our side selling pennants in his colours, and at Chloe's behest I waved one of them over to grab some for us, just as a line of trumpeters filed onto the field.

As they began to play, I wasn't the only one to wince, and a small child in front of me in a flower crown covered her ears at the noise. Luckily they were just announcing the arrival of the Festival Queen, who ascended the stairs and stood at the apex of the balcony, her hands resting on the railing.

I watched as, just as Grey said, a couple – one in a long

white dress with trailing sleeves, and one in an intricate brocade tunic – appeared on the balcony behind the Queen. She announced them to the crowd, who gave a big "huzzah!" to their nuptials, and I joined in, even if I didn't feel particularly like celebrating love in that moment.

I heard Morgan join in, too, and I may have been hearing what I expected to hear, but did she maybe sound a bit unenthusiastic, too?

The couple took their seats, as did the Queen, and then, it seemed, the joust itself could start. Time after time the knights charged at one another, aiming not for each other's torsos but at targets affixed to their opponent's shoulder. Despite the sea of blue and silver on the other side of the arena cheering on the other knight, Sir Maximus was victorious in every single pass. Chloe shushed Phil as he insisted it was staged, instead jumping and cheering for Maximus's attention as he vamped to the crowd after another win. She shimmied in a way I was pretty sure was designed to make her boobs jiggle as much as possible, and I swore I could see his eyes almost fall out of his head as he did a double-take in her direction.

"Slag," Phil teased as she sat down.

"Don't you forget it," she said, sitting back down and crossing her legs.

The joust was, in fact, incredibly cheesy and staged, but the crowd ate up every second of it, and honestly, I did, too. It seemed like a large part of the Renaissance Faire was suspension of disbelief; nobody was bothered with authenticity or plausibility, and they were having way more fun as a result. That seemed to be the name of the game today, after all; Morgan was acting as if the last few months had never happened, and if she could act that well, then I could, too. So I leaned into the excitement as much as I could. I cheered for

Maximus and booed the other knight; I took pictures with the others afterwards at the character boards, letting myself be "duped" into a picture of my face on a tavern wench's body; I did the silly strength test that insisted I was a "sickly child"; I ripped my trousers trying to nock an arrow at the archery range; I even dropped an ungodly amount of money on a metal crown that Chloe insisted made me look like a rakish royal.

"It does look nice," Morgan said as I examined it in the shop's mirror, making me jump about a million miles in the air. I tried my best not to look bowled over, doing the first thing I thought of, which was for some reason to … bow slightly? Why the hell was I bowing?

"Thank you, m'lady."

She smiled and dipped into a slight curtsy in response, despite being in armour, not a dress. "Your Grace."

She turned away to join the others, and I watched her go, wondering how it was possible that we stepped so far back that we were simply good acquaintances again. I stepped forward to follow her out, but as I did, a realisation hit me so hard that it made me physically recoil.

This whole time, I had been convinced that we would either completely disappear from each other's lives, or we'd move past things. Probably the former, given how hurtful we'd both been to each other. And as impossible as that felt, I knew I *could* do it; I'd done it before, after all. And to an extent, I was prepared for that.

But now, as I successfully pretended like everything was fine, and she seemed to be doing the same, I realised that the one eventuality I hadn't prepared for was one where she actually wanted to just be friends again. To have gone through everything we did to just see each other on Mondays and occasional weekends. To laugh at one another's jokes and text each other "happy birthday" and "what was the name of that film you mentioned?" To date other people, and have to meet each other's other people. To still watch each other's futures unfold as if we hadn't once thought we'd be sharing one.

That, actually, sounded like the worst possible outcome of all. And suddenly I wasn't so sure I was capable of pretending after all.

CHAPTER 48
MORGAN

I felt a pinch in my heart as I walked away from Jack, and not just from the embarrassment of having actually curtsied at him – seriously, what the hell was that? – but also because he seemed to be doing ... well, fine. Sure, I'd caught him gazing at me a couple of times, but that was only because of how unsubtle he was. I'd been watching him, too; very closely, in fact. And whilst he wasn't the *most* joyful I'd ever seen him – the crinkly-eyed smiles didn't seem to have made the trip – he was smiling and laughing with the rest of us, and I tried very hard not to take that personally.

The Ren Faire was magical; of course it was. It was always going to be. But it felt like I was on the outside of that magic. Like everyone else was under some enchantment, but I'd succeeded on my saving throw. I wanted to be in it with them. I'd been looking forward to the festival for months, after all. But instead of feeling as immersed as I knew I should be, it all just felt *hollow*.

Throughout the rest of the afternoon, my chain mail

weighed heavy on me. Even with the plastic rings making up the bulk of it, I was still too warm, probably more from lugging it around than from the actual temperature. The afternoon sun was certainly heating things up, but a nice breeze cut through the trees, and there was enough shade that it never got too bad.

I tried my best to stay present as we took in some of the attractions, like archery, at which I was shockingly good, and axe throwing, at which I was shockingly bad; as I pulled my arms up overhead to throw, I ended up flinging the axe backwards and almost taking out a couple dressed as pirates.

"Watch it!" one of them yelled, though I didn't even catch which one, given that I was too busy hiding behind Chloe, who was laughing so hard I thought she might cry.

Besides Jack, the biggest downside was that everything cost money, and we were burning through our cash *fast*. We all grumbled at having dropped two bucks on a "dungeon experience" which ended up just being a maze of dim, damp hallways with plaques about medieval torture methods and mannequins acting them out.

"Honestly," Phil whispered to me as we wandered through, "that stretching rack would sort my back *right* out."

Jack came up behind us in the dark, startling me. "I can help with that," he said, reaching out towards Phil teasingly, who waved him off. Phil jogged ahead to catch up with Fatima, who had sped through after realising what the subject matter was. That's how I found myself walking alongside Jack. I turned back to look for Grey and Chloe, but they were far enough behind that I couldn't see them; just a family with two young boys, who were gawking at each of the scenes.

"Woah, that's so cool," one of them said as they stopped in front of an iron maiden.

"Yeah, so cool," echoed the other, clearly younger, standing on his tiptoes to get a better look.

The older one lost interest and darted past me. I dodged to the side to avoid a collision with the kid, creating one with Jack instead. I felt him tense behind me, but I couldn't move; the little one was running after his brother, and the parents followed behind, gesturing apologetically. Only once they'd squeezed past could I step away from Jack, kicking myself internally for my body's protest at losing contact. I realised that, for the first time since we'd broken up weeks ago, I was alone with Jack. In the dark. With his stubble and his awful yet charming outfit and that stupid crooked crown on top of his wig. He was looking down at the floor, as if he'd had the same realisation and was trying not to be too intense.

"Having fun?" he asked, his gaze fixed on his feet as he leaned against the wall.

"Yeah, definitely," I said, as casually as possible. Why wasn't I walking away? "You?"

He shrugged. "Yeah, it's really cool. Just like you said."

He offered me a smile, but if I'd learned anything over the last few months, it was what a real Jack Evans smile looked like. And this wasn't one. My instant reaction was to ask him what was wrong, but I knew it would be pointless. We both knew this wasn't okay. So I decided to be honest.

"I know this is hard," I said, catching his eye when he looked up suddenly, clearly surprised.

"Yeah," he said, sounding relieved. "Really fucking hard."

I frowned. "I'm sorry. But it's just two days. After that, we can, you know..."

Jack looked at me hopefully, and I paused, wondering what he wanted me to say. What else could possibly follow after what we'd said to each other that night we'd ended things.

"... get some distance."

His face fell. Clearly he had been hoping for something else. But I had nothing else to give him.

"That's not fair, Jack," I muttered at my own feet, as if he'd spoken his hope out loud.

"What's not?" He looked wounded.

"Making me feel like the bad guy." I threw my hands up in resignation and fell back against the opposite wall, letting it hold me up. I could feel the hard pattern of the chain mail through my undershirt.

"I'm not trying to do that," Jack said. "I know I'm the bad guy here."

I let out a frustrated sigh. "See, no, that's not fair either," I said. "You can't make yourself the martyr. That's the whole point."

"How is that the point?"

"Because!" I said, my voice loud enough that it echoed around us. We both looked around to see if anyone would poke their head around a corner, but no one did.

"Because," I said again, quieter this time, "your entire life revolves around this twisted sense of self-sacrifice. Like if you give up everything you want, if you make yourself less important, people will love you more."

I looked up at him again to find his eyes fixed on the wall to my right, and I wondered why I was even bothering. He'd bedded in so deeply to that sense of martyrdom, and honestly, it had been working for him until I'd come along. Did I think it would make him happy in the long run? Of course not. But that was also no longer my problem.

"And here I was thinking maybe you wanted to be friends," he said after a long moment, and my heart sank.

"I don't know, Jack," I said, and clambered for something else to add—

We both know that can only lead to one thing.

I still don't know what the future holds for me.

I'm still in love with you, and being your friend would be too hard.

—but none of those felt helpful, so I just left it. And the silence and stillness between us was long enough that Grey and Chloe finally poked their heads around the corner. I reached my hand out for Chloe, who walked sheepishly over to me and grabbed it. She led me away from Jack, who remained where he was, his jaw set, his eyes glued to the stone wall. And maybe it was just the dim light, but I was almost sure I saw them filling with tears.

By the end of the day, we were all so shattered that we could barely muster enough enthusiasm for a turkey leg. But for Grey's sake, we managed, standing in a circle and dutifully taking bites as Fatima, our resident veggie, stood in the middle and filmed us. It was surprisingly good, actually, but we were all ready to be off our feet, and the staff were walking up and down the festival ground encouraging people towards the exit. So as soon as the camera was off, we started shuffling in that direction.

Back at the house, Phil immediately started on dinner whilst the rest of us disrobed. The spray paint on my chain mail had held up fairly well, and I folded the shirt up as carefully as possible so I'd be able to wear it again. And I hoped I did have an occasion to wear it again, even if I did need to create some distance.

My moment with Jack in the dungeon had confirmed that I needed to take a step back from our D&D nights, sooner rather than later, regardless of my upcoming move. I'd decided I didn't want to – couldn't, even – keep being around him that way. He clearly couldn't handle it, either. After the last couple of weeks, I felt pretty confident that my other friendships would survive me not being in the campaign anymore. But Jack and I could not be friends. I didn't have it in me.

Once I was changed, I snuck out the front door. It had been a busy few weeks making arrangements for the move, and I had some logistics still to deal with. It was already dusk, but I walked down the street far enough that I knew the others wouldn't interrupt.

I took out my phone to make the call, but I saw that I had an email back from my mum. I'd finally responded to one of her updates – the one about her yoga classes – and for the first time in years we were properly talking. Based on the times her emails had come through, I suspected she was getting woken up by notifications so she could respond to me right away. And in just four days, we'd exchanged almost a dozen emails, and I had offered to help her design the logo and website for her travelling yoga studio.

Once I'd responded to *my* mum, I rang Cara's mum. We had a few details to discuss, but most of all I wanted to know how they'd managed to get a moving truck onto the tiny, cramped road outside the house. I had one booked for next month to take away most of the furniture, but I had no idea how they'd load it without blocking the whole street.

I stopped walking when I came to a cul-de-sac, standing next to a McMansion identical to ours until I was done with the call. Then I started back and dialled the second person I needed to speak to.

"Hey Lauren, it's Morgan," I said when Lauren answered the phone at the Rescue.

"Hey! I was just getting Pablo's paperwork in order. Great timing."

I smiled – Lauren had been so excited when I'd filed the adoption application, and she was doing me a massive favour by skipping a bit of red tape so I could take him home before the transfer happened.

"And you're sure it won't get flagged for not having a permanent address?" I asked.

"Yeah, that's fine," she said. "I may have changed your status to 'pre-approved' in the system."

Pre-approved status was usually for applicants who had already rescued before, so they didn't need to undergo a house visit or a background check. Not that I was worried about the background check, but the home visit might have thrown up some red flags if conducted by anyone other than Lauren, given that the house was currently full of moving boxes.

"You're my hero," I said. "I owe you a drink when we get back."

"You bring that cute friend of yours, and you have yourself a deal."

"Deal."

I looked forward to the squeal I was sure I'd get when I let Chloe in on Lauren's terms, but I couldn't tell her yet. Jack cared so much about Pablo, and I wanted him to be the first to know, even if things were going to be different moving forward.

"Just the bank transfer now," she said, "but you can do that when you're back."

"So I can take him home on Tuesday?" I asked, stopping at the end of the drive, my breath hitching. Images flashed through my mind of all the new places we'd explore as a duo; all the new adventures we'd have together. And I had a lot of adventures ahead of me; that much was certain.

"You can take him home as soon as you're back," she said, and I couldn't help myself; I started dancing right there in the driveway.

CHAPTER 49
JACK

The house was only a ten-minute walk from the Ren Faire entrance, but I felt like a weary adventurer by the time I arrived anyway, kicking off my boots, shedding my plastic armour piece by piece in a trail through my room and bathroom. I at least folded the trousers carefully so Phil could mend them. By the time I was done in the shower, all I wanted was to go to bed, despite the smell of food wafting down to the basement.

I grabbed my tablet and decided to have a wander before dinner. I had a nosy in Chloe's giant primary bedroom, which had its own living room and everything; I checked out the deck, where Fatima and Grey were firing up the hot tub; and finally I went upstairs. There wasn't a lot to see, but there were huge picture windows looking out over both the front and back of the house. I looked out towards the festival grounds; from up here I could just about make out the shape of the jousting arena. Then I crossed the room and looked out at the neighbourhood of almost identical houses, wondering why anyone would opt for something so starkly out of place in the landscape around it.

I pulled a bean bag chair up to the window to sketch. I was on a new tablet: a used iPad I'd bought off Amy. I knew she could use the money, and I needed something more sustainable than pencil and paper to use for my course. But sat there, I struggled to find inspiration in the overly manicured neighbourhood; it was like all the soul had been sucked from the landscape when it had been developed. I imagined it as it might have been before, still full of the oak and maple and chestnut trees we'd seen at the festival ground. And that's how I found my muse.

I started sketching out the landscape; it was flat now, but I could tell from the way the trees leaned around the borders that there would have been a shallow gully at one point. So I recreated it as best as I could imagine, with a little stream running through the middle. Then I started to add a Tudor-style cottage beside it, just big enough for two.

Just as I was finishing the shape of the house, I saw movement from the corner of my eye. I looked down and saw Morgan in the driveway, doing the running man with her phone in one hand.

I smiled and watched her until she stopped and brought the phone back to her ear, and wondered who she was talking to that had her so excited. My heart sank when I realised it was probably related to the job; she'd probably got an offer. But on a Saturday? No, something wasn't quite adding up...

"Dinner!" Phil yelled, and I headed back downstairs, reaching the kitchen just as Morgan came through the front door. She had a huge smile plastered on her face, and she searched around, locking eyes with me and opening her mouth as if she were going to share whatever her news was.

But then she clearly thought better of it, or maybe remembered that I wasn't supposed to be that person for her anymore.

So instead she frowned and clamped her mouth shut, filing in line behind me as we queued for dinner.

I DIDN'T QUITE HAVE the stomach for combat once it was full of spaghetti bolognese, but I knew how much Fatima had been pouring into planning tonight's session – it was "the big one", apparently – so I made myself a cup of tea and soldiered on. And I wasn't alone; the kettle took so long to boil on the hob that by the time it was done there was a queue behind me, including Fatima and Grey, who were still wearing their swimsuits.

"Let's aim for eight maybe for our session?" Fatima asked the group as she dropped teabags into a line of mugs one after the other. That gave us about forty-five minutes.

"Finally time to see Ser Prize in action!" Grey said, smiling at me.

"I need a disco nap," Chloe said with a yawn, which set the rest of us off.

"Eight sounds good," Phil said. "Just enough time to mend Jack's trousers and my undershirt before tomorrow."

I headed downstairs to grab said trousers, then followed Phil to his room on the top floor. He had me put them on since the rip was in the pocket, not wanting to get the angles wrong and have it lie funny. I told him it didn't matter, but he insisted, so I used his bathroom to strip off my joggers and put my trousers back on. Phil squatted down to pin them in place, shoving his hand down through the waistband of the trousers so far that, had I not known him all my life, I might have been filing a complaint.

Just as he was finishing the pinning, there was a knock at the door.

"What do you want me to do with the leftovers?" Chloe's voice asked from the other side.

"Hang on," Phil called, then looked up at me. "If you put these on the bed, I can get them mended. Just be careful taking them off."

"Aye, aye," I said with a little salute.

Once Phil left the room, I unfastened the trousers and slipped them off carefully, just grazing my upper thigh with one of the pins. Then, when I was folding them to set them on the bed, I managed to plunge one of them deep into my finger. When I pulled it back, it instantly started dripping blood, and a few droplets got on my white t-shirt.

"Shit," I said, pulling it off immediately. I ducked back into the bathroom and started filling up the sink with water, dunking the entire shirt into it and scratching at the red spot with my finger. I'd seen Mum do this before when she'd cut herself cooking, saying the sooner she got the towel into the water, the less likely it would be to stain.

I turned off the water once the sink was full and kept scratching at the fabric; I was pretty sure it was working, but there was one stubborn spot right by the hem.

I reached for the plug to drain the sink so I could fill it with clean water, but just as my hand came in contact with metal, the door on the other side of the bathroom opened, and Morgan stepped in, her eyes going wide when she saw me.

"What the fuck?!" she shouted. "What the hell are you doing?" Her eyes looked from me – mostly naked – to the sink full of slightly pink water and back again. "Are you cleaning up a crime scene? Is Phil in there with fabric scissors sticking out of his chest?"

I laughed, half in surprise and half at her joke. It came out like a bark. "Just trying to get blood out of my top," I said.

"That's not really helping your case," she said, then reached out towards the sink. "Here, you need to get some clean water running over it."

I smiled. "Thanks," I said. "Good idea."

Once I'd refilled the sink, I stood up straight and suddenly realised just how small the bathroom was. Or maybe Morgan was just standing closer than necessary to me. Either way, I didn't step away, and neither did she. I looked at her in the mirror, trying to catch her gaze, but I couldn't, because it was too busy running over my form. I tried not to flex or reposition, which I knew would give away that I'd seen her, so I just watched her check me out for a solid five seconds before she realised what she was doing. I took advantage of the moment to admire her in return, from the unkempt, very grabbable array of hair falling over her shoulders to the almost-too-short t-shirt dress she wore. I could tell she wasn't wearing a bra underneath.

When she saw me watching her watch me, she looked away, her cheeks flushing pink. But she still didn't move away.

"Jack," she said quietly, and now I turned to face her, my chest just inches from her. She still didn't step away. "I'm so sorry about earlier. What I said was over the line."

"No," I said, shaking my head. I brought my hand up under her chin without even thinking about it, tilting it up so I could see her face. It still took her a moment to meet my gaze, but when she did, the mix of emotions I saw there sent shivers up my spine. "No, it wasn't out of line at all. It was exactly right. You were right. This whole time."

I watched her eyes as she listened to me, my pulse quickening as I saw relief flash across them. Then I dropped my hand, because it wasn't my place to touch her like that anymore; and because if I didn't, I was going to kiss her.

"What you said sucked," I said. "It really, really hurt. And I still don't totally understand why you couldn't let me figure my shit out *and* be with you. But I don't blame you for feeling like it was getting in the way."

"That's not what I meant," she said, her brows pulling up and in, her lips forming into a pout. "It wasn't getting in the way. I just..."

I could see her debating what she wanted to say to me; how far to push this. It felt like we were on the precipice of something; maybe the most honest conversation we'd ever had. So I stood stock still, not wanting to spook her.

"I didn't know what I wanted yet," she said. "And it felt like your baggage was making you pull me in a direction that I'm not even sure *you* wanted for me."

I sort of half-laughed – more of an audible smile, really – and she frowned.

"So in other words," I said, "it was getting in the way?"

She rolled her eyes up and to the side as she thought about that, taking a deep breath. "Yes, okay, fine. It was getting in the way. But *you* weren't getting in the way. And it's important to me that you know that."

"I think I do," I said, and it was true.

As I watched the way she looked at me, her chocolate brown eyes staring into mine, I felt like maybe she still wanted me as much as I wanted her. God, she was gorgeous. And so talented, and so clever. And infuriating sometimes. And I really, really wanted to kiss her.

But I didn't get the chance, because she kissed me first.

Her lips were soft and tentative at first, but the moment I parted mine to taste her, something ignited in her. She reached her arms up over my shoulders, running one hand through the hair at the nape of my neck, biting at my lower lip. I'd made out with Morgan enough times to know what that meant – what she wanted – and I went instantly hard in response.

I reached down to wrap my hands around her thighs, spreading her apart and lifting her up; fuck me, she wasn't wearing underwear, either. I set her back down on the edge of the counter next to the sink, and she pressed her hips up into me and pulled my mouth back to hers with an urgency that left me breathless. I wrapped one of her curls around my finger, ran my thumb over her nipple through her top, traced the curve of her hips. Then finally, I sank my fingers into the wetness of her folds.

All the things I'd been missing most when I was alone at night. All of the moments I'd replayed in the weeks since we'd broken up. They were right in front of me, and I was going to have them all. Taste them all. If she'd let me.

Her hand tugged at my waistband and rubbed up the length of my hard-on, and I knew her *letting* me wouldn't be the problem. I felt like I was about to explode just from a single touch.

"Please," she said, holding me in her hand, tugging me towards her, and she didn't need to ask me twice. I pressed straight into her so quickly it made her gasp. And as I thrust as slowly as I could make myself, all I could think was *Yes. Finally. I'm never giving this up again. Fuck, I love this woman.*

I brought my hand to her face, and then she moved it to her neck, where I squeezed gently, making her gasp in delight. I couldn't help but pick up my pace, somehow getting even harder inside her. Then she began to tighten around me, and I used every ounce of restraint I had left to keep my rhythm, moving my other hand to the spot between her legs I knew would push her just over the edge. She pressed forward against me as she came, pulsing around me, and I wrapped my arms around her as I thrust once, twice, three times more before I came, too, bracing myself against the mirror as she held me close. Then I collapsed against her body as we both breathed hard in time with one another.

Everything went a little fuzzy for a moment whilst I came down from the heat of the moment, and it wasn't until I felt a gentle push against my chest that I even considered moving. I grabbed my wet t-shirt from the sink – it needed a wash anyway, I supposed – and handed it to Morgan as I extracted myself carefully.

"That was incredible," I said as I grabbed my joggers from the floor of Phil's room and slipped them back on. I'd have to go get another top from downstairs, but that was fine. I finally had Morgan back, and I didn't care who knew it.

"Shit," Morgan muttered from the bathroom, and I turned around to see her leaning back against the mirror, her hand on her head.

"What's wrong?" I asked, stepping back towards her and lifting a hand to touch her leg, but she waved me away.

"Don't, Jack," she said, her voice firm. "This doesn't change anything."

I froze instantly. "What do you mean?" I asked, hoping desperately I'd misunderstood her.

"I mean, it doesn't change the fact that you and I desperately need some distance," she said, motioning between us. "It doesn't change any decisions either of us has made."

"What are you talking about?" I asked, the hamster in a wheel that passed for my brain running double-time to try to keep up with this about-face. "We made up, didn't we? Is that not what just happened?"

"No, it's not," she said, pushing me out of her way and jumping down from the sink. "You apologised twice. That doesn't change anything for us."

"How does it not change things?" I asked, feeling like I was having the same fight again, but in reverse. "I don't understand what you want from me here."

She turned back on me. "Look, I'm sorry I let it get this far. But the apologies? They don't mean anything without actions. Acknowledging the problem doesn't absolve you of actually having to solve it. And you haven't solved anything. So no, this doesn't change things between us."

I shook my head. There was so much she didn't know. If she'd only let me explain.

"I know that," I said, my voice weak and wobbly. I didn't know what to say. I wanted to grab her by the hands and tell her that I knew. That I was working on it. That I'd done *so much*, and if only she'd let me prove it to her, things would be different.

But the part of me that still fought against all the change I was making kept me frozen. And when she finally looked me in the eye, I thought my heart might excise itself from my body. She looked so ... determined.

"This can't happen again, Jack," she said, her voice smooth and firm. "This was goodbye."

CHAPTER 50
CAPTAIN MORGANA SILVERSWORD

Huddled behind an overturned table in front of the Adventurers Guild House, the party all wondered if this might be their last fight.

Lord Arnault had retaliated, alright. And now, in the courtyard on the other side of their flimsy wooden barrier, was the sorcerer himself. Plus an air elemental, a fiend...

Oh yeah, and a huge black dragon.

All the Adventurers Guild members in the Capital had come together to fight Arnault off. The elemental wasn't looking great, as much as they could tell how damaged a whirlwind of air actually was. But no one had touched Arnault himself, and as long as he was alive, he could just summon more threats.

The adventurers put up their best defence. Druids turned to panthers and cave bears and even giant scorpions. Rangers rained down arrows from above, lined up on the roof. Rogues darted in, stabbed, and darted out again so quickly they were barely visible. Spells flew in from every direction: fire spells, acid spells, ice spells, and more. Yorick and a handful of other bards played battle tunes, adding an oomph to the hits that did land. And there were so many weapons being swung that Morgana would have been worried about accidental attacks on allies, had the enemies not been so glaringly obvious.

After a group of adventurers, including Gorlag, piled in on it, the elemental went down, dissipating into the air with a scream that tore through the night air. The fiend, however, was proving more difficult. Not only was it getting off so many attacks that it was hard to pin down, but it could fly, too. It took out half the rangers before focusing on the fighters who had taken down the elemental, and Morgana gasped as Gorlag dropped to the ground unconscious.

The dragon was a problem, too, but anybody with eyes or ears would have known that. It was so frightening that adventurers struggled to even face it, and even when they did, many of them paid for it with their lives. It kept swooping down and sending blazes of acidic breath onto those taking cover. It landed on top of the guild house, and Morgana watched as it used its tail to send a barbarian fighter flying into the middle of the square. They didn't get up.

The fiend Morgana was wailing on finally went down in a blaze of fire, blipping out of existence suddenly as it fell. Morgana looked over to see Calamity blowing on her hands, which were still smoking. But she was suddenly struck from behind by a bolt of light from Arnault himself, and Morgana cried out as Calamity fell to the ground.

Adventurers lay unmoving all around her, and Arnault stood, largely unhurt, across the square. Morgana made eye contact with him, and he smiled that unnatural smile again. She tightened her grip on her sword and strode towards him.

"Careful," a voice said, and she turned to see Ser Prize

calling to her from where he knelt next to a fallen mage. "You're just out of his range. Go any closer and you'll get hit."

Morgana wasn't afraid of getting hit. But she was afraid of the fact that Arnault was twitching his fingers again. They needed to finish him off now so they could get clerics in before it was too late. So they could stand a chance against the dragon doing his bidding.

"Then shield me," Morgana said, nodding at Ser Prize. "Because I'm going in."

The two of them strode forward together towards Lord Arnault, who fired off what was probably a warning shot; it deflected easily off Ser Prize's shield. Then they got the main event; a blast of light so strong they had to brace against it. But again, the shield took the brunt, along with a magical extension Ser Prize erected as they pushed forward. Morgana caught Arnault's eye again over the edge of the shield, and his smile faltered; there was fear there now. *Good.*

The dragon must have sensed that Arnault was in danger, because the next thing Morgana knew, she was being slashed across the back by its claw, stumbling forward.

"I've got you," Ser Prize said, laying his hand on the spot where the wound had opened. It felt instantly better, and a lump formed in her throat as she thought about Thrormir. She needed to finish this for him.

The dragon cried out, a horrible roar, and dove at them. But just as Morgana saw it open its mouth to breathe acid at them, Ser Prize's javelin tore through its throat, and it crashed to the ground, taking out an entire building as it did. Morgana hoped there was no one inside, but there wasn't time to worry about that now. They had one more enemy to vanquish.

By the time Arnault realised what was coming for him,

Morgana was on top of him. And though he tried to surrender, though he held up his hands and pleaded for mercy, Morgana had seen enough friends fall for a lifetime. So she lifted her great sword up and swung, taking his head clean off.

CHAPTER 51
MORGAN

It was over. After months of working towards this moment with my friends, both in and out of character, it was finished.

Fatima had done a wonderful job with the finale of our arc, and to everyone else, the tears in my eyes probably made sense as a reaction to what we'd just been through, and the loss we'd nearly incurred. But when I chanced a look up at Jack, I knew that, as sad as that finale had been, neither of us was half as jarred by it as we were by what Jack and I had just done. God, was it wonderful and horrible at the same time; unadulterated bliss followed immediately by the cold shower of reality.

"How's everyone feeling?" Fatima asked, reaching out to put a hand on my arm, her other hand clasping Grey's.

"A bit overwhelmed," Grey said. "Like, good, but also sad."

"Well," Fatima said, "let me read a little something I've prepared." She cleared her throat and looked down at the notebook, which she'd opened to the first page.

"At court, not all is as it seems. And though the story of the brave adventurers who destroyed the Supremacy Sphere will pass into legend, there are new stories to explore and new evils to defeat."

As Fatima continued, telling us about how the Adventurer's Guild was being tasked with an even greater mission, I was only half-listening, because I knew it probably needed to be my last session. Yes, I had a lot of life changes happening. But for Jack's sake, and my own, we probably did need to create that distance I'd mentioned earlier, and sooner rather than later. We clearly weren't capable of maintaining it if we were still around each other.

And though I knew that was probably the right thing to do, he wasn't the only one I'd come to love through this little group playing our silly game each week. I would miss Phil's wit, and of course his brownies. I'd miss Fatima's creativity and kindness. I'd miss Grey's chaotic energy. And I'd miss Chloe most of all, though I also knew – or at least hoped – that saying goodbye to the group wouldn't mean saying goodbye to her, even without sitting across a desk from her.

And then there was Jack, who kept trying to catch my eye. But there were too many things I'd miss about him to think of in the moment, and I couldn't keep playing across from him, wanting him the way I did, if we couldn't be together. If he wouldn't take responsibility for his own future.

As Fatima finished setting the scene for what would be everyone else's next adventure, I expected her to ask us all if we were planning to continue. Bless her, she probably assumed it was a given, and I'd have to bring down the vibe by bowing out.

"But before we talk about continuing," Fatima said, and I looked up at her, surprised, "we're going to have to move from Monday nights."

"Wait, why?" Chloe asked. "We've been playing on Mondays for years."

"Yeah," Grey said, "what's the deal? I've already written it down in my diary for the rest of the year. In pen, no less."

But Fatima didn't answer, instead turning her gaze to Jack. "Over to you, buddy."

"Oh," Jack said, clearly not prepared to say anything. "Okay, um..."

He trailed off, and his eyes found mine for a small moment, but I bailed, looking down at my character sheet instead, fixing my eyes on my atrociously low health, my leg bouncing up and down beneath the table.

"I'm starting a course," he said, and I froze. "It's on Monday and Wednesday nights. So, actually, we can't do Wednesdays either. Hope that's okay."

"Wait, what?" Chloe asked.

"Hey, congrats, mate," Phil said at the same time.

"Thanks," Jack said to Phil.

"Hold on," Chloe said, "what course? What are you talking about?"

"Uh, it's actually an architecture course. Not a degree or anything, just a self-paced intro course with a tutor. Then I can go on to do the actual qualifying ones if I want."

I looked up at the shy smile on Jack's face. I could only imagine what my own face looked like.

"That's so cool," Phil said. "You can finally put all those scribbles to good use."

"What about your dad?" I asked, not thinking about it until the words were already out of my mouth. They all turned to look at me, but I ignored them. I only cared about what Jack was saying. What it meant.

"Dad's cool with it," Jack said, meeting my gaze. "Or, he will be. He knows it's what I want."

It's what I want. Those four words were so innocent, so

simple, and yet they were a tsunami wave crashing over me as I blinked at Jack. Two weeks ago, he hadn't even been able to admit that he didn't want the future he'd laid out for himself. Now, all of a sudden, he not only knew what he wanted he'd actually signed up for a course. Talked to his dad. Made a schedule. The number of steps he had to have taken in the last *three bloody weeks* to be able to say those words?

I didn't know what to think.

"Well, I can do Tuesdays," Grey offered. "Or Thursdays, for that matter."

"Thursdays are better for me," Chloe said.

"Fine by me," Phil added.

They all looked at me; now was the moment. I needed to tell them I couldn't do it. But Jack caught my eye again, and I found I couldn't do it. Those four words had changed everything, and I was at a loss.

"Thursdays are great," I said, too mesmerised by the way Jack's eyes crinkled at the edges to listen to the voice in my head insisting this was a bad idea.

"Great," Fatima said, closing the notebook. "Thursdays it is. Now I don't know about you all, but I'm fucking exhausted."

"Hear, hear," Phil said.

"Huzzah!" Grey cheered.

As the rest of the table got up, Phil patting Jack on the shoulder and congratulating him, I focused in on my bare feet against the cold hardwood floor. Surely, if I concentrated hard enough, I'd be able to actually feel the earth shifting beneath them. The tectonic event that was tonight must have been registering on some Richter scale, somewhere.

"Sorry," Jack said, suddenly the only one left at the table. "I wanted to tell you, but I didn't know how."

I didn't say anything, focused on the way the corners of his mouth kept trying to twitch up into a smile, only to falter and drop back into a straight line.

"And I'm sorry about earlier, too," he said, then quickly added, "actually, no I'm not, that's a lie. I'm not sorry about it."

"You're not?" I asked, frowning.

"Nope," he said, shaking his head. "I'd crawl under this table and between your legs right now if I thought you wanted me to."

My mouth went dry, and the space he'd filled in me earlier throbbed in response, and I gulped to try to silence the traitorous feeling. That was the last thing I needed right now.

"But I heard you," Jack said. "I believe you. If you tell me it's over, then I get it. I don't want it to be, but I understand."

All of a sudden I was struggling to breathe. I pressed my hands hard into one another under the table to try to steady myself.

"This is what I meant earlier," he said, and even the word "earlier" sent a tingle down my spine. But the smile was gone from his face now. "When I said you were right? That wasn't just talk. It wasn't just an apology. I'm actually doing something about it. And you deserve to know that. Because even if you don't want to be with me anymore, you helped me get there. And I'll always—"

His voice broke, but he swallowed hard and carried on, a bit slower, over-enunciating his words.

"I'll always appreciate that you were brave enough to show me."

And with that, he pushed away from the table and left, wiping at his face as he did. And I just sat there for ages, staring at the space he'd occupied. The chair he'd been sitting in when he pulled the rug out from under my best laid plans.

I LAY AWAKE ALL NIGHT, twiddling the crystal Amy had given me between my fingers, replaying everything that had happened. And not just in the dining room; at the gala, at my house, in the bathroom ... there was exactly zero chance of me getting any sleep.

I ended up on the sofa at 2am, drinking chamomile tea – a habit I'd picked up from Jack – and drawing him the way I knew he would look the next day, with that cooked crown and sexy jerkin. (If Past Morgan had ever known that Present Morgan would use "sexy" and "jerkin" together, she would have mocked her mercilessly.) And as his face came to life on my screen, with his green eyes and chiselled jaw, I knew what he'd been saying to me at the table. Jack cared about what I thought. He trusted me. And I was pretty sure he still loved me.

If anyone but Jack had told me that I'd been letting others dictate my life, I wouldn't have listened. I probably would have brushed it off when he'd first implied it if I hadn't already been thinking about it myself. Even Cara; despite hanging on her every word for years, I wouldn't have taken it to heart. I certainly wouldn't have upended my entire life over it like I had now.

But Jack had upended *his* life, too, it turned out. I'd broken up with him, pretended to be fine without him, and then had one last shag before putting the final nail in the coffin of our relationship. Yet he'd still taken what I'd said, what I wanted for him, to heart so much that he was upsetting his career *and* his family dynamic. It made me love him even more.

And it made me hate the way I'd acted, too. When he'd told me to choose him without knowing if he would change anything? I was pretty sure he'd been right. That I should have done it.

Part of me wondered, in fact, if it was too late to do it now.

It was clear as the day that was breaking outside my window that I wanted him, and I hoped that maybe, just maybe, I hadn't screwed everything up beyond repair. I thought about the life that he was going to build now – training to become an architect, finally bringing his creativity to life, not living under his family's thumb – and I knew that I wanted to be there for that. I wanted to be a part of his story, and I wanted him to be a part of mine. And I wanted him to know it.

What I *didn't* want was to crawl back to him and pretend like the last two weeks hadn't happened. Because actually, as embarrassed as I was that I'd so vehemently shut him down before hearing him out, I knew that all of that fallout *had* to have happened to get us to where we were. If we hadn't broken up, maybe he wouldn't be taking the next steps towards his own dreams. I probably wouldn't have been taking mine, either. And to quietly sweep everything we'd been through under the rug would be a disservice to both of us. To how much we wanted for ourselves, and for each other. To how much we loved one another.

He said I'd been brave for showing him the truth. So now I needed to be brave in how I showed him *my* truth: that I loved him. And as the sun peeked over the horizon, I knew just how to do that.

I literally startled myself when the idea came to me, my tea spilling all over my tablet, which was face-down on my lap. I jumped up and got a tea towel from the kitchen, wiping it clean, taking the case off to make sure it was okay. And as soon as I knew it was safe, I set it aside, pulled out my phone, and started typing. I had a lot to do.

CHAPTER 52
JACK

Morgan was nowhere to be found.

Chloe had woken up to a text from her that she would meet us at the Ren Faire, but I knew I'd scared her off. Not least because, when I knocked on her door to see if she was okay, the door swung open to reveal an empty room. Well, empty except for the dress hanging on the back of the wardrobe door.

"Where do you think she's gone?" Grey asked, chomping the end off a strip of streaky bacon.

"Maybe the pharmacy?" Fatima offered. "If she wasn't feeling well, I guess. There was one just past the neighbourhood entrance I think."

But I knew they were wrong. Wherever she'd gone, she was avoiding me. Or, at least, avoiding *us*. And I didn't blame her. But if she didn't want to be with us, I'd have to learn how to be without her. I'd have to learn how to be happy. *So I might as well start now.*

I sat down at the sofa, where I seemed to have left my tablet the night before, to continue my sketch. I decided it didn't matter that I'd started it with Morgan in mind; I deserved to finish it either way.

But when I swiped to unlock the tablet, I realised from the photo of Pablo as the background that it wasn't actually mine but Morgan's. Why was it here? Why was it out of her case? Why didn't she have a password on it? Now that she was doing work on it, she should really have been paying more attention to that kind of thing.

I knew I should have put it straight back down. But I hadn't seen any of her art in weeks, and I wanted to see what she'd been drawing. To feel connected to that part of her. So I opened the app she'd taught me to use, and as I scrolled through her projects, my mouth fell open.

The first thing I saw was me, in the outfit I had laid out downstairs. She'd been a bit generous with the cut of my jaw, but it was amazing to see myself through her eyes. I checked the edit history: it had only been a few hours since she'd worked on this one.

When I scrolled through her recent projects, skimming past the freelance work and gala illustrations, I found dozens of illustrations of me from over the last few months: in my suit for the gala, holding the book she'd given me in Hay-on-Wye, paddling a kayak up a river lined with rhododendron and balsam, on the floor in her lounge with my head leaned back against the sofa... I scrolled all the way back to the beginning of the year, and there was even one of me from then, sat at Fatima's dining table, a D20 die falling from my hand, a huge smile on my face.

I'd known Morgan was in love with me. I never would have had the courage to say it to her otherwise. But seeing all of this – knowing that when she was her best, most creative self, she was thinking of me – I felt that chasm crack open like never before. We were both still literally drawing one another into our lives, so why couldn't we make it work?

But it wasn't real life. It was just a drawing. And if Morgan had wanted to work things out with me, she would have done so last night when we'd made love. She would have changed her mind when I'd told her what I'd been doing to try to make things right for myself. And she would be here now.

But she wasn't. And I supposed that told me everything I needed to know.

AFTER BREAKFAST, I pulled on my newly mended trousers and my jerkin, relying on Chloe to fix the loose tie on the shoulder and help me angle the crown I'd bought just right. She had to pause in the middle of buzzing Grey's head; now that they'd worn their Gorlag outfit, they wanted a clean slate of their natural brown for today's look.

Once we were dressed, we all, sans Morgan, left for the faire. As we went, I looked over my shoulder and could have sworn I saw her standing in the upstairs window, but then the clouds shifted, and it turned out to just be a glare on the window.

We walked over to the festival entrance, admiring again the costumes others had put together. We were all dressed more traditionally "Ren Faire chic" today, as Chloe had called it; she and Fatima wore flowy dresses with corsets over them, Grey wore a lace-up waistcoat over ballooning trousers and shirt, and Phil wore a brocade jerkin not unlike the one the groom had been wearing at the joust yesterday.

At the festival gate, there was a huge group of gender-bent Disney royalty – a bearded hulk of a human dressed as Ariel, paired with a dainty walking ponytail in a Prince Eric costume, and so on – and another group clearly dressed as the Fellowship from *The Lord of the Rings*. I snapped a picture of them to send to Morgan, my thumb hovering over the send button whilst I debated whether or not I should be texting her, before I decided to say "fuck it" and send it anyway. If she didn't want to hear from me, she wouldn't respond.

Inside, the place looked identical to the day before, and it felt like déjà vu to hear the same jokes and lewd comments yelled by the callers and performers. It was fun, but my heart wasn't in it; not without Morgan there. At least yesterday, I'd been able to watch her have fun and know that it was all worth it. But today, everything reminded me of her, and not in a fun way.

After another round of coffee – all iced this time, as it was already warmer than it had been yesterday afternoon – we found some seats at a belly dancing show. I settled down next to Fatima on the end of the row. I hadn't properly spoken to her since everything that had happened with Jared other than to tell her about my course. She seemed to be in pretty good spirits, so I risked bringing the vibe down if it meant maybe getting to commiserate a bit.

"So how are you doing?" I asked Fatima, trying not to sound like I was starting a therapy session, but she clearly got the gist.

"I'm okay," she said, putting on a smile one might describe as "brave". "I mean, better than I thought I'd be. It was a pretty clean break, all things considered."

"That's true," I said, somewhat envious of that. "But you know you don't *have* to be okay, right?"

Fatima caught my eye, and her smile faltered for a moment. "I know," she said, nodding. "But really, Grey's hardly left my side, and Morgan and Chloe have been great, too."

I must have winced slightly at the mention of Morgan, or

maybe Fatima's teacher/DM intuition was at an all-time high, because she narrowed her eyes.

"And how are *you*?"

We'd never actually, officially burst the bubble to Fatima and Grey. We'd been about to when Fatima and Jared had broken up, and Morgan insisted it would have been insensitive to bring it up. But they'd found out; of course they had. I suspected Fatima had known since that day she caught me on my way down the stairs. She'd always been able to see right through people.

Today, I didn't feel like just smiling along, fading into the background. So I decided to be honest.

"Not great," I said, feeling my voice break. "Which seems really stupid to say, given that we were together for what, less than one percent of the time you and Jared were together?"

She shook her head. "It's not about how long you were together," she said, then shrugged as she reconsidered. "Okay, obviously duration plays a part. But with Jared and me, as impossible as it feels, even now, to imagine life without him, we'd at least got to see it through. Our relationship ran its course, apparently. But with you and Morgan..."

"We never got to see what life would be like together," I finished. And that was the killer, wasn't it? All the what-ifs. All the unknowns, which had been the thing to threaten our relationship to begin with, and which were haunting us now. Or, haunting me at least. Was it selfish to hope she was at least slightly haunted, too?

"I guess we'll all have to get used to the unknowns," I said. "She might not even be here a month from now."

Fatima's sympathetic pout sharpened into a confused squint. "Wait, what?"

"She's been looking at jobs in other parts of the country," I said, hoping Fatima didn't find that too triggering. But she didn't look shocked when I told her. Just more confused.

"I did know that," she said, "but—"

Before she could continue, ear-splitting feedback came from the speaker a foot to my left; I actually lifted my hands to my ears in response. A man shouting and whooping came barrelling onto the stage, five elegant belly dancers in a line behind him. The music kicked in, and I could barely hear it through the ringing in my ears. I was almost certain this volume was historically inaccurate.

I tried to catch Fatima's eye, but she'd given up on the conversation. I only half-paid attention; I had one eye on my phone, staring at the message I'd sent Morgan, desperate for the little ticks to turn blue so I knew she'd read it. But with the entire morning gone, I was losing hope.

Just before the show finished, Fatima got up to go to the toilets and said she'd meet us at the joust, so I didn't get to finish our conversation, which I'd of course made all about me. By the time we walked into the arena early to get seats, Morgan was still nowhere to be seen, and I came to terms with the fact that she'd never planned to meet us.

"I feel like I should ring Morgan," Chloe said, echoing my thoughts, pulling her phone out as we settled into the stands, even closer to the middle than we'd been yesterday. But I held out a hand to stop her.

"She's not coming," I said. "Don't bother."

Chloe looked at me and narrowed her eyes. "What makes you think that?"

I shrugged. "A hunch?"

"Bullshit," she said, scowling. "What did you do?"

"Nothing!" I said, in a way that I knew she'd understand to mean "everything".

"Fuck's sake, Jack," Chloe said, smacking me on the arm hard enough that I felt the sting through my jerkin. "Why did you screw this up?"

I levelled my gaze at her, and I must have looked pitiful enough, because her ire quickly melted into pity.

"You really did screw this up, didn't you?" she asked, reaching her arms out to hug me from the side.

"I mean, it was pretty mutually destructive," I said. "But yeah, I wasn't exactly the paragon of good boyfriends."

"It's okay," she said, suddenly very tender, refusing to move her face from my shoulder or her arms from my torso. "You'll be fine. Sounds like you've got a lot going on, anyway."

"Why are we getting all huggy?" Phil asked, climbing over Chloe and me and sitting down right between us, forcing us to scoot apart. He handed me a tub of kettle corn as Fatima and Grey settled in behind us.

"Because Jack's a bad boyfriend," Chloe said, and Phil nodded.

"Yeah, could have told you that," he said.

"From all the time we spent dating?" I asked.

"You couldn't pull me."

"How about we save this little friends-to-enemies-to-lovers arc for after the joust?" Chloe asked, just as Maximus and his opponent came riding out.

As they performed their feats of strength and agility, we all seemed to remember where the huzzahs and boos were meant to go, and it was fun to feel like we were now in on the joke. But I found myself looking over my shoulder subconsciously for Morgan, as if she would appear behind me where she'd been yesterday.

She should be here for this, I thought. *This is all meant to be for her.*

"Did you text Morgan?" I asked Chloe as the trumpeters finished their awful noise and the Queen appeared on the platform.

"Yeah, like, seven times," Chloe said dismissively, looking up at the Queen.

"Welcome to today's joust," she was saying. "Normally we would have a happy pair of newlyweds to preside..."

"Maybe you should text her again," I said quietly.

"Shhhh," Chloe said, swatting at me, looking past me.

"I just don't want her to feel alone," I said.

"Jack—"

"I don't want her to think we're just having fun without her. That we don't miss her."

"Jack?"

"Because it's not the same without her, and it never could be."

"Jack!" Chloe slapped me this time, and as she pointed past me, I realised she wasn't just telling me to shut up. The whole crowd was whispering in confusion, actually. I turned around and followed Chloe's finger, looking at the knights and the host, who were staring up at the platform. Then I followed their gazes to the Queen, who was looking down at someone next to her. Someone shorter than her. Someone in a long blue dress, with ornamental chain mail around her neck.

My kettle corn fell onto the bleachers and my mouth fell open. It was Morgan.

CHAPTER 53
MORGAN

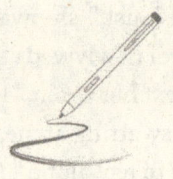

Murmurs of confusion rippled through the crowd, and even the knights looked up at me with scrunched, uncertain faces. But the Queen, who had seemed extremely enthusiastic about my idea when we'd met this morning, cleared her throat.

"Our knights will be demonstrating their strength and bravery today. But we have another contender to introduce; one who wishes to demonstrate her own bravery. May I present to you all Lady Morgana."

"Huzzah!" the crowd cheered, and I did an awkward little wave, a forced smile plastered on my face. I was almost certain I was beet red from head to toe.

"And whose favour do you seek today, Lady Morgana?" she asked, turning to me. She tapped the lapel mic hidden in the intricate beading of her dress, and I leaned in uncomfortably close to her breasts to speak into it.

"Sir Jack Evans, Your Majesty."

A single whoop sounded from the crowd, and I looked out to see Chloe waving her arms around halfway up one side of the arena. I scanned until my eyes finally landed on Jack, the sunlight glinting off his golden hair and the crown perched atop it. I couldn't see his face from where I was, but I could tell he was looking at me.

"Let's help Sir Jack to the front please," the Queen said to the attendants who had been selling regalia just moments ago. One of them waved for Jack to follow her, and it took him a moment to comply, but I felt my whole body relax as he stood up and made his way down to the front.

As Jack leaned against the railing, I could see his face more clearly, and my heart started to beat faster and faster. He looked confused, yes, but he also looked relieved. Maybe even hopeful. And importantly, though his smile was only faint, his eyes were creased at the corners in a way that sent my head into outer space.

The Queen cleared her throat again, but this time it was for me. I looked up at her, and she nodded down at Jack. *Go on*, she was saying. *Show us what you came here for.*

I took a deep breath in and thought about all the things I wanted to say to Jack. All the ways I could tell him what he meant to me, and what I'd learned from him. I stepped forward and put my hands on the balcony, looking down at him, but it wasn't close enough. I knew if I was going to do this I needed to be standing in front of him. Holding his hands.

So I took off running to the back of the balcony, down the stairs, gathering the skirt of my dress in my hand, and then out the doors to the arena. I heard a few gasps, and the knights hurried to move their huge horses back. I was almost certain having guests on the field was a big no-no based on the safety talk I'd had, but fuck it. And when I looked up, I saw Jack vault over the railing and come sprinting towards me, looking like a real-life prince.

I got to him and grabbed his hands as I'd planned, both of us panting as I swallowed hard and met his green eyes with mine. He was smiling down at me, equal parts confusion and delight on his face, and I found all the courage I needed in his gaze. I straightened the chains on my chest and shoulders and smoothed my skirts, then took a deep breath in.

"I love you, Jack," I said, trying to make my voice loud enough for at least some of the audience to hear – that was what had got me up here, in the end: the promise of a show – but it was shaking. I did hear a few people say "awww" though, so I figured it would do. And Jack squeezed my hands as he pressed his lips together in anticipation, spurring me on.

"I know we've been through a lot together in not a lot of time. And I'm not proud of all of that. But I am proud of the person I've become because of you. And important, I'm proud of *you*."

I took a deep breath in, and Jack mirrored it, gripping me tighter. I took a sharp breath in as he stepped just a tiny bit closer, but I forced myself to go on.

"I'm sorry that I pushed you away. That your baggage triggered my baggage, and vice versa. The last thing I wanted to do was make you feel like there was no room in frame for you."

This was it; this was the big moment. The one I needed to be brave for. And looking up into Jack's green eyes, I had never felt braver in my entire life.

"If you'll still have me, I want everything with you. The future, the dog, the house, the babies, the *adventure*. I want it all. And the rest can just be water under the tree."

The whole crowd was silent, and even the far-off noises of the rest of the faire faded into the background. It was just me standing in front of Jack, him staring down at me; nothing else existed in that moment. And whilst I waited for him to respond, it was as if the air had been sucked out of the arena.

"Morgan," he said, then cocked his head to the side, his crown slipping slightly. "Or, Lady Morgana?"

I laughed, and so did he, and the sound was like honey to me. Like sunshine on a cold day. "It's me," I said. "Just me."

"Morgan," he said again. "I am so sorry that I got scared; that I pushed you away. All this time I thought I was the brave one, but it turns out I have a lot to learn from you."

I beamed up at him, blinking back tears. We'd cried enough in the last few days. This was a happy moment; I knew that now from the way he was looking at me.

"I would follow you anywhere," he said, and I could have melted into a puddle right there on the field. "If you'll have me."

"No," I said, shaking my head, and I saw his smile falter. "You don't have to follow me anywhere, because I'm not going anywhere."

His smile cracked wide open and his eyes crinkled at the corners as he wrapped his arms around my waist, dipped me backwards, and kissed me. The whole world erupted with applause, and I could swear that I could hear our friends cheering louder than anyone else.

By the time I was upright again, everything else had been put right, too.

"Let's all raise a cheer for the brave Lady Morgana, and Sir Jack Evans!" the Queen cried. The knights and attendants all shouted, "hip, hip!" and the crowd responded with a deafening "huzzah!"

CHAPTER 54
JACK

"I love you so much," Morgan said as I nuzzled into her neck, the delicate chains cold against my cheek.

Hip hip, huzzah!

"I love you, too," I said in her ear. "And I'm so sorry. But I meant it. You can take the job. No matter where you want to be, what you want to do, I'm there."

Hip hip, huzzah!

"About that," she said, and I pulled back to see a huge smile on her face. "I actually got a different job."

"Oh?" I tried not to sound *too* hopeful.

"Simone helped me get a design job at the Rescue. So looks like I'll be sticking around."

I swallowed hard as I fought back tears. Was this real life?

As the fervour died down around us, I looked up and around and saw the Queen beckoning to us from the balcony. I grabbed Morgan by the hand and climbed the stairs with her, and the Queen presented us to the crowd once more, and they cheered again. Then we were seated, Morgan draped across my lap rather than on her own seat, and the joust began.

"That was hella romantic," the Queen said, dropping out of her Ren Faire voice and into a deep southern drawl.

"It really was," I said, turning to Morgan. "You're my knight in ornamental armour."

"Damn straight," Morgan said, sitting up straighter.

The Queen turned back to the joust, but I couldn't take my eyes off Morgan. She looked more beautiful to me than she ever had, and not just because of the dress, or because of what had just happened. Though sure, that probably had something to do with it.

No, it was because she looked so confident. So completely herself, in a way I'd never seen her. And I hoped I could spend the rest of my life helping her feel that way.

I leaned over towards her, burying my face in her hair by her ear. I felt her shiver in response, and I let myself for a split second think about the *later* I knew would be coming.

"Where will you live?" I asked, fully prepared to ask her then and there to move in with me. But she smiled, and I knew she had it taken care of. Of course she did. She'd thought of everything.

"I'm moving in with Fatima," she said. Suddenly my conversation from earlier made perfect sense; she'd known Morgan was staying in town, because she was part of it. I'd thought she was the one out of the loop, but it turned out to be me.

"She was already panicking about how she'd afford the place without Jared," Morgan continued, "so it was a match made in heaven. I'll have to get rid of a lot of stuff though."

"I'm very good at moving boxes," I said, and Morgan laughed.

"Don't I know it."

We looked out at the joust for a moment, pretending to be interested in what was happening; we were meant to be presiding over it, after all. But if Morgan's thoughts were anything like mine, they were far from Sir Maximus and his opponent.

"So, there's actually more," Morgan said. I leaned my head back and laughed.

"Of fucking course there is. What now?"

Morgan reached down into a pocket in the side of her dress – sorry, Phil had sewn in *pockets*?? – and pulled out her phone. She opened it up, and I watched as she squinted at the screen for a moment before chuckling.

"Hah, the Fellowship. That's funny."

"Come on, you tease," I said, reaching my hands up to tickle her waist. She squirmed in my lap, making my trousers go a bit tight, so I pressed onto her hips to still her.

"Well," she said, "you'll have to be okay sharing me with another guy."

I squinted at her in confusion, and she spun her phone around, a picture of Pablo appearing in front of me. It took me a moment to understand what she was saying, but when I did I grabbed the phone out of her hand, then looked back up at her.

"No!"

She nodded as she smiled, biting at her bottom lip. "We can pick him up on Tuesday when we get home."

I looked up at her with tears in my eyes. "How did you do it?" I asked. "How did you manage to make everything so very right?"

"The same thing as you," she said with a shrug. "I asked myself what I really wanted. The real me, not the me I'd been trying to force. And it was simple. Yes, I wanted to work in design, but I also wanted game nights with our friends. I wanted this dog. And I wanted you. And once I knew that, it felt like a no-brainer."

"Are you sure?" I asked. "Because if that's really what you want, then that's great. But if you want to go to York, if you want to live somewhere else, we can do that. Or you can do that, and I'll support you from wherever you want me. I want you to be happy."

She tilted her face down and rubbed her nose against mine. "*You* make me happy, numpty."

And dammit if the tears didn't start falling at that very minute.

Morgan sat back and laughed. "Numpty? That's what put you over the edge?"

"Shut up," I said, pushing as if to eject her from my lap. "Remember when you used to reward me for showing emotion?"

"I'm sorry," she said in a baby voice, stroking my face, wiping my already-subsided tears away with her thumbs. "A million emotional XP for you."

"Thank you," I said, pulling her in for another kiss. "I couldn't have levelled up without you."

"And what about me?" she asked, sitting up straight and posing as if she was being assessed. "Grand romantic gesture in a foreign country, taking over an entire festival? What's that worth to you?"

"Everything," I said. "It's worth everything."

My phone buzzed in my pocket, and Morgan must have felt it, too, because she looked down at our laps.

"Save the vibes for the bedroom, babe," she said with a laugh.

"Very funny," I said, pulling out my phone to silence it, but not before I saw the text message that had just come through in the Wench Please group chat.

> Get a room!!!!!!!!

"I mean, they've got a point," I said, shrugging up at Morgan, who had read the message, too. "Actually, come to think of it, there's definitely a tree somewhere around here that would be good enough."

Morgan laughed and hit my arm in what I assumed was meant to be a playful punch, but the whole knight thing was clearly getting to her head, as it actually stung a bit. Even so, I could feel my grin extend not only up to my eyes but even down into my chest.

"I love you so much," I whispered in her ear, her curls tickling my cheeks.

"Back at ya," she said, turning to me and kissing me gently on the nose.

"God," I scoffed, "what kind of dickhead doesn't say 'I love you' back?"

Another playful punch in the same spot, and that one *definitely* stung.

"Ouch!" I cried. "Take it easy. You're stronger than you think."

She rolled her eyes. "That's such a cheesy line."

Then she leaned in to kiss me properly, and all the trumpets and gallops and huzzahs faded into nothing. Because I finally knew exactly what I wanted, and I had it right here in my arms.

EPILOGUE
YORICK PROUDHOLLOW

It took a long time to rebuild the Adventurers Guild, but Morgana, Calamity, Gorlag and Yorick were there for every moment of it.

In the weeks following the destruction of the Supremacy Sphere, a lot had happened for Yorick. He and his friends had been honoured by the Queen for their service to the realm, and for weeks they had been the guests of honour at feasts and parties all over the Capital and beyond. But they'd still been grieving their friend, too, and though a statue of Thrormir had been erected in his hometown, it felt like the rest of the people they encountered were keen to brush him under the rug as collateral damage and focus on the near-miss that had been prevented.

So instead of sticking around and pretending they were proud of what they'd done, they went out on missions instead. They'd formed a nice little group; the four remaining from their original party; Ser Prize, who (thankfully) mostly went by Liam these days; and a new druid recruit named Eden. She was younger than the rest of them, and her magic was a bit unpredictable, but she proved herself useful.

It was in the second month after the battle that Yorick received the letter at the guild house from his mother. Which was strange, since his mother had died several years prior. He opened it as he lay in his bunk, the lute he'd been playing discarded at his side.

> *Dearest Yorick, we need your help at home. Your father's unwell, and we need money for a cleric. Please bring some with you when you come. Love, Mum.*

Yorick squinted down at the crooked writing – was he imagining it, or did it look an awful lot like his mother's? – and frowned.

"Check this out," he said, handing the letter down to Gorlag, who was on the bunk below him.

"That's not great," they said after a moment. A long-ish moment; Gorlag wasn't very good with reading. "You want me to go with you?"

Yorick poked his head over the edge of his bunk and met Gorlag's eye.

"My mum's been dead for years."

Gorlag frowned and turned the letter over, examining it. When they did, their face went slack.

"What is it?" Yorick asked, grasping for the letter back. But Gorlag didn't hand it over, just turned it back to show Yorick what they'd found. When he saw it, his own mouth fell open in surprise. How he hadn't noticed it the first time was beyond him. But the wax seal on the letter jumped out at him plain as day now.

Because the shape pressed into the wax seal was a twelve-pointed star.

ACKNOWLEDGMENTS

I've never had more fun writing a book. This story was a culmination of four great loves in my life: telling stories, playing pretend, my wonderful friends, and, you know, actual romantic love. I don't know where or who I would be without all of them. There's a long, long list of people who bolster and inspire me. Dave, Steph, Jim, Cate, Amy, Josie, Rhi, Jess, Chloe, Jepp, et al. – thank you for providing me with endless material for friend group hijinks, and with distractions from deadline insanity. Being your friend is a real privilege.

To my wonderful writing group, thank you for your encouragement. The full days of sprints and the word count challenges have kept me going when deadlines loomed and my well of inspiration ran dry. To Kiera Nixon and Alison Thayer in particular, thank you for keeping me company most evenings whilst we created together. Your encouragement fueled this story as much as any deadline.

Thank you to my wonderful husband Alex for feeding and caffeinating me whilst I wrote, and for listening to me ramble my way into a solution every time I got stuck. You may not be willing to dress up in Ren Faire garb for me (boooooo), but you show up for me in the ways that matter, so I suppose I'll let you off the hook.

Is it weird to thank a dog in the acknowledgements of a book? Actually, don't tell me; I don't care. Thank you to Kirby, my gorgeous Golden Retriever, who fills up my camera roll and quite literally forces me to touch grass.

A million thanks to the wonderful team at One More Chapter and HarperCollins UK. To Jennie Rothwell, thank you for understanding and nurturing the vision for this story, even when you had to learn about D&D to do so. To the gorgeous marketing and design teams and the illustrator of this stunning cover Margherita Abitino, you are such stars - I've been so blessed with perfect packaging every time, so my books always find their way into the right readers' hands. To Emma Petfield in particular, thank you for all your hard work behind the scenes, and for bringing the Ren Faire idea to the party. To Charlotte Ledger, I'll follow you to the end of the earth. Everybody wants to be us.

And to everyone who has commented and watched and messaged as I've worked on this book and shared about it online: your support means the world to me. From the bottom of my heart, thank you. I can't wait to share more stories with you soon.

The author and One More Chapter would like to thank everyone who contributed to the publication of this story...

Analytics
James Brackin
Abigail Fryer
Maria Osa

Audio
Fionnuala Barrett
Ciara Briggs

Contracts
Sasha Duszynska Lewis

Design
Lucy Bennett
Fiona Greenway
Liane Payne
Dean Russell

Digital Sales
Lydia Grainge
Hannah Lismore
Emily Scorer

Editorial
Arsalan Isa
Charlotte Ledger
Bonnie Macleod
Laura McCallen
Janet Marie Adkins
Jennie Rothwell

Harper360
Emily Gerbner
Jean Marie Kelly
emma sullivan
Sophia Wilhelm

International Sales
Peter Borcsok
Bethan Moore

Marketing & Publicity
Chloe Cummings
Emma Petfield

Operations
Melissa Okusanya
Hannah Stamp

Production
Denis Manson
Simon Moore
Francesca Tuzzeo

Rights
Vasiliki Machaira
Rachel McCarron
Hany Sheikh Mohamed
Zoe Shine

The HarperCollins Distribution Team

The HarperCollins Finance & Royalties Team

The HarperCollins Legal Team

The HarperCollins Technology Team

Trade Marketing
Ben Hurd

UK Sales
Laura Carpenter
Isabel Coburn
Jay Cochrane
Sabina Lewis
Holly Martin
Erin White
Harriet Williams
Leah Woods

And every other essential link in the chain from delivery drivers to booksellers to librarians and beyond!

ONE MORE CHAPTER

One More Chapter is an award-winning global division of HarperCollins.

Subscribe to our newsletter to get our latest eBook deals and stay up to date with all our new releases!

signup.harpercollins.co.uk/join/signup-omc

Meet the team at
www.onemorechapter.com

Follow us!

 @OneMoreChapter_
 @OneMoreChapter
@onemorechapterhc

Do you write unputdownable fiction?
We love to hear from new voices.
Find out how to submit your novel at
www.onemorechapter.com/submissions